Ultra Taiwan Fighter

ULTRA TAIWAN FIGHTER

a novel by
Jon Schiller, PhD

BOOKSURGE PUBLISHING
CHARLESTON, SC
2008

First printing

BOOKSURGE PUBLISHING
Charleston, SC 29418
Printed in the United States of America

Jon Schiller author of trading books
Published
Insider's Automatic Trading Strategy
The 100% Return Options Trading Strategy
Self-Adaptive Options & Currency Trading
Options Profit Using Decision Charts
Compilation of Jon Schiller's OEX Options Trading Newsletters

Jon Schiller author of fiction novels
Published
Masada Never Again
Multihulls
Ibex
Soon to be published
Lost in Space

copyright © 2008 Dr. Jon Schiller
jonsch1@verizon.net
http://www.jonschilleroptions.com/
http://wwwjonschblogger.blogspot.com/
ISBN 0-9774305-0-2

Ultra Taiwan Fighter

AUTHOR'S BACKGROUND

JON SCHILLER received the BS in Physics from The California Institute of Technology (Caltech) and the MS and PhD in EE and Math from the University of Southern California where he served as an adjunct assistant professor.

Dr. Schiller was a member of the Scientific Advisory Board in the early 1980's for which he received an Award for Meritorious Service from the USAF.

He was also an executive in the aerospace industry designing avionics Systems for military aircraft and his responsibilities for Middle East business in Iran and Israel involved a great deal of world-wide traveling. He lived in Taiwan for a few months while working on a military avionics Systems contract which provided the geographical and technical background for creating this exciting novel, *Ultra Taiwan Fighter*.

He skippered three Transpacific Yacht Races from Los Angeles to Honolulu, twice winning trophies.

He holds a private pilots license with instrument and multi engine ratings.

The author lived in Europe, mostly in Spain, for 17 years before returning to California in 2001.

LIST OF CHARACTERS

HEADS OF STATE (Actions and words are fictional)

Percival Edwards	President of United States
Deng Xiaoping	Premier of People's Republic of China (PRC)
Chiang Ching-kuo	President of Republic of China (Taiwan) son of Chiang Kai-shek, founder of Republic of China, Taiwan
Rafi Eitan	Prime Minister of Israel

TAIWANESE – REPUBLIC OF CHINA

Dr. Charlie Chang (Cheng-chang)	Program Director Aircraft Industries Development Center (AIDC)
General Huang Ching-lee	Director of AIDC, Taichung, Taiwan
Dr. Chris Haah	Director of Chan Shung Institute of Science & Technology (CSIST) North East of Taipei and Program Director for guided missiles
General David Hua (Ding-fua)	Director General of Ministry of National Defense (MND) in Taipei, nephew of President of Taiwan
Colonel Dr. Jan Wang	Director of Avionics & Systems Integration AIDC Taichung
Ju-ling	Wife of Colonel Wang
Colonel Eddie Chung (Eng-fu)	Taiwan CIA, Taipei with cover: President of Chung-Export/Import Ltd., a trading company
Joy-tung	Playgirl on CIA's Payroll
Mei Lin	Taiwan CIA with cover as dancing partner, used by Colonel Chung to entertain foreign visitors
Colonel Yung Hang-fu	Republic of China Air Force (ROCAF), test pilot for UTF
Su Soong	Director of Singapore Straits Trading Ltd.
Janet Chin	Su Soong's Friend
Major Zin	UTF Test Pilot
Major Hsu	UTF Test Pilot
Billie	Young escort for Mei Lin
Tommie	Young escort for Patricia

CHINESE - PEOPLES' REPUBLIC OF CHINA (PRC)

General Yong Ping-ying	Chief of PRC Air Force
Colonel Zien Yuo	Commander of Third Tactical Air Force Squadron
General Chu	Aid to General Yong
Brigitte Michon (Michov)	KGB Agent
Comrade Yung Hang-lee	Member of PRC Politburo and uncle of Hang-fu Program Director

AMERICANS

Mr. Randy McLyle	Vice President Aeronautical Consultants Inc (ACI), CA
Ms. Patricia Manos	Live-in companion of Randy; and Director of System Analysis at ACI
Dr. Richard Creighton	VP of Tactical Aircraft Programs, Cosmos Aircraft Corporation (CAC), Fort Worth TX
Betty Lou Manfred	Lobby Hostess at CAC
Professor John Marsh	Part time President of ACI and Professor at Caltech, Pasadena
Dr. Willie Rinehart	Director of Tactical Systems, Office of Undersecretary of Defense for Research, Development, and Engineering (OUSDRDE) in Pentagon, Washington DC
Lois Brown	Rinehart's executive secretary
Fred Hanson	DARPA, Director of Advanced Aeronautics
Jerry Taylor	NASA Langley, Director of Advanced Aeronautics

SWISS

Heinz Steinbach	Swiss Banker in Zurich
Gretel Breunner	Assistant to Mr. Steinbach

ISRAELIS

Dr. Yossi Barlev	Mossad agent with cover office in Israeli Aircraft Industries (IAI, Tel Aviv as deputy program manager for *Lavi* fighter aircraft
Colonel David Lahat	Program Manager for *Lavi* in Israeli Ministry of Defense
Dvora Amit	Managing Director for trading company Herzylia-Export/Import Ltd., Herzylia, Israel
Yana	Manager, VIP hotel near Tel Aviv

TABLE OF CONTENTS

Chapter 1

Strategy for Regaining the Mainland

General David Hua's black limousine sped through the streets of Taipei. Less than an hour ago General Hua had received an urgent call from the Presidential Palace asking him to be there at 11 AM. It was the day after Chinese New Year in the Christian year of 1988. General Hua had a nagging head ache from drinking too many holiday spirits the day before. He wondered what this urgent meeting with President Chiang Ching-kuo could be about. A loyal nationalist Chinese, even the Director General of the Military National Defense shouldn't question when he is beckoned by Chiang Kai-shek's son, the authoritarian president of the Republic of China. After all, President Chiang was the moral leader of almost a billion Chinese people. Never mind that only 17 million of these – those living in the province of Taiwan – recognized his leadership. Those ill-informed Chinese living in the mainland provinces of China thought that Premier Deng Xiaoping was their leader. Poor misguided souls!

General Hua thought to himself, "What an honor to be called by the President of China. I can hardly wait until that glorious day when the Republic of China resumes its authority over all of China, not just this one small province where we loyal nationalists live – temporally!" Temporally had been since 1949 when the communist Chinese forces drove General Chiang Kai-shek and his followers to the island province of Taiwan - 100 miles across the South China Sea from the coast of mainland China. Taiwan was now called the 'People's Republic of China' by those misguided Chinese living on the Mainland.

As those thoughts were passing through his mind General Hua's limousine pulled though the Presidential Palace gates guarded by four Chinese guards dressed in their crisp uniforms, helmets with white straps across their chins, and with statue-like expressions on their faces. The entering General was given a robotic salute by the Captain of the guard.

General Hua strode smartly up the steps of the Presidential Palace and walked quickly to the President's office where he was ushered inside by a beautiful 25 year old secretary who was rumored to share the President's bed when his occasional desire for sex occurred.

General Hua was surprised this was a *four eyes* meeting - just he and the President. Usually the room was full of people when he met with the President. General Hua was a trusted confident of the President Chiang – for family reasons. General David Hua was the nephew of the President, educated at the University of California at Los Angeles (UCLA). This is where he picked up the un-Chinese name of David. He still used David because of his wide contacts with Americans who furnished a great deal of Taiwan's (the Republic of China's) military equipment and material. Unlike other countries, however, Taiwan paid Uncle Sam for his military aid, using hard cash earned from its excellent positive balance of trade due to its vigorous export markets.

The President who used General Hua's Chinese name *Ding-fua* said "Please sit down Ding-fua, my beloved nephew. I have an extremely important matter to discuss with you."

"Thank you, Mr. President, my most revered uncle. What is this important matter? I'm at your service, Sir!"

"Ding-fua, I want you to implement my latest plan for regaining the mainland for our beloved Republic of China. After my strategy succeeds, we will be able to return to our homeland, the mainland where we were born and our ancestors are buried! I have had enough of this tiny island and I am sick of the complaints of these native Taiwanese who do not appreciate what we true Chinese are doing for them and their wretched island!"

"And, Uncle Ching-kuo, what is your strategy for regaining the homeland?"

"It is very simple, Ding-fua, very simple. On the false holiday in October that the communist leaders celebrate, they have their total Air Force fly-by while all the leaders stand and salute. We will destroy their Air Force and decapitate all their leaders in a single blow!"

"And how do we accomplish this blow, Uncle Ching-kuo? Our nuclear scientists must have perfected our nuclear bomb, yes?"

"NO, no, Ding-fua, my plan does not need a nuclear bomb. It needs a new fighter, *The Ultra Tactical Fighter!* My nephew in our Central Intelligence Agency, Chung Eng-fu, your cousin, has just informed me of a revolutionary new fighter aircraft being designed in America. We must build this fighter and make it even better!"

"But Uncle Ching-kuo, the Pentagon has repeatedly turned us down when we request a new fighter more advanced than the ancient F-5's we build in Taichung. We wanted the F-16. They refused to sell it to us. Instead they sold it to the communist criminals on the mainland!"

"My dear nephew, I have the greatest confidence in your ability to get the fighter I need to implement my new plan for regaining the mainland. Please report back to me by the end of June regarding you plans to develop and build the *Ultra Tactical Fighter.* I must leave you now. I have a luncheon meeting with a visiting head of state."

Chapter 2

Business Crisis in Pasadena

Randy McLyle woke up early – it was 5 am – with a growing desire for sex. He curled up next to his beautiful roommate and workmate, Patricia Manos. Late last night the pair had fallen into bed after 1 am too exhausted to make love.

The two had been at their office, Aeronautical Consultants Inc. (ACI), until after midnight working on their little company's annual business plan. The business outlook looked bleak unless ACI won a big contract for a proposal their company had sent in. They had teamed with the huge company, Cosmos Aircraft Corporation (CAC) in Fort Worth, for a joint proposal to the US Air Force to design a new *Advanced Tactical Fighter* (ATF). If their team (CAC prime contractor and ACI sub-contractor) won the USAF design contract, then ACI would have plenty of business for several years. If the Pentagon didn't award the prime contract to CAC, then their small company didn't have enough of a back-log to continue operating. It would fail or go bankrupt.

ACI had been struggling for almost a decade to survive with contracts from NASA and the Pentagon (the Department of Defense or DOD). Both Randy and Patricia had invested all their money in ACI. They had worked diligently and intelligently to make a success of their small business. This very morning Randy was scheduled to present the annual business plan they prepared last night to Dr. John Marsh, a Professor at Caltech and the part time president of ACI.

Randy pushed these day-time thoughts from his mind as he continued to caress Patricia. She awoke and returned his kisses and caresses. They quickly made up for their lack of lovemaking the night before and then collapsed into an interval of deep sleep. They were finally awakened at 6 am by their alarm clock radio.

The president of ACI, Dr. John Marsh was a Professor of Aeronautics at the California Institute of Technology on California Street in Pasadena, only a short distance from the ACI office on

Green Street. Dr. Marsh left the running of the business to the Vice President of Operations, Randy McLyle. Dr. Marsh held the majority of the stock in ACI and had the power to fire Randy and Patricia if he didn't like the business plan. Professor Marsh's tenured professorial chair at Caltech isolated him from the financial worries of ACI. If the company went bankrupt, the paper value of his stock would become worthless. He would lose nothing since he had paid nothing.

On the other hand, if ACI filed for bankruptcy, then Randy and Patricia would each lose their life savings, since they had both invested all their money to buy the ACI stock they owned. Of course, they would both lose their jobs if ACI failed.

As usual Professor Marsh was late for the 9 am business review meeting. Randy and Patricia were in the conference room with the colored view graphs they had prepared the night before using the company's personal computer with Microsoft's Power Point program. Patricia flipped through the projection of the view graphs and Randy practiced his speech for the Professor. Professor Marsh finally arrived for the business review meeting just before 10 AM, carrying his battered leather briefcase and explained, "I'm sorry to be late, but one of my PhD students had a minor catastrophe. One of his models went unstable in the hypersonic wind tunnel and did some damage to the apparatus. The director of the wind tunnel was mad as hell. He said we'd have to pay for the damage out of our NASA grant funds."

Randy smiled wryly and replied, "John, we're going to have a catastrophe here at ACI if we don't get some new business soon."

Marsh looked surprised, "But Randy, I thought you told me everything would be great after we win the Advanced Tactical Fighter design support contract."

Randy laughed and agreed, "That's right, John, *if* we win the ATF or Advanced Tactical Fighter. Let me present the briefing Patricia and I prepared last night and I think it will make our financial position crystal clear!"

"OK, Randy, go ahead with your briefing."

McLyle gave the presentation and his final summary chart shows the projected business with and without the Advanced Fighter Design support contract. Randy concluded, "So you see, John, with the ATF contract we will have a good year financially, leading to continued growth over the next five years as the contract continues. Without it, we don't have enough business to support the staff. There won't be enough business to support Patricia and me after August!"

Marsh, sobered by this stark presentation of the business facts of life at ACI, stated, "I see what you mean, Randy. It does look bad without the ATF contract. How about the research contracts you were expecting from the US Air Force this year?"

"John, I'm afraid the expanding Strategic Defense Initiative (SDI) research has gobbled up the aeronautical research funds we were hoping to get. We've tried to get some of the SDI business, but we have the wrong image. They're looking for *Space Cadets, not* aeronautical engineers like us."

At that moment the conference room phone rang. Patricia answered it and spoke for a few moments. Then she turned to Marsh and said, "John, please excuse us while we take this call in the next office. It's from Cosmos Aircraft."

"By all means, take the call. It may be good news!"

Randy and Patricia hurried out of the conference room and rushed down the hall to the office to answer the call from Dr. Richard Creighton, vice president of tactical aircraft Programs at Cosmos Aircraft Corporation in Fort Worth, Texas. Randy pushed the flashing button and said, "Rick, Randy here , What's up?"

Creighton replied, "Randy, I'm afraid I've got bad news. I just received a call from our Washington office. We didn't get the ATF design contract."

Shattered, McLyle responded, "But, Rich, what happened? I thought your congressman from the Fort Worth area assured you he would bring some of the ATF funding to his district."

Creighton replied with a brusque, "Yes, our congressman was right about bringing funding to his district, but I'm afraid the contract went to our big brother across the lake from here – General Dynamics."

Growing increasingly disheartened, Randy retorted, "But, Rich how could we lose? The Air Force evaluators said our design was the most innovative they had ever seen, that it would revolutionize tactical aircraft warfare."

"Well Randy, I guess the evaluators were over-ruled by the Air Force generals in the Pentagon. The feedback we got was that our design was *too far out,* that they wanted a *lower technical risk design – something more conventional."*

Creighton replied calmly, "Randy, you're too much of an idealist! You don't understand how the minds of the generals in the Pentagon work. They don't want to make a mistake. If they selected a *super advanced* design it might flop and their reputations would be damaged. Then they might not get their next star and they would have to retire early!"

Randy responded sadly, "I guess I *am* a hopeless idealist. I thought the generals in the Pentagon were charged with getting the best defense possible for the country within the constraints of technology!"

Creighton brightened and said, "Well Randy, I guess you'll have plenty of time now to work on your other research projects, right?"

Randy answered slowly, "Rich, we've been so busy writing the ATF proposal and then answering the follow-up questions from the Air Force evaluators that we've neglected our other business prospects. We were really depending on the ATF. I'm afraid we're in bad shape business-wise. Do you have any consulting work for us, Rich?"

"I'm afraid not Randy. We at Cosmos were depending on winning the ATF contract, too. Since we didn't get it, we'll have to lay-off a few hundred people. In light of those lay-offs, it's out of the question for us to hire a consultant firm like yours right now. But if something comes up, Randy, I'll give you a call!"

"OK, Rich. Thanks for the call. Keep us in mind."

Randy and Patricia walked dejectedly back into the conference room. Marsh reacted immediately, "Judging by the looks on your faces, it must not have been good news!"

Randy replied sadly, "John, I'm afraid it *was* bad news. Cosmos has just heard they're not getting the ATF design contract. That means the bottom curve on our business chart is what we now project for the future."

Marsh rose slowly, looked at Randy's eyes, and said, "Don't worry Randy, I'll give you and Patricia until August to get some business. That's six months. With your marketing skills, I'm sure you'll come through."

Randy smiled wanly, "That's really fair, John.   Maybe someone else would like to build my design.   It really is revolutionary – *too far out* for the Pentagon Generals!*"*

Marsh laughed and thought a moment.   Then he suggested, "Randy, maybe the Defense Advanced Research Project Agency – DARPA, could come up with enough funds to build a prototype of your design.   Why don't you prepare a un-solicited proposal for them?   My old friend, Fred Hanson, is now director of their advanced aeronautics department.   I'll call him to see if he might be interested."

Randy brightened-up and said, "That's a good idea.   I already discovered when I sent in an un-solicited proposal to government agencies it was a waste of time unless I *first* found someone in the agency who was interested."

Marsh smiled and replied, "Randy I do think selling your ATF design is the best way to stay in business.   Get the proposal ready. Meanwhile I'll call Fred and see if he's encouraging.   Now I've got to get to the campus.   One of my PhD students is waiting to see me.   Good luck!"

Randy responded, "OK, John, and thanks for the six months to find new business."

Patricia interjected, "And John, what happens if we don't find new business by August?"

Walking towards the conference room door, Marsh paused, "I'm surprised you would ask.   In that case, of course, I would accept your and Randy's resignations.   The company won't be able to pay you after August without some new business."

Patricia persisted, "And how about our investment in the company stock? Will you return that?

Marsh replied grimly, "I think you know the answer to that question too, Pat.   The company can't afford to buy back your stock.   You'll just have some worthless stock.   That's one of the risks associated with investing in a small company!" He strode out of the room, leaving Patricia and Randy staring at each other. They walked dejectedly over to the view graph projector, picked up their company plans and walked out, Randy's arm around Patricia's shoulders.

Chapter 3

Taipei Meeting

Eddie Chung strode into the lobby of the Brothers Hotel in Taipei. He found Dr. Chang Cheng-chang having breakfast in the dining room which was just to the right of the desk. Chung seated himself at Dr. Chang's table as Chang finished his morning coffee and greeted Chang brightly, "Good morning, Dr. Chang. Did you enjoy the young lady I sent to your room last night?"

Chang appeared a little embarrassed, and answered, "Why yes, Eddie, of course I enjoyed Joy-tung. When I gave her the 100 New Taiwan dollars for the taxi ride home, she thanked me for making her feel so good. She sent her regards to you, Eddie, - said *she hoped to see the two of us with Mei Lin at the New China Dance Hall tonight for dinner and dancing.* She seemed grateful!"

"Good, good. I like to see our senior AIDC executives relax with a beautiful young girl when you come to Taipei from Taichung. You work too hard, Cheng-chang. You should relax more . We will have dinner and dancing tonight with Mei Lin and Joy-tung after our business is over today. Then you can return to Taichung all relaxed. That should make your wife happy. With your tensions gone, you can make better love with her!"

"Eddie, I like your theories on relaxation. But now we had better leave for our meeting with General Hua. We shouldn't keep the director general of the Ministry of National Defense waiting!"

"My car is parked in the hotel parking garage down below us. We'll be at the MND headquarters building in twenty minutes, in spite of the morning Taipei traffic."

"Do you know what General Hua wants to see us about? The message I got yesterday was a little mysterious. It said *Very urgent you meet with me and Chung Eng-fu tomorrow morning, Ministry of National Defense Headquarters, 10 am. (signed) General Hua Ding-fua.* It must be very important!"

"Yes, Cheng-chang, it is of utmost importance. But we better not discuss it here. My cousin, General Hua, will explain everything."

The two men walked out of the dining room to the elevator in the lobby and descended to the parking lot where Chung's BMW auto was waiting. Chung maneuvered expertly through the chaotic Taipei morning traffic. The pair arrived at the entrance to the MND Headquarters building at 10 minutes 'til 10 am in plenty of time for their 10 am meeting. Chung left his BMW under the watchful eyes of an *unofficial parking attendant* on the street. The pair hurried into the high rise building and took the elevator to the 10th floor. They quickly covered the short distance to General Hua's conference room. His secretary ushered them into the room and immediately brought each man a drink of hot tea in a glass plus a large platter of assorted cookies.

She then said, "Gentlemen, General Hua will be right with you. He's on the phone with President Chiang."

A few minutes later, General Hua strode into the room. He hugged his cousin Chung and shook hands with Chang and stated, "My cousin Eng-fu, it is so good to see you and thank you Cheng-chang for coming up from Taichung on such short notice. I have asked you both to come here to discuss an issue of utmost importance to our nation. I just finished talking to my uncle, President Chiang, who is most anxious that we implement this new project – the Ultra Taiwan Fighter (UTF) - an advanced fighter aircraft. Dr. Chang, I'm naming you Program Director of the UTF, effective immediately. You will report directly to me on this project!"

Dr. Chang was somewhat taken back by this opening statement, and replied, "But, General Hua, this is all so sudden! Just what is the Ultra Taiwan Fighter? What are the UTF requirements?"

I'm sorry Cheng-chang to leap into the UTF so quickly, but I've been thinking about it for over a month now. Let me back up and give you the requirements. Eng-fu here has been working with my Requirements Director to define just what we want in the UTF."

Eddie Chung broke in and said, "Cheng-chang, what we need is an aircraft even more advanced than the American Advanced

Tactical Fighter (AATF) aircraft. That's why we call it the Ultra Taiwan Fighter, or UTF for short!"

"But Eng-fu, what does the UTF have to do?"

"That's easy. It must be capable of destroying our enemy's aircraft, the mainland communists' aircraft, and also of eliminating their leadership *completely*!"

"That's a tall order Eng-fu. Our enemy has the Russian MiG-27 and the American F-16 in their Air Force. And to kill their leadership would require greater accuracy, or a nuclear weapon."

"Exactly, Cheng-chang. The performance of the UTF must greatly exceed that of the MiG-27 and the F-16 and its firepower must have extreme accuracy! But *no nuclear weapons*!"

Dr. Chang reflected for a moment, turned to General Hua and replied, "General Hua, this is a very difficult task for AIDC, the Aircraft Industries Development Center, - to design and build this UTF. We are building the old F-5 under license from Northrop. What you are asking is a quantum leap. We will need outside expertise."

General Hua looked into Changs's eyes, smiled and replied, "Your are right, Cheng-chang. We will need help. My cousin, Eddie Chung, here, points out that you received your PhD at Texas Tech and one of your class mates was Dr. Richard Creighton. Dr. Creighton is now vice president of the Advanced Tactical Aircraft program for Cosmos Aircraft. Perhaps Dr. Creighton can help us!"

"Yes, yes of course! I remember Rich Creighton very well. We both attended our twentieth class reunion at Texas Tech last June. We worked under the same professor for our PhD's. I think Dr. Creighton may be able to help, if anyone in the US can."

General Hua smiled, "Good Cheng-chang. I suggest you call Dr. Creighton today and arrange for a visit to Cosmos Aircraft in Texas as soon as possible. By the way, President Chiang just authorized a budget of two billion dollars or 80 billion New Taiwan dollars for the UTF. The funding will be channeled through our CIA, named after the US Central Intelligence Agency and serving the same purpose. Eng-fu, - that's Eddie to the Americans - will be in charge of administering the funds. We want this project to be *ultra secret*. Please initiate the proper security safeguards, immediately! Only those with *need-to-know* are authorized to know of this project. Is that clear?"

"Yes, General Hua. It is *very* clear. In other words, if we buy any goods or services for the UTF overseas, then the purchasing will be done by Eddie Chung's company, Chung-Export/Import. Ltd., not by AIDC nor the MND. Is that what you mean?"

"Exactly, Cheng-chang. Even though you are a scientist, you have a flair for business – CIA business! Now if you'll excuse me, I have some foreign visitors waiting to see me now. Good luck!"

On the way back to the hotel, Eddie Chung said, "Well, Cheng-chang, we will have a celebration dinner tonight at the New China Dance Hall. Mei Lin and Joy-tung will meet us there. We will dance with the girls after dinner. Then you can take Joy-tung to bed after your midnight call to Texas! It'll be day time there at midnight."

"But, Eddie, won't it be security risk to call about the UTF visit with Joy-tung in my room?"

"Don't worry, Cheng-chang! Joy-tung is cleared for the most sensitive of state secrets. She's on my payroll. Just relax and enjoy her!"

Eddie Chung picked up Dr. Chang at the Brothers Hotel at 6 pm. The New China Dance Hall was an elaborate establishment with bright neon lights illuminating the front of the building. They walked up the entrance stairway, turned left and entered the area of private dining rooms. Eddie opened the door and ushered Chang into the medium sized private dining room. Mei Lin and Joy-tung, both in their mid twenties, were waiting for them. Mei Lin had on a light yellow, tight fitting dress with a slit up the skirt to the top of her thigh. Joy-tung was wearing a similar dark turquoise-colored dress. They were both beautiful and well perfumed.

Joy-tung took Chang by the hand and led him to the guest of honor's place at the head of the table. She held his chair as he was seated. Mei Lin seated Eddie so his back was to the door, indicating he was the host for the group. Each girl seated herself to the right of her companion for the evening.

The waiter, accompanied by two serving assistants, carried in an elaborate tray of Chinese banquet foods. The two girls served their male companions a selection from the many dishes and waited for them to begin eating. Then they served themselves.

The dinner was enjoyable for all!   The girls provided happy, laughing conversations and were very attentive to the culinary needs of the men, giving them personalized service from the array of dishes placed on the dining table, using chop sticks to do the serving.

After a leisurely and pleasurable dinner that lasted almost two hours, the two couples left the dining room and went upstairs to the large dance hall. They are ushered into the darkly lighted room by the hostess, a largish woman in her fifties, dressed in a red Mao-type coat.   She was the owner's wife and greeted Chung happily, "Good evening, Mr. Chung.   Welcome to the New China.   I have an excellent table for you and your guests." She then led them to a booth near the front of the room on the side, about ten feet from the dance floor.   She took their drink orders and left.

Joy-tung turned to Dr. Chang and said, "Dr. Chang, I would love to dance with you.   Are you ready?"

Chang smiled brightly and exclaimed, "Joy-tung I would enjoy dancing with you, but I should warn you, I'm not a very good dancer!"

Joy-tung laughed and beamed out, "I believe you will be as wonderful dancing as you were in bed last night!"

The pair rose and left for the dance floor, followed closely behind by Eddie and Mei Lin.   On the way to the dance floor, Chang whispered in Joy-tung's ear, "You made me feel so young in bed last night.   It was as if I were in my twenties again.   How did you do it?"

As they stepped out onto the dance floor, Joy-tung held Chang tightly, and replied, "I didn't do anything. You just relaxed and let your tensions go while I massaged you.   That's why you felt young! Besides, Dr. Chang, you *are* young,"

Chang pressed his pelvic area tightly against Joy-tung and laughed, "But I'm over forty years old already."

As the two undulated to the romantic dance music, Joy-tung pressed back against Chang and replied, "Dr. Chang, forty is very young.   You'll still be strong in your eighties.   My grandfather, who is 89 just married a twenty year old girl and I'm sure still makes love to his recent bride.   What do you think of that?"

Chang smiled and replied, "I think that's wonderful.   I hope I continue feeling young like tonight."

Joy-tung giggled "Just keep dancing and making love regularly. Then you'll stay young!"

Eddie Chung and Mei Lin dropped Joy-tung and Chang off at the Brother's Hotel just before midnight. Chang and Joy-tung took the elevator to his room on the twelfth floor. While Joy-tung was showering and getting ready for bed, Chang dialed the telephone for an overseas call to Dr. Creighton at Cosmos Aircraft in Fort Worth, Texas. The call went directly through to Creighton's office. His secretary answered with a deep Texas drawl, "This is Dr. Creighton's office. May I help you?"

"Yes, this is Dr. Chang in Taiwan, calling for Dr. Creighton. We're PhD classmates from Texas Tech!"

"Just a moment, Dr. Chang. I'm sure he'll want to talk to you!"

A moment later Creighton answered with his cultured Texas twang, "Why Charlie Chang, it's good to hear from you. How's everything over there in Taiwan – ah, I mean the Republic of China?"

"Rich, everything is great here in ROC. I'm up in Taipei for a short business trip this week. I've got a new project starting down in Taichung. That's what I'm calling about".

"And what can I do for you?"

"We need a new aircraft design. Can you help?"

"Well Charlie, that depends on the Government of the United States of America. You know they have to approve any technical assistance we give your country."

"Yes, yes, Rich, I know that. But do you have the technical capability to help on the design of a really new fighter? And do you have the time available?"

"To be really frank with you, Charlie, we have lots of time just now. We lost the contract for the design of the ATF last month. We had a really superior design, too. A lot better than the one they selected!"

"Rich, can I come to Texas to talk about it?"

"Well, yes, Charlie. When do you want to come?"

"Today's Thursday. How about Monday morning?"

"Boy, you don't waste any time, do you Charlie? Yeah, Monday's fine! I'll make the reservations for you at the Green

Oaks Hotel. It's near our plant here on Lake Worth so it will be convenient to our meeting. Guess you'll be coming Sunday night, right?"

"Right, Sunday at the Green Oaks is fine. See you Monday morning, Rich."

"OK, I'll pick you up at the Green Oaks Monday morning at 8 am. I'll have all of the right people at the meeting. Some have to come from Pasadena! See you Monday, goodbye!"

Having completed his business for the evening, Chang switched to more relaxing activities. Joy made Chang feel twenty years old two nights in a row!

Chapter 4

Fort Worth Meeting

It was late March and Randy McLyle had just spent another discouraging day phoning all of his old customers, business associates, friends in the government and anyone else he thought might have some business for Aeronautical Consultants, Inc (ACI) to perform. Although the words varied from phone call to phone call, the message was clear: 'Sorry, we have no work that we can let out-of-house now. If the situation changes, we'll call you. Don't call us!'

Randy phoned his old friend, Jerry Taylor, Director of Advance Aeronautics at NASA Langley. Jerry answered his own phone with a cheerful, "This is Jerry Taylor, advanced aeronautics. What can I do for you?"

Randy answered, "Hi Jerry, this is Randy McLyle, out at ACI. I'm looking for some new business."

"Why, Randy, I thought you'd be up to your eyeballs on the Advanced Tactical Fighter. I'm just finishing up the TM (technical memo) report evaluating the design. I'll read it to you, kind of summarizes our evaluation: *This report evaluates the ACI design of a candidate for the USAF Advanced Tactical Fighter aircraft. Using ultra-light weight materials this is the most aerodynamically efficient design ever evaluated in the hypersonic wind tunnel at NASA Langley. Its performance is truly outstanding. Our evaluation at the NASA Langley radar range shows this design is essentially invisible to radar because it has an effective cross section of one millionth of a square meter. It is effectively radar invisible!*

"So you see, we think the USAF would be wise to choose your design."

Randy laughed dryly , "That's ironic, Jerry! If only you were on the Source Selection Committee (SSC) in the Pentagon! Our design was *not* selected. The SSC thought our design was *too far out!*"

"That's crazy! Now the USAF won't be able to have your design. They're the losers! But you asked if I could give you a project to work on here. Randy, to be frank with you, my total budget for aeronautical research for the rest of this fiscal year is just over $10,000. I know that wouldn't help you much. Our budget for the next fiscal year is not much more. We just aren't getting aeronautical research funds. All the money's going to weapons research these days! The *Stars War Program* is taking it all!"

Discouraged because this was the last name on his list of people to call for new business, Randy replied sadly, "Well, thanks, Jerry. I appreciate the evaluation of our design. Please send me a copy of your TM report."

"OK, Randy, I'll be glad to. By the way, why don't you call DARPA? They may have funds for an advanced design like yours. Fred Hanson's office at DARPA would be the right one to try."

"Jerry, I'm afraid we've already tried Fred Hanson. ACI's President, Professor Marsh, called Hanson early this month. He was not encouraging. He said all of his advanced aeronautics funding was committed to support the ATF design selected by the Pentagon."

"That's too bad. Sorry I can't help. Good luck, Randy."

"Goodbye, Jerry, and thanks for offering to send me your TM report. It may help get new business!"

Just as Randy hung up the phone, Patricia buzzed him on the intercom. She exclaimed, "I've just been talking to Rich Creighton at Cosmos on the other line. He's got a new project to talk to you about. He's holding, knowing you were talking to Jerry Taylor at Langley."

Randy pushed his flashing phone button and answered happily, "Hi, Rich, what's up?"

Creighton replied cheerily, "Randy, I think we have a customer for your ATF design!"

Randy replied eagerly, "Great! Who is it Rich, the US Navy?"

"No, not the navy! I got a phone call from my old PhD classmate from Texas Tech, Dr. Charlie Chang. Charlie, whose Chinese name is Cheng-chang, is an executive in the Taiwan aircraft establishment called Aeronautical Industries Development Center. AIDC is in Taichung in the middle of the west side of

Taiwan. He asked if we could help him on a new advanced aircraft design. He's coming to my office early Monday morning."

"That sounds interesting."

"Well, Randy, I'll tell him about your design. But don't get your hopes up too high. Remember, the US Government, including the Munitions Control Office (MCO) of the State Department, must OK any technical assistance we provide the Taiwanese Government!"

Randy replied happily, "That shouldn't be any problem. Certainly the State Department will eager to support a free enterprise government like Taiwan. After all, they are not communists like mainland China."

Creighton replied, somewhat condescendingly, "Randy, I'm afraid you don't understand super power politics very well. The US has officially recognized the People's Republic of China, on the mainland. Military cooperation with PRC (Peoples' Republic of China) has been accelerating over the last several years. The PRC is vociferous against the US supporting Taiwan – The Republic of China. !"

Randy asked incredulously, "Well, why in the world not? I thought the US, particularly President Edwards, was staunchly anti-communist."

Creighton replied patiently, "About the only thing both PRC and ROC agree upon is that there is only one China, **not** two! For global strategic reasons, the US agreed during the Nixon years to recognize PRC and to reduce the US Embassy in ROC-Taiwan to a liaison office. This pro-PRC policy is intended to counter the Soviet Union's large military presence in Asia with a friendly Chinese military force."

"How strange that the US would pick a communist government to recognize over a free enterprise government."

"Randy, that is the reality of world super power politics. We can't change that."

Randy questioned, "Well, what do we do next? Can we get the US government's permission to support Dr. Chang or not?"

Creighton replied, "First we have to find out exactly what he wants. Then we have to ask the Pentagon if we can work on the project. Dr. Willie Rinehart in the Pentagon is the key decision maker for such support to Taiwan. If he says *no*, there no hope. If he says *yes,* then a formal technical assistance agreement has to be submitted to the State Department's Office of *Munitions Control.* If some bureaucrat doesn't say *no,* then it will probably be approved. The whole process takes six to nine months."

Randy replied plaintively, "It all sounds so complicated. Do you think I should come to your meeting Monday?"

"No, Randy, I don't thing so. I told Dr. Chang *the people from Pasadena* would be here, but I now believe it would be better for me to meet with him without you there. If it looks encouraging, I'll ask him to stop by Pasadena to see you at ACI."

"OK, Rich keep me informed! Remember, ACI needs the business desperately!"

Gazing out the window of the Delta Airlines' L-1011 Charlie Chang saw Lake Worth to the north. The huge Cosmos Aircraft building and runway were on the north shore of the huge lake. It was late Sunday afternoon, the last week of March 1988.

Chang thought to himself, 'How many beautiful week-ends I spent water skiing on Lake Worth during the four years I attended Texas Tech. The lake looks as inviting as ever, but it's probably a bit chilly in late March. By May it will be warm, even hot. Perfect for water skiing.'

His thoughts were interrupted by the captain who announced the seat belt sign was on in preparation for landing at the enormous Dallas-Fort Worth Airport The big jet turned left over the city of Dallas on a wide base leg heading for the east-west runways. There was a brisk west March wind and the aircraft turned westerly to land into the gusts. The resulting turbulence was uncomfortable, but not bad enough to cause air sickness, to which Chang is susceptible. The jet landed and taxied to the huge Texas sized terminal building. Chang collected his carry-on bag and briefcase, exited the aircraft and strode to the down escalator. Arriving on the street level he found a bus for the twenty minute ride to downtown Fort Worth, then took a taxi for the ten minute drive to reach the Green Oaks Hotel on the west side of Fort Worth.

Chang paid the taxi driver, entered the huge lobby, and walked up to the long desk where he announced to the cute red-headed desk clerk, "My name is Dr. Chang. Cosmos Aircraft made my reservation."

The desk clerk replied in her Texas twang, "Why, Dr. Chang, you've already been checked in by a representative of Cosmos Aircraft who's waiting for you in your room. Here's a second key. You're in the Catfish Suite overlooking the pool. She showed him a map of the hotel and added, "Here's your room, just across from the King's Row Restaurant. Have a pleasant stay in Fort Worth, Dr. Chang."

"Thank you, Miss. With your fine Texas hospitality, I'm sure I'll enjoy my stay."

The clerk grinned mischievously and said, "I'm sure the Cosmos rep waiting in your room will make your stay unforgettable!"

Chang smiled, a little perplexed, and replied, "Thanks!"

Chang strode on through the lobby, passed by the huge goldfish and trout fish-tank, then went past the blue swimming pool to find his Catfish Suite. Walking into the large sitting room he heard a soft, female voice from the adjoining room say, "Dr. Chang , come on into the bedroom."

Chang put down his bag and walked into the next room. Lying in the middle of the bed, completely nude, was a beautiful blue-eyed blonde with long hair and long legs.

Chang gasped at the sight of all this bare pulchritude and managed to say, "Miss, I'm Charlie Chang, and – err- "

The young lady laughed and said, "Don't be embarrassed, Charlie. I'm Betty Lou Manfred. I'm a receptionist over at Cosmos. Dr. Creighton said to come over here and make you feel at home. You poor dear! You must be terribly tired after that long flight from China. You just get undressed and climb into this bed. I'll help you relax!"

Chang was a little embarrassed, but feeling his passion growing, replied, "Betty Lou, pleased meet you. I'm sure you'll make me feel at home. I'll take a quick shower and join you right away."

Charlie awakened about two hours later and mumbled sleepily, "Betty Lou, that was a great way to overcome the jet lag of my long flight from Taiwan. I'm rested now, but hungry."

"Good. Let's get dressed and go enjoy some prime rib and barbequed spare ribs at the Green Oaks' restaurant-night club. The food's great. The music and dancing are even better.

"That sounds like a fine idea. I'm ready for some good Texas barbeque!"

The pair strolled over to the restaurant where they had dinner and then danced until midnight. They then returned to the room and enjoyed a reprise of their lovemaking.

About half past four Charlie partially awoke when Betty Lou, already dressed, bent down and kissed him goodbye, saying, "Honey, Charlie, I've got to get home now. I'm a working gal, you know. Dr. Creighton will meet you for breakfast here at the Green Oaks at about 8:30 AM. See you later!"

Creighton met Chang in the breakfast dining room at 8:30 am. He strode up to Chang's table and exclaimed loudly, "Welcome back to Texas, Charlie." Then he lowered his voice, "And how was Betty Lou?"

Chang smiled broadly and said, "Thanks for the Texas Hospitality, Rich. What a reception for my return to Texas."

After breakfast, the two walked out to Creighton's Cadillac Coupe d'Ville for the drive to Cosmos Aircraft. They drove through the Cosmos guard gate and Creighton parked in a spot right in front of the big lobby. The pair walked into the lobby and were greeted by the receptionist, Betty Lou Manfred who, in a very friendly, but professional tone, said, "Good morning, Doctors Chang and Creighton. Here is your visitor's badge, Dr. Chang. You may enter the classified area now. Right through the door on your right."

Creighton led Chang to the big conference room just off the lobby. Waiting to greet them was a trio of corporate officers: the vice president of public relations, the vice president of marketing and the corporate president.

After the introductions, the president rose and stated, "Dr. Chang, welcome to Cosmos Aircraft. After a short movie about Cosmos and our products, you will be taken on a tour of our plant by my two staff vice presidents and Dr. Creighton. We at Cosmos hope we can help you with your new fighter project. But, frankly, Dr. Chang, the mood in Washington is not encouraging for giving technical assistance to Taiwan – excuse me – the Republic of China. If you were from the Peoples' Republic of China, then it would be a different matter."

Chang was somewhat discouraged by the president's remarks and replied, "But, Sir, I thought your government was strongly anti-communist. Why would your government not help ROC? We are staunchly anti-communist and embody the spirit of free enterprise that we learned well from the United States!"

The president answered sympathetically, "Mr. Chang, certainly if it were up to me, we would help you with your new fighter. But unfortunately, Mr. Nixon played the *China Card* to offset the strategic strength of the Soviets. Unfortunately for Taiwan, that's our government's policy and we at Cosmos have to abide by the decisions that result from that China policy. At any rate I wish you a good visit. Good luck in your quest for technical assistance! I must leave now."

Chang answered dejectedly, "Goodbye, Sir and thank you for your insight into the matter."

Chang then spent the rest of the morning watching movies and briefings about Cosmos Aircraft's capabilities to design and build advanced tactical fighter aircraft: just what Chang needed! He took a long tour of the factory area seeing the production line of new fighter aircraft being built for the US Air Force and US Navy.

Then he was treated to a two hour luncheon in the Cosmos executive dining room. He was surrounded by the top executives of Cosmos. The president joined them for lunch and presented a toast to Dr. Chang's health and to his quest for technical assistance in the US.

After lunch, Chang and his hosts re-assembled in the big expensively furnished conference room. Chang was seated at the head of the big oval table. Creighton was on his right and the two vice presidents of marketing and public relations were on his left.

Creighton opened the afternoon session – it was almost 3 PM by declaring, "Dr. Chang, Charlie, now you've seen our capabilities at Cosmos. And as much as we here at Cosmos would like to help Taiwan – ROC with your new fighter, I'm afraid it's out of the question. While you were on the plant tour, I received a call from Dr. Willie Rinehart in the Pentagon. Dr. Rinehart is director of tactical Systems in the office of the Undersecretary of

Defense for research, development, and engineering (OUSDRDE). I explained your need for technical assistance on your fighter. His reply was, and I quote: *There's no way the Pentagon is going to approve Cosmos to help Taiwan on a new fighter aircraft – it's too high visibility. The PRC would threaten to break diplomatic relations with the US. We can't allow that to happen!* "

Chang looked up sadly and said, "But, Rich, I haven't even told you what our requirements are!"

Creighton looked Chang straight in the eye and replied, "Sorry that's Washington's policy. We can't fight that, no matter what we think personally. However I think there's a glimmer of hope."

Chang's face brightened, "Yes, Rich, and what is that?"

"Well, Willie Rinehart *emphasized* that Cosmos's help would be *too high visibility.* Maybe you should seek help from a smaller firm like Aeronautics Consultants, Inc, ACI, in Pasadena, California. Randy McLyle of ACI was the father of our ATF design. ACI is a very small company. Maybe having Randy help you would be low enough profile that the PRC wouldn't know about it and therefore wouldn't complain. At any rate, it's worth a try."

"Do you really think ACI could help on such a major project as our new fighter aircraft ?"

"Charlie, I'm sure Randy could be a great help. He's a very creative designer. In fact the Pentagon thought his design was *too far out*! Maybe that's just the design you could use."

"In that case it's worth a try. Do you think Randy McLyle has time to help us?"

"Believe me, Charlie, Randy has time. Maybe you can visit him on your way back to Taiwan."

Chang replied, "Good idea. Please call him now. If I take the 6 pm flight from Dallas to Los Angeles, I would arrive at 7 pm this evening. I could meet with McLyle tomorrow!"

"OK, I'll call him right now."

Chapter 5

Meeting in Pasadena

Randy McLyle was sitting at his desk with his head in his hands, staring at the charts showing his company heading for bankruptcy when his phone rang.

Rich Creighton announced, "Good afternoon, Randy. I spent the day here at Cosmos with Dr. Charlie Chang from AIDC of Taiwan. I'm afraid the Government won't let Cosmos help Charlie with his new fighter aircraft design. Dr. Willie Rinehart in the Pentagon said it would be *too high profile* for Cosmos to help."

McLyle was crest-fallen with this bad news and replied, "Wow, Rich! We were really hoping to get some work from this Taiwan project, something that would save ACI financially!"

Creighton replied warmly, "Randy, don't give up. I've suggested to Dr Chang that he come by and visit you in Pasadena on his way home to Taiwan. Since ACI is a small company, you might be given permission to help with the design. You have the advantage of being *low profile.*"

Perceptibly cheered by this news, Randy responded, "Rich, ACI is such *low profile* that we're going to disappear if we don't get some new business soon. We would love to meet with Dr. Chang. When will he arrive?"

He has a reservation on the Delta non-stop from Dallas to Los Angeles. It arrives at LAX about 7 pm this evening. Can you meet him?"

"Yes, by all means, Patricia and I will be delighted to pick him up. How will we recognize him?"

"Charlie's wearing a dark blue suit with a red tie. Also he's wearing the lapel pin we gave him today with a miniature ATF airplane of your design. He should be easy to spot!"

"That sounds like he'll be easy enough to find. Tell Charlie we'll get reservations for him at the Huntington Hotel here in Pasadena. It's near ACI. He should enjoy the environment at the Huntington.

Creighton closed the phone call by saying, "The arrangements sound fine, Randy. I'll tell Charlie right now. Hope it all works out for you. It would be good to see someone implement that design of yours, since the USAF rejected it as being *too far out!*"

"Rich, I certainly hope so. If not I'll be on the streets the end of August. Patricia's in the same boat."

Randy and Patricia were waiting in the Delta arrival area when the L-1011 carrying Dr. Charlie Chang arrived at the LAX terminal, just after 7 pm. Chang was one of the first passengers off the big wide-body jetliner. He had his carry-on bag over one shoulder and was carrying his briefcase full of papers in his left hand. Randy saw his Chinese face and red tie, saw the miniature jetfighter pinned to his label, strode up to him briskly and greeted him, "You must be Dr. Chang. I'm Randy McLyle."

Chang smiled broadly, "Yes, Randy, pleased to meet you. But please call me Charlie. And who is this beautiful lady with you?"

Randy grinned and replied, "This is my colleague from Aeronautical Consultants, Ms. Patricia Manos. She's our expert in Systems analysis. She performs our digital simulations on our personal computers."

"Ms. Manos, it's a pleasure to meet such a beautiful and obviously talented American lady."

"Pleased to meet you, Charlie. Welcome to our sunshine state of California. Pease call me Patricia."

The trio started walking towards the exit. Randy said, "Charlie are these all your bags?"

"Yes, Randy. I learned from you Americans to travel light on business trips. That way the airlines never lose my luggage, right?"

"Right, Charlie. That's the best way. I've started using only carry-ons myself. My car is just across the street in the parking lot."

Charlie replied happily, "Good. It's nice to be in California. There're lots of Chinese here in Los Angeles, aren't there?"

"Yes, there's a large community in Monterey Park close to Los Angeles' Chinatown, which is *larger* than the Chinese community in San Francisco now."

As they walked across the overpass to the parking lot, Charlie commented, "I understand from Rich Creighton that you have reservations for me at the Huntington Hotel in Pasadena. It's a beautiful place. I stayed there during a visit to a seminar at Caltech while I was working on my PhD at Texas Tech."

"I agree, Charlie. It is a beautiful place. One of the highlights of Pasadena, along with Caltech, the Huntington Library and Gardens, the Jet Propulsion Lab, and of course Aeronautical Consultants, Inc!"

The trio quickly found Randy's car and he drove along the LA freeways from LAX to Pasadena. After taking the last exits from the Pasadena freeway, Randy drove the short distance past the stately mansions of Pasadena to the beautiful Huntington Hotel. Chang checked in, put his bag away, and the trio went to the cocktail lounge for drinks.

Over drinks, Chang asked McLyle bluntly, "Randy, do you think you can get permission to adapt your ATF design to our needs for our Ultra Tactical Fighter? It's got to outperform any the PRC's Air Force has."

"First, Charlie, I'm sure that my fighter aircraft design will outperform any PRC airplane. All they have are some old MiG-29's and F-16's. We can fly circles around them. As far as getting permission from the US government to adapt my design to your needs, I'm confident we can get that permission. After all, the Pentagon rejected my design. They thought it was *too far out!* Why wouldn't they let us use it for a friendly country's Air Force?"

Chang grinned broadly, raised his drink glass and replied, "Well, here's to your success in getting permission to use your design!"

Chang, McLyle, and Manos clanked their glasses together and drank to success.

After some conversation about the cultural sights of Pasadena, Randy turned to Charlie and stated, "Charlie we'll pick you up at 8:30 in the morning for the meeting. It's just a short drive from here."

"Good night, Randy and Patricia, see you in the morning. Thanks for everything."

Randy and Patricia chorused their answers, "Good night!"

Dr. Chang's meeting with Randy and Patricia began just after 9 am in their Green Street offices. Chang was seated at the head of the long conference table with Randy on his left and Patricia on his right.

Randy opened the meeting by declaring, "Charlie we're not going to give you a briefing on ACI's capabilities. We know you wouldn't be here if you didn't think we were technically competent to do the design of your new fighter aircraft. We would like you to tell us your requirements first. Then we'll tell you if our ATF design can be adapted to your needs."

Chang smiled happily and said, "Randy, that's a refreshing approach. I spent most of yesterday seeing movies, watching briefings and touring facilities at Cosmos. They never asked me to brief them on our needs. At the end of the day, they said the Pentagon wouldn't let them help us. Rich Creighton suggested you might be able to help, so here I am!"

Randy laughed, "Yeah, I'll bet you had at least three vice presidents and the corporate president who met with you before they said no. Charlie, I'm afraid that's how big aerospace companies like Cosmos operate. We're a little different at ACI. We don't have much fanfare, but we work hard and do good work. We have a Professor from Caltech as our President to give us technical help when needed."

Patricia interrupted and added, "Yes, Charlie, and we really need your business. You'll find us very capable and efficient."

Charlie, now relaxed with this friendly pair, replied, "You're right about the Cosmos *brass* in the meeting. Well let me tell you about our requirements for the new fighter aircraft. We call it the Ultra Tactical Fighter or UTF for short."

Chang spent the next forty-five minutes explaining the details of the requirements for the new fighter. He ended his briefing with a short summary, "So you can see, Randy and Patricia, the UTF should be invisible to enemy radar and air defense sensors. Each aircraft should carry missiles to destroy with certainty 32 enemy aircraft in air-to-air combat or 32 ground targets such as tanks, in air-to-ground combat. Furthermore, the aircraft should be able to maneuver at 20 g's without the pilot losing consciousness by blacking out. It should have a speed of Mach 5 for short distances and Mach 20 for longer distances such as in suborbital flight. As far as the electronics are concerned, it should have radar and other sensors to find the targets, have a good secure communication system, and, at the same time, be immune to enemy countermeasures and defenses."

Randy responded with a deep sigh, "Wow, Charlie! That's a tall order, but guess what?"

"What, Randy?"

"My ATF design meets all of your requirements! It's almost as though you had access to my design in defining your requirements."

Chang thought to himself, 'Eddie Chung in our CIA probably did have access to Randy's Cosmos design. There are enough Chinese engineers working in US aerospace companies who are secretly loyal to ROC (Taiwan) that Chung's intelligence collection network in the US had the details on *all* the ATF designs submitted to the USAF, maybe even before the USAF got them!'

Chang didn't reveal these thoughts to McLyle, but rather replied, "That's excellent, Randy. I'll assure you that these requirements came about from an analysis of our needs. I'm pleased that your design meets our needs."

Randy smiled and stated, "Now, for the sixty-four thousand dollar question. Assuming we obtain permission from the Pentagon to provide you our ATF design, how soon would we be under contract to your organization?"

Charlie, assuming an official business-like air, replied, "First, Randy, any contract would not be with my organization, AIDC. But rather, the contract would be funded by Chung-Export/Import, Ltd., a company headed by Eddie Chung in Taipei. My government thinks all funding for the UTF outside Taiwan should be through Chung's company. It will make it more difficult for our enemy, the *Red Chinese*, to find out about our new fighter project. *Security* you know!"

"Yes, of course, for security reasons. Just how do I meet this Mr. Chung?"

Charlie relaxed from his official air, grinned and said, "Don't worry. Eddie Chung will contact you as soon as I give him the green light. He'll probably want to visit you early in April."

"That sounds great, Charlie. Now we have to keep our fingers crossed. We need the Pentagon's approval."

"OK, Randy, I think we understand each other. I have a 1 pm flight on China Airlines non-stop back to Taipei. If you'll call me a taxi, I'll leave for the airport now. Thanks for everything."

"You're welcome, Charlie. Hope we can work together on this exciting UTF project of yours. There's a taxi stand right outside. You'll be to the airport by 11 am."

Chapter 6

Chung-Export/Import Ltd. Proprietor

Charlie Chang was awakened from a deep sleep by the announcement on the first class cabin loud speaker. The captain of the China Airlines 747-SP announced in Chinese, and then English, "Ladies and Gentlemen, please fasten your safety belts for our approach to the Chiang Kai-shek Airport at Taipei. We will be landing in about twenty minutes. The weather is clear in Taipei, but there are a few scattered thunderstorms that could cause some turbulence."

Chang looked out the window and saw lights in the distance as the wide body airliner approached the north coast of Taiwan. It was almost 8 pm and already dark on the last Wednesday of March 1988. It was less than a week since Chang had left Taipei. He had been half way around the world and back in his quest for help on the new Taiwan Ultra Tactical Fighter (UTF). Chang had called Eddie Chung from the ROC Coordination Council for North American Affairs in Los Angeles – the equivalent of a Consulate – since Taiwan didn't have formal diplomatic relations with the US. Chang gave Eddie a brief summary of his visits in Fort Worth and Pasadena. Chung had insisted on meeting Chang at the airport upon his arrival so they could discuss the next steps toward getting technical assistance for their new fighter aircraft.

After landing, Chang was one of the first passengers off the big jet. He was met at the exit of the jetliner by Eddie Chung, who greeted him, "Cheng-chang, welcome back to China. I have a motor cart waiting to whisk you through passport control and customs. We'll have more time to talk."

"It's good to be home again, Eng-fu. America is a long way from here!"

The pair walked up the stairs from the large arrival lobby to the waiting motor cart. Chang was pleasantly surprised to see Mei Lin and Joy-tung sitting in the back seat of the cart. Chang kissed Mei Lin on the cheeks, and Joy-tung on the lips. Joy-tung whispered in his ear, "Welcome home, Cheng-chang. I will spend the night with you in the Brothers Hotel, if you will permit. Here's your key."

Chang smiled happily and whispered back, "I would love for you to spend the night with me, Joy-tung!"

Chung drove the cart down the long halls of the airport terminal to the passport control window, drove up to the crew window, showed his government ID badge. The officer on duty waived the cart and the four people through passport control. Chang didn't even have to show his passport.

As they waited for the elevator to take them down to customs, Chang remarked, "Eng-fu, your ID works wonders! Usually it takes me thirty minutes to get through passport control."

Chung smiled knowingly and replied, "Cheng-chang, you are too important to the ROC government now to spend so much time waiting for bureaucrats. We must use you time efficiently."

The elevator arrived and the quartet left the cart behind and descended to the ground level. Chung flashed his ID badge and the quartet was waived past customs control and they continued on into the crowded terminal lobby.

As the foursome passed through the underpass to the airport parking lot, Chung announced, "Now, we'll have dinner in one of my favorite restaurants."

Chang remarked, "Eng-fu, it'll be good to have real food again. The Caucasian food is tasteless and so heavy! Even China Airlines serves this kind of food now."

"I agree, Cheng-chang. Even the Chinese restaurants in America serve food I've never heard of before – Chow Mein, Chop Suey, and other inventions of our countrymen who immigrated from the homeland."

The quartet found Chung's BMW. Chang and Joy-tung climbed into the back seat. Mei Lin sat in the front seat next to Eddie Chung. They drove out of the airport parking lot, took the exit road and entered the toll road heading towards Taipei. Twenty-five minutes later, Chang maneuvered the BMW off the wide highway and headed through the streets of Taipei to his chosen restaurant.

They parked in the lot alongside the restaurant and entered the front door, where Chung was greeted warmly by the owner, who led the two couples to a good table near the back of the crowded restaurant.   Eddie Chung ordered a variety of dishes from the menu.   A short time later, two waitresses brought the Chinese feast and placed the dishes around the periphery of a *lazy Susan* in the center of the round table.   As usual, Chung was seated with his back towards the entrance, the indication that he was the host.

The revenue from Chung-Export/Import, Ltd., provided Eddie with a huge expense account that he lavished on friends, business associates, and clients in the expense restaurants, dance halls, and hotels of Taipei and the other cities of Taiwan and elsewhere in the world that he visited.   He took a shopping trip to Hong Kong, a short one and half hour flight from Taipei, with a female companion at least once a month, and stayed in the luxurious Regency Hotel, all paid for by his export/import firm.

Mei Lin and Joy-tung served the two men from the lazy Susan and then served themselves.   The four finished dinner just after 10:30 pm. After paying the bill with his company Visa credit card, Chung explained, "Now Cheng-chang, I'll take you to the Brothers Hotel were we will discuss your trip to the United States.   Mei Lin and Joy-tung have already *electronically swept* the room so we know it is *bug-free*.   We can talk securely there.   After you've spent a relaxing night with Joy-tung, I'll drive you to AIDC in Taichung tomorrow."

"Good Eng-fu.   That sounds like a fine agenda.   My body is confused by the jet lag of the trip to the US and back.   I need a good night's rest before returning to work."

A few minutes later, the quartet arrived at the Chang's suite at the Brothers Hotel.   The two men sat in the living room, while the two girls disappeared unobtrusively into the adjoining bedroom. Eddie Chung turned to Dr. Chang and commanded, "Give me your summary of the trip to the US and your recommendations for the next step in soliciting help for the UTF from the Americans."

Chang responded, "Eng-fu, I gave you a good summary of the trip from the ROC office in Los Angeles before I left yesterday."

"Yes, I know, Cheng-chang, but it was after midnight here when you called and I'm not sure I understood everything you said."

"Well, Eng-fu, the most important point is that Cosmos Aircraft can't help us with the design of the UTF.   Dr. Willie

Rinehart in the Pentagon said *no*. The Cosmos assistance would have *too high visibility* and our enemies on the mainland would put pressure on the American Administration to stop."

"But, Cheng-chang, if we have the design, can Cosmos help by fabricating parts of the aircraft?"

"Eng-fu I didn't ask them about that possibility, but frankly, I think the answer would be no.   Nevertheless, it's worth investigating."

"And how about this Randy McLyle? Do you really believe he can design our UTF aircraft?"

"Yes, Eng-fu. I believe the aircraft he designed for Cosmos would meet our needs. He was highly recommended by Cosmos. Dr. Creighton told me this design Cosmos submitted to the USAF was really McLyle's design. But the USAF rejected it because it was *too far out* !"

"But we want the most advanced design possible for our UTF, don't we?"

"Yes, of course.   NASA Langley performed a design evaluation of McLyle's plans in their hypersonic wind tunnel and confirmed the outstanding performance. McLyle showed me a copy of the NASA TM report. But one problem remains in obtaining help from McLyle and his woman associate, Patricia Manos."

"And what is that problem?"

Cheng-chang said in a serious tone of voice, "McLyle needs permission from the US government before he can provide his design to the Republic of China, even though the Pentagon rejected the design and contracted for a less capable, but lower risk design."

Chung laughed, "Cheng-chang, you scientists worry too much about bureaucratic details. With the budget of two billion dollars that we have and the *carte blanc* from President Chiang to obtain our new Taiwan *Ultra Tactical Fighter* aircraft, we have may options open to us."

Chang looked Chung in the eye and asked inquisitively, "Just what do you have in mind, Eng-fu?"

Chung grinned and responded confidentially, "First, McLyle is a human being, susceptible to greed. We can *buy* McLyle by paying him a sum of, say ten million dollars, for his design. A sum large from the individual's point of view, but small in our two billion dollar budget. Second, we can by-pass the American bureaucracy by offering McLyle an ROC passport and citizenship. After he finishes helping us design the UTF, he can take his million dollars and live anywhere in the world he wants. The US government can't keep him from immigrating."

Chang smiled and replied, "Eng-fu, I'm beginning to see how we can get our UTF design. My estimate is that if we had to do the complete design ourselves, it would cost at least one hundred million dollars, even if we had the technical capability to do it. A payment of ten million dollars would be cheap, about 10 percent of my estimate. What's the next step, Eng-fu?"

Eddie Chung looked at his watch and responded, "It's just after 11 pm here or 9 am in Texas. Let's call Dr. Creighton. You can ask him about the possibility of fabricating parts for the UTF at Cosmos. I would like to visit him and McLyle next week. We should propose a joint venture: AIDC will be the Systems integrator, Cosmos would build the major parts of the airplane and McLyle will be the designer. And, of course, Chung-Export/Import, Ltd. would contract for Cosmos and McLyle's services."

Chang smiled, "Eng-fu, that sounds like a good plan. Let me phone Creighton now. I'll introduce you to him and you can arrange your visit."

Chang dialed Creighton's number from the hotel phone. The efficient Taiwan phone system connected the overseas call in a few seconds. After Creighton answered, Chang said, "Good morning, Rich. This is Charlie Chang in Taiwan calling. I had a good meeting with Randy McLyle and it gave us an idea about how we might cooperate on the project I discussed with you on Monday. Here is Mr. Chung who would like to visit you to discuss our proposal."

"OK, Charlie. Put him on. I'm always glad to listen."

Chang handed the phone to Chung who said, "Good morning, Dr. Creighton. This is Eddie Chung. We have a proposal we would like to make to you that could result in a contract to Cosmos of over a billion dollars. Are you interested"

Creighton replied, "Why yes, of course, Mr. Chung. For a contract that size we're very interested. Just what do you have in mind?"

"Well, Dr. Creighton, rather than discussing this matter on the phone, it would be much better for us to meet in person. Would you be available to meet me in Fort Worth next Monday morning?"

"Sure, I'd love that. I'll make reservations for you for next Sunday night at the Green Oaks Hotel and pick you up there at 8:30 am Monday morning."

"Thank you, Dr. Creighton. I'll see you then. Goodbye."

"Goodbye."

Eddie swung around to face Chang and stated, "Cheng-chang, everything is set for me to meet Dr. Creighton Monday morning. Now, please call Randy McLyle and arrange for me to meet him Wednesday morning."

"OK, Eng-fu, I'll call him now. It's only 7:30 am in California, but he usually gets to the office early."

Chang dialed McLyle's phone number in Pasadena and a few seconds later, McLyle answered, "Randy McLyle here at ACI. Can I help you?"

"Randy, this is Charlie Chang calling you from Taiwan. Eddie Chung would like to meet with you next Wednesday to discuss a business arrangement so we can work together. You remember the project, of course?"

"Yes, Charlie. I remember the project, and yes, Mr. Chung is welcome here next Wednesday morning. Does he need hotel reservations?"

"No, Mr. Chung will make his own arrangements. I'll explain to him how to reach your office. Is 9 am OK?"

"Yes, Charlie, 9 am is fine. I'll see Mr. Chung then. Goodbye."

"Goodbye, Randy, and thanks."

Dr. Chang turned towards Eddie Chung, "OK, Eng-fu. Everything is arranged for you to meet with Dr. McLyle on Wednesday at 9 am next week."

"Good. That'll give me Tuesday free. I have other business in Los Angeles I can attend to. Cheng-chang, have a pleasant night with Joy-tung. Mei Lin and I will go now."

After Chung and Mei Lin left, Chang and Joy-tung spent a passionate hour making love before falling into a deep, restful slumber.

It was the first Monday morning of April 1988. Eddie Chung and Creighton arrived in Creighton's office at Cosmos Aircraft in Fort Worth just after 9 am. Creighton's secretary served the two men coffee and cookies, then closed the door for their private meeting.

Eddie opened, "Dr. Creighton, my company in Taiwan, Chung-Export/Import Ltd., would like to enter into a joint venture with Cosmos Aircraft and Randy McLyle's company ACI for the Ultra Fighter Aircraft of Taiwan. We propose your company will build the major components of the design provided by Randy McLyle. AIDC in Taichung, under the leadership of Dr. Charlie Chang, would assemble the aircraft and test fly it."

"Well, Mr. Chung, that sounds like an attractive arrangement, particularly considering the magnitude of the contract you mentioned – a billion dollars. However, the Pentagon would have to approve the joint venture. As I'm sure Charlie Chang told you, they have already said Cosmos could not help you with the design."

Eddie Chung looked intently at Creighton, "Then if the Pentagon approves the joint venture, you would be willing to help build the aircraft? Is that right?

"Why yes, of course. But that's a mighty big *if*, Mr. Chung."

Undaunted by this pessimistic reply, Chung pressed on with his discussion, "Tell me Dr. Creighton, how do you think we should approach this Pentagon matter? Should someone from our ROC Coordination Office, the equivalent of our embassy, approach the Pentagon people?

"No, no! I think a much lower profile approach would be better. Let Randy McLyle take the proposition to Dr. Rinehart in the Pentagon. Randy has to get permission to provide you with the design anyway. Randy is really motivated to push this through. His company will probably fail if he doesn't get this business."

Chung smiled, "That's a good idea, Dr. Creighton. I'm meeting with Randy next Wednesday morning in Pasadena. I'll tell him you suggested he go to Washington and meet with this Dr. Rinehart to get permission for the joint venture."

Creighton rose to signal the meeting was finished, "Mr. Chung, that's the right approach. I'm afraid there's not much we can do until Randy takes that trip to the Pentagon. Have a good trip to Pasadena!"

The two men shook hands and Chung left Creighton's office and was escorted to the lobby by his secretary. As he left his badge at the front desk of the lobby, the receptionist, Betty Lou, said brightly, "Well goodbye, Mr. Chung, you'll come back won't you. I see from your papers that you're from Taiwan. The same place our visitor last Monday was from, a Dr. Charlie Chang. Do you know him?"

"Yes, Miss, I do know Dr. Chang. We're good friends. Do you know him too?"

Betty grinned, "Just say we had an encounter in the Green Oaks. Do you know what I mean?"

"Yes, I think I know what you mean. I'll tell Charlie hello for you. What's your name?"

"'Jes' tell him Betty Lou sends her warmest regards!"

"I'll tell him, Miss Betty Lou. Goodbye."

Chapter 7

Eddie Chung in Pasadena

Eddie Chung arrived back at the Green Oaks Hotel at 11 am after his Cosmos meeting. He walked through the lobby to the swimming pool located in front of his suite. He found Mei Lin lying in the warm Texas sun in her yellow bikini which showed off her trim body and ample breasts. Seeing Eddie approaching, she called out, "Eddie, you're finished with business already? It's not even lunch time."

"Right, Mei Lin, these Americans don't spend as much time on business meetings as we Chinese. They're always in a hurry. How's the pool?"

"The water's fine. Eddie, get your swimming suit on and I'll race you across the pool."

"OK, Mei Lin, that's a good idea. But first, I've got to call American Airlines to make reservations for us on their 4 pm flight to Los Angeles."

A few minutes later Eddie Chung returned to the pool wearing his red bikini. Chung was 52 years old, but had a trim athletic figure which could be attributed to his daily morning exercises, his frequent athletic dancing (almost every night), and his diet of non-fattening Chinese food. As Eddie walked to the pool, "Mei Lin, we're confirmed on the 4 pm nonstop to LA. Now let's race across the pool!"

The two lined up on the edge of the big swimming pool, as Mei Lin said, "I'll count to three and then let's dive in. One, two, three – go!"

The pair dove into the pool and raced to the other side. It was almost a tie, but Eddie beat Mei Lin by a fraction of a second. He wrapped his arms around her and kissed her.

"Eddie, I have a prize for you, but we have to return to the room for you to collect it!"

Eddie grinned, "Let's go!"

Eddie shook Mei Lin gently to wake her up just before 2 pm. "We better dress and leave for the airport now. We'll have our lunch on the airplane. When we get to Los Angeles, I'll treat you to dinner at my favorite Chinese restaurant in Monterey Park, near our hotel.

"Oh, Eddie, I love to travel with you. Thanks for bringing me on this trip."

"Mei Lin, you are such pleasurable company. I love to have you along. But remember, you have an import mission on this trip. We need Randy McLyle's fighter airplane design. You will play a key role to make sure we get his design and his help on our new Ultra Tactical Fighter Aircraft."

Mei Lon smiled sweetly, "Eddie, I'll do what I can to help. I know how important the UTF is to our country's future."

A few minutes later, the pair were dressed and packed. They carried their small carry-on bags to the lobby and checked out just before the 2 pm deadline. They walked out of the lobby to the black, Monte Carlo rental car waiting in the parking lot. Eddie drove the short distance to the Expressway on-ramp and they headed east towards the Dallas-Fort Worth Airport, passing the high rise buildings of downtown Fort Worth on the way.

They arrived at the Hertz car rental office at the airport, checked in the car and took the Hertz bus to the American Airlines Terminal. They went to the Admiral's Club and obtained their boarding passes for the flight to LAX. While awaiting their flight departure time, they ordered white wine.

As Mei Lin sipped her wine, she asked, "Eddie, just what are the obstacles to obtaining assistance from the Americans for our new Ultra Tactical Fighter?"

Eddie turned serious, "Mei Lin, the greatest obstacle is the American government. They must approve any assistance we receive from the American companies we would like to work with: Cosmos Aircraft and Aeronautical Consultants."

"But surely, Eddie that's no real obstacle. Our country is the *free* China. America has always been friendly to us. We sell so many things to the Americans. They love our products!"

"That's true, Mei Lin. They are friendly, but the reality is that the US recognized communist China, not the Republic of China. This is part or their grand strategy to play one communist giant –

the Red Chinese –against another – the Soviet Union. This is the strategy established by their President Nixon and supported by their subsequent presidents, including the ultra-conservative, communist-hating President Reagan."

"Does that mean the US government will prevent us from building our new fighter, Eddie?"

"No, Mei Lin. They can make it difficult and can oppose it, but we have the resources to build it anyway. Remember, the US government was opposed to Israel's building of their Lavi fighter aircraft but the Israelis built it anyway."

"Perhaps we should seek help from Israel."

"Mei Lin, that's a very good idea. Maybe we should! But first, we have to try to get America's help. At least, I'm sure we will be able to get the design from this American, Randy McLyle."

"But what if the American government says no? What will you do then?"

"Don't worry, Mei Lin. I have a secret plan, and you are part of that plan."

Mei Lin got a pouty look on her face, "But Eddie, I thought you brought me so you could make love to me!"

Eddie patted her on the cheek, "That is important, all right. But your part in the plan is also important!"

Eddie and Mei Lin arrived at the Aeronautical Consultants, Inc., office on Green Street in Pasadena shortly after 9 am on Wednesday. They parked Eddie's rental car in the lot and walked into the reception area of ACI. Eddie was surprised there was no receptionist. He pushed the buzzer as requested by the sign on the receptionist's desk. A moment later Randy McLyle entered the reception area and said, "Sorry, we had to lay off our receptionist because of lack of business. I'm Randy McLyle and you must be Mr. Eddie Chung that Dr. Chang told me about. And who is this beautiful creature with you?" Randy turned to Mei Lin and smiled approvingly.

She returned his smile, "Thank you for the compliment, Dr. McLyle. My name is Mei Lin and, yes, you're right. This is the famous Eddie Chung, president of Chung-Export/Import Ltd., of Taipei!"

Eddie laughed, "Mei Lin is an associate of mine. She's always trying to make me feel important. Actually I'm just a poor struggling business man like you. We also had to lay off our receptionist. Mei Lin had to absorb that duty along with her many others."

Randy responded, "It's a pleasure to meet you both. Please sign the security register here. Government regulations, you know. My associate, Patricia Manos, is waiting for us in the conference room."

Eddie and Mei Lin signed the ACI security register and followed Randy inside the offices. When the trio entered the conference room, Patricia rose, "Welcome to ACI, Mr. Chung. I'm Patricia Manos, director of Systems analysis. I document and analyze the brilliant designs that Dr. Randy McLyle here creates."

Randy laughed, "She really means she sweeps up after me and keeps me from making design blunders! And Patricia, this is Mei Lin, Mr. Chung's associate.

The two women were mutually attracted to each other as they instinctively knew they each were key to the success of the businesses they worked for. Each woman exuded a self confidence and an erotic beauty that their male associates appreciated.

Patricia brought a carafe of coffee and a platter of cookies to the conference room. She said, "Mr. Chung, Mei Lin, may I serve you coffee and cookies?"

Eddie answered, "Yes, Patricia. Thank you but call me Eddie."

Patricia poured the coffee and served the cookies, "OK, Eddie. Now, we understand from Dr. Chang that any business we get from the Republic of China will be through your company, Chung-Export/Import, Ltd. Is that true?"

Eddie smiled, "Yes, Patricia. That's the way my government wants to handle this project. Besides, it'll make it more difficult for our enemy, Red China, to find out about our new UTF project. It makes your participation lower profile, which your government seems to prefer."

Randy added, "Eddie, I'm sure Dr. Chang explained to you that we must obtain approval from the US government to provide you with the design of the UTF."

Eddie replied, "Yes, I understand that formality is necessary. We plan to have Cosmos Aircraft build your design for us, just like the arrangement for the American Advanced Tactical Fighter, if your government had selected the Cosmos/ACI team."

Randy looked saddened, "That's ironic, isn't it? We presented the best ATF design to the US government - it says so in this NASA TM report!"

Randy handed Eddie the unclassified report and continued, "And yet, our own government, the USAF, rejected the plan as being *too far out*! Yet the Republic of China selects our design and you are offering Cosmos and ACI a contract. You're going to get a better fighter aircraft than the US government."

Eddie smiled, "Yes, Randy, it is ironic. But their loss is our gain. Now, we need to know, how do we get permission to use your design? And how is your design documented?"

Patricia laughed, "And to answer your second question first, do you know what this is?"

She holds up a magnetic tape cartridge.

Eddie looked at it, "Yes, of course. It's a magnetic tape with one of your favorite band's music recorded on it."

Patricia replied, "Wrong, Eddie. This is a 30 megabyte computer tape that contains the complete design documentation for our Advanced Tactical Fighter. Uh---I mean *your* Ultra Tactical Fighter!"

Eddie, astonished, "But, aren't you afraid someone might steal the tape and get your design?"

Patricia laughed, "Not a possibility. All the information on this tape is encrypted using the so-called public key encryption code. Only two people know the code: Randy and I. We memorized the code, so it isn't written down anywhere. It exists only in our heads! Without the code, the information of this tape would look like a stream of ones and zeros – meaningless! With the code, it is your UTF design!"

Eddie still looking amazed, "You mean *all* we need is that tape and the code in your head and we have the complete UTF design?"

Randy interrupted, "No, Eddie, not quite. This design on the tape would be our *starting point*. I would have to spend a lot of time adapting or changing the design to meet some of your unique requirements. Patricia would have to analyze that design using some of her analysis Programs, also stored on that tape. Then you would have your complete UTF design."

Eddie smiled, "Then all we need is the tape and you two for a year or so. Then we would have our UTF design, right?"

"Right!"

Eddie Chung stood, somewhat excited, walked around the table to where McLyle was standing, "Look, Randy, I'm prepared to give you a contract today – *right now* – to provide us with your UTF design including the necessary technical support by you and Patricia!"

McLyle rose, faced Chung, "Now, slow down, Eddie. We really want the contract. But you would be wasting your time giving ACI a contract before the Pentagon says we can give you the design."

Chung pressed on intently, "And how soon can you get the Pentagon's approval?"

"I could be ready to present our case to Dr. Rinehart in the Pentagon by the end of this month. But frankly, I have a problem."

"And what is your problem, Randy?"

Randy looked sheepish, "We're out of money. I have no money to travel. Frankly, ACI is almost out of business. If the Pentagon says *no* to helping you, then we're out of business."

"And how much money will this trip to the Pentagon require?"

Randy replied, "Considering air fare, hotel, and everything, about two thousand dollars."

Chung pulled out his wallet, removed twenty crisp 100 dollar bills, laid them on the table, "Randy, here's your two thousand dollars. Please get ready for the trip. Here call me at the number on my business card – collect – as soon as you get the Pentagon answer. In case you get a *no*, I have another idea."

"McLyle slowed picked the money, "Thanks, Eddie. Now I can take the trip. Just what is your idea if Rinehart says no?"

Eddie smiled, ""Let's cross the first bridge first. I'll explain my idea to you if you get a no. In Taipei, not here!"

Chapter 8

Puzzle Palace

Randy McLyle was awakened from a deep sleep by the telephone beside his bed. He picked up the phone and heard a cheery voice, "This the Roslynn Holiday Inn operator. It is 8 am. Time to rise and shine."

McLyle mumbled, "Thank you, operator, for the wake up call."

It was 8 am in Washington DC, but Randy's body was still on California time and thought it was 5 am. Randy looked at his digital watch. It was Tuesday, the last week in April. Randy's appointment with Dr. Willie Rinehart in the Pentagon was at 9 am.

He planned to take the Metro from Roslynn, Virginia, where he was staying, to the Pentagon, a mere ten minutes away. Just as he was getting out of bed, he heard a knock on the door. He realized it was the breakfast he had ordered for 8 am by leaving the request on his outside doorknob. When Randy opened the door, the waiter entered with the tray and set it on the table next to the picture window overlooking Washington, DC and on across the Potomac River. Randy signed the slip giving the waiter a one dollar tip on the six dollar breakfast bill. The waiter left and Randy dug into his breakfast of poached eggs on toast with ham, orange juice and hot chocolate.

As Randy was eating, he looked across the Potomac at the gleaming capitol dome at the far end of Constitution Avenue and the Washington Monument, nearer to the Potomac. He thought to himself, 'Here is where the real power in America now resides. The power used to be vested in the people, but now it's wielded by the bureaucrats in Washington. Their power is independent of the administration in power or the party in control of congress.'

As Randy looked at the Washington Post delivered with his breakfast, he scanned the headlines and read, 'More Indicted in the Government's Expanding Investigation of Insider Trading', 'Defense Scientist Consultant Convicted for Furnishing

Unauthorized Defense Department Information to a large Defense Contractor.' Then he thought to himself, *The pledge of law and order by the Reagan administration is causing many indictments and convictions of the white collar criminals in the US. These are mainly victimless crimes. Meanwhile, it's unsafe to walk the streets after dark in the nation's capitol and in other major cities. And organized crime goes on unabated. Drug abuse and drug traffic is increasing, with over five million of the population having tried drugs, and over a million addicts. It reminds me of my consulting visits to Iran during the last days of the Shah. Every time I would pick up the English language newspaper, I would read about another businessman the Shah had put in prison for charging too much for his products, or some other such seemingly minor offenses. Well, I guess law and order is easier to apply to businessmen that to hardened criminals. The businessmen are easier to catch, because they're unaware that they've done anything wrong until the Justice Department descends upon them!*

Then Randy's thoughts returned to his meeting this morning with Dr. Willie Rinehart in the Pentagon. This meeting brought home to Randy the importance of Washington bureaucrats to the life or death of companies like ACI. If Rinehart said *yes* to Randy's request to furnish his rejected design to Taiwan, Randy's company would become healthy again. If Rinehart said *no*, then ACI would go out of business, and Randy would lose both his job and all the money he had invested in the company.

Randy finished breakfast, dressed, packed his small briefcase and took the elevator to the lobby. He walked the short distance to the Roslynn Metro Station and took the metro car towards the Washington National Airport. He got off at the Pentagon stop, which was just beyond the stop for the Arlington National Cemetery, the burial place of the American war dead, and of the young President Kennedy, assassinated by a mad man's bullet.

Randy took the escalator up from the metro station to the Pentagon Concourse, a huge shopping mall for the thousands of employees of the Pentagon, which was always crowded, even during working hours. Randy knew the Pentagon well. He had served several years as a member of the Defense Science Advisory Council, a group of about one hundred scientists and engineers who advised the Secretary of Defense and his staff on technical matters pertaining to defense. One thing he had learned from his Pentagon service is that a rough measure of the Pentagon official's importance was the distance his office was from the Secretary of Defense's office.

Dr. Rinehart was the director of tactical Systems. He controlled a powerful section of the office of the Undersecretary of Defense for research, development and engineering. In this job Rinehart was responsible for controlling billions of dollars spent by the Pentagon each year on tactical weapons Systems. He also had a powerful say in just who (what countries of the world) could receive which and how many of these American weapons available for export. It was from Rinehart, in his export control role, that Randy expected to seek approval to provide his advanced tactical fighter design to Taiwan.

Randy took the ramp leading up to the second floor of the pentagon, then a flight of stairs up one more level, walked around the *A Ring* to the tenth corridor, walked out to the *E Ring,* turned left and walked the few doors to Rinehart's office number *3B982.* There was a discrete sigh to the left of the door with the title, *Director of Tactical Systems.* Listed was Rinehart's name and the names and titles of his staff members. It was a few minutes before nine when Randy opened the door leading into Rinehart's large reception office. There were several other visitors seated on the brown leather couches, waiting to see various members of Rinehart's staff.

Randy was dazzled by the beauty of Rinehart's secretary. On her desk was a sign, *Lois Brown, Secretary to the Director of Tactical Systems, OUSDRDE.* Lois had long blonde hair, deep blue eyes, and an ample bosom. As Randy approached her desk, she looked up, smiled and said in a warm, friendly tone, You must be Dr. McLyle." Randy nodded, and she continued, Dr. Rinehart is on the phone with the US Air Force Chief of Staff. It will probably be a long call. Something about the new Advanced Tactical Fighter program. If you'll be seated, Dr. McLyle, I'll bring some coffee while you're waiting.

"Why, thank you, Ms Brown. I'll take my coffee black, please."

"OK, coming right up. But, please, call me Lois, Dr. McLyle."

"And Lois, my name is Randy."

A few minutes later, Lois brought Randy a large cup of black coffee in a mug marked *TACTICAL SYSTEMS: THE PENTAGON*. She asked, "Randy, how long are you going to be in town?"

"Well, that depends on Dr. Rinehart. I hope to have an affirmative answer from him this morning. In that case I'll take the 5 pm non-stop back to Los Angeles tonight."

Lois laughed, "Randy, from your telephone message, with your subject, *Tactical Fighter Design* for Taiwan, I can tell you now you're not going to get an answer from Dr. Rinehart today. You should plan on staying until at least tomorrow. He has to check with a lot of people. Taiwan's a controversial place to export military items, you know, because of mainland China.

Randy smiled, "Thanks for the tip. Good thing I didn't check out of my hotel yet. Now I have to decide what to do tonight. Any suggestions?"

"Why, yes, Randy. I know a young lady who would just love to go out to dinner with you for Maine lobster tonight – me!"

Randy laughed, "Lois, if you're right about Dr. Rinehart not giving me an answer today, I'll have to stay over. I've got to know the answer before I go back to California. If I do stay, I'd love to take you to dinner at O'Donnell's for Maine lobster. It's my favorite, too!"

"It's a deal. Oh, Dr. Rinehart's phone light just went off. He's through talking to the General. I'll take you in now. Please follow me."

Lois led Randy into Rinehart's very large office. The wide windows on the outside wall faced towards Washington, DC, with the Potomac, Washington's Monument, and the capitol building clearly visible in the background. This view gave the aura of power to the office. In front of the windows was a large desk with three leather chairs sitting in front of it. The office had a conference table surrounded by enough padded chairs to accommodate ten people. In a corner of the carpeted office there was a red leather couch and three red leather overstuffed chairs around a large coffee table. On the wall behind the couch was a large Mercator projection map of the world. The map had blue pins showing the tactical forces deployed by the US and red pins showing those deployed by the Soviet Union. The office had the atmosphere of a *war room*. The people in the Pentagon tended to think of the world as divided between the blue and red, good and bad, free world and communist. Rinehart used this map in Congressional hearings to justify the tactical weapons part of the over 200 billion dollar defense budget administered by the Pentagon.

Rinehart invited Randy to sit on the couch in front of the coffee table while taking a chair facing his visitor. He turned to his secretary and commanded, "Lois, bring Dr. McLyle and me some coffee." A few moments later Lois served the coffee for the two men in fine China cups along with a tray of *petit fours*.

Rinehart opened the meeting, "Dr. McLyle, I understand your company, Aeronautical Consultants, is interested in providing a design to Taiwan: the Republic of China. Is that right?"

"Yes, Dr. Rinehart. I've been approached by Dr. Chang, program director of the new Ultra Tactical Fighter program at AIDC, to provide them with our version of the ATF design, which was rejected by the Pentagon."

"Your company was teamed with Cosmos Aircraft, as I recall. Yes, I'm afraid our Source Selection Committee found your design to be just *too far out,* too risky a design for us to consider for production. We can't afford to make mistakes, you know like the DIVAD system that Secretary Weinberger had to cancel back in 1985. There was a case of a design that was *too far out.* It didn't work when they tried to build it. We can't afford to let something like that happen to the Air Force's new Advanced Tactical Fighter, can we?"

Randy, looking a little flustered by this verbal attack on his design, stammered out, "Well, I guess you can't afford to make mistakes, all right, but frankly I don't believe the technology nor design we proposed was that extreme. But, since the Pentagon did reject my design, I guess there will be no problem in obtaining permission to adapt it to the new Taiwan UTF, right, Dr. Rinehart?"

Rinehart looked at Randy with a condescending expression, "Now, Dr. McLyle, that logic doesn't necessarily follow. Weapons to Taiwan-ROC is a very touchy issue. We can't afford to upset the PRC. Our relationship with mainland China is too important to the security interests of the US to risk damaging it by furnishing advanced weapon Systems to Taiwan. That's the reason we already turned down Taiwan on their request for the F-16 aircraft."

Randy persisted with his course of thought, "But certainly, the PRC couldn't conceive of a tiny company like ACI furnishing a design rejected by the Pentagon as a threat to their security. Why, they probably wouldn't even know about it."

Rinehart looked intently at Randy, "You must know I have already rejected Cosmos Aircraft's request to furnish your design to Taiwan, *just too high visibility*. Look, Dr. McLyle, it is possible that we may give permission for you to help Taiwan on their new aircraft design, but I can't give you the answer today. There are too many people I have to coordinate with. I think I can have a *provisional* answer to you by, say, 3 pm tomorrow, though."

"Randy's face brightened with this hope, "Yes, I can stay over to meet with you at 3 pm tomorrow. But, one other question, can Cosmos help in building parts for the aircraft after it's designed? We were considering a joint venture. ACI would provide the design and Cosmos would build parts that would be shipped to Taiwan for assembly and integration in the aircraft."

"Dr. McLyle, that's easy! I can give you a firm answer now about Cosmo's building parts for the aircraft. It's *hell no!* Just *too high visibility*. The PRC would raise the devil with the State Department, threaten to break relations, if a big US aircraft company, like Cosmos, built parts for the Taiwan fighter. We just can't afford to let that happen!"

Rinehart rose to signal the meeting had ended, "It was a pleasure to meet you, Dr. McLyle. Stop by and have Lois put our 3 pm meeting on my calendar for tomorrow on your way out."

Randy rose from the couch, began to extend his hand to shake Rinehart's, but Rinehart turned and strode over to his desk. Discouraged, Randy left the office.

Chapter 9

Pentagon Decision

Randy stopped at Lois's desk. She looked up "Randy, I can tell by the look on your face that the news was bad. You do have to stay over, don't you."

"You're right, Lois. Dr. Rinehart said to put tomorrow's meeting down on his calendar for 3 pm."

Lois wrote the meeting on the calendar as she spoke, "Well, Randy, you're lucky the meeting is tomorrow. I thought you might have to wait until Friday for your answer. Taiwan cases are always tough. Now how about dinner for tonight. What time?"

"How about 6 pm? At my room at the Holiday Inn over in Roslynn? Room number 1082."

Lois looked into Randy's face and smiled, "No. I've got to go by my apartment first to get my overnight bag. Don't you think I'll need it?"

He grinned, "Yes, I think you will. Is 7 pm better?"

"Seven's fine! See you then. I'll make reservations at O'Donnell's for 8 pm. Goodbye Randy."

"Goodbye Lois."

When Randy got back to his room, he called Dr. Creighton at Cosmos. As soon as Creighton's secretary put him on the line, McLyle said "Rich, I just finished my first meeting with Rinehart. I'm afraid I have some bad news."

"What's that, Randy?"

""Rinehart gave a firm *no* on Cosmos' participation with ACI to build parts for the ROC fighter."

"Frankly, Randy, I'm not surprised. I didn't want to disappoint Eddie Chung or you by telling you. But, I fully expected Rinehart to say *no* to the idea of Cosmos participating in the program. How about your design for the ROC? What did Rinehart say about that?"

"I have to stay over to meet with Rinehart at 3 pm tomorrow about the design issue. He expects to give me a provisional answer then."

"Good. That's good news, Randy. At least you didn't get an automatic *no* like we got when we asked. Definitely a good sign!"

Randy laughed, "I certainly hope we get an affirmative answer."

"Well, good luck, Randy!"

Randy was awakened by a knock on the door. He looked at his watch, it was 7 pm. He had fallen asleep on the king size bed wearing only a pair of red bikini shorts while watching a movie on the TV during the afternoon. The TV was still blaring with the CBS news. He rose up groggily and answered the door. It was Lois, dressed in a low-cut, white blouse and tight white pants that showed off her ample curves well. She was carrying a small overnight case. She entered. Randy closed the door. She set her overnight case down, grabbed Randy, and kissed him passionately with a deep French kiss.

Lois whispered in his ear, "Randy, I made our dinner reservations for 9 pm, not 8. That gives us two hours. The way I'm feeling after that kiss, we're going to need that much time."

She took off her blouse. Randy took off his red bikini shorts. He turned off the TV and led her towards the bed. She slipped out of her remaining clothes and wrapped her arms around him. Both moved together into the bed. Soon slipped into a short, but deep sleep.

When Randy awakened, he looked at his watch. It was 8:30. He said sleepily, "Lois if you want lobster for dinner tonight, we had better get dressed."

Lois looked up happily, grabs Randy and kissed him passionately, and uttered, "Oh, Randy, you made me feel so good. I want you again tonight, but after dinner. Yes, let's shower and dress. We can take my car to O'Donnell's."

The two took a short shower to wash away the juices of love, then dress for dinner out. They reached O'Donnel's Restaurant right on the edge of the Potomac River just before 9 pm. The head waiter led them to their table. They had a lovely view of the lights on the far shore of the river. Randy ordered a bottle of Korbel's

Champagne Brut as he said to Lois, "This is a good California champagne, better than most French champagnes, and a lot cheaper. It goes great with lobster."

As Lois sipped the Korbel, she exclaimed, "Randy, you're a winner at picking fantastic champagne!"

The waiter brought them each a huge, two pound Maine lobster along with a large green salad, with avocado and tomato slices, topped with a delicious, honey-mustard dressing. The two relished their lobster and champagne dinner. They topped off the main course with a dessert of large strawberries served in thick yoghurt topping.

After dinner they returned to Randy's room in Roslynn. The pair danced nude in the room until almost 1 am when they climbed into bed and enjoyed each other again. Then they fell into a deep, relaxed sleep.

Randy awoke shortly before 7:30 am, finding that Lois was all dressed. She leaned over, kissed him on the lips, and said, "I've got to get to the Pentagon now. See you in the boss's office at 3 pm."

Randy reached Rinehart's office just before 3 pm and went up to Lois's desk. She looked up with a professional smile, no hint of last night's passion, and said "Good afternoon, Dr. McLyle. Dr. Rinehart is ready for you. You may go right in."

Randy smiled, not betraying their night together, "Thank you Ms Brown."

Randy entered Rinehart's big office. He was seated behind his large desk with his back to the awesome Washington DC view. He motioned Randy to take one of the chairs facing his desk. He opened the meeting by saying, "Dr. McLyle, I've staffed your case very thoroughly since you were here yesterday. I had a chance to discuss it with my boss, the Undersecretary in the State Department for Eastern Affairs. I think I warned you that Taiwan weapons cases are a very touchy issue because of our relationship with the PRC."

Randy, looking a little perplexed by this long preamble, asked plaintively, "And, what is the answer? May I provide my rejected ATF design to Taiwan or not?"

"Well, first, Dr. McLyle, I would like to point out to you that it is the Defense Department's design, not your design."

Randy looked confused, "What do you mean not *my* design? I came up with that design. It was paid for by Cosmos Aircraft using their Independent Research and Development (IR&D) funds, *not* Defense Department funds!"

Exactly, Dr. McLyle! IR&D funds were used for the design. And the Defense Department re-imburses Cosmos for their IR&D funds!"

"Well, Dr. Rinehart, you may have a legal point. I don't know. But, as far as I'm concerned, it was my brain that came up with the design, not the Defense Department's. I still believe it's my design. Why, no one in the Defense department even understands my design. Besides, the Pentagon rejected the design as being *too far out,* remember?"

"Yes, of course I remember. Look, let's not drag out this conversation any longer. We have come to a decision. It's final and irrevocable. You will not be permitted to furnish the design or adapt the design to the new Taiwanese fighter aircraft!"

Randy looked crestfallen. The shock of Rinehart's words seeped into his sub-consciousness. Then he replied, "But Dr. Rinehart, without this Taiwan business, my company, Aeronautical Consultants, Inc. is sure to go out of business!"

Rinehart looked Randy straight in the eye and replied harshly, "That's what the free enterprise system is all about. You have the right to succeed and to fail in business. A basic American principle. Don't look for the government for help. You should have gone after American business to furnish weapons to our friends, not yours!"

Randy getting a little angry with this cold statement, protested, "But, I'm not asking the government for help. I'm only asking permission to adapt my design to the needs of a free country - the Republic of China."

Rinehart rose from his chair and said with a tone of finality, "I'm sorry, Dr. McLyle, the US Government only recognizes one China, the People's Republic of China. My answer is final. Now, if you want to consult with the ROC, we can't prevent you, as long as you don't furnish any technical data per the Munitions Control Act that covers technical data."

"But what good is my consulting to ROC without technical data being used?"

"I can't answer that question, Dr. McLyle. Now, good day. I have a staff meeting in a few minutes. Goodbye."

Randy mumbled a goodbye and left the office. As he walked by Lois's desk, she stopped him and said sympathetically, "I can tell from the look on your face that the answer was *no*. I should have warned you that not many Taiwan cases get approved. Goodbye, Randy."

"Thanks, Lois, and goodbye."

Chapter 10

Taiwan Agent

Eddie Chung drove up to the headquarters building of the Ministry of Defense (MND) in Taipei. He had a meeting scheduled this first Friday in May with General Hua, the director general of MND. Dr. Chang had ridden up from Taichung earlier that morning on the MND shuttle, a non-descript Volkswagen–type bus manufactured in Taiwan. Eddie Chang and Dr. Chang were planning to explain to General Hua their fall-back position for getting the Ultra Taiwan Fighter. They needed General Hua's approval before taking the next step. Eddie Chung had received a phone call from Randy McLyle immediately after he got the negative answer from Dr. Rinehart in the Pentagon. McLyle had been very discouraged, but Chung cheered him up by saying that he had a plan that he thought might work. Chung had a meeting in Pasadena scheduled for Monday morning to explain this new plan to Randy.

Chung took the elevator up to General Hua's, strode into the conference room and found Dr. Chang was already waiting. A few moments later, General Hua stalked briskly into the room, walked to the head of the table, turned to Eddie Chung and Dr. Chang and said curtly, "Please be seated, Eng-fu and Cheng-chang. I understand we've a severe set-back in our plans to obtain help from the Americans for our new fighter. And, my dear cousin, Eng-fu, what are you going to do now?"

General Hua then seated himself at the head of the long conference table and looked intently at Eddie Chung for his answer.

"Ding-fua, when I visited Randy McLyle in Pasadena, he and his associate, Ms. Patricia Manos showed me their design. It's stored on a magnetic tape cartridge, just like this."

Eddie, Chung pulled a magnetic tape cartridge from his shirt pocket. It was a recording of music that Eddie played on the tape player in his BMW auto. He handed the tape to General Hua, who looked at it and asked incredulously, "You mean his total design is on a small tape cartridge like this? Why, it's just like the tapes I play in my music recorder."

"Exactly, Din-fua, except that his tape contains encoded digital signals, not music. The crypto code to unlock the information has been memorized by McLyle and Manos so no one can steal their design. The tape has to be decoded, using their IBM personal computers to access the design."

"But how do we get the design? I thought you said the US government wouldn't let McLyle give us the tape."

"The US government doesn't even know the tape exists. All they have are the proposal reports produced from the tapes. With your approval, Ding-fua, I plan to buy that tape as well as McLyle and Manos themselves so they can adapt their design to our UTF."

"Well, Eng-fu, I can understand how you can buy the tape, but how in the world do you *buy* McLyle and Manos?"

Eddie Chung grinned, "Easy, Ding-fua. I would like to make McLyle and Manos an offer of ten million dollars to immigrate to Taiwan, with their tape. The US government can't keep them from immigrating and they won't prevent them from bringing a tape that the USG doesn't even know exists."

General Hua smiled, "But Eng-fu, how do you know that McLyle and Manos will accept your offer?"

"Their company, Aeronautical Consultants, is on the verge of collapse since the Pentagon awarded the ATF contract to another team. One of my ROC CIA agents in the US obtained a confidential financial statement from ACI's bank in Pasadena. Frankly, they have no business and are virtually bankrupt. I know that both McLyle and Manos will be without jobs in August. They'll accept the offer. They have no other choice!"

"Eng-fu, when will you confirm this acceptance? You haven't even made the offer yet, have you?"

"No, Ding-fua, but I have a meeting with McLyle and Manos scheduled for next Monday in Pasadena, California. I plan to start discussions with them. But I want to have McLyle come to Taipei. Then you, Ding-fua, can make the offer. We will pay them out of my CIA funds to make the payment untraceable."

General Hua smiled broadly, "Cousin Eng-fu, an excellent plan! You have my approval to implement this plan. But there's one other matter. Who will build the aircraft, since Cosmos won't be allowed by the Pentagon to take our contract?"

Eddie Chung, smiled, "Ding-fua, that's one reason I asked Cheng-chang to come to our meeting this morning. He has the answer to that question."

Both men turned towards Dr. Chang for his answer. He cleared his throat, "Who, uh – General Hua, I've had my staff conduct a study to determine if we can use the experience we gained building the F-5 fighter under license from the US in order to build the UTF. I have the report here for you to read, Sir, but the short answer is *yes,* we *can* build it."

Dr. Chang handed the thick report to General Hua who thumbed through it and said, "Cheng-chang, I don't have time to read this whole report, but if you say so, I'll go along with your conclusion. But remember, your job is on the line if you're wrong."

"Yes, Sir, I know that. And for that reason we have a back-up plan. We may approach the Israelis to help. They've got their new Lavi fighter flying now, you know. That means they've got the know-how and we know they'll do anything for money."

General Hua looked at Dr. Chang, "And have you approached the Israelis yet?"

"No, Sir. We plan to wait until Randy McLyle is on our team here in Taiwan. He would help us evaluate Israel's capacity to help, if we need the help."

General Hua rose, smiled broadly, "It sounds like we are on the right track for our UTF project. Eng-fu and Cheng-chang, I think your plans, and back-up are sound. Proceed!"

It was the first Monday in May, 1988. Randy McLyle and Patricia Manos were in their Green Street office in Pasadena. The phone rang and Patricia said, "Randy answer the phone. It may be someone with new business."

Randy frowned, walked over to pick up the phone, "Not likely. It seems like we just can't find business anywhere. Even the business in Taiwan that looked so hopeful is dead. Killed by the Washington bureaucracy."

Randy answered the phone and heard, "Randy, this is Eddie Chung. I'm going to be late for our 9 am meeting. Is 11 am OK?

I overslept this morning. The time change from Taipei caught up with me. It'll take Mei Lin and me about an hour to get to your office from our hotel in Monterey Park."

Randy, somewhat dejectedly, "Well, 11 am is fine, Eddie. It isn't as though we are real busy anyhow."

Eddie laughed, "Now cheer up, Randy. You're going to have a lot of business in Taiwan. Just make me your agent."

"Eddie, I don't know how we can get any business in Taiwan. As I explained to you before, the Pentagon turned down my request to give you our design. Dr. Rinehart said I could consult in Taiwan, as long as I didn't furnish technical data."

Eddie went on in a friendly tone, "Don't worry, Randy. We'll talk about it when I get there. You and Patricia plan on having lunch with Mei Lin and me. It'll get your mind off your problems."

"OK, Eddie. See you about 11. And Patricia and I would love to have lunch with you two."

Eddie Chung and Mei Lin finally arrived at the Aeronautical Consultant's office just after 11:30 AM. When Eddie drove up in his rented Hertz car both Randy and Patricia went to the lobby to greet their visitors from far away Taipei. Randy shook hands with Eddie and kissed Mei Lin on both cheeks. Patricia kissed both Eddie and Mei Lin on both cheeks. Patricia and Randy really liked these two charming Chinese people. After Eddie and Mei Lin signed the security register, Eddie took a gift from his briefcase and said, "Here's a little present from Taipei."

Mei Lin added, "We hope you enjoy it."

Eddie handed the gaily wrapped gift to Randy who quickly unwrapped it, being careful not to tear the colorful wrapping paper. It was a decorated metal canister of real Chinese tea.

Eddie added, "Now, you can begin enjoying this tea in anticipation of your trip to Taipei"

Randy looked puzzled, "What trip to Taipei?"

Eddie laughed, "That's what I want to talk to you about. Coming to Taiwan. But first, I have an agreement prepared for you to sign."

As Randy led the visitors to the conference room for their meeting, Patricia said, "I'll make us all tea using this beautiful gift."

Mei Lin smiled, "Patricia, please let me show you how we Chinese make tea.   It's quite different from the English or American tea."

As the two men proceeded to the conference room, the two girls went to the office kitchen to prepare the Chinese tea.

After the two men were seated at the conference table, Eddie Chung opened his briefcase and handed Randy two copies of a three page legal document. Randy took the form, perused it and asked, "Why, Eddie, this is a representation agreement for me and Patricia to consult in Taiwan as individuals. It says nothing about Aeronautical Consultants, Inc. Why not?"

"Exactly, Randy. You already told me that ACI was going to fail. With this agreement, my company, Chung-Export/Import, Ltd, which is already well known in the aircraft industries of Taiwan, will be able to get you and Patricia professional consulting contracts in Taiwan.   That way, you and Patricia can be self employed consultants, not employees of a business, like you are now.

Randy scanned the representation agreement. It seemed fair and straight-forward. Eddie Chung's company would be paid 10% of the value of any consulting contract that he might obtain for them in Taiwan. The agreement was between Randy McLyle and Patricia Manos, *parties of the first part*, and Chung Export/Import, Ltd., *party of the second part*. It promised that Chung Export/Import, Ltd. would work diligently to obtain consulting contracts. It promised that McLyle/Manos would do the work on the consulting contracts obtained in Taiwan.

Just as Randy finished reading the agreement, Mei Lin and Patricia entered the room carrying a tray loaded with four glasses filled with steaming hot water with the tea leaves from Eddie's gift floating on top. The two girls served the tea to the men first, and then to themselves as they sat down at the conference table.

Mei Lin said, "Randy, this is the way we serve tea in China. I hope you like it."

Randy sipped the tea, "This is delicious and it has a nice, fragrant odor."

Patricia echoed, "Yes, I love it. Thank you so much for the gift, Eddie. We'll think of you and Mei Lin as we drink it in the future."

Eddie smiled happily, "I'm very pleased that you both enjoy real Chinese tea. When you come to Taiwan, you can also have real Chinese food."

Randy looked at Patricia, "Patricia, here's a copy of a representation agreement for us to sign. You want to look it over? It looks OK to me."

He handed the copy to Patricia. She spent a few moments reading it, then said, "Eddie, it looks fine except for the percentage of the fee. Ten percent is too much. Change it to five percent and we'll sign it."

Eddie laughed, "Patricia, you're a tough negotiator. Look, I'll make a compromise. Let's make it 10% up to a contract of $100,000, then reducing according to this schedule (which he scribbled out and handed to her): from $100,000 to $1,000,000 a fee of 7.5; any contract over one million dollars, a fee of 5%. Is that fair?"

Patricia frowned and studied the paper for a few moments. Then she answered, "Yes, Eddie, we'll buy that formula!"

Eddie smiled, "Then I'll write in the change. We'll all three initial the changes and sign the agreement. Is that fair?"

Patricia laughed, "Eddie, that's the old fashioned way. Let me enter the document on my personal computer using my optical reader. Then I'll edit in the new words we need and reprint it. Only takes a few seconds."

Patricia took the document over to the personal computer sitting at the end of the conference table. She scanned across each printed line of the document, automatically entering those words into her PC. Then she edited the words to show the changes in the fee to be paid to Eddie's company and pressed the print key. The laser printer zipped out the two copies of the changed document.

Patricia handed Eddie and Randy the two copies, "Voilà! Here are the two edited agreements."

Mei Lin exclaimed, "Wow, Patricia, that was fast! Eddie, it looks like we selected the right pair to be consultants in Taiwan. Our country can use this kind of talent."

Patricia blushed, "Thanks for the compliment Mei Lin, but it's really easy to use the PC. I'd be glad to teach you how in an hour or so."

Mei Lin grinned, "That's a great idea."

Then she turned to Eddie, "Eddie, will you buy me a PC for our office in Taipei?"

Eddie Laughed, "Yes, Mei Lin, right after we get our first million dollar consulting contract for Patricia and Randy. Then I'll have enough money to buy you a computer."

The others laughed at Eddie's little joke.

Patricia got a serious look on her face, "Eddie, Randy and I are willing to sign the agreement now as modified. But tell us, what's the probability that you will get a million dollar consulting contract for us?"

Eddie smiled, "Patricia, I feel the chances are excellent. But first I need Randy and his tape to come Taiwan – soon – to meet the right people."

He turned to Randy, "How soon can you come to Taiwan, Randy?"

Randy looked at his calendar, "Eddie I'm going to be busy with the bankruptcy lawyers for the next 3 weeks. I could come in early June but I have problem, a financial one: no travel money."

Eddie pulled out his wallet and pealed off ten crisp thousand dollar bills, put them on the table, "Randy, you and Patricia sign the agreement and you can consider this ten thousand dollars a *good faith* prepayment for future business, OK?"

Randy looked at Patricia. She nodded and smiled. Randy agreed, "Yes, Eddie, we'll sign. The ten thousand dollars should tide us over."

All parties signed the agreement and then left for lunch together in Randy's car.

Randy headed for a Chinese restaurant on Colorado Street in Pasadena. On the way he explained, "Eddie, we'll order the *Caltech Special.* This is a menu some of the Chinese graduate students at nearby Caltech arranged with the chef here, in order to avoid the usual Chow Mein and Chop Suey syndrome found in most American Chinese restaurants."

Eddie grinned, "That's excellent. I don't recognize most American Chinese food."

When the waiter came, Eddie conversed with him in Chinese and then a broad smile broke out on Eddie's face. The *Caltech Special* is real Chinese food, alright! A perfect way to celebrate the signing of the consultant agreement!"

Chapter 11

Trip to Taiwan

Randy McLyle kissed Patricia goodbye before heading for the crowded China Airlines 747-SP at the Los Angeles International Airport – LAX. The boarding lobby was jam packed with passengers and well wishers for the flight to Taipei. The flight was full. Most of the passengers were carrying lumpy packages aboard. There were a number of small children and infants among them. The Chinese spoken by the passengers sounded like a babbling brook. As Randy was pushed along by the crowd boarding the big Boeing wide-body jet, he noted the intensity with which Chinese was spoken gave one the feeling that the people were angry with one another. He was learning this was the way the Chinese sounded to Americans.

Randy found his inside aisle seat and put his carry-on bag in the overhead baggage compartment. Almost all of the passengers were aboard the plane. The low eight hundred dollar round trip price for a tourist seat encouraged a lot of traffic between Taipei and the West Coast. Soon the turmoil of loading passengers subsided as the people settle into their seats ready for take-off.

A few moments later the 747-SP pushed-back from the jet way and taxied to runway 25-Left on the north side of the LAX airport. A few minutes later the captain received the take-off clearance and the big jetliner roared down the runway, heavy with it's full load of passengers and fuel for the transpacific non-stop flight from Los Angeles to Taipei. Randy glanced at his watch. It was just after 1 PM Los Angeles time, on Sunday. He switched his Seiko watch to *World Time* and set it on Hong Kong (HNK), which was the same as Taipei time. It was just after 5 AM Taipei time, but on Monday because of the date line change between LAX and HNK. The fifteen hour flight was scheduled to arrive in Taipei at 8 pm. The whole flight would be in daylight, except for the last hour or so. A very long day of flying.

The big jetliner climbed out over the Pacific and turned north-westerly on the great circle route to Taipei. Randy looked out the window on the right side of the aircraft and saw the Hollywood Hills to the east and the white beach of Malibu with the movie stars' homes below. He fell asleep reading *Newsweek* magazine.

When he awoke, the stewardesses were rushing around, serving a tasteless dinner to the hordes of people on the packed plane. Randy ate the meal, more out of habit than hunger for the food.   After dinner, the shades were drawn and an obscure Taiwanese movie was shown. Something about a young man in the ROC Air Force and his trials and tribulations. Randy fell asleep again since he couldn't comprehend the movie. When he woke up again, it was dark. The aircraft was approaching the north coast of Taiwan. Large lightning bolts shot down out of scattered thunderstorms as the plane began it's descent for landing at Taipei. The Stewardesses offered Randy a light snack. He gently shook his head. A few minutes later the captain announced the seat belt sign had been turned on in anticipation of their imminent landing at Taipei. Ten minutes later, the 747-SP arrived at the jet way of the Chiang Kai-shek Airport.

Randy was a little slow to get off the airplane, due to the crush of passengers with their many packages stuffed with gifts from the US for family and friends in Taiwan. He made up for his slow exit by walking rapidly, using the moving sidewalks to accelerate his trip to the passport control windows, which he found by following the signs in English. He was in front of the crowd by the time he got to passport control and was one of the first through. The passport control officer checked his visa which was good until the year 1992 for multiple entries to ROC. The officer stamped his passport and waived Randy through. As he was walking out, he was asked by the officer on duty, "Do you have any magazines?"

Randy was surprised by this question. He answered, "Yes, I have a few I brought along to read."

The customs officer looked at the magazines, found a *Penthouse* Magazine among them, and said, "Sorry, I'll have to confiscate this magazine. We don't permit pornography in the Republic of China."

Randy replaced the rest of the magazines into his bag and then walked though the customs entrance into the crowded terminal. He saw Eddie Chung and Mei Lin along with another beautiful Chinese girl, all waving happily to him. Randy pushed his way through the crowd to Eddie. He kissed Mei Lin on the cheeks and shook Eddie's hand, who said, Randy, please meet Joy-tung another member of my staff."

Randy peered at this beautiful creature with long black hair flowing almost to her waist and a classical trim Chinese figure. He smiled, "Joy-tung, I'm very pleased to meet you."

Joy-tung smiled happily, "Oh, Dr. McLyle, you are so handsome!" She then kissed him on each cheek and added, Welcome to Taipei."

Eddie interrupted, "Randy, my car is just across the street in the parking lot. We have a room for you at the Grand Hotel. If you're not too tired from your trip, we plan to take you to dinner and dancing to celebrate your arrival in Taiwan."

Randy laugher, "Eddie, after that food on China Airlines, I'm ready for a good Chinese dinner. And I would love to dance with Joy-tung."

"Good. Let's go."

The quartet took the pedestrian tunnel to the parking lot and found Eddie's BMV parked nearby. Mei Lin entered the front seat with Eddie, and Joy-tung climbed in the back seat with Randy, where she snuggled up close to him.

Randy was amazed at the modern airport buildings and the excellent six lane toll road leading from the airport into the large capitol city of Taipei. On the way into the city, Joy-tung whispered quietly into Randy's ear, "Randy, I hope you invite me to spend the night with you in your room tonight."

Randy looked into Joy-tung's beautiful eyes, "Yes, Joy-tung, I want to feel your warm body next to mine, all night."

Joy-tung giggled, "Oh, Randy, I'll love that!"

Eddie drove down the dark hills ringing the east side of Taipei. He slowed and stopped at the row of toll booths, paid the price, and continued on the six lane freeway leading into the brightly lit city of Taipei. Randy was amazed to see the many high rise buildings and the modern appearance of the city. There was a large classical Chinese structure on a hill to the right of the freeway, its bright red roof corners extended out and ended in upward curving points.

Randy asked, "Eddie, what is that huge Chinese building on the hill there – all lit up?"

Eddie laughed, "That's the Grand Hotel where you're staying. It was originally built by Chiang Kai-shek to remind the people of Taiwan of the grandeur of Chinese architecture on the mainland. The hotel is now operated by the government and is a favorite place to stay for foreign visitors and dignitaries who come here on official state visits."

Randy exclaimed "I've never seen such a grand hotel before."

He squeezed Joy-tung's hand and she returned the squeeze, as she looked into his eyes and whispered, "You will find many pleasures in the Grand Hotel, Randy."

Eddie interrupted their whispered interchange, "Randy as soon as you put your bag in the room, we will go out to dinner and dancing in the city. You're already checked in."

Joy-tung took the room key from her purse, handed it to Randy, and added, "Here's your key. Your room is on the back side with a charming view of Chinese gardens.. We can park the car nearby. It's more private than the rooms in the main building."

"It sounds delightful."

Eddie left the freeway, negotiated the short distance to the hotel, and entered the hotel grounds, driving along the winding road on the east side of the main hotel building. He drove behind the hotel into a section with bungalow type room groupings and parked the BMW.

Joy-tung led the way, saying, "Follow me Randy. Our room is very nearby."

Randy followed her down a short corridor and unlocked the door. The four walked into the comfortable, but smallish room with a double bed and a nice-size bathroom with shower. The floor was wooden in the classical Chinese tradition with a large throw rug covering part of the polished floor.

Randy put down his small carry-on bag, then announced, "I'm ready to go now."

Eddie grinned, "Randy, I'm anxious to show you some real Chinese food tonight. The *Caltech Special* at the restaurant in Pasadena was close. You'll have the *real thing* tonight. But first, I want to tell you what we have planned for tomorrow." He indicated they should sit down, and pulled a list from his pocket.

Randy pulled up a chair and asked, "OK, Eddie. What's the agenda?"

"Tomorrow morning at 10 we have a meeting with a very important person, General David Hua, director general of the Ministry of National Defense. We call it the MND. General Hua is a nephew of our President, Chiang Ching-kuo, the son of our republic's founder, Chiang Kai-shek."

Eddie grinned and went on, "Family relationships in China are quite important, you know. General Hua is my cousin. His job is closer to your Deputy Secretary of Defense. General Hua reports to the Ministry of Defense, but is responsible for the day to day operations of MND. The Minister is responsible for the political aspects of the ministry."

Randy said, "Now, let's go out to dinner. After the food served on the airplane, I'm starved."

The quartet walked the short distance to Eddie's car and headed for dinner.

After a ten minute auto ride through the chaotic traffic of Taipei, Eddie arrived at one of his favorite restaurants. He pulled into the crowed parking lot adjacent to the restaurant and let the other three out. He squeezed the car into a tiny parking space and then joined Randy, Mei Lin, and Joy-tung.

Walking into the restaurant, Eddie was greeted as if he were a long lost relative by the restaurant owner, who in turn, welcomed the 'round eyed' visitor warmly. The owner led the two couples to a choice table overlooking a large fish tank. Eddie was seated with his back to the door, denoting his status as host.

The menus given to the four guests had pictures in them displaying the various dishes to made it easy for Randy to see the food offered. Eddie said, "Randy, you pick two dishes that you particularly like, and I'll order the rest of the dishes for everyone. OK?"

Randy replied, "Well, I love sweet and sour pork, here and fried shrimp, there. Otherwise, I'll trust your judgment."

"Fine, Randy. Those are good choices." He turned to the young waitress who was hovering over their table and ordered in Chinese, pointing to the menu as he ordered each of about ten dishes, including the two Randy selected.

Shortly the waitress brought the four diners' glasses filled with chilled wine. Mei Lin picked up her glass with both hands, extended it in Randy's direction and toasted, "Here's to the success of your and Patricia's consulting in Taiwan. Our country needs your help."

Randy smiled and responded to Mei Lin's personal toast, "Thank you, Mei Lin. Patricia and I would be honored to consult in Taiwan, if we are offered a contract."

Next Eddie Chung toasted Randy, "Here's to a successful meeting with General Hua tomorrow. I hope your contract is so large I only get a five percent fee!"

Eddie and the others joined in laughing at Eddie's little joke.

Next Joy-tung raised her glass for her private toast to Randy, "'Here's to our first night together. I hope it's not the last."

Randy smiled, "You are lovely, Joy-tung. Thank you."

A moment later three young female waitresses carried in three trays loaded with the variety of dishes Eddie had ordered and then arranged them on the table. They brought only chop sticks and China soup spoons for the diners to use. Luckily, Randy knew how.

Mei Lin served Eddie as Joy-tung served Randy his food. The four enjoyed a festive dinner of excellent Chinese food, better than Randy had ever had before in any US Chinese restaurant.

After dinner, Eddie took everyone to the New China dance hall, where they all enjoyed dancing for several hours. Eddie and Mei Lin had several well practiced set dance routines with dips and spins that they followed for each type of dancing: slow-foxtrot, rumba, samba, etc. Randy enjoyed the slow, romantic music, sung by a beautiful Chinese songstress, as Joy-tung's body meshed closely with his. Eddie and Mei Lin dropped Randy and Joy-tung off at the Grand Hotel shortly after midnight.

The couple showered and climbed into bed. They enjoyed themselves immensely. Randy thought to himself, 'Joy-tung! What an appropriated name for the pleasure she gives me!'

Randy's body, now synchronized with Taiwan time, slipped into a deep sleep, curled up next to Jo-tung's delectable body.

Tuesday morning, Eddie Chung met Randy and Joy-tung in the Grand Hotel breakfast room, just after 9. He sipped a cup of coffee with the pair before Eddie and Randy had to leave for their morning business meeting with General Hua.

Eddie drove his BMW toward the high rise MND building, fifteen minutes away in downtown Taipei. An unofficial parking attendant had saved Eddie a good parking spot, right in front of the building, in exchange for a nice tip. Eddie led Randy to the elevator to General Hua's office. The pair walked into the reception office at the end of the hall. Eddie said a few words in Chinese to General Hua's secretary and the two men were ushered into the general's medium-large office. The office was very tastefully furnished including several good Chinese antiques. There was a desk in front of the picture window overlooking the high rise metropolis.

The general greeted Randy warmly, speaking in excellent English, reflecting his education in the United States. "Dr. McLyle welcome to Taiwan and to the Ministry of National Defense. My American name is David, a name I picked up at the University of California at Los Angeles. I graduated there in Engineering in 1957."

Randy smiled as he shook the general's hand, "General Hua, I'm very pleased to be here. So far I'm very impressed with the modern aspects of the beautiful city of Taipei."

"Well, Dr. McLyle, there are many beautiful parts of our island. I especially hope you can visit Sun-Moon Lake in the center of our island, if not during this visit, then during the next. Also please take a few hours from your schedule to visit our National Museum here in Taipei. There you'll see many of our historic treasures"

Randy smiled, "Thank you for your tourist suggestions. I'll try to see as many things as possible during my stay."

General smiled in a friendly fashion, "Let's sit down over here. My secretary has brought some hot tea and cookies for us."

The three men seated themselves comfortably on the couch and soft chairs arranged in the visitor's seating area of General Hua's office with the tea table in front of them. As Randy sipped the aromatic liquid with tiny leaves floating on top of the glass of hot tea, General Hua assumed a serious look, "Dr. McLyle, your visit to our country is an important event. We urgently need our new Ultra Tactical Fighter aircraft to protect our tiny island province of Taiwan against the communist hordes on mainland China. Our President Chiang Ching-kuo has authorized me to allocate a budget of some two billion US dollars, or some 80 billion New Taiwan dollars, to this crucial defense program. We believe that the modernization of our Air Force is critical to the national survival of our Republic of China – the truly *free* China. Frankly, we need your expert assistance to help design this new UTF aircraft that will modernize our Air Force."

"But, General Hua, Mr. Chung must have explained to you that the Pentagon - Dr. Rinehart's office - turned down my request to furnish you with my design for the advanced tactical fighter, even though they decided on another design."

General Hua replied in friendly tone, "Yes, Dr. McLyle, our country is accustomed to being turned down by the Pentagon. First, they refused to let us update our F-5 production line into the improved F-20 fighter model. Next, we tried to buy the F-16, which the US is exporting to many western countries. The Pentagon and the US State Department rejected this request as well. We were left with no alternatives, but to develop our own UTF, much the same way as Israel opted to build their new Lavi fighter aircraft."

Randy interrupted, "Dr. Rinehart did say I could consult for you in Taiwan as long as the consultations didn't involve the providing of technical data. I don't see how I would be of much help to you in your new fighter design with such a restriction on my consulting. About all I could do would be to review your design and critique it. That wouldn't be much help."

General Hua looked at Randy intently, "There is a way you can help our country more directly – and legally. I understand your design is documented on a magnetic tape like this one."

The general pulled a music tape cartridge from shirt pocket and paced it on the table. Randy opened his briefcase and took his tape out of the case and held it up, "Why, yes, General Hua, here is the tape. But I'm afraid that even if I gave it to you, it would be worthless to you. The information on the tape is encrypted, it would be a meaningless jumble of digital symbols: ones and zeros, unless I furnished the encryption code that I've memorized."

Randy handed General Hua the tape, "Here. You can have the tape. I have other copies at home. But there's no way you can use it without the code stored in my brain."

General Hua looked at the tape thoughtfully for a moment, set it down on the table, and then said, "In other words, your giving me this tape in its present form *does not constitute a transfer of technical data.* Is that right, Dr. McLyle?"

"Yes, of course, that's right. It would look like a random series of ones and zeros if you examined it on an IBM personal computer."

General Hua pressed on with his point, "Then the tape would not constitute technical data unless you provided us the encryption key. Right?"

"That's right General Hua, but what is the point you're trying to make?"

General Hua smiled, "Dr. McLyle, if you and your associate, Patricia Manos, immigrated to Taiwan- if we make you citizens of the Republic of China – then, once you are here, you can share anything you want with us, any thing in your brains, as long as you don't bring with you any technical data or other material controlled by the US export laws. Right?"

"That's my understanding of the export control laws, yes. But, General Hua, Patricia and I wouldn't want to emigrate from the US. We're both native born citizens and love America."

General Hua looked Randy straight in the eyes, "Dr. McLyle, I'm going to make you an offer. You are, of course, free to accept or reject it. I hereby authorize Eddie Chung to issue you and Ms. Manos a consulting contract for ten million dollars through his company, Chung-Export/Import, Ltd. You would be obligated to immigrate to Taiwan. We would furnish you both with Republic of China, Taiwan, passports and a prepayment of one million dollars before you leave the US. Your consulting task would be to adapt your design – stored on the tape you just gave me – to our Ultra Tactical Fighter. Your contract obligations would be completed when our UTF completes it first successful flight."

General Hua took a contract out of a manila folder that he had been holding, handed it to Randy and added, "This formalizes my offer."

Randy was dazed by this unexpected turn of events. He looked numbly at the contract as his mind raced along all the possible future effects it could have on his life. He imagined the good life he and Patricia could enjoy with the ten million dollars. They could live in the sun on the Côte d'Azur in France or the Costa del Sol in Spain and never have to work again. He remembered how unfair the Pentagon had been with their position that *his* design was theirs. He especially remembered Rinehart's inference that Randy had sought out foreign business in preference to home-country business – after the countless hours Randy had spent during the Spring of that year pursuing every conceivable avenue of possible new business – to no avail.

Randy suddenly stood up, grinned, and stated, "General Hua, you just made me an offer I can't refuse. Patricia will accept if I do! Here, give me a pen. I'll sign the contract now!"

Chapter 12

Contract Prepayment

It was the morning of the second Friday in August 1988. Randy and Patricia had a meeting scheduled with Professor John Marsh, president of the now bankrupt Aeronautical Consultants, Inc., in Pasadena. Marsh was late for the 9 am meeting, as usual.

As the pair stood in Randy's now bare office, waiting for Marsh to arrive, Patricia started laughing, "Randy, if you had told me a year ago that we would be immigrating to Taiwan, I would have told you that you were crazy. But here we are, our last day in America, waiting for the president of our bankrupt company to give us our final checks and termination notices.

Randy grinned, "Yes, I remember last June when I returned from Taiwan and told you I had signed a consulting contract on my trip, but that we would have immigrate to Taiwan. At first, you thought, I *was* crazy.!"

"I was absolutely sure you had gone off your rocker until you told me the contract was for ten million dollars with a million dollars up-front cash, the payment that Eddie Ching will give us before noon today! I only had to think about it for a few minutes! I realized that with the ten million dollars we would be financially independent and could live anywhere on Earth that we wanted to after we finish the consulting in Taiwan."

"Yes, we certainly did the right thing. I'm sure of that. Besides, we had no alternatives: no business for our old company and no jobs after ACI declared bankruptcy last spring.

Patricia cautioned, "Randy, remember, act sad. Don't give any hint of what we're going to do after Professor Marsh gives us our final checks and fires us."

Randy laughed, "Don't worry. I'll look real sad. Maybe you ought to break down and cry crocodile tears when he hands us the final checks and termination letters. If he asks me what we're going to do, I'll just say, 'John, I don't really know. Guess we'll collect unemployment for a while until we find jobs.' That ought to get to him."

Patricia said, "I would like to feel sorry for him. After all, he is losing his income as president of ACI. But he really didn't work here like we did. And he certainly didn't help with all of the details of the bankruptcy proceedings. We were the ones who had to close up the company's books, fend off the creditors, sell the office furniture, and take care of the other myriad details required. I think the hardest part was closing out the things that went with having had a security clearance here. I nearly went out of my mind trying to follow all the rules for returning all the classified documents to the places they had come from, all double wrapped and by special mail."

Randy continued, "Sorting through all those files cabinets, trying to decide which items to keep and which to throw out, that was a real big job, too. The professor even made us return things to his campus office instead of picking them up himself."

Patricia interrupted, "Randy, I hear Professor Marsh coming in."

A moment later, Professor Marsh joined them in the empty room and said, "Well, Randy and Patricia, this is it. I never thought we'd come to this point. But, I'll keep this final meeting short and sweet. First, here are your final paychecks through today made up by the bankruptcy lawyer."

He handed them the checks and added, "And here are your official termination letters. There are two copies for each of you. Sign one and return it to me. It's for the bankruptcy lawyer."

As he handed the pair the letters firing them, Patricia wailed, "Oh, John, I never thought you would do this to Randy and me. After all, we did to try to make a go of the company."

Marsh seemed embarrassed and mumbled, "Patricia, I'm really sorry, but you know I have no choice. No business means no money. No money means no jobs. Just sign the lawyer's copy, please."

Patricia said with a tone resignation, "OK, John, I understand. Here's the lawyer's copy."

She and Randy both signed and handed copies of their termination letters to Marsh.

Marsh looked over the signatures and sighed, "Well, that's over." He took a deep breath, "What are you two going to do now?"

Randy replied sadly, "John, we just don't know, except that we'll be collecting unemployment checks until we find our new jobs. We are having to move out of our condominium today. We'll send you our new address as soon as we find a room to stay in."

Marsh seemed in a hurry to leave this uncomfortable situation. As he picked up his briefcase, he added, "Well, good luck, you two. Remember, you can always count on me to give you both good technical recommendations with your new employers. I've got to get back to campus, now. May I have your keys to the building now?"

Both Randy and Patricia removed their office keys from their other key rings and handed the keys back to Marsh.

He said, "OK, I will escort you to the front door now. This is a secret facility and you no longer have clearances here, so I can't just leave you!"

The two dejectedly followed Marsh to the front door where he said, "Goodbye and good luck!"

They both mumbled, "Goodbye, John" and headed for their car while Marsh hurried back to his own office.

Randy and Patricia drove up to Eddie Chung's hotel in Monterey Park just before noon. They each had a carry-on bag, packed with clothing for two weeks and a briefcase filled with tools of their trade such as framed college diplomas, hand held pocket calculators, etc. But, in a calculated, deliberated manner, the briefcases were completely empty of anything that could be called *technical data*.

In addition they had two large suitcases in the trunk packed with the personal things they planned to ship to Taiwan. They had disposed of most of their personal belongings, including their cars. Today they were driving a Hertz car that they would turn in at the airport before their 5 pm flight from Los Angeles International Airport.

Just before they got out of the car, Randy looked at Patricia and said, "Now, are you sure you have no regrets at leaving the US and becoming a citizen of Taiwan? If so, this is the time to stop!"

Patricia reached over and kissed Randy passionately, "I'm sure we're doing the right thing, just as I'm sure that I'm madly in love with you, Randy!"

Randy returned Patricia's kiss and said, "I'm sure we're doing the right thing, too. After we finish up in Taiwan and have moved to some place in Europe, I thing we ought to have a baby. After all, we're not getting younger."

Patricia laughed, "In that case, we better get married first."

Randy giggled, "Well, there's plenty of time for that. I've got to get my final divorce decree from Ann first."

Patricia grinned, "Excuses! Excuses! Come on. Let's go in. We don't want to be late for this meeting with Eddie.

"OK. Let's go."

Randy took his briefcase and they each carried one of the big suitcases. Randy locked the car and the two walked into the hotel, took the elevator to the third floor, continued to the suite at the end of the hall, and knocked on the door. They heard a Chinese accented voice, "Just a minute please."

A moment later Eddie Chung came to the door in a white terry cloth bathrobe with the hotel's name on the pocket, "Oh, please come in. Please forgive m - I overslept. It is so hard to adjust to the fifteen hour difference between LA and Taipei."

Eddie led the two into the sitting room and asked them to be seated A few minutes later Mei Lin entered the room wearing her bathrobe. She kissed both on the cheeks, "I welcome both as new residents of the province of Taiwan! Here are your ROC passports." She handed the documents to Randy and Patricia.

Then Eddie unlocked his briefcase, took a thick envelope out and said, "And in accordance with the consulting contract which you both have now signed, here is your pre-payment of one million dollars in cash. Count them. There are 100 ten thousand notes in the envelope."

Randy grinned, took the envelope, "Eddie, we trust you.. I'm not going to count them. But I owe you ten thousand dollars, which you gave me last June so I could afford to take the trip to Taiwan. Here take it."

"No, wrong! You owe me that and fifty thousand more. Remember my 5% fee?"

Randy laughed, "Yes, that's right. I almost forgot. Here. You can take six of these bills back."

Eddie grinned, "No, don't give me the cash. I have plenty now. Just do me a favor, will you?"

"Sure, Eddie, what's that?"

"When you get to Zürich, please deposit the $60,000 to this account number at the Union Bank on Bahnofstrasse."

He handed Randy a slip of paper with several digits written on it.

Randy, looked surprised and said, "But Eddie, how in the world did you know where we were going? We didn't tell anyone."

Eddie grinned, "In my business I have to know many things. Actually your travel record has been in the airline data bank for over two weeks now. If you don't want people to know where your going, don't make reservations. Buy tickets for cash just before you leave."

Randy smiled, "I'll remember that tip in the future. And Eddie, we'll be happy to deposit your sixty thousand to this account number, next Monday morning. Now, Eddie, I have a favor to ask of you."

"And what's that?"

"Patricia and I have two big suitcases here. Will you please take them back to Taiwan with you? We're going to take the slow way to Taiwan via Europe and Singapore. We don't want to have to struggle with these two large things."

"I'd be glad to take them for you. China Airlines gives me special baggage handling services because I fly them so often. They'll pick up your suitcases right from this room and will deliver them to my office in Taipei. I'll store them there until you arrive. Then Mei Lin and I will help you find an apartment in Taichung."

Randy said, "Thanks! Goodbye now. We've got to leave for the airport now. We don't want to miss our flight to Zurich!"

Chapter 13

Gnomes of Zurich

Rand McLyle and Patricia Manos arrived at the airport just after 3 pm the second Friday of August 1988. They had been busy taking care of the last minute details, since leaving Eddie Chung's hotel room. First, they had to stop at their Pasadena bank and cash their final paychecks from their failed company, Aeronautical Consultants, and to close out their joint checking and savings accounts. After their bank transactions, they had just over $15,000 of spendable cash - they didn't consider the 100 ten thousand dollar bills as *spendable*. That would be enough cash for their long, leisurely trip to Taiwan. Since both Randy and Patricia were Mexican food *aficionados,* they stopped off at their favorite restaurant, La Paz, for a final enchilada and taco luncheon before heading for LAX. There, they turned in their Hertz rental car and got on the Hertz transporter bus to the TWA terminal. Their travel agent had delivered their airline tickets the day before. They went straight to the TWA departures lounge and got in the line to get their boarding passes for their non-stop flight from Los Angeles to London. Even with their new found wealth, the pair decided to fly economy class to save money. They were assigned two nice seats close enough to the movie screen for good viewing in the middle section of the wide body 747 airliner.

With over an hour until departure time, they wandered through the airport shops, picking novels and magazines to read on the long flight. Then they stopped in the bar and each had a split of champagne to celebrate the beginning of their new life in Taiwan. Since they did not have to renounce their US citizenship to become citizens of Taiwan, legally they had dual citizenship. They each brought their US passports in case they might ever need them again. As they were finishing their drinks, they heard their flight 760 being called over the loudspeaker system: ready for boarding. They both felt a wave of excitement as they walked towards the departure gate. They were really leaving now!

At 2 pm Zurich time, Randy and Patricia's ticketed Swissair connecting flight from London Heathrow Airport to the Zurich International Airport pulled up to the jet way at the terminal. The two retrieved their carry-on bags from the overhead compartment and scrambled to get off the packed 737 airliner filled with businessmen and August tourists on holiday to Switzerland.

It was a beautiful, sunny day in Zurich. The captain had announced just before landing that the air temperature was a nice, warm 28 degrees Celsius. Perfect weather for a Swiss vacation. The couple exited through passport control, where the passport control officer barely looked at them. They then walked out the *nothing to declare* exit of customs into the Zurich passenger terminal. They stopped to change one thousand US dollars into Swiss francs and got 1500 francs. They took the overpass to the train station and caught a train to the Zurich main train station. They arrived at the hauptbahnhof just before 3 on Saturday afternoon. They had reservations at the Zurich Hotel just a few blocks along the Limmat River from the banhof.

As they got off the train, Patricia looked at her map of Zürich and said, "Randy, this tour guide book said the shops in Zürich close at 4 on Saturdays. That gives us an hour to wander through the stores on Bahnhostrasse before they close. Let's check into the hotel later. We can put our bags in the public lockers here."

Randy replied, "That's a good idea, Patricia. We can also find the Union Bank which is on Bahnhofstrasse. If that's the bank Eddie Chung has his money in, I guess that's the bank we should open our account in as well."

The pair found an open locker and crammed their bags into it, retrieving the key with a one Swiss franc coin. Then they took the escalator from the bahnhof down to the pedestrian tunnel, which was really a large shopping mall for the many pedestrians going to the train station or to one of the tram stops above.

The two glanced briefly at the shops before exiting up the escalator leading to the beautiful shopping street. Bahnhofstrasse began at the hauptbahnhof, paralleled the Limmat River, and terminated at the head of the Zürich See, a 50 kilometer long lake. They strolled along the right hand side of Bahnhofstrasse looking into the variety of shops. They stopped in a *bakerei* and each indulged in a creme filled chocolate tort. A few blocks later they passed St. Ana Gasse and arrived at the St Annahof's Department Store with its fresh fruit and vegetable market in front.

Patricia exclaimed happily, "Oh, Randy.   Let's browse through this department store. I've never been through a Swiss, or any European, department store! Let's see how they compare with those in the old country, the US."

Randy smiled, "Well, OK. You can't spend too much. They close in thirty minutes."

"Randy, I don't want to buy anything, I just want to look. We can return Monday, if I find something to buy."

The pair spent the next half hour wandering through the various floors of this nice department store, looking at the vast variety of goods available.   They stopped to compare prices. Randy used his pocket calculator to convert the Swiss francs into dollars.

After sampling a number of items, Patricia exclaimed excitedly, "Randy, I don't think we would give up anything we were used to in the US, if we lived in Europe. St. Annahof's has everything any department store in the US has, plus a gourmet grocery store in the basement level. The prices seem to be thirty to fifty percent less than in the US."

Randy replied, "Yes, with the million dollars per year we will earn on the investment of our ten million, we can live very well. I'm sure you will be able to buy anything we want or need."

Patricia glanced at her watch, "I think you're right. It's almost closing time now. I guess we better leave the store now."

The two exited through the front entrance and continued their stroll down Bahnhofstrasse. The next building they came to was the Union Bank.   Randy looked at the windows with the red alphanumeric read-outs showing the stock market indices, share prices, etc. and said, "Here's the bank where we'll open our account Monday morning. It looks like they have a full range of financial services, including current market information for stocks."

Patricia replied, "Good. We know where the bank is now. I'll be glad to get the contents of this envelope put safely in the bank Monday."

She patted her purse containing the 100 ten thousand dollar notes.

Randy responded, "Yes, I agree.   It's a new experience, carrying around a million dollars in cash. Well, let's head back to the Hauptbahnhof, get our bags and go to the Zurich Hotel to check in. We can take another walk through the city after we take a nap. I'm tired after that long flight from Los Angeles."

Patricia replied, "That's a good idea. Let's cross the street so we can see the shops on the other side on the way back."

Randy awoke and looked at his watch. It was almost 7 pm. He was curled up next to Patricia's warm, nude body. They both had fallen soundly asleep after lovemaking upon retiring to their room on the 15th floor of their hotel. The room overlooked the city of Zurich and had a beautiful view of the wooded hills surrounding the city on both sides of the lake. Randy kissed Patricia tenderly on the lips.

She awoke slowly and said, "What time is it anyway? My body is all mixed up with the nine hour time change from Los Angeles."

Randy laughed, "Sleepyhead, it's almost 10 am in LA, and nearly 7 pm in Zurich, nine hours later than LA. Let's get up and see what the city has to offer in the evening, OK?"

Patricia, becoming more awake, replied, "That's a good idea. I'd love to see more of Zürich. I'm already convinced it's a wonderful place."

They both quickly showered and got dressed in informal clothes for their evening exploration of Zurich. When they left the hotel, it was just after 7:30 pm, with over an hour of sunlight left. They walked alongside the Limmat River looking at the beautiful old buildings and the swimming swans. When they reached the Rathaus *Bruche* (bridge), they walked into the little square on the bridge and enjoyed the view of the beautiful *Zurich Munster* (cathedral) with its twin towers. They continued their walk past the *Quai Bruche*, where the *Zurich See* emptied into the Limmat River.

As they reached this bridge with the beautiful view of the *Zurich See* stretching many miles to the east, Randy commented, "It's amazing the number of people who are walking. In Pasadena or Los Angeles, hardly anybody walks anywhere. They just drive their cars."

Patricia laughed, "The California cities are so spread out that no one even thinks of walking. The wonderful thing about European cities is that the central part of the city is compact. The cities seen made for pedestrians."

Randy grinned, "You're right. I really love it here. After we finish in Taiwan, maybe we should live in Zurich."

Patricia looked at Randy, smiled, "Randy, you couldn't take the cold winters in Zurich. You're too used to warm weather in the winters like Pasadena. No, Zurich is a good home for our money, but I think we'll want to live in some warmer place, like southern France or in Spain."

Randy laughed, "You're probably right, Patricia. We don't have to worry about that for a while. We'll be busy in Taiwan until the first flight of the UTF."

The couple spent another two hours strolling through the narrow walking streets of Zurich. They had a pizza dinner with beer in one of the sidewalk cafes of Niederdorfstrasse, a popular walking street with many bars and cafes for the young people who crowded the street every night of the week. The two returned to their hotel, exhausted by the unaccustomed activities, at 11:30 pm. They fell right to sleep, too tired even for love making.

Randy and Patricia arrived in the lobby of the Union Bank at just after 10 Monday morning. They explained to one who guards, who spoke excellent English, that they wanted to establish an account and were directed into a room off the lobby. Here they were met by a young man who spent a few minutes interviewing them - a screening progress used by the bank in order to assign the proper banker to the clients. After the short dialogue, the young man concluded the pair were worthy clients of his Swiss bank and said, "Dr. McLyle and Ms. Manos, Mr. Heinz Steinbach will be assigned as your account manager. If you would take the elevator outside my office to the second floor, please give this note to the guard. He will call Mr. Steinbach to come and take care of your needs." He stood up and said, "It was nice meeting you both. Thank you for selecting Union Bank."

Randy and Patricia followed the directions and took the elevator to the second floor. There were two security guards on duty. Randy handed one of them the note from the screening banker. The guard said, "If you would please wait in our library to my right here, I'll notify Mr. Steinbach that you are here to see him. He is just finishing with a client and should be with you shortly."

Randy thanked the guard and the pair entered the large library room which was equipped with soft chairs and a small video screen which continuously read out financial information from around the world. There were also a variety of economic and financial reading materials such as newspapers like the *Wall Street Journal* as well as many reports published by the bank.

Randy and Patricia passed the time waiting for Steinbach by reading the bank's literature. Randy was impressed by the quality of the economic reports and said to Patricia, "Switzerland's banks are amazing institutions. The banking security laws here were set up to protect the many billions of dollars worth of money belonging to foreigners like us who entrust their funds to these Swiss banks. This whole process gives me a sense of security, that our money will be safe here. Do you have the same feeling?"

"Yes, Randy, I do. Switzerland is a safe haven for money. I understand that the Swiss impose no tax on the investment earnings made here. That will be a real plus for us!"

"You're right, Patricia. We should earn at least a hundred thousand per year on the million dollars we'll deposit today. That will certainly be more than enough to live on in Taiwan. When we get the full 10 million dollars here for safekeeping, we'll earn over a million a year, tax free. Darling, we're set for life."

Patricia laughed, 'Yes even the one hundred thousand per year is more than we earned working – slaving is a better word – at dear, old bankrupt Aeronautical Consultants."

At that moment a man about 35 years old, tall and blonde, entered the room, "You must be Dr. McLyle and Ms. Manos. I'm Heinz Steinbach. May I help you?"

Randy rose and shook hands with Mr. Steinbach. Randy responded, "Why, yes, Mr. Steinbach, we have some money we would like to place in a safekeeping account in your bank."

Without batting an eyelash, Steinbach replied, "Fine. Will your funds be in cash or check?"

Randy replied, "The funds are in cash."

Steinbach smiled, "In that case, I'll have my assistant, Gretel Breunner, join me in one of the private meeting rooms to help count your cash. Please follow me."

As the trio passed the guard desk, Steinbach addressed the guard, "Please have Ms. Breunner join us in room C."

"Yes, Mr. Steinbach. I'll call right away."

Steinbach led the pair to a small private conference room with a table and six chairs. A moment later, an attractive young lady about Patricia's age joined them. Steinbach introduced her, "This is my assistant, Gretel Breunner. When I'm busy or unavailable, she can help you with your account. Gretel, this is Dr. Randy McLyle and Ms. Patricia Manos"

After the quartet are all seated, Steinbach asked, "Now, to set up your safekeeping account. First, this is a numbered account that carries the full security and secrecy of the Swiss banking laws. The only way we can disclose your name to anyone is if you give them permission. Or if the money comes from certain criminal activities, like robbing a bank. Otherwise, the security is the best in the world. We never connect your name with the account number for security reasons."

Heinz handed the pair the forms to fill out as Randy explained, "We want this to be joint account with either one of us authorized to withdraw or invest funds from it."

Heinz replied, "That arrangement is fine. Each of you sign the signature card. Now, the only thing remaining is your initial funds for deposit. May I have them now."

Patricia reached into her purse, pulled out the white envelope containing the million dollars, placed it on the table, and said, "Mr. Steinbach, here is a million dollars in cash. We would like you to purchase bearer bonds paying at least ten percent per annum. We prefer Euro denomination bonds, those reported in the *Wall Street Journal,* so we can keep track of their market value."

Steinbach, looking surprised to see so much cash, thumbed through the bills, regained his composure, and said, "Gretel, please count these bills to confirm there are a million dollars here. And, Ms. Manos, I recommend we place 25% of your funds in each of the following Eurodollar bonds: IBM at 9 5/8%; Xerox at 10 ¾%; General Electric at 10 3/8%; and Nippon Credit Bank at 10 3/8%. All of them pay more than 10% except IBM. Of course, everyone should own some IBM."

Randy interrupted, "One other thing, Mr. Steinbach. Before you buy the bonds, please transfer $60,000 to this account in your bank."

Randy handed Steinbach a slip of paper with the account number Eddie Chung had given him. Steinbach took the slip, looked at the number, and said, "Yes, this is one of our bank's safekeeping accounts. I'll transfer the funds today. That's all we need from you. Here is my card with my name and your account number. If you need any help just phone or telex me. Either Gretel or I will take care of your request right away."

Steinbach stood as Gretel reported, "Heinz, I've counted the bills. There are 100 ten thousand dollar bills, a million dollars. Everything looks in order. We'll have to pass them through our currency checking machine, of course, before depositing them."

Steinbach replied, "Fine. Then that's everything. Thank you for your business. Gretel will see you to the lobby."

Randy and Patricia walked out of the bank just before 11 am. Their money was in the bank now, making forty eight dollars an hour for them, without their having to work at all.

Randy said to Patricia, "Well, what shall we do now? I don't know what to do with all this leisure time. We've both worked many more than eight hours every working day for years and years, only stopping to go out to eat, because we were too tired to make the effort to cook at home, and then go home to bed. I'm going to have to learn to spend un-scheduled time."

Patricia replied, "I'll certainly be glad to learn how to do it, however. I bought a Michelin Guide for Zurich and Switzerland. Let's go back to the hotel and research just what to do until next Saturday when our Swissair flight departs for Singapore."

"A good idea!"

Chapter 14

Orient Express

Patricia turned to Randy and said, "I'm glad we upgraded our tourist seats to first class for our long flight from Zurich to Singapore. It seems like a waste of money, but I guess we can afford it now that we're millionaires."

Randy reclined his big first class seat, lifted his glass of champagne, and replied, "Yes, we can afford it now. Isn't it fun, learning to spend money on ourselves instead of slaving to earn it? Wasn't that a great trip we took to Interlaken? Jungfrau is a magnificent mountain!"

Patricia added, "The views from the trains we took from Interlaken to Jungfrau summit were spectacular. And that glacier at the top! I had never seen a real glacier. It was so wonderful to walk into that big ice cave inside it. Just like being in a blue castle. Imagine being *inside* a glacier!"

Randy added, "And I really loved our little hotel overlooking the land and the mountains. The Swiss have a way of making hotels comfortable, don't they?"

Patricia grinned, "The environment was wonderful for lovemaking, too!"

Randy squeezed her hand, "Yes, you were fantastic! I really love you, Patricia."

Their reminiscing about their Swiss adventures was interrupted by the pretty Swissair stewardess bringing them their hors d'oeuvres as the starter for their first class meal service.

Randy looked out the window to the left and exclaimed, "Look, Patricia, we're over the Aegean Sea. See the Greek Isles down there?"

"I hear they're really beautiful. Perhaps we can visit them sometime after we move to Europe from Taiwan."

Randy replied, "For sure! We'll visit all of Europe after we finish in Taiwan. Our trips will be more relaxed than those of the typical American tourist. None of this *If it's Tuesday this must be Belgium* business."

The two finished their in-flight gourmet dinner which featured *château briand* served by the stewardesses from a cart which they pushed down the aisle, cutting the portions to the passengers' individual desires on a hardwood block.

After dinner, they watched two movies: Hollywood's latest attempts at *Rambo* type adventures. Every Russian in sight was *mowed down* by the screen hero's submachine gun. Revolting, but in a *macabre way*, entertaining. Most Hollywood movies required no thinking whatsoever on the part of the viewer, just one action shot after another. Even the language dubbed in made no difference in the viewer's understanding, since the movies were essentially independent of spoken language, instead relying upon the language of frenetic action.

Patricia and Randy fell asleep all curled up together on their reclining seats, with the middle arm removed for better cuddling. When they awakened, the sun was coming up. It was Sunday already. Randy studied the in-flight map, looked out at the ground below, and exclaimed happily, "Look, we're over Eastern India now. It looks almost uninhabited down there. Amazing, that India is one of the most populous countries in the world, but the countryside looks so lightly populated. I guess, as elsewhere, the people just crowd into the cities."

Patricia responded, "I was reading the booklet we picked up at Union Bank last Monday. It compared the wage and salary levels of fifty of the major cities in the world. Bombay is lowest with 6% compared with 100% for Zürich and 141% for Los Angeles."

Randy responded, "Yes, I remember reading it. But the price level for living expenses is 79% in Bombay compared with 100% for Zürich and 141% for Los Angeles. It must be tough to live in the cities of India unless you receive a foreigner's salary."

Patricia sighed, "I'm afraid the world is still full of inequities for many of the people on Earth. I wonder if these unfair inequalities will ever be reduced?"

Randy replied sadly, "Probably not in our life times, but maybe some time in the future."

The pair's musing about the state of civilization was interrupted by the stewardess bringing their breakfast. As she served them, she said, "We'll be landing in Singapore soon. Have you ever been there before? It's such a beautiful city."

Randy smiled, "No, never. This will be the first time ever for us both. What do you suggest we see there?"

The stewardess replied happily, "There are so many things to see, I don't know where to start. Just walking through the shopping streets near the harbor is fun. Also, Tiger Balm Park is a favorite tourist attraction. That's a nice park, not far out of the city on a lake with rental paddle boats and nice open air restaurants."

Randy and Patricia enjoyed their breakfast of French toast with maple syrup and ham, served with orange juice and a plate of tropical fruits. Shortly after, the big 747 airliner started its descent into the city-country of Singapore, which is one of the cleanest cities in Asia, because of its large fine for littering the streets. The police strongly enforce this anti-littering law.

Out of his window, Randy saw the jungles of Malaysia as they approached Singapore from the northwest. Soon the many high rise buildings of the city came into view. The big airliner landed and taxied to the jet way. This city, located just a few degrees north of the equator, has a very even temperature year round, cooled as it is by the sea breezes.

Randy and Patricia retrieved their carry-on bags and briefcases and exited into the terminal for this tropical paradise. After clearing the entry formalities, the pair took a taxi to the Singapore Hilton. They entered the dazzling lobby and were descended upon by bellmen who insisted on carrying their light bags, which they carried themselves the long distance through the airport. The pair checked in at the desk and were assigned a suite on the tenth floor with a beautiful view of the city. As the bell boy showed them how to operate the television and explained the charges for the bar-refrigerator, he handed them two tickets and said, "These are for free drinks in our roof top restaurant. Be sure to try the sate, which is barbequed meat with peanut butter sauce. It's a specialty of Singapore.

When Randy slipped the boy a five dollar tip, he smiled broadly, since service was included in the room charges.

Patricia and Randy were delighted with their beautiful, luxurious suite - a living room and bar and a bedroom with a large bathroom complete with bidet. Both having slept well on the airplane, they decided to explore the city rather than take a nap after their long flight from Zurich.

It was 10:30 am, five and a half hours later than Zurich time. Singapore is one of the few cities in the world to adopt a half hour time zone. Being almost on the equator, Singapore's days and nights are almost exactly twelve hours long all year round. The sun comes up at 6 am and sets at 6 pm. Easy to get used to. There are no seasons. Just a warm tropical paradise with cooling sea breezes all year long.

Patricia and Randy took the elevator down to the lobby and found a taxi waiting in front of the hotel. Randy asked the Chinese driver to take them to a picturesque spot on the water front quay from which they could take a walk.

The cab driver, speaking in excellent English, replied, "Yes, sir. I know just the spot. And I'll drive you past the famous Raffles Hotel on the way."

A short time later, the driver dropped them off at the Singapore quay. They crossed from the street to the waterside using an overpass, and spent a while walking in and out of the variety of shops and admiring the many boats anchored in the harbor. Then they crossed back to the city side of the street and wandered through the town. Randy exchanged two hundred US dollars into Singapore dollars with a Hindu moneychanger whose office was a stool on the sidewalk. Randy received 420 Singapore dollars, about seen percent better than he had received at the airport earlier. The pair noted the anti-litter law was very effective. The city was spotlessly clean.

Since Singapore was a former British Colony, English was the primary language with Chinese Second and Malaysian third. There were a lot of Malaysians, but eighty percent of the population were Chinese.

The pair browsed through a jewelry store and Patricia spotted a beautiful *princess* ring, hand crafted in finely worked gold and set with multi-colored jewels. She fell in love with it. The shopkeeper's asking price was two hundred Singapore dollars.

Randy haggled with him and the two finally agreed to a price of one hundred Singapore dollars.

Then Randy hailed a cab and asked the driver to take them to the aquatic park which the stewardess had told them about. A first the driver was confused, until Randy mentioned the rental paddle boats. Then the driver said, "Oh, you mean *Tiger Balm Park.* Yes! It's only a twenty minute drive from here."

Randy and Patricia strolled through the beautiful green park, where they rented one of the side-by-side paddle boats. They floated almost effortlessly around the small, lovely lake, enjoying the tropical plantings. Then they returned the boat and enjoyed a relaxing luncheon in the waterside restaurant built onto a wooden platform extending out over the water. They learned the park had this odd name because it was built by a local company that also makes *Tiger Balm Lotion*, which is very popular throughout the Far East. They enjoyed strolling through the park, admiring it's colorful statues and looking at the rides. They particularly liked watching the joy on the faces of the young children, while yearning for the day they could have their very own baby.

The pair returned to their hotel suite just after 4 pm and had an erotic session of lovemaking followed by a nap to help adjust to the time change. They awoke refreshed and rested just after 6:30 pm. They dressed in informal clothes for their first night out in Singapore. They decided to try the roof top restaurant at the Hilton. They took the elevator up and were delighted with the tropical paradise restaurant they found there. They had sate, the barbequed meat on skewers recommended by their bellboy, as appetizers with their tropical drinks: Mai Tais. The sweet peanut butter sauce gave a unique flavor to the barbequed meat. Later, they had large broiled shrimp on a bed of curried rice for their main course, with a luscious avocado salad. Dessert was a fantastic fruit cocktail with fresh mangoes, papayas, bananas and oranges. Randy was also served a piece of the Singapore melon-like fruit called *durian.* The waiter explained to Patricia that women don't eat *durian.* As soon as the waiter left, she took a bite anyway. It had a strange musky taste. She decided to leave the fruit to men only.

The couple spent one more relaxing day sightseeing around the environs of Singapore. Their taxi driver guide showed them the place where Japanese soldiers brutally executed hundreds of British people during World War II. The traces of this violence had largely vanished because of the rebuilding of modern Singapore. The recession of the mid 1980's had been replaced by a booming economy, helped in no small part by hordes of Japanese tourists who flocked there in their *eternal tour groups.*

Tuesday morning, Randy and Patricia took their Singapore Airlines flight from Singapore to Taipei, with short stops scheduled for Bangkok and Hong Kong. When the flight made its first stop, at Bangkok, the pair had a few minutes to visit the duty free shop at the airport. Randy found a beautiful pair of earrings that matched the *princess ring* he had purchased for Patricia earlier. He paid a little over twenty US dollars for the earrings. After take off, the pair saw out the airliner windows the river of Bangkok with the many small boats plying the waters, delivering and buying goods at the riverside markets.

As they were served lunch at 37,000 feet on the next leg, between Bangkok and Hong Kong, Randy looked down at the wide Mekong River, winding its way through Vietnam and remarked to Patricia, "Look down at the jungles of Vietnam where so many Americans fought and died. It was a sad period for our former homeland, wasn't it"

"Yes, it was. Even though we were both very young then, I still remember the pain and agony of it, all those bodies returned to the US in the C-141's, anti-war riots in the US, the bombings which killed women and children along with the Vietcong communist enemy. A real nightmare in US history. And what was the outcome? The Soviet navy is now using all those expensive ports the Americans built at the taxpayer' expense. Ironic, isn't it?"

Randy got a sad look in his eyes, "Yes, it is ironic. A war that concluded nothing. Oh, Patricia, I hope our helping the Taiwanese to build a new fighter doesn't result in bloodshed."

"I hope so, too, Randy. It's easy to forget that our new design is meant to kill people, isn't it?"

Randy replied sadly, "I'm afraid I just think of the technical aspects of our design, not the human side, the *deadly* side. Patricia, after this Ultra Taiwan Fighter project is over, let's retire and try to forget we were ever involved in the design of weapon Systems designed to kill people!"

Patricia smiled, "Don't get so morbid, Randy. If we didn't help them with the design, then someone else would."

Randy replied, without smiling, "Yes, I guess you're right. It's still bugging me, though!"

Chapter 15

Taipei Party

The evening mob of well wishers in the terminal of the Chiang Kai-shek Airport made it difficult for Randy and Patricia to find Eddie Chung in the crowd. Then Patricia spotted the beautiful face of Mei Lin and explained, excitedly, "There they are! There they are! Over to the left. See Mei Lin and Eddie standing there?"

Randy replied, "Yes, I see them now."

The pair pushed their way through the noisy crowd to where Eddie Chung and Mei Lin were standing. Mei Lin grabbed Patricia, hugged her, kissed her on both cheeks and said happily, "Welcome to your new home: Taiwan! We are so glad to have you and Randy here."

Eddie Chung hugged Patricia as Mei Lin hugged and kissed Randy a warm welcome. Eddie said to the pair, "We have a nice suite reserved for you at the Brothers Hotel in Taipei. Then, after you get settled in, we have a reception party tonight in the hotel ballroom in your honor. You'll meet all the people in Taiwan that you'll be working with."

Mei Lin added, I hope you're not too tired after your flight from Singapore."

Patricia answered, "No, not at all." She looked questionably at Randy. He nodded his head. Then she continued, "We had a relaxing time in Singapore and it was a just a little over five hours flying time, plus the short stops in Bangkok and Hong Kong. We're ready for the party!"

Just after 8 pm, Eddie and Mei Lin escorted the two new arrivals to Taiwan, Randy and Patricia, up to the hotel ballroom. They could hear the music playing and the guests had already started arriving.

Eddie turned to Randy and said, "The technical elite of Taiwan's aerospace community will be here tonight, all eager to meet the former Americans who are going to help them build the new Ultra Taiwan Fighter."

Mei Lin added, "General Hua is the host tonight. About 9 pm you will join the general and his wife in a reception line to meet all the guests formally."

Patricia responded, "What a wonderful way to meet the people and their spouses that we'll be working with in Taiwan."

Randy added, "Eddie and Mei Lin, thanks for arranging this wonderful party. It really makes us feel welcome in our new home."

Eddie responded, "We want you to relax tonight. We have a busy schedule of meetings for you the rest of this week. Tomorrow morning, you will meet officially with General Hua and some other important people to kick off your consulting contract."

Over a hundred people attended the reception party for Randy and Patricia. They were warmly greeted by all the guests as they stood in the reception line headed by General Hua and his wife. General Hua introduced each guest in turn to Randy and Patricia. His recall of names was phenomenal. He remembered the name of almost every guest. Occasionally, his wife had to help with the wives' names.

There was an elaborate buffet of food and tables for dining and drinking. The dance floor was crowded with couples moving to the music of the live band. The last guest left by 1 am. Eddie and Mei Lin escorted the pair back to their hotel suite. As Eddie and Mei Lin said goodnight to Randy and Patricia, Eddie reminded the couple, "I'll pick you up at 9:30 am in the lobby downstairs. Our meeting with General Hua is at 10 am. See you then."

The pair echoed, "Thanks for the wonderful party. See you in the morning."

It was the first Wednesday of September 1988. As usual, the weather in Taipei was hot and sultry with heavy thunderstorms bringing rain and lightning in the late afternoon.

It was 10 am and already hot as Eddie Chung drove up to the Ministry of National Defense headquarters building in downtown Taipei. He let his passengers, Randy and Patricia, out and he arranged with the unofficial parking attendant to watch his car. The trio took the elevator to the floor where General Hua's conference room was located. Eddie ushered the two into the big room. General Hua was already there with two other men, one in a ROC Air Force general's uniform and the other in a dark blue suit with vest and a conservative striped tie.

General Hua greeted the visitors, "Welcome to the MND, Dr. McLyle and Ms. Manos. I would like you to meet two gentlemen who are responsible for the major segments of our new UTF."

Hua turned to the man in the general's uniform and said, "First, meet General Huang Ching-lee, who is director of the Aircraft Industries Development Center in Taichung where you two will have an office. AIDC is responsible for the aircraft development and integration of the total UTF weapon system."

Randy and Patricia exchanged formalities with General Huang.

Then Hua turned to the second man and introduced him, "This is Dr. Chris Haah, director of the Chan Shung Institute of Science and Technology. Dr. Haah's organization, CSIST, is responsible for developing the guided missiles and avionics Systems that will be integrated into the UTF."

Patricia and Randy shook hands with Dr. Haah, who added, "And tomorrow you two are to be my guests at CSIST, a short drive from Taipei, where we will show you our work on the missiles for the UTF."

Patricia responded, "Thank you, Dr. Haah. We will look forward to that visit. I have Programs on our magnetic tape – the one Randy brought that contains his aircraft design and my analysis Programs - to evaluate the effectiveness of the missiles against various enemy targets."

General Huang said, "And next week, after you finish your business in the Taipei area, you will come south to Taichung to begin your work with us at AIDC."

Randy laughed, "You are all very well organized. We look forward to working with such talented organizations as CSIST and AIDC."

Patricia added, "Yes, I can see you are truly professional."

General Hua interrupts, " Lady and Gentleman, we have many important matters to cover this morning. First, I have asked Colonel Eddie Chung to present my briefing on our requirements for the Republic of China's new Ultra Tactical Fighter. Then I would like for Dr. McLyle to present a briefing on his advanced tactical fighter aircraft design that will be adapted to our UTF."

Both Randy and Patricia were surprised to hear General Hua refer to Eddie Chung as a colonel. They had believed he was just a businessman, not a part of the ROC government. They would never learn for sure that he was a colonel in the ROC CIA.

Randy responded to General Hua's outline of the meeting by saying, "General Huang, I have briefing charts summarizing the highlights of my aircraft design contained on this magnetic tape. Randy held up the tape and added, "It's the tape I gave General Huang in June. Now, I can provide the code so the information contained on the tape can be *unlocked!* I can use the IBM PC at the end of your conference table for projecting on the color video monitor here."

Huang responded, "Excellent, Dr. McLyle. But first, my briefing of our need for the new aircraft. Colonel Chung, please present my briefing."

Eddie responded, "Yes, General Huang. I will now begin your presentation."

Eddie Chung spent the next forty-five minutes presenting the requirements for the new Ultra Taiwan Fighter aircraft. Randy and Patricia interrupted the briefing with frequent and penetrating questions. Eddie could answer all their questions in complete detail. This technical expertise and knowledge shown by Eddie had never been revealed to the couple before. They were impressed.

After Eddie completed the briefing, General Huang turned to Randy and said, "Now, Dr. McLyle, that you see what we need, please tell us how your design fits our requirements."

Randy walked to the IBM personal computer at the end of the table, turned it on, and waited while the computer whirred away, loading the information stored on the tape onto the computer memory disk. After the PC finished booting and showed a colored page, Randy exclaimed, "OK, the briefing is ready to begin." He pushed the *begin* button, returned to his seat, and said, "General Huang, I programmed the computer to speak to you using a *synthesized* human voice. It never makes a mistake."

The computer started speaking using a sexy female voice for describing the colored charts of the *Advanced Tactical Fighter* aircraft. When one of the men in the audience interrupted to ask a question, the computer, using a voice recognition feature, answered the question in the same female voice.   Only occasionally did Randy have to help out, answering the question himself.

At the end of the briefing, General Huang rose and said, "Dr. McLyle, your computer presented a thorough and excellent summary of your design. It does appear that your design and our needs are closely matched."

Randy replied, "Thank you, General. I think the adaptation of my design to your requirements will be straightforward. With Patricia and me here to work with your people, I feel confident you will have the best fighter aircraft in the world. But I have a final question about the aircraft project. Are you sure you can build such an advanced aircraft? Do you have the manufacturing capabilities?"

General Hua got a serious look on his face and replied, "Dr. McLyle, at the present time, I and my advisors hold the opinion that we can build the UTF here in Taiwan. But, I would like to make a request of you."

Randy smiled, "And what is that, General Huang?"

"When the preliminary design of our new UTF is completed next June 1989, I would like to meet with you and review this question before we actually start building."

Chapter 16

Missiles

The countryside of Taiwan was verdant from the heavy rains. Randy and Patricia were riding with Eddie Chung to the secret facility of the Chan Shung Institute of Science and Technology in the northeast corner of Taiwan, about fifty minutes' drive from downtown Taipei. Randy and Patricia checked out of their room at the Brothers Hotel and moved to a hotel much closer to CSIST, not far from the Chiang Kai-shek airport. Since they will be visiting CSIST for the next two days, they want to avoid the drive back to Taipei at the end of the work day

Driving along the two lane highway, passing through rice paddies on either side of the highway, Eddie Chung said, "We will soon be passing by the *Eye on China* Amusement Park. We have constructed *in miniature* many of the famous monuments and geographic wonders found in Mainland China at the park, so that our children will not forget the cultural glories of *all* of China. Mei Lin and I will escort you on a visit to the park Saturday morning. I think you will enjoy it."

Patricia replied enthusiastically, "Oh, thank you, Eddie. We would love to visit the park. It sounds like an easy way to visit Mainland China, right here in Taiwan."

Ten minutes later the trio arrived at the huge secret facility of CSIST. Eddie stopped at the security building and obtained badges for Randy and Patricia authorizing them to enter the guarded premises. They left their passports as collateral for the badges. Eddie showed his identity badge to the guard at the entrance who waived Eddie's BMW car, carrying Eddie and his two passengers, through the gate. Except for the exceptional security at the entrance gate, the CSIST facility looked more like a college campus than a weapons research and development laboratory. Based on the size of the facility and the number of buildings, Randy estimated there must be between ten and twenty thousand workers at CSIST, making it a major employer of scientists and engineers engaged in weapons R&D.

Eddie drove to the headquarters building which was flying the ROC flag. He parked in front and escorted his two companions into the multistory building. They took an elevator to the top floor and Eddie led them to a large conference room. Dr. Chris Haah, whom Randy and Patricia had met the day before in General Hua's office, greeted them at the door, and said, "Welcome to CSIST Dr. McLyle and Ms. Manos. I believe you met my senior staff at your reception party. We will brief you on the missiles we plan to utilize in the new UTF aircraft."

After shaking hands with the many members of Dr. Haah's senior staff, Randy looked around the room and saw a number of full scale models of air-to-air and air-to-ground missiles on display in the large conference room.

Randy said, "Are these the missiles you plan to use in the UTF?"

Dr. Haah laughed, "Oh, no! These are older missiles that were either procured from the US or designed and built here at CSIST. They are used on our old F-5 fighter aircraft. The missiles for the UTF are much more advanced."

Randy responded, "Dr. Haah, before we go into your description of the missiles for the UTF, I should make sure you understand my advanced aircraft design assumes the missiles will be carried internally to the aircraft, not on the wings, like on your F-5's."

"Yes, Dr. McLyle, we understand that point very well. Remember, we have excellent intelligence information from some of the Chinese engineers employed in the US aerospace companies."

Randy looked surprised at this answer, and asked, "But, isn't that illegal? To obtain classified information from Chinese engineers in the US?"

Eddie interrupted and answered, "Randy, in the intelligence collection business, nothing is illegal. Unless you get caught."

Patricia added, "Well, Eddie. I certainly hope you're right. The US government is very tough on spies, even ones from friendly countries like Taiwan and Israel."

Randy declared, "Look, Eddie. Patricia and I don't approve of espionage."

Eddie replied, "Good. Then we can rest assured you won't tell any of our secrets to your former country can't we?"

Randy, surprised by this reply, "Well, yes of course! We believe responsibility goes with citizenship!" Then he turned to Dr. Haah, "Let's get on with your briefing on the missiles for the UTF."

Dr. Haah replied apologetically, "I'm sorry, Dr. McLyle and Ms. Manos, I didn't intend to offend you by my remarks. I just thought any knowledgeable person, like you two, would know that small countries like Taiwan and Israel would have to depend upon espionage and covert operations to get the technology we need to overcome the huge numerical advantages of our enemies."

Randy replied, "Frankly, I never thought about your problems before this year. I've always been too busy creating new designs to even think about espionage, except for being sure I always followed the security rules for any classified information entrusted to me. As far as my advanced tactical fighter design is concerned, it was not classified."

Eddie Chung interrupted and cautioned, "Randy, your design wasn't classified in the US, but here in Taiwan your design is classified *Top Secret.* Understand?"

Dr. Haah added, "And what you will hear about our new missiles is *Top Secret* as well."

Randy and Patricia chorused, "Yes, we understand."

Dr. Haah, who has been sitting at the head of the long, oblong conference table, rose and walked to the front of the room, carrying a stack of colored, transparent view graphs. He placed the first on the view graph projector with the title projected on the big white screen: *UTF Missile Overview.*

Then he said, "I will present an overview of the air-to-air and air-to-ground missiles we plan to use in the Ultra Taiwan Fighter aircraft. Then during the next two days, specialists from my staff will present you with all of the details."

Dr. Haah gave an excellent description of the missiles intended for the UTF. He made the following points:

Number 1. The missiles must be designed so that the UTF can launch the missiles and then leave in order to avoid the danger of being shot down by enemy defenses. Once they have been launched, the missiles must be smart enough to find the targets and to destroy them. The missile must have a long range so the UTF aircraft doesn't have to get too close to the enemy defenses.

Number 2. Each missile must be designed so that it contains eight mini-missiles, each capable of hitting and destroying a different target. With four missiles carried by the UTF, then 32 different targets can be destroyed by a single aircraft, in a matter of a few seconds.

Number 3. The missiles must be completely immune to enemy countermeasures, such as jamming and decoys. In other words, whatever the enemy might do to try to confuse the missile and make it miss the targets, the missile must be smart enough to avoid the enemy tricks and to still hit the targets. Stated another way, the missile must have enough different types of *eyes* and *ears*, or sensors, to look at the target plus a sophisticated brain, or computer, to be able to think about what its eyes and ears sense in order to avoid the tricks of the enemy.

Number 4. The same missile design must be programmable to be an *air-to-air missile* capable of shooting down enemy aircraft *and* it must also be programmed to become an *air-to-ground missile* in order to destroy enemy targets on the ground. The pilot should be able to reconfigure the missile's program *in flight* in order to adapt to his needs for air-to-air or air-to-ground combat.

Number 5. Finally, the missile design must be smart enough that the human pilot is not overwhelmed by the decision making process of what target to attack. The aircraft avionics and the missile computer must help the pilot with the targeting job.

After Dr. Haah finished, his staff members gave many more briefings covering the details of how the missiles would to their job. These briefings lasted two days.

At the end of the second day of briefings, Randy rose, faced Dr. Haah, and said "Now, I've heard your plans for the UTF missiles. But I'm afraid you have two problems you haven't yet solved."

Dr. Haah appeared surprised and asked, "What are they, Dr. McLyle?"

Randy answered slowly and clearly, "In order to accomplish your ambitious plans, you will need two major scientific breakthroughs. *First,* you can't get all the electronics you need to do all those things into the small volume of the missile without some electronic findings. And *second,* the multiple independently targeted sub-missiles will need a huge advance in the presently available computer algorithms. Without these two *quantum leaps,* the UTF will be just an expensive one man transport."

Eddie Chung stood, looked Randy straight in the eyes and replied, "Randy, the Israelis have solved those two problems. We merely have to figure out how to obtain that technology from them."

Chapter 17

Taichung

Randy and Patricia enjoyed the trip to Taichung, the major city on the west side of the island of Taiwan. Eddie Chung indicated several points of interest as he drove rapidly along the super highway and then through the city streets until he parked in front of a three storied apartment building. He led the couple inside and held open the door of an apartment.

Randy and Patricia walked into the large, three bedroom flat. It was tastefully and completely furnished, including even dishes, glassware, stainless steel flatware, and pots and pans. The living room had comfortable, soft chairs and a couch, placed so they surrounded a large carved, coffee table, plus a bar with four stools. On three walls were beautiful oil paintings showing two Taiwanese still life scenes and a beautiful landscape of rice paddies with water buffaloes. There was a hand carved wooden statue of an eagle standing in the corner of the living room, a specialty from a small town about thirty kilometers north of Taichung.

The dining room featured a large dining table and chair set, plus a built-in wooden credenza and display shelves, complete with linen tablecloths and napkins. The master bedroom had a made-up double bed with bedspread, dresser, and adequate closets for their clothing. There was also big, beautiful crystal chandelier.

The nice sized guest bedroom had twin beds. An additional bedroom was outfitted as a home office, with two desks and chairs and a cabinet for filing papers. Randy and Patricia were surprised to note that an IBM personal computer *clone made in Taiwan* was sitting on each desk plus a laser printer to be shared by the two computers that were linked to permit easy transfer of files from one computer to the other.

Patricia exclaimed, "Eddie, I can hardly believe that a furnished apartment in Taiwan comes with two personal computers."

Eddie grinned, "General Hua authorized me to buy the two IBM PC *clones* from his discretionary budget. He said, 'I want to make sure Dr. McLyle and Ms. Manos can work at home on our UTF design whenever they want to. Be sure each computer has the latest *Windows and* Office software to make it easy for home use.' So this is what I bought. They cost less than half what they would in the US."

Randy said, "They look like great machines. Just like the IBM PC we used to have at our old Pasadena office."

When Patricia entered the kitchen, she exclaimed, "Oh, Eddie. I love this room! It has everything: a big refrigerator with freezer, a great stove, lots of cabinets, and even a dishwasher. And look at all the pots and pans." She turned to Randy and added, "Oh, Randy, we'll hardly have to buy anything for housekeeping."

Eddie responded, "That's the idea. We want you two to work on the fighter design, not spend a lot of time setting up house. There's one more thing you haven't seen: the laundry room."

Just behind the kitchen was a laundry area with a washing machine and dryer plus a wash tub.

Patricia exclaimed, "Eddie this apartment has everything. I'm afraid to ask how much the rent is per month."

Eddie grinned, "It's pretty expensive. Twenty thousand New Taiwan dollars per month."

Randy pulled out his pocket calculator, "That's only 500 US dollars per month. An apartment like this in Pasadena, California, would cost more than two thousand dollars per month."

Eddie smiled, "Just another advantage of living in Taiwan. Our living expenses are much less than in California. Another advantage of this apartment is that it is right next door to the Presidential Hotel. They have some nice restaurants there and you can catch a taxi to downtown Taichung just in front of the hotel. Taxis here are so inexpensive that it's hardly worth owning a car."

Patricia responded, "Eddie, we love the apartment, it furnishings, its location, and its price. But who do we pay the rent to?"

Eddie smiled broadly, "That's easy. You pay me the rent. I own the apartment. But to save you the trouble, I'll just deduct the rent from your contract payments, so don't worry about paying the rent. Your credit is good."

Patricia laughed, "That's easy, Eddie. I was reviewing our contract last night. We get a two million dollar payment when we complete the preliminary design review and another two million when we complete the critical design review."

Eddie added, "That's right, Patricia, and you get the final five million dollars when we have the first successful flight. We hope that flight will be in July 1991, less than three years away."

Randy asked, "Does that mean we can rent your apartment for the next three years, Eddie?"

"That's no problem, Randy. Here's a three year lease for you to sign. The rent will be adjusted annually to compensate for the cost-of-living index."

Patricia laughed, "Eddie, you think of everything. I'll bet you even have a used car to sell us."

Eddie grinned. "Yes here are the keys. It's a white Toyota sports car. You owe me 7,000 dollars for it. It's in the parking garage below. I'll deduct the cost from your next payment, too!"

Randy replied, "We'll take it. I'll bet your easy payment terms are the best in Taichung!" He signed and handed the papers to Patricia so she could do the same.

Eddie laughed, "I thought you'd take the car. Now you have a way to get to Sun-Moon Lake this week-end. It's only about an hour and a half drive from your apartment."

Eddie picked up his copy of the lease agreement and added, "I'll leave you two to get settled in your new apartment. One more thing …"

"What's that?" Randy and Patricia choroused.

"General Huang is giving a dinner party to welcome you to Taichung, home of AIDC, tonight. I'll pick you up here at 7 pm. The dinner's just next door at the Presidential Hotel."

Randy replied, "Great! See you then, Eddie."

That evening Eddie Chung escorted the happy couple to the Presidential Hotel. They entered the large and beautiful lobby which featured black marble decorations and rich Chinese carpets. They climbed up the wide stairway to the second floor and walked into a private dining room. Randy and Patricia were to be treated to another ceremonial Chinese dinner party, intended to entertain honored guests in an intimate, friendly atmosphere with good food, drink, and fellowship. The official host was General Huang, director of AIDC. Also attending were Dr. Charlie Chang, program director for the UTF, Colonel Dr. Jan Wang, director of avionics and systems integration for the UTF, and finally Colonel Yung Hang-fu, the chief test pilot assigned to fly the new fighter. As usual, Eddie Chung's seat was arranged with his back to the door, indicating he would pay the bill for tonight's festive dinner. After the round of greetings and introductions were finished, the guests seated themselves with Patricia, the only woman, at General Huang's right and Randy at his left. The over guests arranged themselves around the circular table with their distances from General Huang denoting the importance of the individuals.

With this elaborate *pecking order* established, General Huang proposed a toast, "To the success of our new *Ultra Tactical Fighter* with the help of our new citizens, Dr. McLyle and Ms. Manos."

The toast was drink with a very pleasant rosé wine made in Taiwan. While waiting for the waiters to bring the food, the various Chinese guests followed the delightful custom of *one-at-a-time* toasting either Randy or Patricia. This personalized toasting made the pair feel at home and savor the good fellowship expressed towards them by the other guests.

The food was served and was a true Chinese feast offering a wide variety of choices. Some delightful to the palates of Randy and Patricia, some a little strange to their taste. All-in-all, they enjoyed the dinner very much.

At the end of the meal, General Hua rose and said, "Lady and gentlemen. I have an announcement to make. I hereby appoint Dr. McLyle as my chief scientist for the UTF and Ms. Manos as the deputy chief scientist. In their new positions, they will report directly to my office."

Then he turned to Randy and Patricia and said, "I have arranged for a new office for the two of you in our headquarters building, just down the hall from my office. It is completely equipped with two IBM compatible personal computers for you to use. And Mr. Chung has agreed to release one of his staff members to be your personal secretary. Her name is Joy-tung, a very talented young lady. If you'll please stand, I'll present you with the keys to your office."

Randy and Patricia stood, accepted the keys, and shook hands with the general. Patricia responded, "Thank you, General Huang, for the honored positions, the new office, and a personal secretary. How wonderful."

Randy thought to himself, *Joy-tung is very talented. I remember my night with her very well*. And then said, "Yes, General Huang. We truly appreciate your recognition of us and the beautiful new office complete with computers and a private secretary."

General Huang added, "Saturday mornings are work days at AIDC, but since this is your first weekend in Taichung, I order you to take tomorrow, Saturday, off. I think you should do some sightseeing around Taichung: Sun-Moon Lake, our Buddhist temples, etcetera. I have assigned Colonel Jan Wang to escort you to these places. You will both be working closely with Jan. He received his PhD in aeronautical engineering from Caltech in Pasadena, where you used to live."

Patricia and Randy spoke as one, "Thank you, General Huang."

The next morning, Jan Wang and his wife, Ju-ling, picked up Randy and Patricia at their apartment at 9 am for their guided tour of central Taiwan. The quartet got into the Wang's four door black Ford, manufactured in Taiwan. As they were turning onto the toll highway to go north, Patricia remarked to Ju-ling, "I'm trying to learn to read Chinese writing. I notice that Taipei and Taichung both have two symbols, and first symbols are the same."

Ju-ling replied, "Very observant! Taipei means city in the north of Taiwan. Taichung means city in the middle of Taiwan. The first common symbol means Taiwan, the second symbol for Taipei means north."

Patricia responded, "Then many of the names of places have two symbols, right?"

"Right! I'll help you learn our language. We can start by reading signs as we drive along today."

At the toll booth, Ju-ling pointed out the symbol for an automobile, "It's rectangular shape makes it look a little like the undercarriage of a car with two axles. The booth for trucks uses the same character but precedes it with the symbol for big. The booth for automobiles precedes the character with the symbol for little."

Twenty minutes later Jan Wang took an exit from the north-south highway and entered a small village west of the highway. Almost every shop featured large, carved wooden statues, similar to the one in Randy and Patricia's living room in Taichung. The quartet spent an hour wandering through the many shops looking at the fantastic wooden figures. There were dragons, lions, horses, tigers, eagles, and even nude women. The statues were fabricated by a number of artisans from this village using large blocks of wood. The artisans used a combination of carving and a blow torch to achieve the proper shapes. As a result of the flame technique used, the statues had a black charred appearance. They were very imaginative and reasonably affordable, considering their size. A large statue's asking price was about forty thousand New Taiwan dollars or 1000 US dollars. A small one was one fifth that price. By bargaining, one could reduce the price by ten to twenty percent of the asking price. Randy and Patricia enjoyed seeing where and how their wooden eagle was made, but decided one statue for their apartment was enough.

After leaving the statue village, Jan Wang announced, "Next we'll head for a town south of Taichung. There's a Chinese museum that shows how the villagers from this part of Taiwan lived several hundred years ago. There were several sample rooms furnished with authentic furniture from the past eras."

Patricia responded, "Oh, that's great. I love Museums."

Ju-ling added, "Nearby the museums is one of the largest Buddhist temples in Taiwan. We'll visit the temple so you can see how our people worship."

Patricia replied, "That would be lovely, Ju-ling."

The quartet spent the rest of the afternoon visiting the museum and temple. Randy and Patricia were particularly impressed by the large temple with its alter filled with burning incense. Ju-ling and Jan led the pair to a special room in the temple with glass jars lining the wall on a ledge up high. Ju-ling explained, "These jars contain the remains of the deceased after they have been cremated. The presence of stones among the residue is an indication of the holiness of the person. The more stones, the holier the person was during life."

Colonel Wang pointed proudly to a jar with several of the largest stones. "That jar holds my grandmother's remains. See the stones, she was very holy!"

Ju-ling added, "Our family is a very proud of grandmother. She was 94 when she died."

Wang added, "My grandfather was very lonely after my grandmother died. But he cured his loneliness by marrying twenty year old girl. She keeps him very happy. He is 97 years old now."

Randy said, "That's amazing, for your grandfather to marry a twenty old. Isn't that unusual for such an old man to marry such a young girl.?"

Wang grinned, "We Chinese hold old age in great reverence. It is common for elderly men like my grandfather to take a young girl for a bride. The old man enjoys sleeping with the young woman. The young woman enjoys the prestige the age and wealth of her elderly husband brings to her."

Ju-ling interrupted, "Randy and Patricia, our sightseeing for the day is over. There is a restaurant nearby that features a type of chicken we Chinese love. It's about twenty minutes away. Tomorrow we will take you to Sun-Moon Lake and spend all day Sunday there, enjoying the beautiful scenery."

Patricia responded happily, "We would love to have dinner with you now. The trip to Sun-Moon Lake tomorrow sounds very nice."

At the restaurant, Wang ordered a Chinese delicacy – *barnyard chicken* – for all four diners. Randy and Patricia were surprised when the chicken was served . The flesh was dark colored, almost black and was very tough and difficult to chew. Patricia exclaimed, generously, after tasting it, "This is very interesting chicken. The meat is very firm, and the color is different."

JU-ling laughed and explained, "We Chinese believe *barnyard chicken* to be the best and most healthful chicken you can eat. The chicken is allowed to roam around the barnyard, eating grubs and worms. That's why the chicken's meat is so black. The meat is firm because the chicken gets a lot of exercise running around the barnyard. It's not like the pampered chickens grown in buildings and stuffed with food to make them fat, fast, for the market. This is a *natural* chicken!"

Randy, who could hardly chew the chicken and who found the color repulsive, smiled stiffly and replied, "Yes, this chicken is very – *different!*"

After dinner, the Wang's dropped Randy and Patricia off at their apartment about 8 pm, and Wang said just before he drove away, "We'll pick you up at 9 in the morning for the trip to Sun-Moon Lake."

Randy and Patricia enjoyed the first Saturday night in their new apartment watching an American movie on TV with Chinese subtitles. It was an interesting experience seeing the flow of Chinese characters as the actors said their lines. After a session of love-making, they fell into a relaxed sleep, enjoying their new home in Taichung.

Randy and Patricia spent a very delightful Sunday with the Wangs, enjoying the sights of the beautiful Sun-Moon Lake situated in the ridge of mountains which ran through the center of Taiwan. They learned the Chinese consider the only correct way to visit the lake included an overnight stay at the hotel there. The true nature lover would get up early to watch the sun come up through the mists rising off the lake, especially at the time of a full moon. They decided they would do that some time in the future when there was a full moon.

When they returned to their apartment Sunday night, Randy remarked to Patricia, "Well, the *Taiwan Holiday* is over now. Our real work starts tomorrow."

Patricia replied, "Yes, you're right. Do you really think you can be ready for the Preliminary Design Review, PDR, by next June? That's only eight months away!"

Randy grinned, "Yes, Patricia, no problem. The real problem is building the aircraft after the design is completed. I'm *not* convinced the Taiwanese can do it. My design used a much different technology than the F-5's they have built at AIDC. I'm afraid they are going to need outside help."

Chapter 18

Design Begins

The second Monday in October 1988.

In the privacy of their new office Randy expressed his concern about the ability of the Ultra Tactical Fighter organization to understand the details of his design, "Patricia, I'm really worried that Charlie Chang's organization is so bureaucratic that it can never implement my design. They're organized more like a military outfit than a hard-hitting design team.

Patricia responded, "Well, for heaven's sake, why don't we meet with Charlie and explain your concerns? After all, we are General Huang' chief scientist and deputy chief scientist now. We have a responsibility to speak up."

"That's a good idea, Patricia, I'll call him now and set up a meeting - today if possible."

Patricia, Randy, and Charlie met in the small conference room attached to their offices on the second floor of the AIDC headquarters building. Randy and Patricia's new secretary, Joy-tung, served the trio Chinese tea with cookies. Randy opened the meeting by saying, "Charlie, you have a big responsibility as program director for the new UTF aircraft. Patricia and I want you to be successful. We have a vested interest in your success. Half of our contract payment depends on the first flight."

Charlie smiled, looked Randy in the eye, and said, "Randy, just what do you have in mind? Remember, I spent four years going to graduate school in Texas. I can sense when an American, or a *former* American wants to say something, but is afraid to offend the person he's taking to."

Randy grinned, "Charlie, you are very perceptive. Look, Patricia and I have been working with your people now for a few weeks and I can see some things I think need changing. Your organization was set up to build the F-5's from plans that were already completed and following procedures that had already been tried out in the US when they built the first F-5's. Now we are trying to design a new and more modern airplane. Your people have never done this before. They need a different plan of organization. I think you need to set a special UTF design team, one that cuts across this military-type organization you have here at AIDC."

Chang interrupted, "You mean a UTF *matrix organization* like Cosmos Aircraft proposed for the Advanced Tactical Fighter, right? Remember I spent a whole boring day at Cosmos listening to briefings giving descriptions of their plans for building the ATF that they didn't get to build for us. You are talking about a UTF Program Organization that reports straight to me, the program director, right?"

Randy smiled broadly, "Exactly, Charlie. You must have been reading my mind. The team should be divided into sub-teams to perform the various detailed jobs called for by my overall design."

Charlie realized he had a good ally, a powerful friend, in Randy, and responded, "Good. That's exactly what I want, too. I approached General Huang with such a proposal last month, but he turned me down. Said he wanted to build a strong, functional organization for the long term, not one just for the UTF program."

Randy saw that he and Charlie were on the same side, "Let's work out a plan for a team organization to run the UTF program – one we work out together – and present to General Huang. I'll explain that we can't guarantee the schedule will be met without such an organization. He'll buy it. Believe me!"

Charlie smiled enthusiastically, "I think you're right Randy. General Huang is under a lot of pressure from General Hua to meet a flight date of July 1991. He wouldn't want to jeopardize that schedule."

Patricia added, "I sounds to me like you two are in complete agreement. I'll project two charts onto the PC video screen, one showing the aircraft and it's subsystems and one showing the design tasks that have to be done. That should help you two define the kind of organization you need."

Chang responded, "Good idea, Patricia. And Randy, you list the team breakdown you think we should have to do the job. I'll list key people I think should be assigned to the team."

Randy replied, "OK, that should be easy. And Patricia you can create the organization chart we come up with on the PC and get a print-out, can't you?"

"Right, we should have the new organization defined before lunch, with your brains and my PC."

Looking at the two charts up on the personal computer screen, Randy explained, "Charlie, I think we should have the following subteams: *aeronautical configuration, stability and control, propulsion, cockpit controls and displays, avionics*, and *weapons*."

As Randy spoke, Patricia created an organization chart on her computer screen. She set up a series of boxes with the name of one of the six subteams in each box. Charlie supplied the name of a leader for each box and Patricia typed the name in the correct box.

Patricia added, "Randy, I think you've forgotten two subteams that should be added to the UTF organization."

Randy, looking surprised, "What are those two, Patricia?"

"A *human-factors subteam* to make sure the pilot can do everything required to fly the airplane and fire the weapons. And a *missions and tactics subteam* to evaluate whether or not the theoretically designed airplane can do what the real aircraft has to do in actual combat."

Charlie grinned broadly, "Randy, you have a smart deputy. I think those two subteams are needed, also."

Randy replied, "I agree. Let's include them!"

Charlie supplied the names for the two additional subteam boxes, and Patricia entered the new subteams. "Voilá! You now have the UTF organization. See it on the screen?"

Randy and Charlie examined the new organization they had created. Each suggested a few minor revisions which Patricia corrected on the screen. When both agreed the organization was optimal, Patricia pushed the *print* button on the PC and the laser printer connected to the computer printed out four copies of the organization chart. They each kept a copy and Charlie took an extra copy to give to General Huang and said, "I'll set up a meeting for the three of us and General Huang right after lunch. If he approves it, we'll have a meeting of the new team leaders at 3 today and explain to them how the new organization will work, OK?"

Patricia and Randy agreed, "Sounds great, Charlie!"

The trio had their meeting with General Huang at 1:30. Randy opened the meeting by saying, "General Huang, Dr. Chang and I have defined what we think is a very effective *matrix* organization for the UTF team It has the advantage of focusing your AIDC manpower to complete the UTF design and fabrication on schedule. It retains your existing functional organization, but assigns people from that organization to the UTF organization.

Chang handed the general a copy of the organization chart they had prepared before lunch. He looked at the chart, and said "I see what you've done. It looks like a good team organization. But I have question."

Randy asked, "What is your question, Sir?"

General Huang looked at Chang with a serious expression on his face and asked, "Some of these key people will have two bosses. Just who decides about things like salary increases, reprimands and firings? Which boss?"

Chang answered, "Sir, the answer to that is easy. Both bosses have to sign salary increases or other such personnel action papers. They both have to agree."

Huang asked cautiously, "And what if the bosses can't agree?"

Randy, sensing that Chang doesn't have a good answer to this question interrupted, "Why, in that case, General Huang, the dispute should be assigned to an arbitration council of three managers, appointed by you, Sir. But really, I think such disagreements would be rare."

General Huang arose, grinned broadly and stated, "I think your organization will work. I approve it, effective immediately."

Huang signed the organization chart and then added, "You may issue this chart to all personnel today. Thank you, lady and gentlemen."

Randy and Patricia worked hard the next several months defining the design of the Ultra Tactical Taiwan Fighter. The new UTF team organization turned out to be extremely effective. Randy's overall design was adapted to the needs of Taiwan for a new modern fighter. The UTF team members expanded on the details of Randy's basic design . Patricia evaluated the design by periodically using her combat engagement simulation program.

The new theoretical aircraft performed brilliantly in the simulations.

Finally, in early June 1989, some nine months after Randy and Patricia began work in Taichung, the preliminary design was completed. The UTF team was ready for the formal *preliminary design review.* If the PDR was successfully approved by General Hua, General Huang's boss, then Patricia and Randy would receive another contract payment, this one for two million dollars.

Chapter 19

Preliminary Design Completed

The large auditorium was filled with people attending the formal *preliminary design review,* PDR in aerospace-ese. The front row was reserved for the top brass headed by General Hua, director general of MND, down from Taipei, along with his staff. General Huang, director of AIDC, and Dr. Chris Haah, director of CSIST, were seated to General Hua's left. Dr. Charlie Chang, program director for the UTF, Randy McLyle and Patricia Manos were also seated on the front row. The second row was filled with the second echelon brass including Colonel Jan Wang, director of avionics, Colonel Yung, the UTF test pilot, and the always present Eddie Chung. The seats in the rest of the auditorium were taken up by the engineers and scientists working on the details of the UTF aircraft design.

It was the first Monday of June 1989. Everyone was happy that this important milestone of completing the preliminary design review had been met and on schedule. Randy and Patricia were particularly happy. If General Hua certified at the end of today's meeting that the *PDR milestone* was successfully passed, then Eddie Chung would transfer two million dollars to their Swiss bank account.

Charlie Chang climbed up the stairs to the stage and walked to the microphone equipped podium. The drapes covering the large back-illuminated screen were withdrawn and a slide with an artist's rendering of the *Ultra Tactical Fighter* was displayed on the screen. In the upper right hand corner of the slide was a modernistic logo of *AIDC* and in the upper left corner was the logo of *MND*, giving the authority of the *Ministry of National Defense* to the briefing.

Dr. Chang addressed the audience in English, the technical language of AIDC, for his opening remarks, "General Hua, General Huang, ladies and gentlemen, today we present the results of the new Ultra Tactical Fighter aircraft design. The meeting today marks a major milestone in our UTF program, the PDR! By our formal regulations, the preliminary design will be documented in a written report to be submitted a week from today. Now, our chief scientist, Dr. Randy McLyle, will present the overall design of the UTF, Randy"

Randy replaced Chang on the podium. Aided by a detailed plan-view of the aircraft projected onto the screen. Randy gave his summary description of the fighter. "The UTF is a flying-wing configuration with no bumps or stores, like missiles and fuel tanks hanging below. Everything is internal to the flying wing. The antennas are conformal. In other words they are part of the surface structure of the flying wing. Everything is smooth. This is the way we make aircraft *stealthy*, that is, *invisible* to enemy radar and anti-aircraft detection."

General Hua interrupted with a question, "Dr. McLyle, a flying wing seems to be very narrow. How do you get a pilot and his ejection seat installed?"

Randy smiled, "General, that is one of the design compromises we made. We eliminated the ejection seat. The pilot lies prone on a specially fitted foam couch. This way, the pilot can take twenty g's of acceleration during combat turns, without blacking out."

The general pressed his point, "But, Dr. McLyle, what if the aircraft is hit by enemy fire and the pilot has to eject?"

"General Hua, our studies show that the probability of losing the aircraft is so low that we would lose a pilot once in every 100 years!"

General Hua rose, getting red in the face, and said in a strident voice, "Dr. McLyle, that philosophy is completely unacceptable in a military aircraft. I don't want to lose even one pilot. Remember what happened to the *US Space Shuttle*, Challenger! NASA assumed the space shuttle would never crash and they lost seven crewmen. *No*, I must insist that you include an escape capsule. Something to give the pilot a chance of survival if hit during combat, even if it is very unlikely. Else, I won't approve the PDR!"

Randy, taken aback by General Hua's strong stand, backed down and said, "OK, General Hua, we can make the pilot compartment into an escape capsule. But it will add one hundred pounds of weight to the vehicle. That'll reduce our range by 5%.

General Hua said as he sat back down, "That's an acceptable compromise, Dr. McLyle. Make the change!"

"Yes, the change will be made. Now to continue: the propulsion will be by dual ram jet engines. Since ramjets don't operate below a speed of Mach one, we use a re-usable solid propellant rocket booster for take off to get up to speed Mach one."

General Hua asked another question, "Dr. McLyle, isn't that a rather revolutionary propulsion system for the UTF?"

Randy grinned, "General Hua, that's a very good question. There are three advantages. *First*, we can take off vertically without needing an airfield. These aircraft can be launched from anywhere – a rice paddy, from the top of a building, from the back of a truck- *anywhere.*

Second, we get enormous speed. We cruise at Mach 5 or about one mile per second, 3600 miles per hour for short distances of up to 500 miles. For longer distances, up to 3000 miles, we go *suborbital* at a speed of Mach 20 or 4 miles per second, 14,400 miles per hour!"

General Hua, with a happy expression on his face, replied, "That is amazing! We will have the most revolutionary fighter aircraft ever known with that kind of speed and range. That's more than I could have hoped for!"

Randy continued with his summary of the UTF design, "The cockpit controls and displays are designed to permit the pilot to cope with all the complexity need to fly the aircraft and to fight the battles, both *air-to-air* and *air-to-ground.* To do this we provide all the visual information by a special optical device built into the pilot's helmet that projects images onto the pilot's visor. In addition, our computer employs what the engineers call *artificial intelligence* to make decisions in split seconds during combat."

General Hua interrupted again and asked, "Dr. McLyle, I'm confused. You mean you don't have all the dials and gauges found in a regular cockpit panel? You just shine light on the pilot's visor? How in the world does that work?"

Randy smiled broadly, "I know it's confusing at first. Everyone is used to the cockpit and all the hardware, dials, gauges, video tubes, etc. But the UTF does away with all that hardware.

It's not needed anymore. Not with the helmet optics available now and the computer software that makes it all work correctly. The optics mounted on the helmet project an *image* of what the dials and gauges look like. The optics are such that he sees these objects no matter what direction his eyes are looking. We even project the outside world on this screen before the pilot's eyeballs. The pilot doesn't look out the window. There isn't one. The picture of the outside world is created by the aircraft's sensors: the radar, the infrared sensors, the ultraviolet sensors, etcetera. The *artificial intelligence computer* interprets all this information to tell the pilot what to do.

General Hua sighed, "It sounds very complicated to me. Are you sure it will all work?"

Randy replied, "Yes, General, it is complicated, but we have the optics and the software working *now* in our simulation laboratory. Our test pilot, Colonel Yung Hang-fu, has *flown* it in the simulator."

General Hua turned to Yung, who is seated behind him and asked, "Hang-fu, as one pilot to another, does it all really work?"

Colonel Yung, dressed in his ROC Air Force uniform, rose and answered, "Yes, General Hua, it really does work. At first I was really skeptical. But after Ms. Manos showed me some of the tricks of the simulation, I got used to it. I have over one hundred hours of simulated combat time now. Our system *always* destroys the enemy!"

General Hua relaxed, laughed and said, "Well, Hang-fu, if you can fly it, I guess I could learn to fly it, too. Remember, I was your instructor in flying school."

Yung grinned and stated, "Of course, you could fly it, General Hua. You taught me *almost* everything I know about flying!"

Laughter rose from the audience.

General Hua then turned to Randy and said, "Dr. McLyle, please forgive me for my rude interruptions, but the UTF is such a fantastic machine, it's hard to believe that we can design, much less build, such an aircraft. Tell me about the weapons. How to they work?"

Randy replied, "General Hua, the UTF contains four *smart* guided missiles designed by Dr. Chris Haah and his team at CSIST. Each missile can be programmed by the UTF computer to be either an air-to-air or an air-to-ground weapon. Each missile contains eight sub-missiles that are individually targeted and guided to *kill* a target."

General Hua asked, "You mean we can destroy up to 32 targets with one UTF? One UTF can kill 32 enemy aircraft?"

Randy replied, "Yes, Sir, *or* it could destroy 2 targets on the ground: tanks, ammunition storage bunkers, or even individual soldiers. The accuracy is better than two inches, even for targets over a hundred miles away."

General Hua asked, "But, how does the pilot know what the targets are from a hundred miles away?"

Randy replied, "Easy, General Hua. The missile transmits the images of what it sees with its *electronic eyes* over a radio link to the airplane. The image is projected onto the visor of the helmet described earlier, and the pilot can see everything. He can help our *artificial intelligence computer* pick out the right targets to destroy."

General Hua asked, "And, could it recognize a tank or even the face of an enemy officer?"

"Yes, Sir, it could. The pilot could even hit some enemy officer he didn't like."

There was more laughter from the audience at this macabre comment.

General Hua persisted with his question, "And Dr. McLyle, wouldn't the enemy be able to jam the radio link between the missile and airplane?"

Randy smiled, "Another good question, General Hua, but no. The enemy can't jam our communication links because we use a *pseudo-noise coded spread spectrum radio link*. The enemy can't jam them if he could. The signals look like radio *noise*, not radio signals. Because of the special coding it would take an enormous amount of jamming to jam our signal. More jamming than the enemy has."

General Hua responded, "Dr. McLyle, the UTF looks like a fantastic aircraft, the *Ultra Tactical Fighter!*"

Randy smiled broadly, "Yes, Sir! It is a fantastic aircraft. That completes my design summary. The rest of the day will be spent by various members of our design team going into all the *gory details* of the design."

After all the briefings had been completed at the end of the day, Randy returned to the podium and said, "So you can see, our preliminary design of the Ultra Tactical Fighter, the UTF aircraft, is completed. It's speed and range exceed the original requirements, and the combat capability meets all the needs. And as you heard Colonel Yung say in his briefing, 'It's a fighter pilot's airplane!' So General Hua, that completes our preliminary design review, -- and the *escape capsule* will be included!"

General Hua rose, strode up to the podium, faced the audience and said, "Ladies and gentlemen, fellow officers, congratulations for completing the preliminary design of our Republic of China's new tactical fighter aircraft. This new aircraft is crucial to the defense of our nation. I hereby approve the satisfactory completion of the PDR!"

Then he turned to Randy, who was still standing next to the podium and said, "I would like to see you and Colonel Chung for a few minutes, in your private office – *now!*"

"OK, General Hua. I'll see you there."

Ten minutes later, General Hua and Eddie Chung entered Randy's office in the AIDC headquarters building. Randy and Patricia rose from their side-by-side desks when the visitors arrived.

General Hua faced Patricia and said, "Forgive me Ms. Manos, but I need to meet with Dr. McLyle alone about a very sensitive subject. If you don't mind."

Patricia, upset by this *male chauvinism*, almost said, *But I do mind.* Instead she smiled graciously, and replied, "No, I don't mind at all, General. I have to go to the rest room anyway. I understand you Taiwanese say, 'I'll go sing a song!'"

As Patricia left, General Hua nodded to Eddie Chung, indicating that he should shut the door for privacy. General Hua began the closed door meeting by saying, "Dr. McLyle, I understand from my cousin, Eng-fu, here, that you have reservations about AIDC's capability to build the aircraft you have designed. Is that right?"

Well, yes, Sir. I do have reservations. Frankly, I think you need outside help from some country that has the level of technology needed to build this airplane. The technology is just not here in Taiwan to do it"

"I understand from Eng-fu that Israel probably has the right technology to help. Do you agree?"

Randy answered, "Yes, Sir. I believe they could help because of their experience building the *Lavi* fighter. You are certainly not going to get any such help from the US. Their relationship with Mainland China precludes that possibility."

General Hua looked Randy in the eye and said, "We have problems dealing with Israel on a government-to-government basis. Taiwan has some large multi-billion dollar contracts with Saudi Arabia and other Arab countries. Our economy couldn't withstand losing those contracts."

Eddie Ching interrupted, "Ding-fua, don't worry about the Arabs finding out about our working with the Israelis. We can do it in a clandestine way, using a deep cover to hide the relationships."

General Hua looked at Eddie Chung and said, "Eng-fu, how do we do that?"

Eddie grinned, "Easy, Ding-fua. We cooperate with the Israeli Mossad to work out the details of the deep cover. I've already contacted Dr. Yossi Barlev of Mossad. He's willing to work with us. All we need is for you to approve a trip."

General Hua asked, "A trip to where? And who would go?"

Eddie smiled broadly and replied, "To Israel, Tel Aviv. Randy McLyle and I would go, as two business men meeting with another businessman."

General Hua then asked, "But wouldn't using Taiwan passports raise flags there?"

Eddie answered happily, "No problem, Ding-fua. Randy and I would use Singapore Passports. Here they are!"

Eddie placed two passports on the table. They look very official. One with Eddie's picture and the other one with Randy's. Each carried a fictitious name.

Eddie added, "Israel does a lot of business with Singapore. These passports would survive any Arab surveillance of activities between an Israeli trading company, operated by Mossad, and Chung-Export/Import, Ltd. We have a Singapore subsidiary already set up."

General Hua rose, grinned and said, "Eng-fu, it looks like you've given this matter a lot of thought. I hereby authorize your *top secret* trip with Dr. McLyle to Israel. You are instructed to negotiate a *Memo of Understanding (MOU)* to get Israel's cooperation to build our UTF aircraft. You should leave as soon as possible!"

Chapter 20

Singapore Office

Randy McLyle was awakened from a deep sleep by the pretty China Airlines stewardess. She was offering him and Eddie Chung, who was sitting next to him in their first class seats, luncheon. Randy looked at his watch as the stewardess was placing the luncheon tray on his seat table. It is just after 12:30 Singapore time. They would be landing in just less than two hours. It was the second Tuesday in June, 1989, just a few days after General Hua authorized their trip to Israel to seek help in building the new the new UTF aircraft.

Eddie Chung turned to Randy and said, "You've been out like a light, Randy. My office manger, Su Soong, will meet us at the airport. We'll go to my Singapore office, near Raffles Square, so you can get to know Ms. Soong better. She will be a key link in our work with the Israelis."

As Randy finished tasting the first bite of his sweet and sour chicken, he asked, "Just how do you expect Su to help with the Israelis?"

Eddie answered, "We'll have all our telex communications go through her office as relay point, to improve security and keep our true relations with the Israelis clandestine."

Randy laughed, "That sounds pretty complicated, Eddie. Why don't we just communicate directly with the Israelis?"

Eddie grinned, "Randy, you really are naive! The intelligence communities of the world love to intercept telex messages in order to glean information about what's happening in the world. The Arabs intercept messages from and to the Israelis, the Mainland Chinese intercept messages to and from Taiwan, the KGB and NSA intercept messages from everyone. We just don't want anyone to know what we are doing with the Israelis."

Randy smiled, "Yes, Eddie, I guess I am naive. You mean *Orwell's world of 1984* is already here? We've lost our privacy? I don't see how they can listen to all the communication traffic and find out anything."

Eddie answered, "I guess *1984* is here, at least in international communications. The only way to have privacy in telexes is to use tricks to keep what we're doing clandestine, like we are going to do. As to how they do it, the answer is computers. They feed all these messages through huge supercomputers. The computer software that gleans intelligence from the world's babble uses *key words* to identify messages of interest."

Randy groaned, "Eddie, it sounds too complicated to me. I think I'll just stick to simple things like designing advanced tactical fighters. I understand that. This intelligence business – *bah*, I'll leave that to others."

The China Airlines 747-SP pulled up to the jet way at the Singapore Airport just before 2:30 PM, right on schedule. Randy and Eddie cleared the entry formalities quickly and continued on into the arrival lobby. Waiting near the door they came through was a beautiful Chinese girl, who was quite tall and had a well proportioned figure. She was wearing a white linen *Mao* jacket and slacks. Eddie exclaimed to Randy, "There's Su Soong waiting for us."

When Su saw Eddie, she rushed over and greeted him with a kiss. Then Eddie made the introductions, "Su, this is Randy McLyle. Randy, Su Soong. Su's manager of my office here."

Su shook hands with Randy and said, "Oh, Randy, I'm so pleased to meet you. I should warn you, I'm attracted to round eyes, especially handsome ones like you!"

Randy laughed, "Don't worry Su. I'm attracted to beautiful Chinese girls like you!"

Eddie smiled, "You two have all night to work out your mutual attraction problems. Let's get over to the office now. We want to finish our business discussions before dinner time."

Randy took Su's hand and led her towards the exit as he replied, "OK, let's go Eddie. Su, I hope you can have dinner with us tonight."

Su smiled sweetly, "Of course, Randy. I've reserved all night for you."

She led the pair of men to her car parked in the airport parking lot. It was a white, four-door Mercedes. Twenty minutes later, the trio arrived at the ten story office building a short distance from the famous *Raffles Square*. Su left the car with a street parking attendant who assured the safety for a small fee. They took an elevator to the eighth floor and enter a small office with a metal name plate that read: *Singapore Straits Trading, Ltd.* The office had three desks and a sitting area with a leather couch and chair. The office was equipped with telephones, a telex machine, and an IBM compatible personal computer with a communication modem connection to the telephone and telex (the precursor to Internet).

Randy commented when he saw the computer, "Looks like you're all set to communicate with anyone in the world."

Su smiled, "Yes, the personal computer saves us at least two office workers. I can run the whole office by myself this way. Please be seated on the couch over there. I'll be back soon with tea and cookies for you to enjoy during our discussions."

Su joined the two men in the sitting area a few minutes later, carrying a tray with hot tea in three glasses and a small dish of cookies.

As Eddie sipped his tea, he said, "Su is cleared for top secret, so we can discuss the UTF project with her freely, Randy."

Eddie then explained to Su that he and Randy expected to make an agreement with the Israelis to assist in building the UTF aircraft. Then he said, "Su, all contracts with the Israelis will be signed with the name of Singapore Straits Trading, Ltd. The relationship between the Israelis and ROC must be completely clandestine. All telexes and mail will pass through your office to help keep the relationship hidden. Do you understand?"

Su smiled, "Yes, of course. We'll use code words on the open telex to keep from triggering the enemies' telex interception computer programs. To begin with, we'll call the UTF the *Universal Textile Fabricator.* We'll establish a list of clothing-related words to stand for the various aircraft words Randy expects will be used. That's better than using encryption. The enemies' super computers really go to work, if we send encrypted messages. This way, we can fool their computers."

Eddie grinned, "Good thing, Su. You have the idea. Now you and Randy make a list of code words for the various aircraft words

Randy expects he will use.   Then we'll have a fool-proof way of keeping our business with the Israelis *private* – and *secure*!"

Randy and Su spent the next hour making up the code word list. Su entered the list in the PC computer and printed a copy each for Randy and Eddie. When they are finished, Randy said, Eddie, now that we have the codebook completed, let's check into the Hilton and have dinner."

Eddie grinned and agreed, "OK! Then we'll go dancing. Su has a nice girl friend that helps her in the office part time. She'll join us for dinner and dancing. Chinese men should never be lonesome on trips, right?"

Randy smiled, "right! We Chinese men should never be lonesome. Dancing sounds like a good idea."

Su dropped Randy and Eddie off at the Singapore Hilton and said, "Janet Chin and I will join you for dinner at 7 pm. We'll come up to your rooms. I've already checked you in. Randy, here's your key, room 1012 and Eddie, here's your key, room 1014. They're nice connecting suites with good views overlooking the city."

Randy replied, "See you at 7 pm. We could have dinner and dance here at the hotel, up on the roof. It's really nice."

After putting his bag in his room, Randy took a shower and fell asleep. Just before 7 pm, he was awakened by a warm nude body cuddling up to him. He was startled to find Su Soong next to him. She whispered, "Don't worry. It's just me. I left a message with Eddie that we would meet him and Janet up at the roof top restaurant at 8:30. He won't mind. Janet's in bed with him."

Randy wrapped his arms around Su and they enjoyed their time together. They even had time to doze for a short time.

Then Randy kissed Su awake and whispered, "It's time to shower, dress, and go up for dinner."

Su answered sleepily, "OK Randy. Let's get ready to meet Eddie and Janet now."

When Randy and Su reached the roof top restaurant, Eddie and Janet were already seated at a table near the dance floor enjoying a glass of tea. Eddie introduced Janet to Randy and then waved to the waiter to bring the elaborate tray of hors d'oeuvres he had already ordered. The tray included broiled beef brochettes on a stick with the local unique peanut butter sauce as a dip. After they finished the appetizers, the waiter brought a complete Chinese dinner with seven different dishes plus fried rice with tiny pieces of shrimp in it.

The dance band was playing soft music and Randy and Su danced to the lovely strains in the delicious tropical air on the roof top. They gazed at the glittering lights of the city as they glided about the dance floor. Eddie and Janet were dancing a stylistic routine featuring many low dips and gyrations that Eddie learned in a Taipei dance school. Shortly after midnight, as the quartet was sipping tea – no one ordered alcoholic drinks – Eddie announced to the others, "We better call it a night and go to bed now. We'll have to get up early to catch our 8 am flight. Su and Janet will drive us to the airport."

Randy squeezed Su's hand and replied, "That's a good idea, Eddie. What time should we leave the hotel?"

"We'll leave at 7 am. That should be plenty of time. Shall we have breakfast in our rooms or shall we eat together in the breakfast room downstairs?"

Randy and Su rose to leave as Randy replied, "The service is always so slow in a hotel breakfast room. We can eat together in your room, if we open the connecting doors between our rooms." As Eddie nodded agreement, Randy continued, "Remember to put your breakfast order on the doorknob. Good night."

Randy and Su returned to his room and had another erotic session in bed before falling into slumberland. When Randy awoke in the morning, Su was already up and dressed. She looked like the efficient business-woman she was. Randy thought to himself, *My night in bed with Su was wonderful. That seems to be the way things are done in Taiwan and I guess I need to go along with it. But it doesn't affect the way I feel about Patricia. I still love her and want to marry her.*

Patricia Manos received a call in her hotel room at the Brothers Hotel in Taipei. After driving up from Taichung with Randy to see him off for his trip to Israel, Mei Lin had suggested that Patricia spend the night in Taipei at the Brothers Hotel and have dinner with her. That would avoid another long drive from

Taipei back to Taichung the same day. Patricia had decided to take Mei Lin's suggestion and stay over. She knew it would be lonesome alone in the apartment, particularly the first night Randy was away. She welcomed the company, since she was very fond of Mei Lin anyway. As she answered the hotel phone, she looked at her watch. It was 5 pm.

She answered, "Hello, this is Patricia."

Mei Lin was on the line and said cheerfully, "Patricia, this is Mei Lin. I hope you won't be offended but I'm bring two handsome young men along to have dinner with us. We don't believe a Chinese woman, like you, should be lonesome when her man is on a trip. OK?"

Patricia laughed, "I guess you're right, Mei Lin. We Chinese women shouldn't be lonesome when our men are away. Yes, bring them. I hope they're cute."

Mei Lin laughed in return, "Yes, Patricia, they're both very handsome and young, only twenty five, but very discrete. They never kiss and tell, - anyone!"

Patricia giggled and answered, "That is young! I hope they are discrete. I've never been out with another man since I've been living with Randy. But then I've never been Chinese before either! I guess I'll go along with the customs of my new country."

A half hour later, Patricia answered a knock on her hotel room door. It is Mei Lin with two very handsome young Chinese men, both very well dressed. Patricia invited the three to enter. Mei Lin smiled as she introduced her companions, "Patricia, these are Billie and Tommie. We'll just use first names tonight. More friendly. Right? By the way Tommie is yours. I'm already promised to Billie."

Patricia laughed, kissed both men on the cheeks, and said, "Tommie, you are a beautiful hunk!"

As she pointed to the bed, Tommie took her in his arms, kissed her passionately on the lips, and whispered in her dear, "I'll show you how Chinese men make love. You'll love it."

Patricia pressed her body against Tommie's and whispered her reply, "Oh, you feel good next to me. Yes, I want you to show me this Chinese way – everything!"

Mei Lin interrupted, "Enough of the whispering! Let's leave for dinner now. We're dining at the New China dance hall. We have a private dining room downstairs. Later, we'll go upstairs and dance."

Patricia still holding Tommie next to her said, "I'm ready. I don't feel lonesome now."

The quartet took a taxi from the Brothers Hotel through the heavy afternoon traffic to the New China dance hall. It was just getting dark and the gaudy lights were lit on the front of this popular dance hall. Since Taiwan is close the equator, their days do not grow much longer in the summer. Mei Lin paid the taxi and led the other three through the entrance and continued toward the private dining room she had reserved for their discrete dinner party. They reached the room and were greeted by two waitresses who seated them. Mei Lin turned to the waitresses and said, in Chinese, "Bring the usual full dinner I like. And give special consideration to my *round eyed guest.*"

Shortly afterwards, the first waitress served each diner two glasses, one of red wine and one of white wine. The second waitress brought a tray of food dishes and placed them on the *lazy Susan* in the center of the round table. Tommie took one of the empty plates and served a portion of each dish to Patricia, using chop sticks to serve. Billie did the same for Mei Lin. Then the two young men served themselves. Patricia was by now quite expert with chops sticks. She dipped into the variety of dishes which she enjoyed very much.

When the first dishes of food were only about half finished, the first waitress cleared them away and the second waitress brought another new set of different dishes. Patricia and Mei Lin were again served the new culinary delights by the two young men. Billie and Tommie each drank toasts to Mei Lin, Patricia and to each other in the warm Chinese custom at group dinners.

After finishing the gourmet meal, the quartet walked up the stairs leading to the room where they would dance. The dance hall was dimly lit by candles on the tables and small white lights around the edges of the room. There were flashing lights on the dance podium that flickered in beat with the dance music when the *modern music* group was playing. Soft dance music was played by a second *Benny Goodman* type band. The music never stopped. At the end of each hour, the lights got very dim and the bands started playing a soft tune. One at a time, each band member left quietly and was replaced by a member of the second band, still playing the same tune. It was a very romantic atmosphere, and very discrete.

The hostess seated the quartet near the dance floor and brought a round of hot tea for everyone, since no one wanted alcoholic drinks after the dinner wine. Patricia and Tommie walked to the dance floor followed by Mei Lin and Billie. Tommie held Patricia very close during the slow dance tunes. Tommie was also a good dancer to the fast tunes. He expertly controlled her body and sent her on exhilarating spins and twirls. Patricia felt ten years younger dancing with this young, virile Chinese man

Shortly after midnight, Mei Lin announced, "It's time to go now. I'll pay the bill and we'll leave."

As the quartet exited onto the street garishly lit by the bright lights on the front of the dance hall, Mei Lin hailed a taxi and gave instructions to the driver to take Patricia and Tommie to the Brothers Hotel. As the pair drove off together in the first taxi, Mei Lin hailed a second to take her and Billie to her apartment.

Patricia and Tommie had lots of fun and games in her hotel room that evening and then dropped off into a beautiful, dreamless sleep.

Tommie was gone when Patricia woke up in the morning. She thought to herself, *Did last night really happen, or did I just dream it?*

Then she thought of Randy and of how much she loved him, *I still love Randy. Last night, if it really happened, was just an erotic incident, meaningless except for the temporary feelings of sex. It doesn't threaten my wonderful, warm relationship with Randy at all.*

Chapter 21

Dinner in Tel Aviv

Randy McLyle was excited to be coming to the Holy Land. He had never been to Israel before. His maternal grandfather had visited Israel as a boy and had told him about the wonderful sights in Old Jerusalem and the other holy sites like Nazareth, the Sea of Galilee, and Abraham's Tomb in Hebron. Randy hoped he could see some these holy places while he and Eddie Chung are in Israel, but he realized they would be busy. He looked out the window of the Japan Airlines 747 that brought them from Singapore to Tel Aviv. He admired the blue Mediterranean Sea sparkling in the mid afternoon sun of this warm June day. When the aircraft begin its descent for landing at the Ben Gurion Airport, he studied the beaches stretching north and south of Tel Aviv and the high rise apartments of Herzylia to the north and of Tel Avis proper in front of the airplane. He noted that Tel Aviv suffered from the same smog problem that his former home in the Los Angeles Basin had. The grayish-yellow pall hung over the center of the city.

As they approached the airport his view changed to the fertile green fields of Israel. The Israelis had truly transformed the dessert into a garden by irrigation and fertilizers. To the east beyond Tel Aviv he contemplated the rocky hills leading into the old, most holy city of Jerusalem. The big 747 flew a wide down wind leg towards the east, turned north on its base leg and then banked steeply to turn onto its final approach, landing to the west into the brisk afternoon wind blowing in off the Mediterranean

After they touched down the Japan Airlines plane taxied up to a concrete ramp and stopped its engines. The stewardesses warned the passengers to stay seated. There would be a security check. A few minutes later the front door was opened and Randy watched four burly Israeli security men entering the aircraft carrying Uzi machine guns.

Randy turned to Eddie and asked, "What in the world is this all about?"

Eddie grinned and replied, "The Israelis are very security conscious. They had stopped these security measures on arriving airliners for awhile, but after last years' attack by a group of Japanese Red Guards, they reinstated the post landing security checks. They are particularly nervous about airplanes from the far east since they've had two attacks now from that sector. Just relax."

Randy whispered, "Well, I don't like the idea of guards entering a civilian aircraft carrying loaded machine guns."

Eddie laughed and replied, "It's a lot better than terrorists carrying loaded machine guns! They would shoot you. These guards won't.

Randy whispered back, "That's a relief. I wasn't sure when I saw the suspicious look they gave me when they passed by our seat and asked to see our false passports."

Eddie smiled, "They're searching for people who fit a certain list of characteristics. Maybe a *round eyes* and a *Chinese man* traveling together fits one of their suspicious profiles!"

A few minutes later, the stewardess announced, "You may de-plane now. Welcome to Tel Aviv."

Randy and Eddie retrieved their hand baggage and scrambled down the stairs to the tarmac below. There they were greeted by one of the guards carrying an Uzi, who asked, in good English "Are you Mr. Chung and Dr. McLyle?"

Randy, realizing their passports didn't show those names, whispered to Eddie, "What shall we say?"

Eddie ignored Randy's question and replied to the guard, "Yes, Sir, we are. We are here to meet Yossi Barlev."

The guard replied, "Then follow me, please."

The pair walked behind the guard who held his finger on the Uzi trigger the whole time, which made Randy a little nervous. They reached a black Chevrolet Impala parked behind the security truck the guards had used. The car had one-way windows which were darkened so no one could see who's inside. The guard opened the back door and barked, "Get in, please."

The two men crawled into the back seat. Seated by the window was a youngish looking man in his early thirties, about Randy's age. He smiled and said, "Welcome to Israel, Mr. Chung and Dr. McLyle. I'm Yossi Barlev. My boss decided it would be better if we handled you two as secret VIP visitors. Less likely the Arabs or the Red Chinese would learn of your visit. This project is too sensitive for us to risk anyone finding out that you came to Israel. We are going to drive you straight to our secret VIP quarters. Having you stay in a public hotel is just too dangerous. You will forego all the entry and exit formalities. That way no one but friends will ever know you were here."

Randy smiled, "Gee, Yossi, I've never been involved in this *cloak and dagger* stuff before. I'm just a simple airplane designer."

Yossi laughed, "Randy, don't be so modest. We Israelis know you're one of the best designers of advanced aircraft in the world. You're probably more famous than you realize. We know all about your advanced tactical fighter design for Cosmos. We thought the Pentagon was stupid for not picking your design. We know it was the best. We evaluated all of them."

Randy, surprised by all this knowledge, exclaimed, "How in the world did you know? Even though my design was not classified, I understood the Pentagon kept wraps on all the ATF designs."

Yossi smiled, "Let's just say *we have our ways*. A small country like ours has to keep up with what's happening in the world. We have to know what our enemies and our friends are doing as well. It's important for our survival!"

As this conversation had been going on, the driver, who wore an Army master sergeant's uniform, drove across the tarmac towards a heavily guarded exit from the airport. The guards, armed with Uzi's had the driver roll down the car window. One looked inside, smiled when he recognized Yossi, and waived the car through the gate. The driver took highway 12 towards Haifa, but soon turned off and headed towards the Tel Aviv suburb of Ramat Gan. The driver turned onto a wide driveway leading to a large building on a knoll. It appeared to be a very large estate. There was an armed guard partway up the driveway, hidden from the street that passed outside. The guard looked in the back seat, visually identified Yossi and then waived them through to the inner grounds. The main building of the estate was about three hundred meters from the main gate. The road leading to the estate had several sharp turns and was lined on either side with thick evergreen hedges.   When the building loomed into sight after making the last curve, the passengers discerned a wide circular driveway leading up to the front door.

Yossi announced, "This your *hotel* during your stay in Israel. Many famous people have used this *VIP hotel*. And as far as you are concerned, the bill is all paid by the State of Israel."

Randy, curious about the VIP treatment for him and Eddie, asked, "Yossi, what famous people do you mean?   Like movie stars?"

Yossi laughed, ""Oh, no, not movie stars, but *heads of state*, particularly Arab leaders who visit Israel clandestinely. I can only mention those Arab leaders whose visits to Israel later became public knowledge, like President Anwar Saddat of Egypt. He stayed here before his historic visit to our Knesset in Jerusalem. King Hassan of Morocco once stayed here before he met with our former Prime Minister, Shimon Peres."

As Yossi led the pair up the broad marble steps of the mansion, Randy persisted with his questions and asked, "But why are we being given such ostentatious treatment? We're not heads of state. There must be other private places where you could hide us."

Yossi looked Randy in the eyes and said, "Our Prime Minister, Mr. Rafi Eitan, the former General, received a call from your President, Mr. Chiang Ching-kuo. He said you and Mr. Chung are his personal representatives. So, as far as we are concerned, you and Mr. Chung will be treated like you are the representatives of the President of the Republic of China. You have *head-of-state status* in our country!"

Randy smiled and exclaimed, "Wow! I'm really impressed. Aren't you Eddie?"

Eddie smiled faintly and replied, "I'm sure Yossi and his Prime Minister realize how important our program – the Ultra Tactical Fighter – is to both our countries. We are talking about a program that can significantly improve the survival of two small countries beset by enemies with populations many times larger than our own."

They entered the large reception room which was decorated in the style of the old English mansion it once was, with a pink marble floor, large crystal chandeliers, rich oriental carpets, and several masterpiece paintings adorning the walls. There was one beautiful young lady attending a desk. She was dressed in a stylish black dress with a glittering diamond and emerald necklace on her ample bust.

Yossi led Randy and Eddie to this young lady and said, "Dr. McLyle and Mr. Chung, please meet Yana. She is your host in our VIP hotel. She acts as the manager, concierge, communications specialist, and so forth. All telephone calls in and out of the facility go through Yana, to ensure privacy and security."

Yana grinned happily and said, "Oh, Yossi, you make my job sound so glamorous. I'm really pleased to meet both of you. Welcome to our VIP hotel. If there's anything you need, any time of day or night, just dial 12 on your room phone. I'll answer. Yossi already has the keys to your adjoining suites on the top floor. We have a buffet breakfast every morning from 7 am to 9 am, with lots of fresh fruits and orange juice. Enjoy your stay."

Randy and Eddie chorused, "Pleased to meet you, Yana!"

Yossi led the two men, who were carrying their small carry-on bags and briefcases to the elevator. They exited on the third floor and walked to the end of the hall to two huge suites, each with a formal living room, two bedrooms, and two baths. There was a well stocked liquor cabinet behind the bar. A refrigerator next to the bar had a good supply of soft drinks and snacks. The windows overlooked a large, formal garden with lawn, a variety of flowers and semi tropical plants, and a big fountain which splashed into a pond with white swans swimming in it.

As Randy put away his personal effects, he said to Yossi, "This suite and the view of the grounds are both gorgeous."

Yossi replied, "I'm glad you like it, Randy. Getting back to business matters, I know you're tired after your long flight from Singapore. That's a four and a half hour time change. It's 5:30 pm now. My associate, Ms Dvora Amit, and I will return at 9 pm to have a private dinner with you in a small dining room downstairs, just the four of us. We'll go over the agenda for your visit here the rest of the week, if that's OK with you."

Randy replied, "Great, Yossi. See you then. I'll tell Eddie of the plans. Goodbye."

Yossi smiled, "Shalom, Randy. See you at 9."

Randy was awakened from a sound sleep by the jangle of the telephone next to his bed. He groped in the dark for the phone and answered sleepily, "Yes, this is Randy McLyle."

A sweet, female voice came on the line, "Good evening, Dr. McLyle, this is Dvora Amit, Yossi's associate. Yossi and Mr. Chung are already down here in the dining room. Eddie thought you might have overslept your nap."

Randy answered apologetically, "Yes, Dvora I guess I did, but it'll only take me a minute to get ready for dinner."

Dvora continued, "If you would like, I'll come up and get you in about five minutes and escort you down."

A few minutes later Randy answered the door. It's Dvora. She was a stunning beauty with reddish brown hair and deep green eyes. She was dressed in a low cut white blouse and tight black pants that showed every curve of her trim body. She announced simply, "I'm Dvora. You must be Randy."

"Right, Dvora, come in. I'm almost ready."

Dvora smiled shyly and responded, "Take your time, Randy. We have all evening if you wish."

Randy picked up on Dvora's last comment and responded, "Dvora, you're a beautiful young lady. I'm sure we can find things to talk about and do all evening – all night – if you're willing."

Dvora laughed and said forthrightly, "Randy, I'm going to be your constant companion during your visit to Israel. Considering the magnitude of the program we are going to discuss, it's very important to the security and economy of my country. I would love to spend the evening – and perhaps all night – with you. That way I can protect one of our country's valuable assets – you!"

Dvora showed Randy the way to the small private dining room on the ground floor. The room was richly furnished with a beautiful Persian carpet in delicate shades of turquoise displaying repeated patterns of Ibexes, the mountain goats of Iran. The walls were paneled in a light walnut, and hung with paintings from the fifteenth century. The four place table was set with white linen, sterling silverware, and a large silver candelabra. A magnum of Israeli champagne from the Carmel winery was cooling in a silver champagne chiller filled with ice and sitting on a stand beside the table. Yossi was sitting with his back to the door with Eddie to his right. The two men rose as Dvora and Randy entered the room.

Yossi smiled and said lightly, "Dvora, I see you found Randy. Eddie was just outlining the requirements for Randy's new Ultra Tactical Fighter aircraft. Randy, he suggested that you give me a few more details of the design. But first, please be seated and let's begin to enjoy dinner."

Randy was seated to Yossi's left and Dvora was seated opposite Yossi. Just as they all got seated, Yana entered the room dressed in a beautiful long, tight fitting, white evening gown, adorned with a large beaded flower design. Her diamond necklace resting on her ample bosom, gleamed in the reflected glow of the candles. Yana took the champagne bottle and expertly poured each guest a glass of the bubbly liquid .

Then she said, "Yossi has selected a special menu for everyone this evening. To start, we have a nice Mediterranean shrimp cocktail served with a piquant sauce. For your salad course, we have a salad with tomatoes and avocado slices served on a bed of fresh spinach with mustard-honey dressing. For your main course, we offer large shrimp from the Gulf of Aqaba cooked in a delicate lemon and vermouth sauce with a touch of yogurt to give it body. Finally for dessert, we have fresh Israeli strawberries served with thick sweetened yogurt. Does that menu meet with your desires?"

Randy exclaimed, "Yana, that sounds like a fantastic dinner. I'll love it – everything!"

Eddie looked at Yana's large breasts just above his head, and said with a grin, "Yana, that includes everything I want tonight except for one thing."

Yana blushed at Eddie's veiled hint and replied demurely, "Mr. Chang, I'm sure we can fulfill your every desire. As I said earlier, call me on extension 12 and tell me your desires – later."

With that comment Yana swept out of the dining room to bring their first course.

After she left, Yossi said, "Yana is cleared for the highest of state secrets, so you don't have to be careful what you say in front of her. For your information, your program - the Ultra Tactical Fighter - and our cooperation with you is *special compartmentalized secret or SCS*. Now Randy, give me a brief summary of your fighter design, and then try to tell me where you need help from Israel. Especially, where do you see holes in your current technology.

Randy smiled, "Yossi, I'm not sure how technical to be…"

Yossi laughed, "Get as technical as you wish. I have a PhD from Caltech in aeronautics. Your former associate, Professor Marsh, was chairman of my doctoral committee. I'm presently assigned as deputy program manager for the Lavi aircraft."

"Wow! You really are well qualified. I will give you a brief verbal overview tonight. I brought some colored view graphs. They're stored on this computer tape." Randy pulled the magnetic tape cartridge out of his shirt pocket and added, "If you have an IBM compatible personal computer, I can use it to print out these view graphs for you tomorrow."

At that instant Yana entered carrying a tray with the shrimp cocktail appetizers. Yossi smiled and said, "I thought you might need an IBM PC. Why wait until tomorrow?" He then turned to Yana and said, "Yana, please bring the IBM PC computer with the color monitor. Dr. McLyle needs it for our dinner conversation."

Everyone laughed at Yossi's comments, but Yana said simply, as she served the shrimp cocktails, "No problem, Yossi. It's just next door on a wheeled cart. I'll roll it right in before serving your salads."

Randy grinned, "What service, Yana. That computer will make it much easier for me to brief you."

Eddie quickly jumped up, saying, "Let me help you with the cart, Yana." And he followed her out of the room. As soon as they were out of earshot of the diners, Eddie told Yana what he desired later tonight. As hoped, she agreed. They wheeled the cart back into the dining room.

Eddie turned to Randy, "Randy, does that tape have your UTF design details stored on it.?"

Randy, a little surprised at the question answered, "Why, yes, Eddie, it does. Why do you ask?"

Eddie grinned, "If we are able to reach an agreement with Yossi, we'll leave a copy of your tape so the Israeli's have the design to work from."

Yossi seemed perplexed by Eddie's comment, "Surely you don't believe we can reach an agreement this week, while you're here, do you?"

Eddie looked Yossi in the eye and replied in a serious tone, "Certainly we expect to negotiate an agreement while we are here. Randy and I expect to take back a *Memo of Understanding, MOU* when we return to Taipei. General Hua said we shouldn't come home without a signed *MOU.* I'm authorized to sign and commit a contract value for the Republic of China."

Yossi smiled and added smoothly, "Good. I'm authorized to sign an agreement for Israel, but for the large amount of the contract we expect – one billion dollars – our Prime Minister and his budget director will need to see the *MOU* before I sign it."

Eddie with a negotiator's frown on his face, said. "Yossi, I don't remember saying anything about a billion dollar contract."

Yossi replied firmly, "Now, Eddie, let's not play games! We know you offered Cosmos Aircraft a billion dollar contract to build the UTF for you. We wouldn't expect any less!"

Eddie looked shocked, "Yossi, how did you know about our offer to Cosmos? It sounds like one of the executives at Cosmos betrayed our confidentiality."

Yossi smiled and stated calmly, "Eddie, you know we have our way of getting vital intelligence information, just like ROC's CIA gets information. No executive at Cosmos betrayed your confidentiality. But let's use the billion dollar figure as a target, OK?"

Eddie smiled, "OK! We'll use that as a target amount. But that doesn't mean I agree to it!"

Yossi nodded and responded, "There's a saying that the Chinese are the Jews of the Orient! Yes, I think we understand one another. Now let's see Randy's colored briefing on the IBM PC."

Randy loaded his tape into the computer's disk memory, pressed a few keys, and called up the first slide onto the computer screen.

Randy said, "Yossi, so we don't interfere with the enjoyment of the fantastic meal Yana is serving us, I've programmed the computer to present the slides and explanations for each slide using the voice synthesizer. I've made the voice sound like that of a beautiful young lady."

As the title slide, saying *Ultra Tactical Fighter* came up on the PC monitor screen, Yossi raised his champagne glass and said,

"Here's to Randy's automated briefing and to the billion dollar *MOU* we hope to sign before you leave!"

Eddie, grinned, "Yes, here's to our half billion dollar *MOU!*"

Yossi laughed, "Eddie, let's negotiate the price later. Shalom!"

Everyone chorused, "Shalom!"

As the computer presented Randy's briefing, the quartet enjoyed the *Symphony of Shrimp* dinner served by Yana. The briefing finished just as the group finished their strawberry dessert. Randy turned to Yossi and asked, "Now, that you see my design, do you think you Israelis can built it?"

Yossi thought for a moment and then replied, "Randy, before I answer your question, I'd like you to tell me just where you think the deficiencies are. In other words, what do you think Taiwan needs help with?"

Randy responded, "Yossi, other than needing help to build the aircraft, I think there are three technical areas in which we are deficient in Taiwan. Maybe you have the needed technologies. *(1) the electronics will never fit in the space available. (2) the, multiple independently targeted warheads in the missiles will never work unless we have the right software algorithms. And (3) we need help on the ultra light, super strong, structures of the aircraft.*"

Yossi smiled, "Randy, I think we have just what you need. We call our technologies *METS, MITS,* and *ULS.* We'll tell you about these three technologies at our meeting tomorrow morning at 9 am. I'm sure there are things you and Eddie would rather do now than talk about airplanes!"

Randy looked at Dvora and Eddie grinned at Yana.

Randy smiled, "Right, Yossi, We'll see you in the morning. We'll be ready to leave by 8 am. OK?"

"OK, Shalom!"

Chapter 22

Tel Aviv Agreement

Randy returned to his room with Dvora just after midnight. As he closed the door, he caught a glimpse of Yana entering the adjoining suite with Eddie Chung.

Randy said to Dvora, "Would you like something to drink before bed?"

Dvora smiled and replied graciously, "Yes, thank you, Randy. It is so warm here in June that I get thirsty. I'll take a tall glass of Orangiata with ice, please."

Randy went to the refrigerator by the bar and poured an Orangiata for Dvora and a Coke for himself. He said, "Dvora, we spent so much time talking about the new UTF airplane design, I didn't find out much about you, except that you're beautiful and charming. Tell me about yourself, what you do, where you live, things like that."

Dvora blushed as she responded, "Thank you for the compliment, Randy. Well, let's see. I'm manager of a trading company located in the suburb called Herzylia, just north of here. It's called Herzylia-Export/Import Limited. My office is in one of the high rise buildings on the beach in Herzylia. I live in an apartment adjacent to my office, so I don't have to commute in the awful traffic around Tel Aviv."

Randy asked, "And what role will you play in the UTF program?"

"Any contract that results from the agreement Eddie Chung will negotiate with Yossi Barlev will go through my company, Herzylia-Export/Import Limited. This business arrangement will hide the project from the enemies of Israel and Taiwan."

Randy switched on the radio, tuned in soft dance music and said, "Enough of this business talk. Let's dance."

Dvora replied, "That would be nice."

Randy pressed close to Dvora's soft body and moved to the sweet strains of the music. After a half hour of dancing, the two slowly undressed, took showers and climbed into the big double bed in one of the bedrooms overlooking the garden. The soft moonlight fell into the room from the almost full moon overhead. Randy and Dvora enjoyed the pleasures of each other's bodies before passing into Dreamland.

The next morning Randy and Dvora joined Eddie Chang in the breakfast room. They were the only guests, and Eddie invited Yana to join the other three for breakfast. She consented. Randy noted that she wore a relaxed, happy look on her face. He assumed it was the result of the night she spent with Eddie in his suite.

Just as the quartet was finishing breakfast, Yossi Barlev arrived and called out, "Shalom! I hope you all had pleasant dreams last night. The driver is waiting outside to take us to our meeting at Israeli Aircraft Industries. "

Yossi led Randy, Eddie and Dvora to the waiting car and added, "Our meeting this morning will be with Colonel David Lahat, who is program manager of the Lavi fighter program at IAI."

In the car, Eddie asked, "Yossi, will Colonel Lahat brief us on the three technologies you mentioned last night?"

Yossi replied, "You mean *METS, MITS* and *ULS?* Yes, he and his staff will give you a thorough briefing today. The more I think about Randy's computer briefing last night, the more I'm sure our technologies are the key to the success of the UTF aircraft."

By now the car was approaching the guarded gate at the exit from the *VIP villa.* Randy laughed and said, "Yossi, I certainly hope so. I'll be glad to learn what your acronyms mean."

Yossi grinned, "Don't worry, Randy. After Colonel Lahat and his staff brief you, you'll be an expert on these technologies."

Dvora added, "Yes, Randy. You will be impressed. A lot of people believe the US leads the world in technology. But we Israelis believe that in these three areas we are the leaders!"

Twenty minutes later the car carrying Yossi, Dvora, Eddie and Randy arrived at the IAI (Israeli Aircraft Industries) guard gate. The guard looked into the car, recognized Yossi and waived the group on through the entrance. Soon they pulled up to the IAI headquarters building in the large complex adjacent to the Ben

Gurion airport. The quartet exited the car and Yossi led the others into the IAI chairman's reception area. They were met by the chairman and Colonel Lahat. After the introductions everyone was seated in a modernistically furnished room with comfortable leather chairs and couches. A beautiful young lady brought Turkish coffee and a tray loaded with chocolate confections for the group.

The chairman opened the discussions by saying, "Welcome to Israel and to IAI, Dr. McLyle and Mr. Chung. Our program manager, Colonel Lahat, and his staff will give you a most interesting briefing this morning on some of our new technologies. Let me assure you your project, the Ultra Tactical Fighter, will be handled with the utmost secrecy and discretion by IAI."

Then the chairman turned to Dvora and said, "This young lady, Dvora Amit, will handle all contractual matters that may arise from any agreement negotiated here, though her company, Herzylia-Export/Import, Ltd.   This arrangement will insure the secrecy and privacy of this project. Believe me, our government considers the UTF to be extremely important to the future of Israel, as I know it is important to your government. Our Prime Minister authorized me to delegate the responsibility for the Israeli side of the negotiations leading to an agreement to Dr. Yossi Barlev. And Mr. Chung, we have been advised by your government that you are the delegated negotiator for the Republic of China, Taiwan."

Eddie replied, "Thank you very much for your courtesies to me and to Dr. McLyle. We look forward to a smooth cooperation between Israel and ROC on the UTF aircraft."

The chairman rose and said, "Now, if you'll forgive me I have to leave for Jerusalem now. I'm supposed to explain our over-runs on the Lavi fighter to the Knesset this afternoon, a job I don't relish. Good luck on your negotiations."

The group rose as the chairman left. Then Colonel David Lahat turned and addressed the group. "Please be seated. Now that the reception is over, we'll get down to business. We have prepared briefings covering the three Israeli technologies that would apply to your new fighter aircraft, the UTF."

Randy interrupted, "David, before you give the briefings could you explain briefly the meanings of these strange acronyms – *METS, MITS,* and *ULS?* "

Lahat laughed, "Yes, of course. We all get wrapped up in our acronyms, don't we? First *METS* stands for **M**olecular **E**lectronics **T**echnology **S**uper-microminiaturization. This is a new circuit technology developed at our Weitzman Institute of Technology in Rehovat. In all other countries of the world now, computer circuits are placed on the flat surface of a chip. Here at IAI our circuitry is integrated at the molecular level into a three dimensional block of material. So instead of having flat circuit chips, we have circuit blocks. A *METS* block contains a million times more circuit elements than in the densest circuit chip."

Randy exclaimed, "You mean, with METS you can get up to a million more circuit functions than with chips?"

David replied, "Exactly! In other words, if a computer memory chip contained a million bits before, we can have a block with a thousand billion bits. Put another way, if your super computer took up the space of a cubic meter before, it will be shrunk to a cubic centimeter with METS, and be thousands of times faster besides!"

Randy replied happily, "Your METS technology should solve our computer problems for the aircraft and the missiles. But is this METS just an idea, or can you really build them?"

David smiled and pulled out a small, dark block, about half the size of gaming dice. The die had a small tube, about the thickness of a piece of spaghetti attached to one face. He replied, "See this METS block? It performs all the functions of an old IBM 370 computer, except it's a million times faster, much cheaper, and, as you can see, a tiny fraction of its size. That tube coming out of the side is a light pipe which allows the computer inside the block to send its results to a video screen, other computers, etcetera, all at the speed of light. It really works. We'll give you a demonstration later."

Randy said, "Now I understand METS. What is MITS?"

Lahat smiled and answered, "I understand from Yossi that your aircraft missiles use independently targeted submissiles to increase the number of targets each missile can destroy, right?"

Randy nodded and replied, "Right. Each missile has eight submissiles, each of which must destroy a different target, if our UTF is to be effective as a fighter. I see that your METS technology makes it possible for us to get the computer electronics we need into each submissile, since the blocks are so small but still so powerful. But we have a second problem. These submissiles have to be able to do so many things that we don't know how to write the software to control the submissiles. It's a very complex problem."

Lahat continued, "Our MITS solves your software problems. MITS stands for Multiple Independently Targeted Submunitions. We have developed fool-proof algorithms and the software to implement them."

Randy asked, "And are you sure it works?"

Lahat answered grimly, "Unfortunately, we Israelis have been in a continuous state of war with our Arab neighbors for many years. We get to test our weapons in real warfare. Here are some pictures of our attack against the Syrians in the Bekaa Valley of Lebanon that we occupied last year, late 1988. One shows one of our aircraft launching just two missiles, one air-to-air and one air-to-ground. One photo shows how one missile destroyed eight of the Syrian's new MiG-29's. Another photo shows how the other missile destroyed four tanks and four anti-aircraft missile sites. Not a single civilian was injured even though the tanks and missile sites were interspersed among the civilian population."

Randy looked carefully at the photos, handed them to Eddie to examine, and said, "These photos are really convincing. Looks like MITS technology is great. Just what we need for our UTF missiles!"

Lahat added, "Finally, the third technology is **Ultra Light Structures** technology, using materials like carbon fiber and Kevlar fiber materials. The new materials give high strength and light weight. They are also less visible to radar, which helps to *hide* any aircraft made out of these materials from enemy radar."

Randy asked, "And, have you actually used ULS technology yet?"

Lahat replied, "Yes, we build about 50% of the Lavi using ULS materials. It has proven very successful in reducing weight and increasing structural strength."

Randy replied, "David, I'm so impressed with your three technologies that I think we can skip the briefings you planned."

He turned to Eddie and Yossi Barlev with a smile, "You two can start your negotiations right now. Eddie, IAI has convinced me they have *exactly* the technologies we need to make our UTF aircraft a complete success."

At the end of the day, after tough negotiations between Yossi and Eddie, a *Memorandum of Understanding* was ready to be signed. While the men were negotiating, Dvora had typed the five page document using a word processor in the conference room. She made the necessary changes and additions in real time. Yossi transmitted a copy to Jerusalem to the Prime Minister's office for review. Thirty minutes later Yossi received the word that he could sign the MOU!

Before signing, Eddie Chung stood before the small group – Yossi, Randy, Dvora, and David – and announced, "We accomplished our objective. Yossi, I appreciate your agreeing to nine hundred million dollars rather than the billion dollars you originally insisted upon. I think the agreement is fair. We grant you co-production rights of Randy's design in return for your METS, MITS, and ULS technologies. My company in Singapore will send Dvora's company a contract for one hundred million dollars immediately so you can get started. Per the MOU your contract negotiators will meet with ours soon to complete the final contract for the nine hundred million. Shalom!"

Yossi rose and added, "Eddie, you were a tough negotiator. I hated to leave that one hundred million on the table, but that's the aerospace business. This MOU should increase the defense capabilities and security of both our small countries. Shalom!"

Friday night, Mei Lin and Patricia met Eddie and Randy at Chiang Kai-shek airport in Taipei. The quartet had a small dinner party celebration at the Grand Hotel where Randy and Patricia would spend the night before driving back to Taichung. They all drank to the success of the cooperation between Israel and Taiwan in building the new UTF airplane.

Randy and Patricia had each found the hours long and lonely while they were apart. The longer their lives had been intertwined, the more they found themselves relying upon the companionship and friendship of the other. That night they renewed their pledge of love in the privacy of their hotel room.

Chapter 23

Green Light in Taipei

Patricia woke Randy up by rubbing his ears. Randy asked sleepily, "What time is it anyway?"

Patricia laughed, "Sleepyhead! It's 9:30 already. Time to get up. Eddie left a message with the hotel operator. It said, *We have a meeting with General Hua this morning at 11 am. Will pick you up at 10:30. Eddie.* So you can't sleep any longer."

Randy groaned, "Well my body thinks it's four in the morning. That's the time in Israel. This flitting around the world in jets sure wrecks the body's clock, doesn't it?"

Patricia smiled sympathetically, "Oh, my poor baby, suffering from jet lag. The best cure is to get up right now, go down to the hotel breakfast room and have ham and eggs. Then you'll be ready for your meeting with General Hua."

Randy climbed out of bed, staggered into the bathroom, and took a shower. As soon as he was dressed and wide awake, Patricia asked, "Guess what? I got some good news this week."

Randy replied as they started out the hotel door for the breakfast room, "Yeah, what's the good news?"

"Heinz, our Swiss banker, sent a telex confirming our two million dollar progress payment arrived this week in our account. I sent him a telex asking him to put it in Eurodollar bonds paying at least 10%. I got the confirmation back by telex already. Our funds are now earning an average of 10.5%."

Randy asked as they entered the elevator to go downstairs, "So how much do we earn per month? Enough to live on?"

Patricia laughed and replied, "Considering our total monthly living expenses are just about a thousand dollars per month, yes, our funds earn enough to live on. I figure over $26,000 per month. That's more than 300 thousand dollars per year.!"

Randy grinned, "I guess that's enough, all right! Looks like money's one thing we don't have to worry about."

Randy and Patricia were the only ones in the Grand Hotel elevator. She grabbed Randy and gave him a big hug, "Right, Darling. All we need now is each other and our love."

As the elevator door opened on the breakfast room floor, Randy grinned, gave Patricia a quick peck on the cheek and replied, "Right, Baby! Our love is the important thing now – and enjoying life together!"

Randy and Patricia had a quick breakfast in the dining room. Just as they were finishing, Eddie called a *good morning* to them, and then joined them at their table. He had a cup of coffee while they were waiting for their bill.

Eddie explained the reason for the upcoming meeting. "General Hua wants to go over the Israeli agreement with us. He has to meet with President Chiang Monday afternoon. That's why he wanted to meet with us this Saturday morning."

Randy responded, "General Hua should be happy with the MOU with the Israelis. It makes the UTF program feasible, now, in my opinion."

Eddie responded, "Yes, I agree, Randy, but President Chiang is unpredictable sometimes. His behavior is affected by his unchallenged power for so many years. As you know, we don't have opposition political parties here in Taiwan."

Patricia said, "Yes, I was really surprised reading the newspaper here. The government is always putting someone from one of the unauthorized political parties in prison here. That never happens in the US!"

Eddie frowned and corrected her, "What do you mean *never*! I recall during Watergate that Haldeman, Erlichman, Mitchell, and Dean were all put in prison."

Randy protested, "But Eddie, that was for criminal activities – spying on their political opponents and then lying about it."

Eddie snorted, "If every politician in the world were put in prison for spying on their political opponents and lying, there wouldn't be many politicians walking around."

Patricia looked at her watch and replied, "Eddie, you may be right. But you better leave for your meeting with General Hua right now. It's almost 10:30."

Eddie rose and said, "You're right, Patricia, Randy and I had better go. Mei Lin said she would come over and have lunch with you today. Randy and I should be back by 2:30. We'll have lunch with General Hua."

Randy kissed Patricia good bye and hurried off after Eddie.

The two arrived at General Hua's office just shortly before 11. His secretary led them into the general's office for their morning meeting and took their orders for refreshments. Both ordered Chinese tea. General Hua greeted the two men warmly and directed them to be seated on the leather couch in one corner of his office. He sat across from them in a matching plush leather chair. As soon as they were seated, the secretary served the men their hot tea in glasses along with a tray of assorted cookies. Hua opened the meeting by saying, "Eng-fu, I understand your trip to Tel Aviv was fruitful and that you have brought back a signed Memorandum of Understanding."

Eddie handed General Hua a copy of the MOU and replied, "Yes, Ding-fua, our trip was very successful. Randy and I were both impressed with the technology they offered us. We are convinced they can build the prototype aircraft. And then they can help us build the production aircraft here in Taiwan."

General Hua answered, "Yes, but what technology did they offer? Will it really help?"

Randy responded, General Hua, they offered us three key technologies: METS or **M**olecular **E**lectronics **T**echnology **S**uper-microminiaturization, MITS or **M**ultiple **I**ndependently **T**argeted **S**ubmunitions technology, and ULS or **U**ltra **L**ight **S**tructures technology. They also showed us enough evidence that we are sure these technologies are real! As Yossi Barlev said *With these three technologies, we'll have the best fighter aircraft in the world!"*

General Hua grinned broadly and replied enthusiastically, "Great! That's exactly the kind of results I hoped for from your trip. Let me read the MOU for moment, please."

General Hua perused the MOU and responded, "Eng-fu, everything looks good except the price. I really expected you to get the Israelis to accept the agreement for 800 million dollars, not 900 million."

Eddie protested, "But, Ding-fua, you gave me a negotiating range of 700 million to 999 million. I had a hard time beating the

Israelis down from a billion to 900 million. Somehow they had learned we had offered Cosmos aircraft the higher price. Besides, these three technologies are a bonus we didn't expect to get. They alone are worth 400 million."

Hua nodded and replied, "When you put it that way, I guess you're right. I hope our Uncle Ching-kuo sees it that way, too. You had better come with me to my Monday afternoon meeting. Two nephews can placate an irascible uncle more easily that just one!"

Eddie smiled, "Ding-fua, I'll be pleased to accompany you to the meeting with Uncle Ching-kuo."

General Hua rose and announced, "Congratulations for bringing back the MOU, Eng-fu, even if you did leave a hundred million on the table. Let's go to lunch and celebrate the Israeli agreement."

Eddie and Randy both rose, as Eddie said, "Now, Cousin Ding-fua, don't rub it in. The Israelis thought they were leaving a hundred million on the table. That means it was a successful negotiation, right in the middle of what we wanted and the Israelis wanted. Nine hundred million is a good price!"

General Hua and Eddie Chung arrived at President Chiang's outer office a few minutes before 2 pm Monday afternoon. The President's secretary greeted the two men, "Good afternoon, General Hua and Colonel Chung. The President is ready for you. You may go right in."

The two men entered President Chiang's office. The President arose and motioned for the two men to sit in the chairs in front of his desk. He said "It is good to see my two nephews this rainy August afternoon. I hope you bring me good news about our agreement with the Israelis."

General Hua smiled and said, "Yes, Uncle Ching-kuo. We do have good news. The Israelis signed this Memorandum of Understanding with my Cousin Eng-fu, here. It provides for the Israelis to build the prototype aircraft and for us to share production."

The President asked impatiently, "Yes, yes. But how much will it cost us?"

Hua replied, "We negotiated the Israelis down to nine hundred million dollars, well within our budget range."

The President got red in the face and exclaimed angrily, "You consider 900 million a good price. That's too much for the Jews! I thought you'd get the agreement for eight hundred million!"

Hua managed to keep his voice calm as he replied, "But Uncle Ching-kuo, we got the Israelis to give us the rights for three new technologies. They're worth a lot more than 100 million. These technologies will make the UTF the best fighter plane in the world."

The President, calming down, asked, "Just what are these three technologies?"

Hua explained in some detail the METS, MITS, and ULS technologies the Israelis were going to transfer to Taiwan. He also explained the advantages these technologies would give to the capabilities of their new weapons system. He emphasized the MITS would in fact allow them to decapitate the Red Chinese leadership with a single aircraft, when they were ready to attack.

After the long explanation, the President stood up and said enthusiastically, "I'm really proud of my two nephews for pulling off this agreement. I think, now, that it's a real coup! Really worth the 900 million it costs. I'm going to call the Israeli Prime Minister now and give him the green light."

Then the President turned to Eddie and said, "Congratulations, Eng-fu, you did a really good job to negotiate this agreement which obtains MITS, METS, and ULS for the Republic of China."

A few minutes later, the President's secretary said, "Mr. President, I have Prime Minister Eitan of Israel on the phone for you."

The President picked up the phone, flipped the speaker switch so that Hua and Chung could hear, and said, "General Eitan, I've just reviewed the MOU your Dr. Barlev signed with my Colonel Chung. I want you to know that you have the green light to proceed with our mutual project."

The Prime Minister responded, "President Chiang, thank you for the green light. I already have the team formed under Dr. Barlev and they're starting work. When can we come to Taipei to sign the definitive contract?"

Hua whispered in the President's ear, "Tell him it will be ready to sign next Monday."

When President Chiang relayed this information to Prime Minister Eitan, he replied, "OK, Mr. President, I will send Dr. Barlev and Ms. Amit to Taipei to meet with your Colonel Chung next Monday. Please show them the courtesies of my office. They're my personal representatives."

"Shalom!"

"Shalom!"

Chapter 24

Israelis in Taipei

General Hua had insisted upon coming to the airport with Eddie and Randy to meet Yossi Barlev and Dvora Amit. The trio were now waiting in the VIP lounge, reserved for diplomatic visitors, for the arrival of the Singapore Airlines flight carrying Yossi and Dvora. The airliner was due to arrive at 6 pm, just a few minutes from now. Su Soong had phoned Eddie earlier that afternoon from Singapore saying that Yossi and Dvora had safely departed Singapore for Taipei. Su had explained to Eddie that the meeting had been successful and that they had worked out all the details for their mutual business on the *Universal Textile Fabricator*. They had also agreed upon the contracts between Singapore Straits Trading Ltd., and Herzylia-Export/Import Ltd., so the payments of money in the future would move smoothly through those companies, and not indicate any governmental ties between Israel and Taiwan.

A few minutes later, Yossi and Dvora were escorted into the VIP lounge by a plain clothes security agent who had brought them straight from the airliner. Eddie popped up from his seat when he saw them enter. He thanked the security agent for bringing the important guests from their flight. Eddie then escorted the pair over to General Hua and introduced Yossi and Dvora to him.

General Hua greeted them warmly and said, "Welcome to the Republic of China, Ms. Amit and Dr. Barlev. My limousine is waiting just outside to take us all to dinner."

Eddie Chung added, "And all the passport and customs formalities are waived for you, since you are diplomatic guests of our government."

Yossi replied, "Thank you so much for your kind reception. Ms. Amit and I are honored to join you for dinner. And we certainly appreciate all the special considerations you have shown us here. We feel that it protects the privacy and secrecy of our UTF business."

The group exited the VIP lounge to the black Mercedes-Benz limousine waiting to whisk them into Taipei for their welcoming dinner. Thirty minutes later they pulled up to a special entrance to the Grand Hotel. Eddie Chung led the group to a private dining room in the diplomatic section of the hotel. They were met by Mei Lin and Joy-tung who assisted in seating the guests. Joy-tung was seated at General Hua's right, Mei Lin to the right of Yossi, and Dvora to the right of Randy.

As soon as the guests were seated, three beautiful young Chinese waitresses dressed in ceremonial costumes entered carrying the elaborate array of dinner dishes. Each guest was served a glass of Taiwan champagne from a magnum resting in an iced receptacle. Joy-tung served some of each exotic dish to General Hua and Eddie. Mei Lin served Yossi and Randy. Randy served Dvora.

General Hua proposed a toast, holding his glass out in front of himself with both hands, the right hand actually holding the glass and the fingers of the left hand resting gently against the side of the class, "To the success of the UTF and to the cooperation with our friends from Israel!"

Everyone drank to this toast and then enjoyed the meal and companionship during this elaborate ceremonial Chinese feast.

At the end of dinner, General Hua rose and said, graciously, "I'm sorry to leave you now, but I have some important matters to attend to. I'm sure that Colonel Chung will properly attend to your post dinner entertainment."

Joy-tung left unobtrusively with General Hua.

Eddie said, "There is a small, secluded dance hall in this section of the hotel. I suggest we all go upstairs and enjoy the rest of the evening dancing."

Yossi grinned as Mei Lin pressed his hand and said, "Eddie, that sounds like a good idea. I'm sure Yossi needs some relaxation after his long flight from Singapore today."

The three men and two women left the dining room and took an elevator up to the dance hall. As the hostess seated the group, a beautiful young Chinese girl slipped into a seat next to Eddie. Now everyone was paired up for Dancing: Dvora and Randy, Yossi and Mei Lin, and Eddie with the young girl. The happy group spent the next two hours dancing to the strains of the two orchestras that provided continuous dance music.

While dancing closely, Dvora invited Randy to spend the night in her room. Yossi invited Mei Lin to spend the night with him. Randy and Mei Lin both accepted their invitations.

Shortly after midnight, Eddie announced, "We have a business meeting at 9 am in General Hua's office. We had better leave now. Mei Lin will show you where your rooms are located. I'll pick you up in the morning at 8:30. Goodnight."

Everyone chorused, "Good night." Eddie paid the bill and left with his beautiful, young, Chinese companion.

The meeting in General Hua's office in the Ministry of National Defense headquarters building began promptly at 9 am on the last Tuesday in August 1989. The participants were seated around the general's conference table. General Hua's legal aide had prepared copies of the definitive contract that described the obligations of the parties: Herzylia-Export/Import Ltd., proxy for Israeli Aircraft Industries, and Singapore Straits Trading Ltd., proxy for Aeronautical Industries Development Center.

General Hua opened the meeting by stating, "Dr. Barlev and Ms. Amit, here is the contract we have prepared. We hope that it meets with your approval. If there are any changes, they must be agreed to by Colonel Chung and Dr. McLyle. My legal aide will enter any agreed to changes into the PC word processor here on the table. I believe this contract is merely an expansion of the MOU signed in Tel Aviv. So, agreement should be easy."

Yossi replied, "General Hua, one key provision I must insist upon is the payment schedule we require. I brought a copy of our proposed schedule. I hope it meets your approval."

Yossi handed out copies of the payment schedule to General Hua and Eddie Chung. Eddie looked at it and said, "You propose that we pay you two hundred million dollars upon the signing of the agreement, 300 million upon approval of the full scale mock-up, 300 million upon delivery of the first prototype, and 100 million upon delivery of the first production model."

Yossi replied, "Yes, Eddie, that's right. We think that's a fair payment schedule."

Eddie and General Hua conversed together in Chinese for a few moments. Then Eddie responded, "We agree the payment schedule is fair, but General Hua and I insist upon one change."

Yossi asked, "And what's that, Eddie?"

We believe payment for the first prototype should be *after* the first successful flight in Taiwan, not merely upon delivery. What if it is defective?"

Yossi and Dvora put their heads together for a short conference in Hebrew. Then Yossi replied, "I'll agree to that change with the additional stipulation that the first flight be within thirty days after delivery. We don't want to wait too long for our payment."

General Hua responded, Dr. Barlev, we'll agree to that stipulation." Then he turned to his legal aide and instructed, "Major, please enter the payment schedule as agree to into the definitive contract."

Yossi said, "Genera Hua, we need about thirty minutes to read the contract to determine whether or not we have any further requests for changes."

General Hua replied, "That's fine, Dr. Barlev. I'm going to leave now and let you and Colonel Chung hammer out the details. I'll return just before lunch and see what progress you're making. And then we'll all have lunch in the MND dining room upstairs."

Yossi replied, "Thank you, General Hua. That is fine. We'll see you later. Shalom."

Hua smiled and repeated, "Shalom."

General Hua returned just after twelve noon. As he entered the room, both Yossi and Eddie rose with broad grins on their faces. Yossi said, "General Hua, we have some good news for you. We have reached agreement on the definitive contract and we have both signed it. Everything is *green-go* now, contractually speaking.

Eddie added, "Yes, Ding-fua, here it is, all signed and sealed. We quickly agreed to several minor items. The only problem that took any time was the clause referring to third country sales. I insisted that Israel give the Republic of China right to approve sales to third countries since we have paid for the development.

After some haggling over the contract wording, Yossi finally agreed."

General Hua looked surprised, "But I thought it would take at least two days to get agreement on the contract. It's so complex."

Dvora laughed and said, "General Hua, Su Soong had a copy for us to review when we got to Singapore. We had a chance to spend all day going over the contract with her. We had a list of the changes we wanted when we arrived here this morning."

General Hua turned to Eddie and said, "Eng-fu, that was a good idea to have Su Soong present Dr. Barlev and Ms. Amit copies of the contract in Singapore."

Eddie smiled, "Ding-fua, I can't take the credit for that idea. It was Su's idea. She's a sharp business woman."

Dvora added, "Yes, General Hua, she is. I'm sure that Su and I can work well together. It should make our cooperative project, the Universal Textile Fabricator, go smoothly."

General Hua looked perplexed as he asked, "What in the world is the Universal Textile Fabricator?"

Eddie laughed and said, "Ding-fua, that's our telex code word for the UTF aircraft."

"Good thinking!"

Chapter 25

Critical Design Review

The Critical Design Review, CDR, was conducted in Taichung at AIDC beginning on the last Monday in September, 1989. All the key actors in the Ultra Tactical Fighter aircraft program were present. Yossi Barlev and Dvora Amit were there from Israel. Randy McLyle and Patricia Manos had been watching and analyzing the detailed design as it progressed. General Huang, Dr. Charlie Chang, Colonel Wang, and the test pilot, Colonel Yung were there from AIDC. Dr. Chris Haah and his staff, the designers of the advanced missiles, were there CSIST. And finally, General Hua was presiding over the entire proceedings, down from MND in Taipei. Also, the full scale mock-up was finished and ready for all the reviewers to touch, feel, see, and crawl over and through.

General Hua opened the CDR on the first day with the warning, "First of all, I would like to remind everyone in this room that the UTF carries the highest security classification: Special Compartmentalized Secret. You each must take personal responsibility for seeing that none of the information about this fighter falls into enemy hands."

Then he turned to Randy McLyle and said, "Most of the credit for this UTF design goes to Dr. McLyle, thanks to his creative brain. Also he was alert enough to see that we in Taiwan needed some specialized help."

He turned to Yossi Barlev and added, "Dr. Barlev has taken Dr. McLyle's design and added some new technologies: METS, MITS, and ULS, to come up with what I truly believe will be the best fighter aircraft in the world. Dr. Barlev advised me this morning just before the meeting started that IAI will deliver the first prototype to AIDC in early July of 1991, so that we can plan on the first flight of the UTF immediately afterward, less than two years from now!"

Then he addressed the whole audience, "Now, let's get on with the CDR. I expect you all to critically examine this design to identify any changes that must be made. After this week, the design will be *frozen* for the first prototype. Good luck!"

The remainder of the morning, Yossi and Randy presented briefings covering the details of the aircraft design. Just after lunch, Dr. Haah, director of CSIST presented the details of the advanced missiles to be carried by the UTF.

Dr. Haah in his opening remarks said, "The METS and MITS technologies transferred to us by the Israelis have removed any final doubts that our missile can do the job we intended. Designing a missile to carry out both the air-to-air and air-to-ground missions was very difficult. But Yossi sent some of the top Israeli missile designers to review our missile design. They suggested a few changes which have been made. They gave our design the *green light*. We now feel confident it will do the job."

Late in the afternoon, the group toured the super secret hanger which housed the full scale mock-up of the UTF. Dr. Charlie Chang, the UTF program manager, presented the briefing on the details of the mock-up. He said in his opening remarks, "We also benefited from the Israeli technology transfer. The METS and ULS technologies allow us to make the electronics small enough and the aircraft light and strong enough to perform its mission!"

After Dr. Chang's presentation, the test pilot, Colonel Yung Hang-fu, who would fly the prototype in July 1991, gave a briefing from the cockpit. He said, "Ms. Patricia Manos has provided a very realistic simulation for our new UTF aircraft. I've flown it many hours now, so that I feel completely at home in this weird cockpit. As you can see, I'm lying prone so that my body can withstand 20 g's of acceleration without my blacking out. All the cockpit information is projected on my helmet visor. We call it the *Virtual Cockpit*. We've replaced all the normal cockpit instruments and hardware with software and some fiber optics. Really advanced! It's really going to work!"

At the end of the last day of the CDR, General Hua mounted the podium in the auditorium and addressed the participants, "Ladies and gentlemen, congratulations on completing the design of the Ultra Tactical Fighter aircraft! The audit team has made a comprehensive list of the changes to be made, all minor. I hereby approve the completion of the major milestone called the *CDR*!"

Then he turned to Yossi Barlev and said, "And, Dr. Barlev, you are hereby authorized to have IAI begin construction of the first prototype to be ready for first flight in July 1991. My authorization will be confirmed though our normal communications channels."

Su Soong was sitting next to Dvora Amit and whispered, "Dvora, I'll give you the authorization before you leave. That'll save a long telex, right?"

"Right! Shalom, Su!"

Later that night after they finished making love, Patricia turned over and said to Randy, "Darling, we'll receive another two million dollar cash transfer to our Swiss bank account now. I figure our monthly income will be over 43 thousand dollars a month. That's over half million dollars per year!"

Randy groaned, put his arms around her and said, "What a thing to figure out after making love. But I love your figures as well as your figure. Good night darling. I love you."

"I love you too!"

Chapter 26

First Flight

On the first Sunday of July, 1991, a special El Al 747 airliner pulled up to a hanger at Israeli Aircraft Industries. Yossi Barlev was personally supervising the loading of a strangely shaped package into the huge uniquely modified cargo bay of the big wide body aircraft. It fitted nicely into the specially designed cargo area. It is marked in black letters, *Universal Textile Fabricator.* It's destination was marked Singapore Straits Trading Ltd. And the manufacturer was listed as Herzylia-Export/Import Ltd. After the big package was loaded, Yossi climbed up the boarding stairs into the empty aircraft and seated himself next to Dvora in the first class section.

Yossi said, "The UTF prototype is safely loaded. Now the pilot can taxi over and pick up the passengers for our regular El Al flight 007 from Tel Aviv to
 Singapore."

Dvora smiled, "It's been a tough job, building the first UTF in only twenty-one months, hasn't it?"

As the big aircraft began to taxi from the IAI ramp over to the regular passenger boarding tarmac on Bin Gurion Airport, Yossi replied, "Yes, it was a tough job. If it hadn't been for two things we could never have done it on such a short schedule."

"And what two things are those?"

"First, Randy's design was very thorough, well thought out, and easy to fabricate and assemble. Second, our experience building the advanced Lavi fighter really prepared us to tackle this more advanced aircraft."

Dvora added, "Well, anyway, it's a nice feeling to be finished. And, we'll get another 300 million dollar progress payment after the first flight next week."

Yossi reminded, "If successful!"

Dvora got a quizzical look on her face and replied, "You don't have any doubts, do you?"

Well, not really, but a lot of things could go wrong. There's a lot of complex hardware and really sophisticated software. And it all has to work right."

Dvora asked, "But didn't you do extensive testing of everything in the simulation at IAI? I thought all that testing would catch all the bugs."

Yossi answered, "Well, we did do a lot of testing, but it would take a hundred years to test *everything*. That's why we have to fly the airplane. To make sure everything really works."

Dvora smiled, "I'll keep my fingers crossed."

Yossi replied, "Me, too!"

When the big 747 arrived at the Singapore airport, it discharged all the passengers except Yossi and Dvora who rode the 747 and its UTF cargo as it taxied over to a special bonded warehouse. Sitting on the tarmac next to the warehouse was a China Airlines 747-SP, also with a cargo area custom designed to receive the very special package

Su Soong met the El Al airliner accompanied by a special customs agent. He was special because he was authorized to approve the transfer of the package from the El Al 747 to the China Airlines 747 without any customs duty or inspection. Su had assured his cooperation in this touchy transfer by transferring a hundred thousand US dollars to his secret Hong Kong bank account and she had spent the last several nights in his bed attending to his perverse sexual desires. Forty-five minutes later a special crew from the China Airlines 747 had transferred the special package. Su joined Dvora and Yossi in the first class section of the China Airlines 747 before it taxied back to the airport jetway to pick up its regular passengers for the non-stop flight to Taipei of flight 004.

Soon all the passengers were loaded onto flight 004 and it departed for Taipei. After the 747 reached cruising altitude, Su went up to the flight deck, knocked on the door and showed the crew her ROC CIA identification. She said to the flight engineer, "I need to use one of your secure communications channels for an official message to Taipei. It's very important!"

"OK, Ms. Soong, no problem. Here, use this channel. It goes directly to the officer-of-the-day at CIA headquarters, Taipei."

"Thank you, Sir. This message will only take a moment."

Su picked up the radio microphone. She entered the code of the day by depressing the special buttons on the face of the radio set. This provided encryption for the maximum security communication. She called over the mike, "Hello, Home Office, this is 069 calling."

Immediately a female voice replied, "Hello, 069, this is Home Office, go ahead, please."

Su replied, "Yes, Home Office, 069 here. Please give the following message to 079. *Your Universal Textile Fabricator will arrive aboard flight 004 at 6 pm today. Have friends aboard. Regards, 069.* Thank you, Home Office, out!"

"Roger, 069, Home Office will comply with your request immediately. Out."

Su turned to the flight engineer, and said sweetly, "Thank you, Sir. I'm all finished."

The flight engineer replied, "Good. Would you like a cup of coffee here in the cockpit?"

"No, sir, I'm sorry. I've got to get back to my seat."

"How about a date tonight in Taipei?"

"Sorry, Sir, but I'm busy. Maybe some other time, perhaps in Singapore."

The flight engineer replied eagerly, "Great, I'd like that. See you later."

"So long."

Su returned to her seat across the aisle from Dvora and Yossi. She said, "Eddie knows we're on the way. He and Randy will meet us at the airport to see that the UTF is safely loaded on the C-130 for the flight to Taichung. We'll fly down with the UTF. Then we'll all have dinner together in Taichung tonight to celebrate the arrival of the UTF."

Dvora replied, "Su, that will be nice. We've all worked so hard to get the UTF ready for its first flight. When do you think that'll take place?"

Su smiled and replied, "I'm not sure about that, Dvora. Better ask Randy when we get to Taipei. My guess is less than a week, though."

After landing in Taipei, a plain clothes security agent met the trio and led them to the VIP lounge where Eddie and Randy were waiting to greet them. They all followed the security agent to a Volkswagen-type bus waiting to drive them to the tarmac where the C-130 was parked. Twenty minutes later a truck carrying the big package arrived and drove up the wide ramp at the rear of the C-130 transport aircraft. The group of five buckled themselves into the passenger seats in the big plane, the clamshell doors at the rear closed, the turboprop aircraft taxied to the active runway and received immediate clearance for take off.

A few minutes later the big transport leaped into the air with its precious cargo: the prototype Ultra Tactical Fighter aircraft. When they reached cruising altitude a master sergeant in the ROC Air Force served the quintet coffee and cookies for the short half hour flight from Taipei to Taichung.

While sipping the coffee, Dvora asked Randy, "How long will it take until we're ready for the first flight?"

Randy answered, "We have a few thing to do, like loading the software into the flight computers, installing the solid propellant rocket boosters and running system integration checks. We're scheduled to fly Friday morning. We *must* be ready on time. President Chiang is flying down with General Hua to witness the first flight!"

Dvora said, "That's exciting! And just think, Colonel Yung will be the pilot. He's so cute. I'd love to dance with him sometime."

Randy laughed, "You'll get your chance tonight. He's going to join us for dinner at the President Hotel where you'll be staying."

The C-130 landed on the airport at Taichung just after 7:30. It taxied up to the super secret hangar at the AIDC facility where the final system integration and ground tests would take place. As soon as the rear cargo doors were opened, the truck carrying the UTF package backed out and drove into the hangar where it was unloaded by a crane. A group of technicians swarmed over the package, removed the precious cargo from the container, and started connecting cables and other items to the prototype.

Colonel Jan Wang, director of avionics and systems integration, was there to supervise the work. He greeted the quintet who had escorted the UTF to Taichung, and then turned to Randy and said, "We'll be working around the clock getting ready for Friday morning's flight. General Huang said we must be ready for take off no later than 9 am. That's shortly after President Chiang and General Hua will arrive from Taipei."

Randy exclaimed, "It looks like you have the *cream of the crop* out here working on the plane tonight. I'll see you first thing in the morning. I have to escort our VIP visitors from Israel to their hotel for dinner. They'll join me in the morning to see how things are going."

Colonel Wang replied, "Fine, see you then.   The most important happening tomorrow morning will start at 10 am. Colonel Yung will *fly* the aircraft which will be connected to the flight simulator. Patricia already has the mission plan on the flight tape ready for loading into the flight computer just as soon as we get power applied to the bird!"

"I want to see that. Colonel Yung is having dinner with our guests tonight.   We'll make sure he's all relaxed ready for the *simulated flight* in the morning."

Dvora, who overheard Randy's conversation with Colonel Wang, whispered in Randy's ear, "Don't worry. After I finish with that beautiful hunk in bed tonight, he'll be completely relaxed and ready to fly."

Randy whispered back, "That lucky dog! I know he'll be relaxed after a night with you."

After seeing that the UTF prototype was in good hands, the quintet that escorted the aircraft to Taichung left for dinner. On the way to the Presidential Hotel in Taichung, Eddie turned to Dvora and Yossi and said, "Don't worry about your bags. The driver will see that they are safely placed in your suites. Mei Lin has already checked you in and has your room keys. She and the other dinner guests will meet us in the dining room."

Yossi replied, "Thanks, Eddie. You're really efficient. It'll be nice to see Mei Lin again."

Eddie led the other four up to a private dining room on the second floor of the hotel. Waiting to greet the new arrivals were General Huang, director of AIDC, Patricia, Mei Lin, Joy-tung, and the test pilot, Colonel Yung. Mei Lin oversaw the seating of the guests and made sure everyone was properly paired off for the evening as well as for all night! Joy-tung was seated to General

Huang's right, Mei Lin to Yossi's right, Dvora to Colonel Yung's right, Patricia to Randy's right. Eddie, with Su Soong on his right, was seated with his back to the door, indicating, in the Chinese custom, that he was the paying host. General Huang was the ceremonial host.

After they had all been seated, the young waitress served them each a glass of bubbling champagne. General Huang then proposed a toast, "To the safe arrival at AIDC of the UTF prototype. Shalom!"

The other guests chorused, "Shalom!"

Then Colonel Yung stood, "And here's to the first flight Friday. I'm really going to put that *mother fucker* through the paces. I hope you built it good and strong!"

Everyone chorused, "Here! Here! To the first flight!"

After the toast, Yossi turned to Colonel Yung and said, "Don't worry! We built the bird plenty strong – but remember, this is a *control configured design*! The software has to work right, too!"

Colonel Yung grinned, "Yeah I know. I just hope these software weenies haven't *fucked up*. If so, I'll find out Friday. I'm going to fly it through every maneuver known to a fighter pilot. And we know a whole bunch of tough maneuvers!"

A few moments later, Dvora whispered into Yung's ear, "Hang-fu, I'd like to make sure you're relaxed for your flight tomorrow. Please stay with me tonight."

Yung looked at Dvora's body greedily and whispered back, "You betcha! I just love to screw round eyes specially those built like you, Doll!"

He then kissed Dvora on the lips as she squeezed his hand in anticipation.

Everyone was seated in the grandstand erected for the VIP's who were there to witness the first flight of the Ultra Tactical Fighter. There are speakers set up so the observers could hear the communications between the ground controller and Colonel Yung. There were three large screen TV monitors to show the images projected – one from the nose of the UTF aircraft, one from the chase plane following the UTF, and a third connected to the sight head of the missile being fired. Earlier that morning a committee composed of Dr. Charlie Chang, Yossi, and Randy had met to review the flight readiness. They had given the *green light* for the flight to begin at 1000 exactly.

The sleek, stealthy aircraft was sitting on its tail in the bed of a truck about a kilometer in front of the reviewing stand. Colonel Yung walked out to the plane shown on one of the TV monitors wearing a white scarf and his modernistic helmet with the virtual cockpit visor. He looked more like an astronaut than a fighter pilot. The UTF was almost a space vehicle since it reached the fringes of the Earth's atmosphere in its suborbital mode. Spread out in the field about two kilometers from the viewing stand were eight simulated ground targets: four tanks and four dummies dressed in Red Chinese army uniforms. A group of supersonic target drones were flying overhead. The countdown for takeoff began, "Ten, nine, --- three, two, one, GO!"

Colonel Yung pressed the takeoff button. The solid propellant rocket booster ignited. The strange looking aircraft leapt off the truck bed on a tail of white flame with almost no smoke visible. The booster dropped away as the dual ramjet engines propelled the aircraft beyond Mach 2.

A few seconds later the controller reported, "The UTF has achieved a cruise speed of Mach 5, or a mile per second. Everything looks normal."

Colonel Yung reported over the loudspeaker, "This is a *hot mother*!" Real flying is a lot more fun than flying the simulator! Watch those supersonic target drones. I'm going to go after them, now!"

One of the video screens in front of the viewing stands showed the missile in its air-to-air mode being launched from the UTF. Another monitor showed the image the missile's seeker saw. At first the eight drones appeared like a *blob* in the middle of the screen. Then the missile got closer, the individual drones became visible. Suddenly the missile seemed to explode in the sky as the eight submissiles were deployed. A few seconds later there were eight simultaneous explosions overhead as the eight drones were hit by the deadly submissiles and rained down in burning pieces from above.

Colonel Yung's voice came on the speaker as he exclaimed, "Yowee! What a machine! What a missile! Did you see that? All eight killed with one *fucking* missile!"

A moment later, Colonel Yung's voice came back over the speaker, "Now, I'm going to get those ground targets out in front of you. I'm switching to the *air-to-ground* mode. Got it!"

The video screen showed the area of the ground targets seen by the aircraft's sensors. Then Yung's voice came over the speaker, "Here goes! I'm going to kill those *fuckers* on the ground now!"

The video screens in front of the viewing stand showed the missile zipping away from the aircraft towards the ground. Another video screen displayed what the missile's sensors saw. At first it started heading towards the target blob. The individual targets became visible a few seconds later. The viewing audience watched the missile seem to explode into eight pieces about two thousand feet above the ground. The eight submissiles sought out the four tanks and four dummy soldiers. Every one achieved a bull's eye. The eight objects were destroyed in front of the eyes of the spectators.

Colonel Yung's voice exclaimed over the loud speakers again, "Did you see that? Four tanks and four enemy officers destroyed with *one* missile! This is a real fighting machine!"

The UTF then pulled up and could hardly be seen visually, but the chase plane managed to keep the UTF clearly on the audience viewing screen in front of the first flight viewers.

A few minutes later, Colonel Yung's speaker voice was heard, "Now that we have seen the missiles work, I'm going to really put this *mother fucker* through its paces and see if it knows how to fly in tight combat maneuvers. Here goes!"

The UTF aircraft underwent a number of violent maneuvers in the blue sky overhead.

Then Colonel Yung shouted over the speaker, "Oh, *shit!* It's in a flat spin. I can't pull it out. I'm below ten thousand feet. Here goes!"

The video screen showing the spinning UTF aircraft was watched in horror by the participants. There was an explosion and parts of the UTF aircraft fell burning from the sky. A moment later the piece that used to be the center section developed a streamer that slowed it down. Then a large chute deployed. The escape capsule floated down.

Colonel Yung's voice came over the speaker, "There must be a software glitch. Got to be fixed! I'm OK!"

Everyone in the strands had been holding his or her breath. Now one could hear a sort of moan for the loss of the plane and of relief for the saving of the pilot.

General Hua leaned over to Eddie Chung and said, "Eng-fu, I'm sure glad I insisted on an escape capsule! We needed it, didn't we?"

Eddie looked at him glumly and replied sadly, "Yes, we sure did, Ding-fua! We sure did!"

Chapter 27

Crash Cause

It was the last Monday in August 1991. The crash investigators had been working tirelessly for many long hours since *Black Friday,* the day of the crash. They had reported their findings to General Huang, director of AIDC.

General Huang telephoned General Hua, "I'm happy to report that the crash review team has found the cause of the crash. Colonel Yung said as he was descending in the escape capsule, *There must be a software glitch!* Well, Colonel Yung's intuitive feelings turned out to be correct. There *was* a software fault. A careful review of the flight tapes showed that there was lock-up of the software in each of the four redundant flight computers. The software simply locked up and stopped working. There was not time to reset the computers and start over. I know my secretary is always complaining, *Oh, General Huang, I just lost the last three pages I typed. The software locked up again. The cursor won't move. Nothing happens!* Well, the same type of thing happened with our software in our four flight computers. As a result when Colonel Yung entered the spin, there was no control. The airplane crashed. Fortunately, the escape capsule firing mechanism is independent of the flight computers. Otherwise, Colonel Yung wouldn't be here to tell us what happened."

General Hua asked incredulously, "You mean all four of our expensive flight computers did exactly the same thing? Nothing?"

General Huang replied seriously, "Yes, General Hua. All four did the same thing – nothing! Because all four flight computers had the same software loaded in them I'm afraid there was a *common failure point* in our quadruple redundant system that we somehow overlooked during the software development.

General Hua pursued his questioning relentlessly, "Are you were there wasn't some structural failure? Some defect in the prototype airplane IAI built?

General Huang replied, "General Hua, there was absolutely no evidence of structural failure. It was definitely the software!"

General Hua asked, "Well, what are we going to do to fix the problem? Do we know how to fix the problem?"

General Huang replied, "Yes, Sir. We do know how to fix it. Randy McLyle suggested using Fault Tolerant Software, or FTS for short. FTS involves using a slightly different version of software in each of the four redundant flight computers, so we can make sure that all *four* computers don't lock up at the same time."

General Hua asked, "You mean that by using four separate versions of the software we have redundancy in the software just like the redundancy we have in the computer hardware? But isn't that a terribly difficult job? It took almost two years to develop the first version of the software, the version that failed in flight."

"No, General Hua. It isn't a big job. Patricia Manos developed a technique to generate the other three versions from the original version. Her technique assures that no more than one version would lock up at any given time."

General Hua asked incredulously, "How can you be sure it will work?"

"We have the software loaded into the flight simulator. We tried to test every maneuver we could think of that the aircraft could execute. With the old software, we can reproduce the maneuver where we got the software lock up and lost the UTF in the uncontrollable flat spin. With the new software in the simulator, if we *fly* the same flat spin, we can recover from it. Everything works. I can show you in the simulation room, if you wish."

General Hua replied, "No, that's not necessary."

He laughed and continued, "Maybe you can install your FTS concept on my personal computer to make its word processing software work all the time. My secretary also complained about losing several pages she had typed when the software locked up."

General Huang continued, "We have more good news. Due to the Israelis' concurrent production line, they say the prototype replacement will be delivered before the Chinese New Year, less that six months from now. It will be the first plane on their production line. The next test flight can be scheduled for the week before Chinese New Year, 1992. And, the Israelis say they'll deliver two more planes in July 1992."

General Hua grinned and responded, "That's sooner than I expected. Looks like we'll have something special to celebrate for our New Years this coming year."

Then he asked, "And when will the first production aircraft be completed at our facilities here at AIDC?"

"General Hua, the Israelis are already here helping to get our production line going. We'll have our first three production aircraft completed by October 1992."

General Hua grinned, "That means we'll have six UTF aircraft ready by October. Right?"

General Huang replied, "Yes, Sir. But remember because of our effective missiles, that equivalent to having one hundred and twenty conventional aircraft."

General Hua smiled broadly, "Yes, the UTF is very effective. The MND is getting it's money's worth. President Chiang will be very pleased with all this good news. Understandably, he was very distressed to witness the crash."

As he hung up, General Hua turned to Eddie Chung, who had been sitting listening to the conversation on the speaker phone, "Cousin Eng-fu, I think we can tell Uncle Ching-kuo that Plan A can be executed in July, 1992!"

"Yes, Ding-fua, it looks that way!"

Chapter 28

Next Flight

At dinner that night, Patricia said to Randy, "I'm glad General Hua approved of our software fix for the next flight."

Randy replied, "Me, too! It's really too bad the prototype plane crashed. It means we didn't get our five million dollar payment. I had thought we would be married and in Europe by now."

Patricia laughed, "Well, Randy, it's not so bad here in Taichung. After all, we're making over 500 thousand dollars per year in interest from our bank account in Zürich now. And your final divorce decree came through, so we can get married any time we want to now.

Randy said, "Let's get married just before we leave Taiwan. We'll ask Eddie to be our *Best Man,* OK?"

Patricia responded, "That sounds wonderful. I'd like Mei Lin to be *Maid Of Honor*. It's agreed, OK?"

Randy grinned broadly, walked over, put his arms around Patricia, hugged and kissed her as he exclaimed, "Yes, Darling, it's agreed. We'll get married and move to some sunny spot in Europe."

"Oh, Randy, I love you. That's a wonderful plan!"

The second prototype had been delivered by Herzylia-Export/Import Ltd. to Singapore Straits Trading Ltd. The special 747 SP of China Airlines had delivered the UTF to Taipei. The C-130 transport had carried it to AIDC in Taichung. The stealthy new aircraft had completed its hangar testing at AIDC. It was ten days before the Chinese New Year in 1992. All the key personnel had been assembled in the AIDC theater for the final flight readiness review for the test flight scheduled for later that week.

General Hua mounted the podium and addressed the group, "General Huang, I want you to know that it's mandatory that this next flight be totally successful! If there's another failure, I can assure you – heads will roll! President Chiang has hinted as much to me already. Even though I'm his nephew, I would be finished. And if I'm finished, Ching-lee, you're finished!"

General Huang rose and responded firmly, "Now, Ding-fua, I understand that. Everyone here understands we are responsible for the failures as well as the successes. But let me assure you, we are ready for the next flight. Our testing has been extremely thorough. We haven't left a stone unturned."

Colonel Yung rose and added, "That's right, Ding-fua. We are really ready this time. I can assure you as one pilot to another, this *mother fucker* is going to work and work good!"

General Hua smiled, "Well, I feel better after those reassuring comments. I just want everyone to understand this program is extremely crucial to the survival of our nation. I'll sit down now and hear your final review."

Randy, Yossi, Charlie Chang, and Colonel Wang presented a polished set of briefings detailing the preparations for the next flight. The briefings were followed by a demonstration in the super secret hangar with test pilot, Colonel Yung, giving a simulated flight demonstration which showed that the software fixes worked. At the end of the day, General Hua again mounted the podium in the auditorium and announced, "Congratulations. I'm convinced you are now ready for the next flight. I hereby give you the green light to conduct the next flight Friday morning. This time we'll have the flight *without* President Chiang present. If all goes well, we will provide a special demonstration later for him."

The sleek UTF aircraft blasted off in front of the audience for the second attempt at a successful flight. A few seconds later, the solid rocket booster dropped away and the dual ramjet engines were actuated. Colonel Yung's voice came over the loud speaker in front of the observers, "This time I'm going to begin by putting this bird through a series of maneuvers to make sure the software fix works in flight. The first maneuver will be the spin that caused us to crash last July. Here goes!"

The video image from the chase plane showed the UTF plane enter a violent spin that turned into a flat spin. The new aircraft was spinning helplessly towards earth like a big acacia leaf floating down from a tree. A loud gasp was heard from the audience as this dangerous maneuver was executed. The altitude was announced by the chase plane as being nine thousand feet, lower than the altitude at which Colonel Yung had activated the escape capsule in the first flight, the one that crashed. All of a sudden the spinning stopped and the sleek plane went into an almost vertical climb to gain altitude.

As the crowd applauded wildly, Patricia stood and yelled with excitement, "It worked! It worked!"

Just then Colonel Yung's voice was heard over the loudspeaker, "We really fixed this *mother fucker!* The software fix works! Now I'm going to put this bird through the other maneuvers."

During the next ten minutes the UTF aircraft showed on the screen, as seen from the chase plane, going through other test gyrations. After each maneuver, the UTF recovered smoothly to straight and level before beginning the next exercise. When the last maneuver was finished, Colonel Yung announced on the speaker, "I'm completely satisfied the software fix does it. Randy's FTS is great!. Now, to get those targets."

This time there were sixteen drones flying in two clusters separated by about ten nautical miles. The aircraft in each cluster were in a tight formation. Two video screens each showed one of the two clusters of target drones. The third video showed what the aircraft sensors saw – two blobs on the target display, just like the scene projected on Colonel Yung's helmet visor. Two air-to-air configured missiles struck out from the UTF aircraft. The two video screens switched to the scene as viewed by the missile sensors. As the two missiles drew closer to the two clusters of drones, the individual target drones could be seen. Then each of the two missiles separated into eight submissiles. Each submissile headed for an individual target drone. The chase plane showed all sixteen drones falling from the sky in flames, fatally hit by the sixteen submissiles.

Colonel Yung yelled into the speaker, "Yippee! Sixteen enemy aircraft downed with just two missiles. I've got two more missiles left. Now to kill those enemy targets in the field in front of you."

Just a half kilometer away were four jeeps, remotely controlled. Each carried one dummy driver and one dummy gunner. Standing near the jeeps were four dummy enemy soldiers. A kilometer away were four dummy tanks and four dummy *surface-to-air* missile sites on the ground. One missile headed for the four jeeps and four dummy soldiers. The second missile headed towards the dummy tanks and dummy missile sites.

The audience saw each of the two missiles separate into eight submissiles. The sixteen submissiles headed for the sixteen ground targets. Sixteen puffs of smoke appeared and explosions were heard as the submissile warheads struck their targets. Each target was killed - right on! The four tanks and the four missiles sites were destroyed by the eight submissiles from one missile. The four jeeps and four soldier dummies were destroyed by the eight submissiles from the other missile. The four soldier dummies were obliterated. The tanks were left blown apart with their fuel burning. The jeeps and missiles sites were gone.

Colonel Yung yelled into the mike, "Mission accomplished. I'm coming home."

A few moments later the sleek, stealthy aircraft landed on the runway in full view of the audience in the viewing stands. Everyone cheered. General Hua took the microphone he was handed by an aide and exclaimed, "Congratulations, General Huang, to you and your UTF team members. We have a successful flight. We are ready to demonstrate the UTF to President Chiang, the day after New Years."

Patricia turned to Randy who was sitting next to her in the viewing stand and whispered, "We've passed the last milestone. The successful first flight. Now we'll get our final payment of five million dollars. We can set the date for our wedding and start planning our move to Europe!"

Randy grabbed Patricia, hugged and kissed her, and told her, "Oh, Darling, I forgot to tell you. General Huang asked us to stay over until October of this year when the first UTFs made by AIDC will be finished. He said they might need our help during the production phase of the program and it's only eight more months. He offered us a bonus of half a million dollars, plus he said he would pay all the costs for our wedding."

Patricia asked, "And what did you tell him?"

Randy grinned, "I told him yes."

Mei Lin was waiting at the aircraft when Colonel Yung crawled out of the body-contoured cockpit. She grabbed Yung, kissed him passionately, and said, "Hang-fu, come to room 812 in the President Hotel after your debriefing. I'd like to *reward* you for your successful flight."

Yung exclaimed, "To hell with the debriefing. They have all my comments on the flight tapes. Let's go to your room now! I've always wanted to fuck you, Mei Lin!"

Chapter 29

Plan *A* Ordered

The day after the Chinese New Years celebrations had been completed, the long black presidential limousine pulled up to an observation tower located on a remote section of the huge AIDC grounds. Located a prudent distance away from the tower was a simulation of the reviewing stand which was always used by the Red Chinese leadership to review the annual October Parade celebrating the communist party victory in Mainland China over the Nationalist forces of General Chiang Kai-shek, many years before. Mounted on the platform were dummies dressed and made to look like the current Mainland Chinese leaders.

General Hua and Eddie Chung helped President Chiang climb the steep, circular stairway leading up to the glass observation tower that resembled an airport control tower. When the trio reached the platform level, General Hua pointed to the mock viewing stand a safe distance away and said, "Uncle Ching-kuo, as you can see, we went to a lot of expense to duplicate the reviewing stand our enemies on the mainland use for their big October military parade. Nobody has seen the simulated target except the three of us and three of Eng-fu's trusted aides who set up the display. Even Hang-fu, who will fly our new Ultra Tactical Fighter and who will implement *Plan C* next October doesn't know the details of the target he is destroying today."

A few moments later, Colonel Yung reported over the loudspeaker in the observation tower, "I'm now ready to destroy the ground targets. Missiles one and two are now configured for *air-to-ground*! I'm now one hundred nautical miles from the target. There, I can see the target on my zoom radar. Missiles away!"

Two minutes later the three men in the observation tower saw the puffs of smoke high in the sky above the viewing stand as the two missiles separated into sixteen deadly, homing projectiles, each one targeted for the head of one of the sixteen enemies leaders. An instant later, all sixteen dummies disappeared into a cloud of black smoke as the sixteen warheads exploded on contact.

President Ching arose from his chair and exclaimed excitedly, "Ding-fua, we're ready to recapture the mainland! What a fantastic weapon we've developed."

General Hua put his hand on the President's shoulder and said firmly, "Not quite yet, Uncle Ching-kuo. We won't be ready for *Plans B and C* until next October when the enemy has the real parade. Meanwhile we have to execute *Plan A.*"

The President protested, "But aren't you ready for *Plan A* now?"

General Hua smiled, "Almost, but first we want to show you how we will execute *Plan A*. We have sixteen supersonic drones flying now which simulate eight of the enemy's F-16's and eight of his MiG-29's. Please watch now."

A moment later Colonel Yung reported on the loudspeaker, "I now have sixteen of the enemy aircraft in view on my target sensor display. I'll use my last two missiles configured *air-to-air* to destroy them all. Missiles away!"

The video monitor showed the two missiles zipping towards the target drones. The separation of the two missiles into sixteen submissiles showed clearly on another video screen. Each submissile sought out its own target drone. A few seconds later the sixteen target drones exploded on impact from the submissile warheads. The video screen showed the dripping fire and smoke from the destroyed drones.

General Hua exclaimed loudly, "See, Uncle Ching-kuo, our UTF will obsolete nuclear war."

President Chiang arose and said, "I don't know about that, Ding-fua, but I'm convinced we can eliminate the leadership of the mainland and retake our homeland with the help of this flying weapon. Congratulations to both of you for a convincing demonstration!"

A few days later General Hua and Eddie Chung were summoned to the Presidential Palace by President Chiang. The two men were ushered into the President's sitting room by his attractive young secretary. The President motioned for the two men to be seated as his secretary poured them tea and served them cookies.

The President opened the meeting, "I was very impressed with your demonstration of the capabilities of our new Ultra Tactical Fighter. I've consulted with my senior advisors and they all agree we are ready to implement *Plan A*. I hereby direct you to implement *Plan A* as soon as possible."

Eddie Chung grinned and said, "Good, Uncle Ching-kuo. The Red Chinese are getting bolder and bolder over-flying our territorial waters with their fancy new F-16's and MiG-29's. They know we can't touch them with our old F-5's. I just received a report yesterday that they were over-flying our waters with fifteen F-16's and fifteen MiG-29's three times per week."

General Hua smiled and added, "Uncle Ching-kuo, we can eliminate all thirty of those advanced aircraft with a single UTF with it's four missiles configured for *air-to-air*."

The President rose and said, "OK, OK, my two nephews. Enough taking about it. Let's *do* it!"

Chapter 30

Plan *A* Preparations

Mei Lin and Hang-fu were awakened by the jangle of the telephone. Hang-fu answered. It was Eddie Chung, who said, "Hang-fu, this is Eng-fu in the lobby. It's 9:30. Are you ready to leave for our meeting with General Hua now?"

Hang-fu answered sleepily, "Eng-fu, I'll be right down just as soon as I get dressed. Guess I'll skip breakfast this morning."

Eddie laughed, "Well, hurry, Hang-fu, but don't worry about missing breakfast. I'll stop at a little cafe on the way and get you some hot rolls and coffee. You can eat your breakfast as we drive to the meeting. That way we'll be on time."

Hang-fu, now wide awake, answered, "OK, Eng-fu. I'll be down in a minute."

When Hang-fu got to the lobby of the Brothers Hotel, Eddie Chung was waiting for him. As they walked outside to his car, Eddie asked, "How was Mei Lin, Hang-fu?"

Hang-fu grinned, "She's one of the best I've ever had!"

Eddie patted Hang-fu on the shoulder and responded, "Yes, she's one of my favorites, too. I tried something new last night – I slept with my wife."

Eddie swished through the heavy morning Taipei traffic, crowded not only with cars, but with seemingly thousands of motor bikes, many carrying two or more passengers in addition to the driver! He arrived at the main entrance of the MND building in plenty of time for their 10 am meeting, even though they made the promised short stop to pick up Hang-fu's roll and coffee.

When they reached General Hua's office, his secretary was putting a tray with three hot teas in glasses and a small plate of chocolate confections on the coffee table. She quickly left the room and discretely closed the door, as General Hua motioned the pair to sit down on his couch. He seated himself opposite the two men and said, "Hang-fu, I selected you for a special mission. No one else is to know about this mission – not even your boss, General Huang."

Hang-fu grinned, "And just what is the mission, Ding-fua? Not flying your girl friend over from Hong Kong, is it?"

General Hua smiled briefly, then with a serious look on his face, replied, "No, Hang-fu, this is a really important mission. We want to teach our enemies over on the mainland a lesson. They've been flying over our territorial waters with several squadrons of F-16's and MiG-29's several times a week. They know we can't touch them with our F-5's. Our F-5's are outclassed."

Hang-fu grinned and exclaimed loudly, "Well, I can sure shoot down those *mother fuckers* with the UTF. Probably do it with only two missiles, too!"

General Hua smiled, "Exactly, Hung-fu, exactly. Our super secret *Plan A* is to do just that. Use the UTF to shoot down the enemy planes intruding into our airspace."

Eddie added, "But, Hang-fu, our intelligence reports show that they usually send about thirty aircraft on these over-flights. They're really arrogant. You'll probably have to use all four missiles."

Hang-fu laughed, "Big *fuckin'* deal So I'll use all four missiles to shoot their asses out of the sky. When do you want to do it, Ding-fua?"

General Hua answered, "President Chiang said he wanted to do it as soon as possible."

Hang-fu exclaimed, "Wow! Even the President's in on the act! Well, this is mid March. I'd like to do it right away, but—"

General Hua interrupted a little haughtily, "But what, Hang-fu? Let's do it now."

Hang-fu answered seriously, "Ding-fua, you said you would like to teach them a lesson. I want to be sure we complete the mission successfully. We get our next UTF from the Israelis in July. I think we should wait until July so we have a back up UTF, just in case. Remember, we're already lost one. We don't want to attempt this mission and end up embarrassed. We want to *do* it."

General Hua thought for a moment and then replied slowly, "Well, Hang-fu, you have a good point. We don't want to fail. President Chiang would really be upset if we tried and failed. OK,

I'll explain our rationale to him for waiting until July to execute *Plan A*."

Hang-fu responded, "One other thing, Ding-fua."

"What's that?"

Hang-fu answered, "I want to get some help from Patricia Manos to work up a simulation and tactics to make sure we get them all."

Eddie Chung responded, "Hang-fu, that's a really good idea, but we have to be careful to keep this project secret. Maybe we can bring Patricia into the picture without letting her know about *Plan A*. She can be told it's just a theoretical exercise."

Hang-fu stubbornly insisted, "No, Eng-fu, that won't work. She's got to know. I want her to work with the intelligence data you folks in the CIA are collecting. I want our simulation to be like the real thing. Then I'll be sure we'll shoot down every one of these *mother fucking communists.*!"

General Hua responded, "That's logical. OK, it's all right to bring Ms. Manos into the picture. She can be the fifth person in Taiwan to know about *Plan A*, besides we three and the President."

Patricia woke Randy up in the middle of the night and said plaintively, "Randy, something's bothering me."

Randy said sleepily, "Patricia, it must be four in the morning. What in the world could be bothering you?"

Sobbing quietly she answered, "It's my --, my conscience!"

Randy, becoming more wide awake, asked, "You have a new lover and want to leave me. Is that it?"

Patricia forced a smile, "No, silly. Nothing like that. I'm not supposed to tell you about it."

"What do you mean?"

"It's a super secret project I've been working on. Eddie Chung said, *Don't tell anybody!*"

Randy, now wide awake, said firmly, "Patricia, you can tell me! I'm not going to tell anyone. Remember I have a SCS clearance just like you."

"I know, but Eddie said it was even more classified than SCS. I'll tell you as long as you make sure Eddie never knows you know!"

Randy said seriously, "You know you are much more important to me than Eddie. I don't want you worrying about something I know nothing about. Of course I promise to keep your information secret."

Patricia replied slowly, "Well, the Taiwanese are planning on shooting down a lot of Red Chinese Air Force airplanes, about fifteen F-16's and fifteen MiG-29's, using the RTF with Colonel Yung as pilot."

Randy asked incredulously, "You mean Hang-fu's going to fly over the mainland and shoot down a bunch of their aircraft? That could provoke a war!"

Patricia answered, "No, actually he's going to shoot them down over Taiwan's territorial waters They've been over-flying ROC territory now for over a year, several times a week."

Randy replied "Well, that different. That's a clear provocation by the Red Chinese. They should expect to be shot down."

Patricia replied with a loud sob, "But all those pilots – they'll be killed and I will have helped plot their murders. That's what's bothering my conscience."

Randy held Patricia closely to comfort her until she stopped crying. Then he added, "Look, Patricia, you won't be personally responsible. This is a geo-political matter beyond your control. The Red Chinese are provoking this action with all their over-flights."

She replied, "Thanks! That helps a little."

Randy continued, "Remember, too, those are professional military pilots flying those airplanes. It's not like the Russians who shot down the South Korean 747 Airliner flying over their territory. These planes have ejection seats. If the plane is hit by a missile, the pilot can eject and be saved. Hang-fu won't be murdering anyone. He'll be eliminating a threat to his home: the flying of enemy military aircraft over his territorial waters."

Patricia, becoming calmer, said, "Randy, after you put it that way, my conscience feels a lot better. But I'm still glad I told you."

Randy smiled and said, "And look, just so your conscience won't bother you about telling me, I'll tell Eddie I know and *why*! Don't worry he'll understand."

Patricia smiled, "My conscience is happy now. I can go back to sleep."

Randy laughed, "Well, I can't! You've got me wide awake. I want to make love to you now."

The final briefing for *Plan A* took place in the secret vault in AIDC. The vault was specially constructed to make sure no enemy listening devices could see or hear what took place in this hidden chamber. It was the first Tuesday in July. The second UTF was safely in the hanger, ready as a back up, if Colonel Yung should need it to carry out *Plan A*. There were four people present in the vault: Randy, Patricia, Eddie and Hang-fu. After Randy confessed to Eddie that he knew about *Plan A*, Eddie formally included Randy in the inner circle.

Eddie opened the meeting, "Our agent on the mainland informed us that there will be another over-flight of our territorial waters tonight. There will be sixteen F-16's and sixteen MiG-29's in the whole flight, divided into four groups of eight aircraft per group."

Hang-fu said excitedly, "Great. That means we'll use four of our missiles configured for *air-to-air*. We won't waste a single submissile."

Eddie continued. "But there's one complication. There's a big typhoon, Typhoon Linda, moving up into the China Sea. It'll be between us and the mainland by the time the flight of enemy aircraft reaches our territorial waters."

Hang-fu replied, "That's no problem for us, Eng-fu. I'll fly well above the highest clouds. But those poor bastards will be down in it at their altitude of 50 to 60 thousand feet."

Eddie asked, "But, won't they cancel out with all that weather out there?"

"Hell, no! Those yellow-livered bastards will think we can't see them with radar. The sneaky devils love a good cloud to hide in. They'll come."

Patricia added, "Eddie, when I realized this mission would be flown during the typhoon season, I made up flight profiles for the simulator that included typhoon weather. Hang-fu has already spent many hours practicing with exactly the conditions we expect tonight."

Hang-fu said excitedly, "You bet your ass, Eng-fu. I'm ready for those *mother fuckers* tonight. They're as good as dead!"

Patricia gasped at his comment.

Randy interjected, "Hang-fu meant the aircraft would be dead, not the pilots. Right, Hang-fu?"

Hang-fu laughed and said, "Yes, that's what I meant. Those pilots will eject just like I did in the first UTF test."

Eddie added, "Our navy patrol boats are ready to pick up the pilots from the sea. We want to embarrass the enemy by liberating their pilots to the freedom of Taiwan."

Patricia asked with surprise in her voice, "You mean the Red Chinese pilots would want to stay in Taiwan? Instead of returning to their families?"

Eddie laughed, "Patricia, everyone wants to escape from Red China, even their pilots!"

Chapter 31

Plan *A* Mission Completed

General Hua, Eddie Chung, Randy, and Patricia were in the special observation tower on the secret area of AIDC where President Chiang had witnessed the destructive power of the UTF a few months earlier. They concentrated on the faint glow from a light on the back of the truck holding the sleek UTF sitting on it's tail and mounted on the solid rocket booster all ready to go. There was a special encrypted radio transceiver in the observation tower along with the three video monitors that would let the trio watch the *Plan A* mission as it progressed. The voice channels and the video channels were encrypted and used the special spread spectrum wave form that made the interception and jamming of the signals from the UTF virtually impossible.

As Colonel Yung crawled into the cockpit of the UTF, he flashed a signal from his hand held laser flashlight to a receiver in the tower. When Eddie saw the laser receiver light flash, he said to the others, "That's Hang-fu's signal that we can talk to him soon. First, he has to crawl into his prone cockpit position and enter the code of the day into his transmitter."

Colonel Zien You was sitting in the cockpit of his F-16 aircraft. He looked to the right and to the left at his two wing men who were waiting on the wide runway for their leader to flash his navigation lights off as the signal they were about to take off on tonight's mission. It was another mission to harass their enemy, the Chinese Nationalists, on Taiwan. As they did routinely, they would penetrate Taiwan's airspace at very high altitude and watch for the Taiwanese surveillance radar to show up on their radar warning receivers. They wanted to make sure the Nationalists knew their airspace has been penetrated. Colonel Zien thought to himself, as he looked at the two sleek MiG-29's on either wing tip and the two F-16's right behind him, *We'll show those dirty fascists on Taiwan that we can enter their airspace any time we want. Those F-5's of theirs can't touch our F-16's and MiG-29's!'*

Colonel Zien was the leader of this evening's intrusion. He had 32 aircraft including his own: sixteen F-16's and sixteen MiG-29's organized into four groups of eight. Colonel Zien's group would be the leaders tonight.

Suddenly the green light on Colonel Zien's special coded panel came on, along with a high pitched *beep, beep, beep.* It was his authorization from the control tower that his flight of 32 planes were cleared for takeoff. Colonel Zien jammed the throttle forward into the afterburner position as he turned off his navigation lights to signal the other seven in his group to follow him down the runway for a formation takeoff. The other three groups followed at ten second intervals. Seventy five seconds after Colonel Zien received the green light, all 32 aircraft were airborne, climbing to their cruise altitude of 55,000 feet.

As he climbed out, he remembered the weather briefing they had received thirty minutes before mounting their aircraft. There was a nasty typhoon named Linda between the mainland and Taiwan. The weather briefer had assured them that if they would head for a point halfway between Taipei and Taichung and then turn directly towards Taichung, they would avoid the worst build-ups. They would be able to thread their way through the big cumulus cloud build-ups associated with the typhoon. The tops of these monstrous clouds reached to almost 80,000 feet. There was no hope of going on top. They would just have to go around them. They were using their forward looking radar in the weather mode to see the centers of the cumulus clouds and avoid them.

As usual this harassment mission proceeded smoothly without any problems, other than threading around the huge clouds in their path. Some forty minutes after takeoff, they reached the point where the weather man said they could turn south towards Taichung for this evening's penetration of Taiwan's airspace. Sure enough, the weather radar showed that to be a good track. They would fly within three miles of the coast line before turning on their afterburners and turning back towards the mainland. Colonel Zien thought to himself, 'If we're lucky, we'll cause some sonic booms so those fascist bastards will know we visited them again tonight!'

Hang-fu's voice came over the loudspeaker in the tower, "White Team, this is White Stallion, ready to launch when you give the word, over."

"White Stallion, this is White Team. We read you loud and clear. We just received word that Red Team has departed from their home base. We estimate your liftoff will be in ten minutes. We will advise as soon as we have radar confirmation that Red Team is entering White Team's space, over."

"Roger, White Team, White Stallion here. I'm ready to rip. I've got four red hot pokers to jam up Red Team's ass. All configured and checked out for air-to-aid mode."

"Roger, White Stallion, understand. Be patient. You'll have your chance soon."

Several minutes later a voice came over the loudspeaker, "White Team, this is White Surveillance. We have Red Team in view on *Big Eye*. *Big Eye's* predicted vector predicts they will enter White Team's space in three minutes and two zero seconds. Penetration will be in sector x-ray."

"Roger, White Surveillance, understand penetration in three minutes and two zero seconds."

"That's affirmative, White Team. Will advise of any change. White Surveillance out."

A minutes or so later, White Surveillance reported, "White Team, this is White Surveillance. Red Team just went into afterburner. They turned south and will enter White Team's space in ten seconds. Oh, they just penetrated sector victor-two. Out."

"Roger, White Surveillance. Out."

Eddie exclaims to the others in the observation tower, "Those bastards really have their nerve. They're penetrating our airspace right here off the coast from Taichung."

Then he switched on the transceiver connected to the UTF and reported, "White Stallion, you are cleared for immediate lift off. Red Team just penetrated sector victor-two. Good luck!"

"Roger, White Team. Those *mother fuckers* will be sorry this time. Here goes. Out."

The quartet in the observation tower concentrated on the white flame from Hang-fu's solid rocket booster. The initial acceleration of 20 g's made the UTF, which could be seen dimly from the rocket's glare, seem to leap into the sky. In a few seconds the plane disappeared into the overcast above.

Less than two minutes later, Hang-fu's voice came over the loud speaker in the tower, "White Team, this is White Stallion, have Red Team in sight on Little Eye. Confirm Big Eye's position report. Expect action in thirty-five seconds. Current distance 69 nautical miles at 12 o'clock from my position."

The four observers gazed at one of the video monitors in the control tower, watching the radar image of Little Eye. The thirty-two Red Chinese aircraft looked like four blobs separated by short distances.

General Hua exclaimed excitedly, "Our enemies are about to receive an expensive lesson. This will teach them not to over-fly our territorial waters."

Several seconds later, the loudspeaker blared again, "White Team, this is White Stallion. My four red hot pokers are on their way. Headed right at Red Team. Impact in 40 seconds!"

The quartet in the tower fixated on the image as seen by two of the four missiles which were heading for the four blobs of Red Team's 32 aircraft. The blobs grew in size. After about 30 seconds, the blob that each missile was headed for got bigger and the quartet made out the eight smaller dots, one for each of the eight aircraft in the blob. The video screen went blank for a second when the submissiles were deployed. The screen then showed one of the submissiles headed for the aircraft it was homing on. Then the screen went blank again.

Hang-fu yelled into the mike, "I think I got every one of those 32 *mother fuckers*!"

The other speaker came on and reported, "White Team, this is White Surveillance. All Red Team's targets have disappeared from Big Eye. Out."

Eddie yelled, "We really did it, Ding-fua! We taught the bastards a lesson."

Then Eddie switched on the mike and said, "White Stallion, White Team here. Big Eye confirms that Red Team is gone! Congratulations!"

Colonel Zien had just noticed from his inertial navigation set that they were about three minutes from the point of turning back, when suddenly the missile attack section of his threat warning panel lit up like a Christmas tree. He reached over and switched on the missile jamming and countermeasures systems. A few seconds later he saw his two wing men explode in brilliant white flames. An instant later he felt a sickening jolt to his aircraft as one of Hang-fu's red hot pokers struck his jet engine intake. He barely had time to punch the eject button before he lost consciousness.

The next thing Colonel Zien remembered was a bright light shining in his face. Two sailors were grabbing him by the parachute shrouds still attached to his chest pack chute. They were shouting in Chinese, "Colonel, don't worry. You're safe now. You're going to be OK now, and *free,* too!"

Colonel Zien shoot his head to clear his brain. He realized he was wet and floating in water. The two husky sailors lifted him up and pulled him into the big eight man rubber inflatable dinghy. Another sailor jammed the throttle on the 100 horsepower outboard engine forward and the boat headed for a patrol boat a short distance away. Colonel Zien looked behind him in the boat. He was surprised to see two more pilots, one from a MiG-29 and another F-16 pilot, from his flight.

He muttered to one of them, "What the *fuck* happened anyway?"

The other pilot mumbled, "Colonel, Sir, I don't know. The last thing I remember was a big flash and I punched out!"

One of the two sailors who pulled Colonel Zien out of the water said, "Don't worry, Sir. You'll be safe inside Taichung Harbor within an hour and a half. We just got word the center of Typhoon Linda is headed our way. We've got to get out of here."

Zien shocked by all this news, asked, "You mean your ship's from Taiwan, not China?"

The sailor replied proudly, "Taiwan *is* China, Sir. The Republic of China."

Zien said nothing else and a sullen look settled on his face. The men and the dinghy were hoisted out of the water by a hook and cable. By now the waves were breaking over the sides of the patrol boat. As soon as they were aboard, the engines of the patrol boat roared into action and it started cutting though the rough water heading for port.

The sailors led the three pilots from the rubber dinghy into the ship's ward room. Colonel Zien was amazed to see fourteen other of his pilots: a total of seventeen survivors from his ill fated flight!

Randy and Patricia, tired by the evening's excitement, left the group and returned to the privacy and quiet of their Taichung apartment. General Hua and Eddie Ching hurried to the AIDC headquarters building where they planned to telephone President Chiang, using a red secure phone in the secret vault. But before making the call, they waited until Colonel Yung joined them, having already landed safely from his mission.

A few minutes later Colonel Yung swaggered into the secure vault, laughed and boasted, "Just think, Ding-fua, the enemy now has 32 fewer fighter aircraft! Bet they'll stop this *shit* of flying over our territorial waters all the time now!"

General Hua responded, "Yes, Hang-fu, I think we taught them a lesson! I'm going to call President Chiang now. Eng-fu and I waited until you got here before placing the call to give the President the good news."

General Hua reached President Chiang on his private red phone, and said excitedly, "Uncle Ching-kuo, we did it! We really taught the enemy a lesson. *Plan A* has been successfully accomplished."

The President said happily, "Congratulations to both my nephews and Hang-fu. I want you all three to join me in the Presidential Palace at 3 pm tomorrow. You will all be awarded medals!"

Chapter 32

PRC Gets the Word

General David Hua, Eddie Chung, and Colonel Yung were ushered into President Chiang's office by his beautiful young secretary, who directed them to the sitting area. General Hua and Eddie Chang were surprised to find the President in a very bad mood. They had expected he would be happy because of the successful execution of *Plan A*.

The President opened the meeting by exclaiming, "We just received a radio report that Premier Deng Xiaoping just announced, *32 of our aircraft were lost in Typhoon Linda.* The enemy doesn't know we shot down their planes!"

The three visitors looked at each other in amazement. This was a development that had never occurred to any of them. There were a few moments of silence. Then Eddie Chung said, "Uncle Ching-kuo, why don't we tell our enemy what happened?"

The President was surprised with Eddie's suggestion, "And, Eng-fu, just how do we tell them what happened?"

Eddie grinned, "Easy, Uncle Ching-kuo. One of my female agents, Mei Lin, knows General Yong, head of the enemy's Air Force."

The President asked, "What do you mean, Mei Lin knows General Yong?"

Eddie smiled, "General Yong thinks Mei Lin is one of *his* agents. She gives him information *that we want him to know* about our Air Force when she slips onto the mainland to sleep with him."

The President smiled craftily, "That might just work, Eng-fu. How long will it take for Mei Lin to – er – *explain the facts* to General Yong?"

"Sir, if you authorize the operation, she can be in his bed tomorrow night. Mei Lin can make sure that General Yong understands what happened to this thirty two aircraft, that it was not Typhoon Linda."

The President grinned happily, "By all means, I authorize the operation. Go with it!"

The President smiled as he picked up the medals he was going to award to the three men and said, "In the name of the Republic of China, I hereby award these medals to you three patriots for a job well done: executing *Plan A!*"

He handed each of the men a medal and a certificate with the Presidential seal embossed on it. He added, "Eng-fu, Ding-fua, and Hang-fu, you richly deserve these medals and our Nation's Certificate of Highest Merit! Congratulations!"

The President personally pinned the medals on the lapels of their coats and then handed them their certificates.

He then said, "Eng-fu, please get Mei Lin to the mainland as soon as possible!"

Mei Lin's China Airlines flight from Taipei arrived in Hong Kong just after 7 pm. She took her small overnight bag and hailed a taxi. She told the driver to take her to the frontier of the People's Republic of China. The driver expertly wove his way through the chaotic Hong Kong traffic. Forty minutes later, Mel Lin paid him and walked across the frontier as she submitted her PRC passport to the guard. Thirty minutes later, she boarded a train for the trip to the big PRC Air Force base located near the coastline directly across from Taiwan. She arrived in the train station there just after 10 am. She walked the short distance to a familiar hotel where she checked into a room. Mei Lin thought to herself, *I had better spend a few hours sleeping this afternoon. I won't get much sleep tonight. General Yong is a real animal in bed!*

Mei Lin awoke just after 6 pm, all refreshed and ready for the active night that lay ahead. She laid out her fanciest, sexiest clothes. She then picked up the phone and called General Yong's private number.

When the general answered, Mei Lin said in her low, sexy voice, "Ping-ying, this is Mei Lin. I'm back. I've got lots of good information for you."

General Yong asked, "Where are you staying? The usual place?"

Mei Lin laughed, "Yes, Ping-ying, the usual place and the usual room."

General Yong replied, "Good! I'll send my staff car to pick you up. I'll meet you at the officers' club where we can have drinks and dinner. My driver should be there within twenty minutes."

Mei Lin responded, "Oh, Ping-ying, I can hardly wait to feel you again. It's so lonesome when I'm away from you."

General Yong responded, "Mei Lin, you couldn't have come at a better time. My wife's out in the country visiting her mother. You can stay in my quarters this time."

"I can hardly wait, Ping-ying."

Just as Mei Lin finished putting on her perfume and make-up, she heard a knock on her door. She called out, "Who is it?"

The voice on the other side of the door said, "Miss, this is General Yong's driver. Shall I wait in the lobby for you?"

"No, no, I'm ready. I'll be right out."

The driver, a lieutenant colonel, led Mei Lin down the stairs and out to the black staff car. On its front fender there was a flag with four red stars denoting General Yong's rank as a four star general, head of the PRC Air force. The driver opened the back door for Mei Lin and she entered. When the car arrived at the guard gate of the Air Force Base, the two guards carrying machine guns waived them through the entrance. A few minutes later, the staff car pulled up at the officers' club. The driver led Mei Lin into the bar where General Yong was sitting in a booth with several other Air Force officers. When General Yong saw Mei Lin approaching his booth, he motioned to the other men to leave. They discretely slipped away as Mei Lin joined the general.

General Yong stood up, grabbed Mei Lin and kissed her passionately. He then said, "How've you been, Mei Lin? I've really missed you."

Mei smiled sweetly, "Ping-ying, it's so nice being back in the People's Paradise. I just hate being with all those fascists on Taiwan."

General Yong patted her on the backside and responded, "Yes, I know. It must be horrible living among those *Nationalist Pigs*, but you are providing a valuable service for the motherland."

Mei Lin exclaimed, "Oh, Ping-ying, I've got some really valuable information this time. It's about …"

Yong interrupted and said, "Mei Lin, you've got all night to tell me your information. First, let's have dinner and then go to bed. I listen better in bed."

Mei Lin laughed, "Ping-ying, you're so eager in bed. You won't hear anything until after I've satisfied you."

"You may be right, Mei Lin. But dinner first anyway. My private dinning room is set up for the two of us."

General Yong led Mei Lin the short distance to the private dining room. The table was set in red linen with ivory chop sticks. Mei Lin sat on General Yong's right. Shortly after they were settled, three waiters dressed in crisp black uniforms carried in a variety of dishes. Mei Lin served General Yong and then served herself. Mei Lin thought to herself, *The People's Republic certainly doesn't stint on food. This meal is just as elaborate as any found in the finest restaurants in Taipei.*

After the fantastic feast, General Yong's driver took the pair to the general's private quarters on the Air Force base. His house was a grand edifice with several bedrooms and a lovely garden in an enclosed patio. General Yong led Mei Lin into the master bedroom and said, "You can use the connecting bathroom. I'll go down the hall and use the other bathroom and shower."

They both finished their showers and climbed into bed. Then began a period of warm love-making until they fell into a relaxing dream world.

The next morning Mei Lin and General Yong showered and dressed. His orderly served them a hearty breakfast. As they were drinking their orange juice, General Yong, said "Now Mei Lin, I can listen. Tell me this new information you brought for me."

Mei Lin smiled and said, "Ping-ying, your airplanes weren't lost in Typhoon Linda. They were shot down by *the Nationalist Pigs.*"

General Yong got a pale look on his face as he exclaimed, "Mei Lin, that's not possible. There's no way the Nationalist's F-5's could shoot down our F-16's and MiG-29's"

Mei Lin replied, "Ping-ying, they didn't use their old F-5's. They have a new airplane called the Ultra Tactical Fighter. Really high performance. They used this new airplane to shoot down your aircraft."

The general asked incredulously, "We had no idea they had a high performance airplane. How many did they use?"

Mei Lin responded, "Twenty-five." She thought to herself, *That's what Eddie said to say.*

General Yong replied incredulously, "But we didn't see anything on our radar."

Mei Lin lied, "The pigs are very clever. They hid behind Typhoon Linda, so your radar showed the weather clutter and not the planes."

Yong jumped up and exclaimed, "Oh, my god! I had better call Premier Deng right away and tell him. He personally announced on PRC radio that our aircraft were lost in Typhoon Linda."

Chapter 33

First Taiwan Made UTF

Three months after the destruction of the thirty two PRC aircraft, Randy heard Patricia sobbing in the bathroom. They had just returned from their office at AIDC. Randy rapped on the bathroom door and asked, "What's wrong, Darling? It sounds like you're crying."

Patricia opened the door rushed out, put her arms around Randy and sobbed, "Oh, Randy, it's horrible. Hang-fu just told me this afternoon there were only seventeen survivors from the UTF attack. That means fifteen men died. We really did contribute to their *murders*!"

Randy, shocked to hear this sad news, stroked Patricia on her back in an effort to comfort her, and responded, "But, they had intruded into Taiwanese airspace. They should expect to be shot down."

Patricia pushed him out to arms length and exclaimed angrily, "Randy, you're beginning to sound like a warmonger. Trying to justify a horrible deed. After all, they weren't entering Taiwan's airspace to bomb and kill people, just to test their ability to do so. They thought ROC only had slow old F-5's. Our UTF ambushed and murdered them! There's no other word that fits!"

Surprised by Patricia's strong reaction, Randy reflected for a moment and responded, "Yes, Patricia. I'm afraid you're right. We did contribute to their killing. I designed the airplane. You devised the tactics that Hang-fu used to shoot them down."

Patricia reacted, "And when I originally protested that it amounted to murder, Hang-fu said they would eject and be saved just like he was when the first UTF crashed."

Randy said sadly, "Yes, I remember. I believed Hang-fu, too. But we hadn't counted on the difficulty of rescuing the pilots in the stormy China Sea in the rough seas caused by Typhoon Linda."

The pair walked into their comfortable living room. Randy poured both a glass of white wine from the bar refrigerator as they settled into the soft leather couch. Randy put his arm around Patricia and said, philosophically, "You know, Patricia, we've both been involved in this weapons business for all our professional lives. Designing fighter airplanes and the tactics to use them to destroy targets all seemed so abstract. Until you realize they are really designed to kill the *people* in the targets as well as destroy the machinery --- airplanes, tanks, jeeps, or whatever!"

Patricia replied in an equally philosophical mood, "Up to now it has seemed like war games! Now the weapons you designed and the tactics I devised on the simulator actually killed real people. Men with wives, girl friends, children. Randy, we were part of a conspiracy that murdered them. There's no other way to look at it."

Randy replied sadly, "Patricia, you're absolutely right. But the strange thing is that no one will ever charge or prosecute us for the murders. In fact I forgot to tell you. President Chiang is going to present us both with medals for meritorious service to the Republic of China this week after the rollout of the first Taiwan-built UTF."

Patricia replied, "That's really ironic. We contribute to the murder of fifteen men and we receive medals of commendation from the President. What a rotten business!"

Randy replied, "That's not different from President Reagan awarding medals to the military leaders who participated in the bombing of Libya back in April of 1986.

Patricia protested, "But, that was really quite different. Libya and its leader, Gadafi, had been supporting international terrorism and killed innocent people."

"Maybe so, Patricia, but the bombs the US planes dropped that went astray killed innocent civilians in Libya. Those pilots didn't intend to kill the civilians any more than Hang-fu intended to kill the pilots of the airplanes he shot down. Both were by-products of military actions."

Patricia grabbed Randy in her arms and cried, "Let's get married, leave Taiwan, and forget we were ever in this horrible business of killing people, even in the name of defense."

Randy kissed Patricia passionately and answered, "I've already asked Eddie to be our best man. We'll get married as soon as possible after Thursday's roll out. Eddie said he would be busy for a few days after the roll out."

Patricia smiled happily, "I've already asked Mei Lin to be maid of honor. She said she would be out of town for a few days before the roll out but that any time after that would be fine."

Randy asked, "What shall we do after we leave here?"

Patricia answered, "That's easy. Let's go to Zürich for our honeymoon, count our money, and decide where we want to live and what we want to do then – not now!"

Randy laughed, "Your plan is a winner. We'll do it!"

On Thursday morning, the first week of October 1992, the observation stand was full of spectators who had come to witness the roll out and first flight of the first UTF aircraft built in Taiwan. The first row in the stand was occupied by President Chiang and the top political leaders of Taiwan. Randy and Patricia were seated on the second row along with the top brass of AIDC and CSIST, builders of the advanced fighter aircraft and of the aircraft's weapons systems. In the third row were the country's top military brass.

A cheer rose from the crowd as the truck carrying the stealth aircraft and it's attached solid rocket booster pulled into view. Colonel Yung stood proudly beside the new aircraft, wearing his silvered astronaut-type uniform, holding his helmet under his left arm. Hang-fu waved recognition to the crowd as they cheered him and his new aircraft. Randy turned to General Huang who was sitting next to him and said, "General Huang, this is a first to have a roll out and the first flight on the same day."

General Huang smiled happily, "Yes, it is only possible because of the thorough testing and systems integration done by Dr. Chang and his team here at AIDC. The simulations devised by your *bride-to-be* helped a great deal too."

Randy laughed, "I didn't think you knew of our impending marriage. We haven't sent out the invitations yet."

General Huang grinned, "The word gets around fast about such happy events. Actually, Colonel Chung *leaked* it to me."

"I hope you can come to our wedding. We'll be leaving Taiwan for our honeymoon afterwards. We want to say goodbye to our friends during the reception at the Grand Hotel."

"Don't worry. I'll be there even if you don't send an invitation."

"You're on the list, Sir."

Just as Hang-fu was about to start his work of flying the new UTF aircraft, Mei Lin finished her work, in bed with General Yong Ping-ying, commander of the PRC Air Force. The two were sitting up in bed. Mei Lin said, "Show me again, Ping-ying, where you'll be standing during the big military parade next week. I want to be able to pick you out. I won't be very close to the reviewing stand, you know."

"Yes, I know, Mei Lin. I can't very well get you into the family's seating area. My wife will be there. Here, I'll show you where I'll be."

General Yong reached over to pull the seating plan from a drawer in the bed side table. He said proudly, "Look here, Mei Lin. I'm only nine places away from Premier Deng this year. Last year I was twelve away from him. I'm moving up fast in the Politburo. Who knows, maybe I'll go from the military to politics someday soon."

Mei Lin exclaimed, "Oh, Ping-ying, I'm so proud of you for moving up so quickly. But, for you to become a political member of the Politburo, doesn't that mean someone has to die first?"

"Yes, of course it does. But those old farts are so old now, they're dropping off like flies. One died just last week and was replaced by Comrade Yung. He was way back in twenty-ninth place."

Mei Lin said, "That's strange. The name of the pilot who shot down your planes in July is named Yung. Colonel Yung Hang-fu."

"Comrade Yung has a nephew living among the Nationalist Pigs. His nephew has hindered his progress up the ladder. But he's such a loyal party follower and a brilliant strategist that he was finally allowed into the inner circle."

"May I have a copy of the seating plan? I would love to have it as a souvenir of this year's parade."

General Yong laughed, squeezed one of her bare breasts, and said, "Of course, Darling. I have another one at the office. Just don't tell anyone I gave it to you."

"You can be sure of that, Ping-ying!"

General Yong handed her the seating plan, and said, "I don't want…. to seem like I'm throwing you out, Mei Lin. But my wife will be home in a few hours. I've got to make sure my orderly gets rid of all of the evidences of your having been here!"

"I understand. I wouldn't want to cause a scandal. A messy divorce could harm your rapid rise in the Politburo, Ping-ying."

The general put his arms around her and gave her one final passionate kiss. Then he said, "Mei Lin, you're really wonderful. So understanding and so good in bed."

Mei Lin got out of bed, carefully folding the seating plan and placing it in her purse. She said, "Oh, Ping-ying, I can hardly wait until I can sleep with you again. But I need to dress and go now."

Colonel Yung Hang-fu, the test pilot, donned his astronaut type helmet, climbed into the cockpit of the first UTF to be built in Taiwan, and a few minutes later called the control tower, "White Stallion Two, ready for lift off. All checked out and ready to."

"White Stallion Two, you are cleared for immediate lift off. Have a good flight."

The audience heard the interchange on the loudspeaker in front of the viewing stand. A roar of delight went up. Then the white flame of the solid rockets lifted the sleek aircraft into the blue sky above. The video camera from the chase plane focused on the UTF so the observers got a clear picture of the airplane on the monitor as the booster dropped away and the ramjet engines accelerated the craft along. Today there would be no live munitions firing, only a variety of activities in the air to put the plane through its paces.

After twenty minutes of grueling maneuvers, Hang-fu exclaimed over the loudspeaker, "This bird is ready to go. It's even better than the ones the Israelis built."

A yell of national pride erupted from the crowd of spectators. A few minutes later, the sleek plane touched down on the runway in front of the observers. They all rose from their seats and applauded along with the cries of joy after the first flight of their fantastic new plane, built right here in Taichung by AIDC.

President Chiang was led to the podium at the front of the observers' stand by two of his security guards who took positions on either side of the podium, while he rambled into a long, but laudatory speech, on the accomplishments of the Republic of China in the aerospace field, citing the UTF weapon system as the culmination of their success. He ended the speech by saying, "And, will Dr. Chang, Dr. McLyle, and Ms. Manos please come forward for the recognition they so richly deserve."

General Hua rose to lead Randy and Patricia down the steps to the podium in front. He whispered into Randy's ear, "I just authorized Colonel Chung to transfer the half million dollar bonus to your account. Your contract is completed today!"

Randy squeezed Patricia's hand as he exclaimed softly, "Yippee, we can get married now. Hope you can come to our wedding, General Hua."

As they got close to the podium, General Hua whispered, "Of course, but now for your medals!"

President Chiang gave a short speech in Chinese for the benefit of the observers and then finished in English, "And so, Dr. McLyle and Ms. Manos, please accept these silver medals and Certificates of Meritorious Service for your role in our new UTF weapon system. And Dr. Chang, here is your gold medal for directing this magnificent team that built our new fighter, right here in Taiwan!"

General Hua carefully pinned the medals on the three. They turned and shook hands with the President who handed them their certificates while the crowd clapped vigorously.

Chapter 34

Authorization for Plans *B & C*

Eddie Chung parked his black BMW in front of the MND building in Taipei and hurried inside, heading for his 10 am meeting with General Hua. Less than an hour ago, Mei Lin had handed him the seating plan for the Politburo members at the big October military parade to be held near Beijing next week. She also brought a diagram of the order of flight of the big fly-by which was one of the main features of the parade. The order of flight diagram was an unexpected bonus. Mei Lin had used a tiny hidden camera to take a picture of it when she found it in General Yong's home office.

Eddie glanced at his watch as he entered the elevator. It was just before 10 am. Hang-fu should have been airborne thirty minutes ago on the test flight of the third AIDC built UTF aircraft. Eddie thought to himself, *After today we will have a fleet of six UTF's ready to execute Plans B and C, three built by the Israelis and three built by us.*

When he strode into General Hua's reception area, his secretary greeted Eddie, "Good morning, Colonel Chung, General Hua is on the phone with the President. As soon as he finishes you may go right in. By the way, I received a cryptic message for you from General Huang a moment before you arrived. He said, *Tell Colonel Chung that Hang-fu's flight was A-OK!* He said you would understand."

"Thank you. I do understand," replied Eddie who seated himself and began reading a newspaper to pass the time.

Soon General Hua's secretary announced, "Oh, Colonel Chung, the general's off the phone. You may go right in."

General Hua motioned for Eddie to be seated on the couch opposite his arm chair as his secretary served the two men hot Chinese tea in glasses with a tray of cookies alongside. After they interchanged pleasantries, Eddie gave Hua the good news about the morning's test flight, "Ding-fua, General Huang just left word that

Hang-fu successfully completed the test flight of our sixth UTF, the third we built. Looks like we're almost ready for *Plans B and C* next week."

I was talking to Uncle Ching-duo on the phone. He wanted to meet with us at 2 pm this afternoon to hear details of executing *Plans B and C."*

Eddie reached into his briefcase and pulled out the two papers that Mei Lin had just given him.

"Cousin Ding-fua, my agent Mei Lin delivered these two documents to me just an hour ago, straight from General Yong!"

General Hua picked up the seating plan for the PRC military parade and said, "I see mostly the same old names in the Politburo. Oh, I notice General Yong moved up a few places this year. I'm glad to see the communist enemy recognizes the talent of Air Force pilots."

Eddie laughed, "They recognize the talent of their CIA even more. The CIA director is in fourth place."

Hua smiled knowingly as he continued to scan the seating list, "Well, there are probably a lot of good men among these thirty Politburo members. Too bad they've all got to go according to *Plan C*. By the way, Eng-fu, who is this comrade Yung in position 29? A new face. I don't remember him before."

Eddie exclaimed. "Oh, I hadn't noticed that myself. That's Colonel Yung's uncle, Yung Hung-lo, an old party strategist. So he's finally been promoted to the Politburo. We had a devil of a time pushing Hang-fu's security clearance through because of his uncle. It's a good thing he doesn't know his uncle will be one of his victims – I mean targets."

Hua raised an eyebrow and exclaimed, "Wow, that's right. We better not let Hang-fu see a copy of the chart. I'll have a sanitized version prepared. We'll show him that. He has to see the physical layout of his – er – targets before he fires his air-to-ground missiles at them. We couldn't very well ask him to eliminate his own uncle. Are you sure he won't find out?"

Eddie answered, "Cousin Ding-fua, you and I are the only ones who have seen this chart, except for Mei Lin. Being one of my agents she won't talk to anybody about it. Besides she probably didn't even notice the name among thirty. Even if she did, Yung is a common name. She wouldn't necessarily connect it with Hang-fu."

Hua smiled slightly, "Then you do see a small probability of a leak – from Mei Lin to Hang-fu right?"

"Well, maybe a small possibility. I'll warn Mei Lin to tell no one, especially Hang-fu, if it would make you feel better. Of course, she is unaware of *Plan C*."

"No, that's not necessary. That's like telling her not to divulge state secrets to unauthorized persons. She's too well trained to do that. Beside the fact that she doesn't know about *Plan C* reduces the probability even further."

General Hua picked up the other document, and asked, "What in the world is this? It looks interesting."

Eddie responded, "It's a bonus Mei Lin picked up. She found it in a desk drawer in General Yong's home office. She took pictures of it with her micro-spy camera. I developed the film just before leaving the office to come here. I haven't had a chance to study it very carefully."

General Hua exclaimed excitedly, "Fantastic! Eng-fu, this should be a great help for planning *Plan B*. It shows the order of flight, the number of each type of aircraft, and the exact time the lead plane of each type is to fly in front of the viewing stand. Also, it gives the initial point twenty miles away. They're supposed fly in a straight line from the initial point to the viewing stand on a true heading of 240 degrees and a ground speed of 200 knots."

Eddie replied, "That is a stroke of luck to get this information! It will take all the uncertainty out of executing *Plan B*. But, Cousin Ding-fua, we have a problem in working out the detailed plan."

"And what's that?"

"Well, you told Patricia Manos and Randy McLyle that their contract is all finished. We need Patricia to help plan the mission, in view of all this new intelligence information about the fly-by."

General Hua pondered a moment and then asked, "Have they left Taiwan yet?"

Eddie replied, "No, they're getting married Sunday afternoon at the Grand Hotel. Here's your invitation. I'm to be best man. They're leaving Monday morning on the Singapore Airlines flight to Zürich."

"Good. That's several days away. Plenty of time to run all the simulations with the pilot, right?"

"Yes but how do we get her to do it without a contract? She's busy getting ready for the wedding."

Hua grinned, " Easy. With money! Tell her we'll give her a little 250 thousand dollar wedding present if she'll do this thing for us. OK?"

Eddie stood, laughed, "Yes, I'm sure she'll buy that. Particularly, if I assign Mei Lin to work full time getting everything ready for the wedding, so Patricia doesn't have to worry about the details. She can concentrate on the simulation of the – er – war games Right?"

"Right, Eng-fu. You go get Patricia's agreement to help right now before our meeting with Uncle Ching-kuo. I'll see you at the Presidential Palace at 2 pm."

Eddie Chung got back to his office just after 11am Mei Lin was delighted when she heard she would be given several days off to help Patricia take care of the details for her wedding. Eddie dialed the telephone number for Randy and Patricia's apartment in Taichung. Patricia answered the phone. Eddie explained his proposition for her to help plan an exercise for the next few days, starting that afternoon.

After hearing the proposition, Patricia responded, "But Eddie, are you sure this is an exercise and not some attack against real airplanes and targets? It's just war games?"

Eddie said reassuringly, "Yes, yes. Just a war games exercise next month. The Air Force wants to show the President what their new fleet of six UTF's can do against drones and ground targets., down south of Taichung in our bombing range there."

Patricia answered somewhat reluctantly, "Well, OK. I'll do it. But I sure wish you had thought about it last week or last month. I'll need to meet with Mei Lin and tell her what still needs to be done for the wedding. I haven't seen her since her trip to Hong Kong."

Eddie laughed, "Don't worry, Patricia. She's back. I just told her of her new duties to help you. She's on her way down to Taichung now. She'll meet you in your apartment by 2 pm. Thanks for helping us out."

Eddie Chung met with General Hua in the outer Presidential office ten minutes before two. While waiting for their 2 pm meeting, Eddie explained to the general that he had made all of the arrangements for Patricia to help with the simulation training for the mission called *Plans B and C*. Then he suggested to General Hua that the two of them travel to Taichung and explain the details of the plans to the six pilots who would fly the mission.

General Hua responded, "Cousin Eng-fu, while you were busy arranging for Patricia's help, I called General Huang and asked him to set up a meeting of the six pilots and Patricia with us in secret at AIDC later this afternoon. I've arranged for my helicopter to take us from the helipad here at the Presidential Palace to the pad at AIDC in Taichung immediately after we finish with the President. We should be there by 4 pm."

Eddie grinned, "Cousin Ding-fua, as usual, you are way ahead of me. We'll see that the simulation training gets properly kicked off, in the right direction. Remember though, I told Patricia that they were *war games* simulations."

"Right! *War games*!"

The pair were ushered into the President's office by his beautiful young secretary, who looked especially relaxed this afternoon. Eddie thought to himself as he noted her coiffure was slightly out of place, *It looks as though my uncle had a little sexual diversion with his lovely young plaything during his three hour lunch today.*

The elderly, but alert, President opened the meeting by stating, "Of course, since the October Parade is next week, and our new plane seems to be ready, I hereby authorize you to execute *Plans B and C*. Now tell me some of your details, my nephews."

General Hua responded, "Thanks to the services of one of Cousin Eng-fu's beautiful female agents, we have the seating plan for the Politburo and the order of the fly-by"

He handed the President the two documents, who looked at them carefully for a few moments and handed them back. He turned to Eddie and said, "Good work, Eng-fu. Impressive information.

Eddie answered, "Thanks, Uncle. Mei Lin knows her way around the enemies' bedrooms."

The President continued, "But how are you going to shoot down all those airplanes with only six fighters?"

Eddie responded, "We don't have to shoot down *all* their aircraft to effectively destroy the enemy's Air Force, only their front line fighters: their F-16's and MiG-29's."

General Hua added, "That's right, Uncle Ching-kuo. They have 160 F-16's and MiG-29's. Five of our UTF's with four missiles each having eight independently targeted submissiles will kill all 160 planes. The remaining planes are transports, helicopters, and really old fighters that are no threat to our F-5's. They could take them out any time."

The President asked, "And the leadership? How do we decapitate the thirty Politburo members?"

Hua answered, "That's easy, Sir! We send our ace, Hang-fu, after them with our sixth plane. He will fire his four missiles, each with eight submissiles targeted for one of the thirty. We send two each for the Premier and Vice Premier, just to make sure."

The President laughed, "I hope we don't get accused of overkill! Sending two after the Premier and Vice Premier."

Eddie laughed, "Sir, there won't be many left in the PRC leadership to accuse us of anything. But tell us, what do we do next? I mean, after we successfully complete *Plans B and C*?"

The President's face became grim, "That's when our responsibility for all of China will begin, my nephews. Eng-fu, by your latest Intelligence Report, you have a half million trusted agents ready to rise and assume all the current political positions. Ding-fua, by your latest Military Intelligence Report, you have a quarter million trusted agents ready to assume all the top military positions. Your trusted agents will offer the incumbents two choices, either become their deputies or be executed. They'll become deputies, don't worry. Meanwhile, I'll announce on radio beamed to our people on the mainland that I'm their new leader and demand their allegiance to their new government. All one billion of them!"

Chapter 35

Detailing the Execution

General Hua and Eddie Chung jammed on the flight helmets handed them by the helicopter crew chief and boarded the well equipped military helicopter whirring on the helipad of the Presidential Palace. As soon as they were fastened into their seats by the crew chief, he signaled the chief pilot. The pilot immediately adjusted the RPM to the take-off range and pulled back on the collective pitch causing the big specially equipped chopper to leap off the ground.

Eddie Chung leaned over and yelled into Hua's ear, over the rotor noise, "Well, Ding-fua, we're *green-go* for *Plans B and C.* Just think of it, this time next week, we'll be in control of all of China, not just Taiwan."

General Hua grinned and yelled back, "Yeah, just imagine! I think I would like to try being Minister of Defense. Too bad we have to shoot down so many of *my* planes. What job do you want?"

By now the noise had been reduced to a comfortable hearing level. Eddie Chung laughed, "I want to be Head of Intelligence! It's the plushiest job in government. Nobody can really check-up on what you're doing, because almost everything you're doing is too secret for anybody to know about. If you want to do something shady, just classify it to a very high level. Then none of the watch dogs can find out about it. Ridiculous, isn't it?"

General Hua grinned, "You may be right, Eng-fu, but I like the ministry of defense job. It's got the real power and money in government. Besides, you've got all those generals and admirals kowtowing to you, hoping to get the money for their special projects. And just in case, you've got their loyalty. That is, if you'd like to move up."

Eddie laughed, "You mean, if you want to pull a military coup, right?"

"Right!"

"Remember, Intelligence is there to kick you up, if you need help."

General Hua said, "Getting back to reality, Eng-fu, we've got to get the mission planned and well worked out first."

Eddie replied, "We have to give instructions to the two teams this afternoon. The *simulated training flights* are just a matter of *crank grinding*."

Hua responded, "I guess you're right about the crank grinding, but what two teams do you mean? I was thinking about only one team. "

Eddie laughed, "You don't have a devious mind like I have. There's no reason for the five fighter jocks, who are going to shoot down the 160 F-16's and MiG-29's, to know about the Politburo targets. So we will brief them on the order of the fly-by and then excuse them from the meeting. Only Hang-fu and Patricia need to know about both parts."

Hua responded, "Good thing Eng-fu. But why do Hang-fu and Patricia need to know about both plans?"

"Patricia needs know so the two attacks are completely timed to interleave in the proper sequence. We want the leadership to be hit just a few seconds before the aircraft are hit. Otherwise, the leadership would know something was wrong and would duck or run and hide."

Hua said, "Excellent, Eng-fu. I hadn't thought of that. And if the leaders' stand is hit too soon before the airplanes are hit, the planes' pilots might panic and break formation. Right?"

Eddie grinned, "Right! Now you've got it. If the planes in the fly-by broke formation and dispersed, it would make it almost impossible to pick out the 160 specific aircraft we want to destroy."

General Hua appeared more relaxed now, and said, smiling, "Eng-fu, I feel much better now that we have our scenario worked out. With our six aircraft at 150 thousand feet altitude, a hundred miles away, the enemy will never know what hit them. What a perfect set up the October military parade is for eliminating our enemy's leadership and his Air Force."

Eddie replied, "We should be through explaining the scenario to the two teams by 5 pm. Then I've got a special treat for you tonight, Ding-fua. You've been working too hard lately, and so have I. To help us relax, I've arranged for two twenty-one year old girls to meet us in our hotel at 6. We'll have dinner, dance, and then make love all night. How does that sound?"

"Eng-fu, that sounds like paradise! You do have a good mind!"

The big chopper was set down on the helipad outside the AIDC headquarters building just before 4 pm. The two men strode from the helicopter to the entrance of the building and went directly to the secret vault where the six pilots and Patricia were sitting at the oblong conference table sipping tea. The seven rose as the pair entered. The six pilots saluted the general smartly. Hua returned their salute.

General Hua opened the meeting, "We have a war games exercise planned at our bombing range south of Taichung in early November. Since President Chiang is going to personally witness these war games, I want the simulation training to be as realistic as possible."

Eddie Chung added, "For purposes of the war games we want to simulate an operation against the PRC Air Force during their annual October military parade and fly-over held near Beijing. So the geography of the fly-by should be in accordance with this fly-by schedule."

Eddie handed everyone a copy of the order of flight, and stated, "Since the fly-by is scheduled to pass the reviewing stand at exactly 12 noon local time, the strike on the enemy aircraft has to be timed to fit that schedule."

General Hua added, "And, Gentlemen, the objective of your war games exercise is to pick out the 160 F-16's and MiG-29's from the more than five hundred aircraft in the fly-by. We want each of the five pilots for the air-to-air attack to be assigned 32 targets to kill with your four air-to-air configured missiles."

Eddie smiled, "Yes, we don't want to waste even one of the 160 submissiles by killing the same aircraft twice."

The pilot's laughed and Hang-fu responded, "General Hua, I think our mission is very clear. Patricia and we pilots should be able to work out all the details of this mission and have a few hours of simulation training under our belts by this time tomorrow. Is there anything else?"

General Hua looked at Eddie Chung for guidance. Eddie whispers something into Hua's ear. Then the General said, "We have one other matter for just the pilots. Patricia, may we ask you to leave for a short time? Have a cup of coffee down the hall or perhaps *sing a song*? This next discussion is at a clearance level beyond your access. Do you mind?"

Patricia smiled, ""No, sir, I don't mind at all. Maybe I should *sing a song*, if this meeting is going to last much longer."

Hua smiled, "Thank you, Patricia. We'll need you for another thirty minutes after we finish with the pilots."

After Patricia left the room, General Hua rose and said, "Gentlemen, this is not a war games exercise as we stated in front of Ms. Manos. It's the real thing. This plan has the highest security clearance. The code word for your mission is *Plan B*. You are going to destroy the heart and the threat of the PRC's Air Force next week – Monday – once and for all! Your simulation training should be taken seriously. Tell no one else about these plans, not your wives nor girl friends, not your fellow pilots. And especially not Patricia Manos. You must be ready to take off under my verbal orders at exactly 11 am local time Monday morning. This is an extremely crucial operation, authorized by President Chiang himself. Now, go and do your training and do a good job. Good luck! "

There was a low murmur of excitement among the pilots as they heard this news about their mission.

General Hua added, "You may all be excused now, except Colonel Yung who will be assigned as back up in case one of your aircraft or missiles should malfunction."

The other five pilots rose, saluted smartly, and started to exit.

Eddie called to a young major in the group nearest to him and said, "Please ask Ms. Manos to rejoin us in the vault."

"Yes, Sir. I will, Sir."

A few minutes later, Patricia rejoined the three men in the vault. General Hua rose, "Now, for the air-to-ground part of the war games exercises. We classify these as small, soft targets."

Hua handed the others copies of the *sanitized* seating plans and added, "Hang-fu, your mission is to destroy these thirty soft targets with your missiles configured in the air-to-ground mode."

Hang-fu responded, "But, Ding-fua, I have enough submissiles to destroy 32 targets. What do I do with the extra two?"

Hua answered, "Target the extra two submissiles on the soft targets in positions one and two on the diagram."

"Yes, Sir. That's easy."

Patricia looked at General Hua and asked, "Looking at your diagrams, the soft targets look like humans. Who are they?"

Eddie answered, "Patricia, they are supposed to be a group of Air Force brass reviewing a big fly-by of their aircraft. You know, something generals like to do."

"But why do you want to kill them, even in a war games exercise?"

General Hua answered, "Patricia, we don't really want to kill them. It's just that we want to show the President that not only can we shoot down a lot of airplanes, but also at the same time, we could destroy closely grouped ground targets, even foot soldiers, if necessary."

Patricia, not satisfied with this answer, retorted, "Well, that seems like a waste for a war games exercise. Why not destroy a group of tanks instead?"

General Hua said firmly, "Patricia, I'm afraid the Advisory Group in the Ministry of National Defense selected these target examples for the war games. I'm not free to change their selections."

Patricia replied, "Well, it seems really dumb to me, but we'll work out the simulation to destroy them. Any other constraints on the attack we should know about?"

General Hua replied, "Yes, Patricia and Hang-fu, there is an important restraint. The ground targets should be destroyed first and then within a few seconds the aircraft should be destroyed. This order of destruction is very important."

Eddie Chung added, "One other thing. If you look at the diagram for the fly-by, you will see that all aircraft in the fly-by line up four abreast and fly in a straight line from the initial point to in front of the reviewing stand, a distance of twenty nautical miles. It's important to wait until all the aircraft are strung along this twenty mile line before attaching them."

Patricia responded brightly, "I see. I think I have the picture now. I'll get the simulation program written tonight. The training simulation can start at 8 am tomorrow morning." She stood up, getting ready to leave.

General Hua stood also, grinned broadly and said, "That's wonderful, Patricia. Thanks for coming back and helping us with this simulation. I really appreciate it. Sorry the meeting lasted so long."

He then turned to Hang-fu and said, "Please stay over a few minutes, Hang-fu. We need to brief you on one other matter before you leave."

After Patricia had left, Eddie Ching made sure the vault door was safely closed and locked to give the three remaining participants in the meeting complete privacy. Then General Hua looked Hang-fu straight in the eye and said, "Hang-fu, your targets next Monday are the enemy's evil ruling group – the Politburo. The code name for your mission is *Plan C*. You must not fail. Your President is relying on you. Your nation of a billion people are relying on you to root out this evil nest of communists once and for all. Then all our people can be free once again. Not just the ones in Taiwan! Understand?"

"Yes, Sir! I understand. Don't worry, you can depend upon me!"

During the next two days, Patricia and the six pilots worked hard at the simulation training until all six pilots could execute their portions of the mission easily and repeatedly. The aircraft and ground targets were all destroyed each time they ran the realistic war games simulation.

At 2 pm Saturday, Hang-fu crawled out of his simulation cockpit and exclaimed, "Patricia, we're all six ready for the war games now. You go home and get ready for your wedding tomorrow. I'll be there with Mei Lin. I'm going to enjoy seeing you as a bride instead of a *computer nerd*!"

Chapter 36

The Wedding Night

Patricia left the simulation laboratory, exhausted from the long hours she has spent the last couple of days working so hard on the simulation training for the war games. She drove home through the north gate of AIDC and wound her way through the narrow streets of the village bordering the big aerospace complex. She was careful to avoid the chickens, pedestrians, bicyclists, mopeds, and occasional car. She smelled the pungent odors from the roadside cafes, food stands, and open sewers. She suddenly felt she would miss these odors when she left Taiwan. At first they had been strange to her nostrils. Now they smelled like *home*.

But in her heart she realized she and Randy wouldn't be happy for long in Taiwan, now that their contract was finally finished. The culture was just too different from the one in which they both grew up. Even though she and Randy had learned enough Chinese to read the local newspaper and to name the foods in the markets, their friends were the people they have worked with, who all speak English. Randy and Patricia had found it was easier to read a language than to understand it when people spoke it to them. Even harder was being able to say the words in the correct cadence and tone for the natives to understand their heavily accented Chinese.

When she walked along the sidewalks of downtown Taichung on her frequent shopping trips, she was the only Caucasian in a sea of oriental faces. Even though she was only 5 feet 4 inches tall (1.63 meters), she stood out like a giant in the crowd. The short stature of the Chinese, she decided, must be due to generations of undernourishment on the mainland, since Taiwan was a prosperous, well fed nation. She recalled the economic statistics from last year. Taiwan had a positive balance of trade of over twenty billion dollars. Not bad for a population of seventeen million – almost 1200 dollars for each man, woman, and child.

On the way home this afternoon, she stopped at the row of shops a couple of blocks from their apartment. This was a special night, the last night in their apartment that they've lived in for almost exactly four years now. Patricia was going to prepare a last home-cooked dinner for Randy. She bought fresh shrimp, a variety of fresh vegetables, and thinly sliced lean beef and pork. She bought mandarin oranges and vanilla ice cream. She planned to combine these ingredients into some six dishes which were her interpretation of authentic Chinese food a la Taichung. She and Randy had both stayed thin and kept their youthful appearance eating this healthful Chinese food and doing regular exercises. They had received pictures from their previous friends in the US who were beginning to suffer from middle age spread with puffy faces and veins probably clogged with cholesterol from eating too much fatty food including fatty beef.

As Patricia drove to their apartment with her groceries, she thought, 'I hope when Randy and I are in our early fifties like Eddie Chung, that we are as slim and healthy looking as he is. It must be the diet and exercise of his life style. Since we've adapted a similar life style, we should keep it up and benefit as we grow older in our super-early retirement.'

Patricia arrived at her apartment door with her four plastic bags filled with the special groceries. Mei Lin met her at the door and exclaimed, "Patricia every last detail is ready for your wedding. All you have to do now is get dressed, walk up to the minister and say, 'I do'!"

Randy came into the entry hall and took the grocery bags. He added, "Yes, Patricia, and everything is all packed ready for our honeymoon trip and the boxes are all packed with the things Eddie will store and ship to us later when we get settled in Europe."

Patricia laughed, "Wow! You two have been busy while I've been slaving away at the war games simulation. Guess what? We're all finished. Hang-fu and the other pilots are all ready for their demonstration next month."

Randy grinned, "Now you can relax and just get married to me!"

Patricia replied, "First, I'm going to cook you a final Chinese dinner in our dear Taichung apartment. Mei Lin, you're invited to stay for dinner, too."

Mei Lin said, Thanks, Patricia dear, but I've got to get back to Taipei. I promised Eddie I'd have dinner and go dancing with him tonight. You know how much Eddie enjoys such evenings."

Patricia smiled, "We'll miss you, but we understand. Thanks for all your help with the wedding. Well check into the Grand by 11am tomorrow. That should be plenty of time to get dressed for the 12 noon wedding. Right?"

Mei Lin smiled, "That schedule sounds fine, Patricia. Here's the key to the bridal suite. You're already checked in. The manager is a friend of mine and gave me the key before I left Taipei. I'll see you in your room to help you get dressed. Eddie will be there to help you, Randy. I've got to go now. Goodbye!"

Randy and Patricia chorused, "Goodbye and thanks!"

The marriage ceremony started on time at 12 noon in a special chapel for weddings at the Grand Hotel. There were over two hundred guests, friends and associates of Randy and Patricia from their four years in Taiwan. General Hua from MND, the top brass from CSIST, AIDC, and the many engineers and scientists they have worked with. Most were accompanied by their spouses or lovers. It was a happy supportive group of guests.

The pair were married by a Presbyterian minister Mei Lin helped to find. The chapel was decorated with many colorful flowers. The pre-vow music was beautiful and tasteful. The ceremony was formal and traditional. Patricia's flowing white gown was complemented by the pastel colors of the dresses worn by Mei Lin and the three bridesmaids from Eddie's office.

Randy with Eddie as his best man and three engineers from AIDC as ushers looked handsome in their tuxedos. The minister asked the inevitable question of both Patricia and Randy, They responded with firm *I do's* and the minister pronounced them *man and wife*, followed by the traditional nuptial kiss.

The newly married pair walked back up the aisle where Eddie and Mei Lin met them and whisked them to the large ballroom, where the reception line formed and the reception feast begun.

Two large dance bands had been hired by Eddie, one to play romantic music, one to play disco music. Over a dozen white coated waiters circulated through the crowd serving French Champagne and hors d'oeuvres. After the reception line was finished and the guests had danced for several melodies, Eddie mounted the stage and announced that the formal sit down dinner would commence.

A flock of waiters carried in a huge variety of Chinese dishes, especially chosen by Eddie Chung, which were served to the guests. The band number one played soft music during the dinner as the guests enjoyed the elaborate wedding feast. It concluded with slices of white cake cut from the multi-tiered, frosting covered wedding cake Mei Lin had ordered made by the hotel pastry chef.

Finally, at about 6 pm, as the guests began to disappear, Eddie again mounted the stage and announced the bride would be throwing her bouquet. Patricia climbed the stage and tossed her bouquet high into the air. Joy-tung was the lucky maid who caught it. Tradition said she would be the next person to be married. Joy-tung returned to her handsome escort amid the teasing words of her friends as to whether or not this was the man she would marry. Patricia noted Mei Lin was on the arm of Hang-fu.

Patricia and Randy exited the room under a hail of rice. They ran to the elevator and returned to the bridal suite where they spent all evening making love. Their Singapore Airlines flight was scheduled to leave at 9 am in the morning.

Immediately after Randy and Patricia left the ball room, Mei Lin and Hang-fu departed for her Taipei apartment. As they drove along in Hang-fu's low-slung Toyota sports car, Hang-fu declared, "Mei Lin, I've really missed you. Being with you really helps me relax before my high tech flights. I've got to leave before dawn for a very important mission. I have to check a lot of last minute details before the mission begins at 11 am."

Mei Lin kissed Hang-fu's ear as she replied, "Oh, I hoped you could take the day off so we could make love all day. I guess we'll just have to settle for all evening. It's early and I don't need dinner after that feast. Do you?"

Hang-fu laughed, "Mei Lin, all I want right now is to make love to you all evening. No food, just you."

Mel Lin responded, "Oh, good!" Then she reached over and hugged and kissed him at the next stop light.

Inside Mei Lin's apartment, the couple quickly undressed, showered and jumped into bed for their sexual activities. Just before Mei Lin fell asleep, she said drowsily, "Hang-fu, I didn't know you had an uncle who was a VIP in the communist party on the mainland."

Hang-fu laughed, "Yeah, he's caused me a lot of problems with security clearances over the yeas. But I wouldn't say he's much of a VIP. He's just a strategist for the party, sort of a communist intellectual, not much of a do-er."

Mei Lin smiled, "Well, he's been promoted to the Politburo now. He's number 29 in succession for the head of the PRC. I'd say he is a VIP now!"

Hang-fu got a shocked look on this face that Mei Lin couldn't see in the dark of the bedroom. He tried to regain his composure. He hoped his voice wasn't betraying his inner emotion as he said, "Well, it's nice to have a famous uncle, even if he is a communist. Let's go to sleep now. I've got to leave early, remember ?"

"Yes, Hang-fu I remember."

As Hang-fu waited for Mei Lin to fall asleep he was thinking to himself, *I've been assigned to execute my own uncle. My ancestors would punish me in eternity for doing such a dishonorable act. I can't do it! I'll bet Eng-fu and Ding-fua know my uncle will be on the platform. That's why the seating diagram didn't have names. Mei Lin works in Eddie's office. She must have seen the diagram with the names. How else would she have known. Just wait! I'll show those bastards! They can't make me disgrace my ancestors. Family is more important than government!*

Chapter 37

Revenge

Hang-fu waited what seemed to be an eternity, to be sure Mei Lin was sound asleep. It was really only about forty minutes. He slipped quietly out of bed and looked at his watch. Just past midnight. At this time of night he could probably make it to Taichung in two and a half hours. He can't afford to get a ticket. He doesn't want to risk being jailed by an irascible policeman for speeding. Fortunately he had a speed radar warning device that had proved reliable in the past. He dressed quickly, took his overnight bag and slipped out the door. He was lucky Mei Lin didn't wake up or even stir. In the morning when she finds him gone, she'll just think he left a little early for Taichung.

He thought to himself, *A good loving really makes a woman sleep soundly.*

He took the elevator down and nodded to the doorman of the apartment as he exited to the street. He started his car. Ten minutes later he was on the multilane toll road heading towards Taichung. Being a Sunday night, the traffic was light, picking up a bit as he approached Chiang Kai-shek Airport that had a few post midnight departures of jumbos for various destinations. He headed down the toll roads, only stopping at the three toll gates. He cruised at 180 kilometers per hour, slowing to 110 when his radar warning receiver lighted up. He avoided all tickets. As he drove along, his adrenalin supply made him very alert. He mapped out his plan of action step by step in his mind. He must do what family loyalty dictated. Time was very critical. He must also work out a plausible story for the security guards. He rehearsed the story in his mind over and over until it sounded logical and credible.

At just before 3 am he turned off the toll road onto the Taichung off-ramp, a curvy interchange. He skidded as he executed the sharp turn a bit too fast but recovered safely. He drove as fast as possible on the surface street towards downtown

Taichung.   He turned off along the convoluted streets leading through the quiet village outside the north security gate of AIDC.

The gate guard turned out to be an eager young man who insisted that he stop and open his trunk to allow the guard to inspect for bombs or other contraband.   Hang-fu protested to the young guard, "Look at my pass! I'm a full colonel! Besides, I'm on a special mission for the President!"

The guard, knowing his power, replied, "Colonel, Sir!   I wouldn't care if you were a four star general of a mission for Buddha.   There ain't going to be no bombs through this gate on my watch. So just be patient."

The guard poked around in the messy trunk, saluted, and said, "Colonel, Sir, you're clean. You may pass."

Hang-fu curtly returned the salute, climbed into his car and roared onto the grounds of the huge AIDC facility. He looked at his watch. 3:15 am. He mentally figured how long it would take to get ready.

He computed all the steps necessary. Then thought to himself, *I should be all ready by 4:15, -- 4:30 at the latest.   Good! That should give me plenty of time.*

Hang-fu arrived at the secret hangar housing the six sleek UTF fighters at 3:25 am.   The two guards challenged Hang-fu as he drove up to the hangar entrance. He got out of his car, showed his badge and said, "I'm the pilot of UTF-007. I've got to check out all six planes to be sure they are ready for the mission in the morning."

The lead guard said, Sorry, Sir, but you are only permitted to check out your own plane, 007. Strict orders from General Huang. Of course, it you'd like me to call him and get to countermand our orders, that would be fine. No other way! Sorry!"

Hang-fu responded angrily, "That's a hell of a way to treat a senior colonel. Don't bother calling General Huang. I'll report your attitude to him in the morning."

The guard replied sarcastically, "Oh, thank you, Sir. I wanted another commendation from the general."

Hang-fu said resignedly, "Well, at least, open the hangar door for me so I can roll my plane, 007 out onto the ramp for its final check out."

Sorry Sir, that won't be possible. General Huang's instructions are the hangar doors are to remain closed until 8 am. But if ---"

Hang-fu interrupted disgustedly, "I know! You'd call General Huang. OK, I'll do my check out in the hangar. But I'm going to write you both up for interfering with an important mission."

Hang-fu suddenly realized the roof of the hangar would slide back, making a large opening, big enough for him to lift off through. The guard's refusal to allow him to move the planes outside would make it more difficult, but not impossible to destroy the other five aircraft 002 through 006. When he entered the hangar he was shocked to see only three aircraft, not six!

He thought to himself, *I could ask the guards where the planes are. But they probably wouldn't tell me. The question would arouse their suspicions. The only logical space they could be was in a second secret hangar about a half kilometer away. General Huang probably decided to move the other three for security. In case of a hangar fire, at least not all six aircraft could be destroyed with one fire. General Huang was very safety and security conscious.*

Hang-fu went over to his aircraft number 007 which was sitting upright on its solid rocket booster on the back of a transporter truck. He climbed into the truck bed, walked around and visually inspected the aircraft. Everything looked normal. He checked the fuel tanks. They were full. He looked into the cockpit. Everything looked normal there, too. He looked up at the sliding roof.

He thought to himself, *That's the first piece of good luck tonight! I'm under the center of the hangar roof aperture. All I've got to do is actuate the roof opening motor on the control board in the back of the hangar and I've got stars above.* Hang-fu looked at his watch. It was 3:40 am He thought to himself, *I had better get into my flight suit and get this mother fucker ground tested. I should be able to blast off by 4 am – the perfect time.*

Hang-fu rushed back to the pilot's locker room and donned his silver flight suit. He grabbed his space helmet with the special visor. He then strode to the electrical switch panel and discovered he needed a key to actuate the roof opening switch.

Oh, hell! he thought, *I don't have any idea where that fucking key is. I'll have to take the face off the panel and jump a wire across the switch to actuate the opener motor. I'll have to use one of the battery jumper cables from the corner over there.*

Hang-fu got the cable, found a screw driver and wrench to take off the switch panel. Then he returned to the panel, gently set down his helmet as he thought to himself, *I've got to be careful not to bust my helmet. Its anthropomorphically fitted to my head and eye-balls. It has all my cockpit instruments projected on it.*

Hang-fu found it difficult to get the panel off. He stripped some screw heads and had to go back for some long nose pliers. After some agonizingly slow work, he finally got the panel off and found the proper connections for the sliding roof motor switch. He put one end of the battery jumper cable on and was about to connect the other end when he thought, *If I open the hangar now, the guards are sure to hear the noise and come in to investigate. I'll tell them I have to see the stars to adjust my sextant, -- but they may have orders to keep the roof opening closed. No, I'd better wait until the last minute after the plane's preflight check is completed. Then open the roof!*

Hang-fu headed back to the UTF, climbed up on the truck bed, and clambered into the cockpit. He looked at his watch. It was already 4:07 am. The cockpit check would take at least 10 minutes. He suddenly remembered a special hangar cleaning crew would come into the hangar at 4:30 am. Only thirteen minutes tolerance. He went through the elaborate computer controlled check out procedure. He confirmed the new mission tape Patricia had made for him Saturday was loaded. He then realized he had to reprogram this latest mission – the escape mission. He called up the fight map on his video screen. He moved the airplane shaped cursor in order to trace the flight trajectory to the airbase on the mainland where he planned to land. A few minutes later, this new flight trajectory was loaded. He checked his missiles. They checked out OK. He configured two missiles for the air-to-ground mode. He would have to destroy the other five UTF's on the ground. He configured the remaining two missiles for air-to-air operation in case someone was dispatched to intercept him, which wasn't likely.

When Hang-fu finished his checkout, he looked at his watch. 4: 26. Just four minutes until the maintenance crew was due. He scrambled out of the cockpit and ran to the electrical panel at the back of the hangar. He carefully placed the other terminal of the battery cable on the proper point. The roof started sliding back slowly. He knew it took at least thirty seconds to open fully. He dashed back toward the airplane.

Suddenly remembering his helmet, which was still sitting on the floor next to the roof control panel. He dashed back for it, then rushed toward the plane.

As he reached the truck, the two guards entered the hangar and yelled, "Hey, what's going on here? That roof isn't supposed to be opened! Orders from General Huang."

As the guards started running towards Hang-fu, he clambered up on the truck bed, scrambled into his cockpit, and slid the hatch closed. The two guards got to the truck just as Hang-fu was safely inside the plane. The roof aperture was now completely open. The guards, seeing they couldn't get to the pilot in the cockpit, started running towards the electrical panel to close the opening. Just as the reached it, Hang-fu pressed the lift off switch. At that same instant the guards initiated the hangar closing switch. The hangar was filled with clouds of white smoke as the sleek UTF accelerated off at 20 g's vertically. It took just two and a half seconds for the plane to roar past the closing roof aperture. There was plenty of room to clear. Hang-fu was home free, almost.

Hang-fu thought, *Now, I have to destroy those other five UTF's so they can't come after me. But first I've got to get altitude and get oriented to find those two fucking hangars.*

Meanwhile the guards called General Huang at home to report the theft of the UTF. General Huang immediately called General Hua on the red phone and asked for authorization to shoot down the UTF. General Hua, realizing he was overstepping his authority, authorized the shoot down. Then he called the President and told him.

The President screamed, "Kill the traitor! Why would a loyal ROC citizen do such a thing?"

General Hua answered "Uncle Ching-kuo, he probably found out his uncle would be on the Politburo reviewing stand. That's the only thing that could explain this act."

The President answered, "No, there's one other explanation. The Red Chinese have offered ten million dollars in gold to any of our pilots to defect with a plane. That's to counter act our offer of two million dollars for the same act."

Huang replied, "Well, at any rate, I have authorized him to be shot down."

"Good, my nephew. Good!"

General Huang was lucky. He reached two of his UTF pilots, Major Zin and Major Hsu, who were staying in the flight crew quarters only three minutes away from the flight hangars. He explained briefly to the pilots what happened and ordered them to get over to their UTF's as fast as possible, to launch immediately and to shoot down Hang-fu. The pilots rushed over to the hangars already dressed in their flight suits with helmets. As they drove onto the ramp about thirty meters away from the first hangar they saw sixteen brilliant flashes from two of Hang-fu's air-to-ground missiles. Hang-fu had targeted the submissiles to explode around the foundations to make the hangars to collapse. He was successful with one hangar. It collapsed completely and exploded into an orange ball of fire, destroying the two UTF's inside.

The second hangar was only partially damaged since due to the oblique angle of the projectiles, they missed the foundation by a few inches. Two of the UTF's in this hangar were undamaged. Zin and Hsu scrambled into these two UTF's as they bypassed some of the ground test procedures and, less than a minute after arriving, both pilots had ignited their solid rocket boosters and were airborne shortly thereafter.

Hang-fu attempted to assess the damage before departing. He wanted to make sure he had destroyed all five UTF's. *If necessary,* he thought, *I'll launch a third missile to finish off the mother fuckers.*

Much to his surprise and horror he saw the solid rocket booster flames of the two UTF's on his IR (Infra-Red) sensor just as they blasted off. This was the only moment the stealthy UTF's could be seen by sensors.

Hang-fu thought to himself, *They can't see me and I can't see them with our radar or other air-to-air sensors. The only thing that may work is eyeballs. Shall I hang around and shoot them down? Or head for the mainland?*

Hang-fu's fighter pilot instinct won the argument. He decided to engage them visually and try to shoot them down. It was just past 5 am now, still dark on the ground. But at 150 thousand feet of altitude, he was in bright sunlight. He asked his in-flight computer to predict the position at which the other two aircraft would reach the cruise altitude of 150 thousand feet. Sure enough, a few seconds later he saw the two sleek aircraft visually less than a kilometer away. He pressed the air-to-air missile firing switch before the other two pilots saw him. To be certain of hitting the planes he targeted four submissiles for each aircraft. Fifteen seconds later, he saw two brilliant white explosions as the remaining two UTF's of the ROC Air Force rained towards Earth. The pilots, Zin and Hsu, didn't have time to escape in their capsules.

Hang-fu headed for his ancestor's homeland. Four thousand years of Chinese culture had won out over the loyalty to a forty-four year old government.

.

Chapter 38

Ancestors Appeased

Hang-fu looked down as he flew north and saw the dawn light began to grow on the ground ahead. Overhead the sky was still black with a glimmer from the setting moon. He felt relaxed now. He was really home free. No other aircraft in China could touch him. He even had one more missile in reserve, just in case. But he didn't expect to have to use it. Ten minutes later he started his descent for landing at the Air Force base where General Yong was headquartered.

He thought to himself, *Here I am getting ready to land at the airbase where the 32 planes I shot down were based. Now to hope they don't shoot me when I roll back the canopy. Not much chance of that. They'll be too curious.*

The UTF was like the US Space Shuttle in that it had to land dead stick, without propulsion power. The design compromises to achieve performance and reduce weight led to using the ramjet engine which doesn't work below Mach 1. So when Hang-fu slowed down below Mach 1, the ramjet was extinguished and the engine stopped. He deployed the spoilers and quickly decelerated to 200 knots. He followed a steep 20 degree approach path, just like the Space Shuttle. The control tower operators hadn't seen his plane yet. It was too high and too stealthy to see. At 200 feet higher than the runway, he brought the nose up, flared out, and then touched down on the runway surface. Instantly he heard on his UHF emergency channel the control tower operator yelling, "Unidentified aircraft, you are not authorized to land here. Take off! Take off immediately!"

Hang-fu replied calmly, "Sorry, tower. I'm out of fuel. I'm Colonel Yung. I have a present for General Yong: this aircraft. I've just defected from Taiwan."

The tower operator said, "Yes, Sir. Understand, please turn off at the next high speed turn off. We're calling General Yong now. You'll be met at your plane by military police. Please don't resist. Welcome home to China!"

The military police set out a ring of armed guards around the UTF. Then they drove Hang-fu to General Yong's office.

Hang-fu was led into the Air Force headquarters building by four guards armed with submachine guns. They marched him down the hall with two guards in front and two guards behind. Hang-fu was still wearing his silver flight suit and his helmet, with the visor lifted. He looked like an alien from outer space. When they reach the general's outer reception office, his chief of staff, a one star general named Chu greeted the sergeant of the military police with a curt, "Thank you, sergeant. We won't need you or your guards any longer. Colonel Yung is a guest of the People's Republic of China. Make sure you keep a twenty four hour security guard on the colonel's airplane. It's very valuable.

The sergeant replied, "Yes, Sir! The guard for the aircraft is secured, Sir, twenty four hours per day."

Then General Chu turned to Hang-fu and said, "Welcome home to China, Colonel Yung! General Yong is on the telephone. Just as soon as he finishes, you can go right in. We all had to be up extra early this morning. This is the day of our big military parade, you know. The whole Politburo will be on hand to watch the Air Force fly-by. We have to leave for the parade area soon as it's a two and half hour flight from here."

Hang-fu responded, "Yes, I know all about your military parade and fly-by. That's why I'm here."

General Chu smiled, "Oh, I see General Yong's off the phone now. I'll take you in."

General Yong said cordially, "Welcome home to China, Colonel Yung. Do you mind if I call you Hang-fu? You may call me Ping-ying. It seems like I've known you for a long time now."

Hang-fu puzzled, responded, "Of course you may call me Hang-fu, General – er Ping-ying. But how did you know my name?"

Ping-ying laughed, "I'll be frank with you, Hang-fu, but I expect you to be discrete. Mei Lin, one of our agents from Taiwan, told me your name last August shortly after you shot down our thirty two F-16's and MiG-29's over the China Sea. I sleep with Mei Lin when she visits to give me such information."

Dumbfounded, Hang-fu responded, "Ping-ying, we have something in common. We both sleep with Mei Lin. When she told me in bed last night my uncle was in the Politburo and would be standing on the reviewing stand, I just couldn't go through with the mission."

Now Ping-ying was surprised, "What mission, Hang-fu? What mission?"

Hang-fu replied calmly, "We were going to use our six UTF aircraft to fly a mission against your military parade. The other five aircraft were to destroy your remaining 160 F-16's and MiG-29's. My aircraft, UTF number 007, sitting on your ramp, was supposed to execute the thirty Politburo members with my 32 submissiles. But when Mei Lin told me my own uncle would be one of the victims, I knew I couldn't do it. So I stole the UTF and here I am."

Ping-ying, dumfounded himself by Hang-fu's revelation, asked, "And what about the other five aircraft? Will they try the mission without you?"

"Not really, Sir! I destroyed three of them on the ground. I saw them burning with my electro-optical zoom sensors. The other two I shot down with one of my remaining two missiles. I saw them explode and burn with my own eyes. The only remaining UTF is parked on your flight ramp, outside!"

Ping-ying whistles, "Wow! What a story. Hang-fu, I'm utterly amazed. I hardly know what to say except, thanks for my life and your uncle's life. Wait until I tell this story in the Politburo meeting this morning. Well, I have some good news for you!"

Hang-fu asked, "And what is that, Sir?"

"You're going to meet Premier Deng and your Uncle Hang-lee at 10 am in the Premier's special parade headquarters. During the parade, he is going to present you with your prize and medal for bringing the homeland an aircraft from Taiwan. But he wants to meet you first. I talked to them both while you were waiting outside my office."

Hang-fu was surprised by this news and asked, "What prize and what medal? For What?

Ping-ying answered, "Our country awards a prize of 10 million dollars and a PRC hero's gold medal to any Taiwan pilot who defects and brings a Taiwanese aircraft with him. Didn't you know?"

Hang-fu, overwhelmed by this news, broke down and sobbed, "No! I had no idea! I'm just glad I stopped the idiotic *Plans B and C* – those are the code words for the mission we were to fly today."

Ping-ying walked over and wrapped his arm around Hang-fu's shoulder to comfort him, and said, "Hang-fu, I know this is an emotional experience, but you're among friends now. My private jet is waiting outside to take us to the parade. We're going to display your UTF in a military transport in the parade. Premier Deng thought of that. Today will be a really golden day for you."

General Yong's eight place executive jet landed at the military airport near the parade site at 9:30 am. General Yong and Colonel Yung boarded a military helicopter to carry them to Premier Deng's parade headquarters. General Chu stayed behind to arrange for the transport of the UTF-007 to the parade site for display during the parade.

Fifteen minutes later the helicopter sat down on the helipad next to the Premier's temporary headquarters. General Yong led Hang-fu into the building. They walked to the Premier's office and were ushered in by his military aide.

The Premier rose to meet the young man who had delivered the valuable present to the PRC. Hang-fu was amazed at how physically vigorous the Premier was. The Premier said, "General Yong, welcome to the People's Republic of China. We are so happy to have you here. You probably don't remember your Uncle Hang-lee, here. You were a baby when your father took you to Taiwan."

Hang-fu felt tears welling up in his eyes as he shook the Premier's hand and hugged and kissed his Uncle Hang-lee on both cheeks. Then Hang-fu realized the Premier had addressed him as general, not colonel, and he said, "But Premier Deng, I'm a colonel, not a general."

The Premier smiled happily, "You were a colonel in the Taiwanese Air Force, but you are a one star general in the Chinese Air Force. Congratulations on your promotion!"

Uncle Hang-lee added, "Congratulations, my nephew Hang-fu. You did a brave thing this morning. Your family, your country, and your people all appreciate your brave act."

General Yong added, "Premier Deng and Comrade Ying, you both need to know the full story of what General Yung did today. Then you will really appreciate his brave act."

General Yong explained *Plans B and Plans C* to the two men and detailed how Hang-fu destroyed the other UTF's before flying across the China Sea.

Now Premier Deng and Comrade Yung had tears in their eyes as they both hugged and kissed Hang-fu and thanked him for saving their lives.

The PRC October military parade was a colorful and impressive affair. There seemed to be over a million Chinese people crowding the wide avenue that all the massive military hardware rolled down past the Politburo's reviewing stand. Today a young man, General Yung Hang-fu, was seated next to his uncle Hang-lee, watching the parade. After the massive satellite launching rocket booster rolled by, the first of 500 military aircraft flew over, four abreast, at an altitude of a few hundred feet. The display of majestic airpower was overwhelming. And then, timed with the last over-flight plane, the sleek UTF-007 was rolled out on a truck and stopped in front of the reviewing stand.

Premier Deng rose and the vast crowd applauded and cheered wildly to see their leader there in person. He prepared to address the crowd over the powerful audio system. At the same time, his image and words would be broadcast throughout China and the world by satellite TV and radio. His speech would be translated into a multitude of languages. He was going for maximum impact on world opinion.

At the same time, Comrade Yung led his nephew to a position next to the Premier, who began his speech:

"Comrades and citizens of the world, I'm going to award the People's Republic of China's Hero's Gold Medal to General Yung Hang-fu, who is standing here beside me with his uncle, Comrade Yung Hang-lee. I draw your attention to this unusual airplane poised in front of me called the Ultra Tactical Fighter. For flying this combination rocket-airplane here from Taiwan, I hereby award

General Yung ten million dollars in gold to use as he sees fit. I have one other citation to make to General Yung. It's the Chinese Award of honor. As a result of his actions today, I'm alive along with the other Politburo members as well as the pilots of the one hundred and sixty F-16's and MiG-29's that just flew overhead. We all thank General Yung for our lives. By foiling the plot of the Taiwanese leaders *called Plan B and C*, I and my previously named comrades are alive this very moment. Our lives were to be extinguished under those plans ten minutes ago. I sincerely hope that I can prevail upon President Chiang to give up his insane idea of recapturing the mainland and to join the People's Republic of China as a peaceful, but autonomous part of the motherland. The Politburo has authorized me in a special session this morning to make Taiwan a formal offer along these lines. Over four thousand years of Chinese history dictate that he should agree."

Chapter 39

New Life

The television showed the big military parade near Beijing. There seemed to be an endless stream of war machines, tanks, armored carriers, smartly marching soldiers, etc. Then a fly-by of airplanes four abreast showed on the screens and the Politburo dressed in Mao coats were shown sitting in the reviewing stand. Randy was sitting in their Singapore Hilton Hotel suite living room reading the English language newspaper while watching the TV from time to time, while Patricia was in the bathroom putting on her make-up ready to go out for dinner. They had decided to break up their long flight to Zürich by stopping over in Singapore, a city they had both enjoyed when they stayed here before.

All of a sudden Randy yelled, "Patricia, come quick! You've got to see this. I can't believe it. Hurry!"

Patricia rushed into the living room with her lipstick half applied and asked, "What could it be, Darling?"

Then she looked at the screen and saw what Randy was excited about. The screen showed Premier Deng giving a speech and Hang-fu standing next to him, smiling. Also on the screen was a good picture of the Ultra Tactical Fighter sitting on a truck right in front of Premier Deng.

Randy gasped, "What in the world has happened. How did Hang-fu and the UTF get to Beijing?"

Patricia exclaimed, "Listen, here's your answer!"

"And I award a prize of 10 million dollars in gold to General Yung to do with as he pleases."

The pair, glued to the TV, heard the rest of the Premier's speech. At the end, visibly shaken, and angry, "Patricia exclaimed, "So that's what the *war games* we simulated last week were all about. I was tricked!"

Then she turned to Randy and asked pointedly, "Was there a fly-by of, say, 500 airplanes four abreast during the parade?"

Randy answered, "Why, yes, but how did you know? You were in the bathroom."

Ignoring his question, she said with tears welling her eyes, "And look! There are the thirty Politburo members sitting in the reviewing stand just like the diagram we simulated last week end!"

Randy walked over and took Patricia in his arms. Flabbergasted by her violent reaction, he asked, "What in the world are you taking about? You sound crazy!"

She wiped her eyes and spit out, "No, I'm not crazy, just naive! Randy, do you realize that I participated in a plot to execute the Politburo members of the People's Republic of China, using the UTF you designed? Furthermore, *Plan B* was to shoot down the 160 aircraft the Premier mentioned! Oh, Randy, I was tricked!"

At last Randy understood what Patricia had been telling him. He asked, "In other words, last week end while Mei Lin and I were getting ready for the wedding, you were simulating *Plans B and C* so the Taiwanese could attack the PRC military parade today, right?"

"Exactly! Exactly! I was told it was for a war games exercise next month that President Chiang was going to watch. What he was really trying to do was to re-take the mainland for the Nationalists by decapitating the communist leadership in Beijing!"

Randy commented, "It sounds like Hang-fu did the right thing. Plans B and C and the UTF could very well have precipitated the nuclear holocaust of World War III"

Patricia, aghast at this speculation, asked incredulously, "But how? How could the UTF and Taiwanese plot do that?"

Randy said, "Let me describe the scenario and see if you agree. *First*, the PRC launches a ballistic missile attack against Taiwan to punish them – in fact, eliminate them altogether. This would take, say ten ICBM's (Inter Continental Ballistic Missiles) with MIRV's (**M**ultiple **I**ndependently-targeted **R**eentry **V**ehicles) to destroy Taiwan, its military forces and most of its population.

"*Second*, the Soviet Union ICBM surveillance system detects the Chinese ICBM launches. If they wait long enough to determine the direction of the ICBM's are headed, and they are headed for Russia, it would be too late to retaliate. The Soviet leadership assumes that the Chinese are attacking the USSR and launch a retaliatory attack against China using, say, 50 of their vast ICBM arsenal. That's enough to destroy PRC's missile silos and a few hundred million Chinese.

"*Third*, the United States ICBM surveillance system detects the large Soviet ICBM attack. The American leadership assumes this is a pre-emptive attack by the Russians to destroy the US Minuteman missiles and MX (Peacekeeper) missiles in their silos. *Peacekeeper* – that's really *Doublespeak*, straight out of the book *1984*! Therefore, the US launches a counterstrike force against the Soviet Union with, say, 200 ICBM's with about a thousand nuclear warheads. Enough to destroy the Soviet war-making potential and half their population.

"*Fourth*, the Soviet Union detects the incoming missiles from the US and launches an attack against the population centers and missile silos of the US. Enough warheads to kill half the US population."

Patricia sat silently a moment, absorbing the impact of this terrifying drama. Then she exclaimed, "Randy, your scenario sounds very plausible, even probable. All from six UTF's that we designed and the *war games* simulation I designed"

Randy comment, "Exactly! A scenario, if not a blueprint, for how the nuclear holocaust could visit our blue-green earth, caused by a purely regional conflict using a small number of potent forces. It would eliminate civilization as we know it."

Patricia responded, "Randy, the Nuclear Powers – the US and the USSR – might be forced into these hair-trigger decision windows because of the short flight time of the ICBM's. I know we have both been critical of the Star Wars program, but right now it seems to be the only hope we have of preventing this Mutually Assured Destruction, MAD, as it is often referred to in the aerospace industry."

Randy added philosophically, "Well, Patricia, as we observe the world go by in our early retirement in Europe, let's both hope that the Superpowers come to their senses and negotiate a meaningful disarmament agreement. But I can see that unless all nuclear powers agree to destroy all nuclear weapons, which is unlikely, the world will still need a nuclear shield. Call it Star Wars, if you wish, but it will be needed!"

Randy and Patricia arrived at the Zürich airport late on Wednesday during the last week in October 1992. The pair took a train to the Zürich Hauptbahnhof and arrived there just before 5 pm. They had only two carry-on bags and it was a sunny autumn day, about 19 degrees C, so they decided to walk the short distance to the Zürich Hotel. They exited through the back of the station and walked through the beautiful green park called Platzpronenade. They strolled along the Limmat River enjoying the swans and ducks swimming there. They crossed the Drahtsmidlesteg (footbridge), crossed the Neumuhte quai and entered the lobby of the black, high rise Zürich Hotel. They found their suite on the tenth floor was ready for them. They took the elevator up to their room, unpacked their bags, and sat down to enjoy the view of the Zürich See, the big lake extending some fifty kilometers east of Zürich, while having a split each of champagne from their room refrigerator. They decided to take a nap to recover from their long flight from Singapore. When they woke up, it was 9 pm. They felt really refreshed now.

Randy suggested, "Let's walk down the Niederdorfstrasse, the night walking street, look at the people for a while and then have dinner."

Patricia exclaimed happily, "Oh, Randy, you have such good ideas. I'd love that!"

The pair strolled down the brightly lit Limmat Quai looking into the shop windows which held all kinds of appealing merchandise. When they reached Muhle, they turned north until they intercepted Niederdorfstrasse. They turned and strolled up and down the length of the walking street until Randy said, "Let's stop here and have a beer and a pizza for appetizers. Then we can walk back to that little restaurant that serves cheese fondue and have that for our main course. How does that sound?"

"Good. I feel like pizza and fondue tonight. Right now I'm thirsty for good German beer."

The couple easily found a table for their beer and pizza. Later they strolled back to the street and enjoyed a pot of bubbling fondue which they ate by putting small cubes of French bread on their forks and then dipping them into the goat cheese mixture.

Feeling the effects of the jet lag setting in, the pair returned to their hotel, watched a sexy movie on the room TV until 1:30 am and then tried out some of the sex positions from the movie before falling into Slumber land.

The next morning at 10 am Patricia telephoned their banker, Heinz, and made an appointment through his assistant, Gretel, for 11 am, to go over their accounts and investment strategies. After dressing, the couple took a leisurely stroll down to Bahnhofstrasse and enjoyed window shopping on the way to the bank. They arrived at the bank just before their appointment time and took the elevator to the second floor where they informed the guard on duty that they had an appointment with Mr. Heinz Steinbach. The guard ushered them into the reading library to wait for their banker. A few minutes later, Mr. Steinbach and his assistant Gretel arrived.

He opened the meeting by saying, "The growing size of your account with my bank has contributed greatly to my Christmas bonus for the last four years. Here's the latest statement for your account, showing a balance of over twelve million dollars.

Heinz handed Patricia the statement. It showed their current account to be worth $12,050,332.55

Patricia looked over the statement carefully and then handed it to Randy for his perusal.

She turned to Heinz and said, "This looks very good, and our current annual income is $1,132,731.26 or 94,394.27 per month. Would you recommend any changes to our investment portfolio?"

Heinz smiled and replied professionally, "No, I think your portfolio is optimally arranged right now. I'd recommend an annual review about this time of year to see if the market conditions then suggest any changes."

Randy commented happily, "Mr. Steinbach, we appreciate the professional manner in which you are managing our account. Now the only thing we have to do is to decide where to live."

Heinz responded, "Thank you, Dr. McLyle. I can't tell you where to live, but here's the latest issue of a booklet prepared by our bank that tells how much it will cost you to live in some fifty major cities around the world."

Patricia turned to Gretel and said, "Ms. Breunner, I'll bet you have some non-financial ideas about good places to live in Europe. We love the beauty of Switzerland and want to visit here frequently, but we think we want to live someplace warmer, like southern France or Italy."

Gretel grinned and answered, "As a bank official, I can't tell you where to live either, Mrs. McLyle. By the way, congratulations on your recent marriage. But, I just returned from my August vacation in Marbella, Spain, on the Costa del Sol. I know I would enjoy living there if I wanted a warm climate. With your income, you could have a really luxurious apartment on the sunny beach in an English speaking barrio. There are lots of Brits and Americans living there."

Patricia rose and said, "Thank you both for your advice. We'll see you next October, if not before."

Patricia and Randy went to the St. Annahof Department Store and bought maps and Michelin Tourist Guidebooks of southern France, Southern Spain and Italy. They returned to their room, ordered lunch from room service, and studied the maps and guides.

Soon Patricia said, "There seem to be many places where we could live happily in Europe. I thing Marbella sounds really good as a place to start. They have had a fascinating history according to those guide books. Maybe we could write a book about that if we find we need to do something to keep busy. Whatever we do, it must have nothing to do with weapons or war games!"

Randy grabbed Patricia, hugged and kissed her, and said, "I agree! Marbella, Spain it is! Let's move there in a week or two – as soon as we get tired of Switzerland, or it gets too cold."

Chapter 40

Exchange

The revelations given to world TV and it's enormous audience by Premier Deng about the Taiwanese had been very embarrassing to President Chiang. He appeared on a satellite TV press interview in Taipei organized by his Minister of Public Relations in order to counter the *lies* put forth by Premier Deng and the *traitor pilot*, General Yung Han-fu. During the press conference, the President was asked many probing questions by the veteran international press corps. The President stuck doggedly to his story that the PRC Premier was stating the *Big Lie*. The press corps tended to believe the President. They had a natural tendency to believe the free world leaders and discount what communist leaders, like Premier Deng, said in public.

Nevertheless, there were still serious doubts in the minds of some of the most knowledgeable and senior members of the press corps. These same reporters were given an opportunity to interview General Yung a few days after the big October military parade. This youngish general's hair raising story was very believable. He went into a lot of detail using charts and diagrams to explain the Taiwanese plot against the PRC leadership. President Chiang's denial did not wipe out the memory of this fighter pilot's story. The fact that the PRC leadership permitted such an open press conference in Beijing was in itself a very unusual event. Nevertheless, Taiwan was left with a slight credibility edge in the battle of minds.

After the Presidential press conference ended, the President called General Hua and Eddie Chung into his office and said, "My nephews, Ding-fua and Eng-fu, I'm afraid we're not going to be able to recapture the mainland this year. The failure of *Plans B and C* has been a deep shock and a disgrace to me. I wonder if I'll ever fully recover. But, time will tell. In the meantime, I want you two to get back our UTF aircraft. We can't let the enemy keep it."

General Hua asked, "How do we get the UTF back? I don't know where to start."

President Chiang smiled understandingly, and replied, "Use our bargaining chips. We have seventeen pilots we can trade for the airplane. Simple, yes?"

Eddie Chung added, "Uncle Ching-kuo, that's a brilliant idea. I suggest we send my agent, Mei Lin, to sleep with General Yong, Tell him what our offer is and feel him out."

The President asked cautiously, "But isn't it a little dangerous to send Mei Lin back to the mainland? Won't General Yong know by now that Mei Lin used the charts he gave – or that she stole – for us to plan the mission for *Plan B and C*?"

Eddie grinned and said, "No, Uncle Ching-kuo. I think that Mei Lin will be safe. We know now that Mei Lin told Hang-fu about his uncle being in the Politburo. That is what caused Hang-fu to defect. I'm sure that General Yong considers Mei Lin a heroine now. He believes she is a reliable double agent. Her telling Hang-fu even though it was without knowledge of *Plans B and C,* adds to her credibility with General Yong."

The President smiled, "Nephew Eng-fu, that reasoning is a little convoluted for my old brain to absorb, but I'll buy your conclusion. Yes, send Mei Lin to get the negotiations rolling. It just might work."

Mei Lin was a little hesitant to cross the frontier from Hong Kong to the People's Republic of China, but she accepted Eddie Chung's assignment to become the go-between for the exchange of the seventeen Red Chinese Pilots for the Taiwanese UTF aircraft. Eddie assured her that no harm would come to her. She wasn't so sure. She thought to herself, *When I get off the train near General Yong's Air Force base, instead of checking into my usual hotel, I'll call him from a pay phone in the train station. If his reaction seems threatening, then I can escape in the crowds at the train station.*

With this mental plan, Mei Lin crossed the border into China and took the overnight train. The next morning when she reached her destination, she phoned General Yong's private phone number. When he answered, she said, "Ping-ying, I have a message for you from General Hua in Taipei. He wants to exchange your seventeen pilots for the UTF."

"Mei Lin, where are you? It sounds like an interesting proposition. But I need to ask you a few questions first."

Mei Lin replied cautiously, "Well, I'm in Hong Kong. I wanted to see how you felt about the proposition – and about me. You know I gave the parade seating plan to my control officer in Taipei.".

Ping-ying responded, "Yes, I know, Mei Lin. I also know that you made a copy of the fly-by plan. Hang-fu told me all about it. He also told me you told him about his uncle being promoted to the Politburo. That's what caused Hang-fu to defect, - and that's what saved my life, along with the others."

Mei Lin said, "Ping-ying, please believe me, when I tell you I didn't know about any plans to kill people in that viewing stand. I didn't dream that was what they wanted to use it for."

"Ping-ying said kindly, "Mei Lin, of course I believe you."

Mei Lin asked gingerly, "Then you're not mad at me?"

Ping-ying answered in a friendly tone, "No, Mei Lin, I'm not mad. But you've been playing with fire! You could be *burned* by either the Taiwanese or the Chinese, if you keep up this dangerous life of yours."

Mei Lin broke down and sobbed, "Yes, Ping-ying, I know it's dangerous – what I've been doing. I want to get out of this dirty business, but I feel trapped."

Ping-ying comforted her over the phone, "I'm sorry you are unhappy. I have some ideas about how you can get out of the espionage business, if you really want to. When can I see you?"

Mei Lin feeling it would be safe to see Ping-ying now, answered, "I lied to you. I'm not in Hong Kong. I'm in the train station here. I'll check into my usual hotel in a few minutes. I need to get cleaned up after my overnight train trip How about an hour?"

"Fine, Mei Lin. My wife is in town, so I'll meet you at your hotel. I've really missed you!"

When General Yong arrived in her hotel room, Mei Lin was dressed in a tight white silk chemise with a long slit up one leg. Ping-ying reached out for her, kissed her passionately, and whispered, "Mei Lin, you are so lovely. I can't think of business until I've had your luscious body once again."

Mei Lin complied by slipping out of her clothes. Ping-ying did the same.

An hour later their passions were satiated and, as Mei Lin lay curled up and relaxed in Ping-ying's arms, he said quietly, "Mei Lin, when you return to Taipei, you may tell General Hua that I'm very interested in the exchange of the UTF for our seventeen pilots. But I just talked to Premier Deng before coming to see you. He said he wants the exchange to be part of a larger accord. Premier Deng will be contacting President Chiang soon. He will have an offer that can't be refused."

Surprised, Mei Lin asked, "Can you tell me anything about the offer?"

Ping-ying smiled, "No, Mei Lin, I'm sorry, but I can't tell you about the offer. But I can suggest a way to get out of the dirty business you're in."

Mei Lin looked questionably at Ping-ying and asked, "How?"

"Simple. After you deliver my message to General Hua, return to China and marry Hang-fu. He told me he was in love with you, Mei Lin. Being the wife of an Air Force general is a good life. You'll like it."

"He said he loves me? You're sure? Oh, tell him I love him too, and I'll be back. Soon!"

Chapter 41

Chinese Accord

The BMW drove rapidly down the streets of Taipei through the heavy morning traffic. The black, expensive car stopped in front of the Ministry of National Defense. Eddie Chung paid the unofficial parking man his usual bribe and then led Mei Lin into the building The pair took the elevator to General Hua's floor. Eddie strode rapidly down the hall to Hua's office followed closely by Mei Lin. Hua's secretary escorted the pair into the general's office.

After exchanging pleasantries, General Hua asked, "And what news do you have for me from General Yong?" He directed the question to the pair, not sure who would respond.

Eddie answered, "Ding-fua, Mei Lin just returned from Hong Kong this morning from the mainland. General Yong told her that he was interested in the exchange of the seventeen Air Force pilots for our UTF, but that it had to be part of a larger accord."

General Hua looked inquisitively at Mei Lin and asked pointedly, "Mei Lin, what did he mean by a larger accord? What else did he say?"

Mei Lin looked at Eddie Chung for permission to answer. He nodded permission to go ahead. Mei Lin replied with hesitation, "Sir, I'm not exactly sure what he meant by a larger accord. But he did say that Premier Deng would be calling President Chiang soon with an offer he can't refuse!"

"Do you have any idea what he meant?"

"No Sir. Only that he mentioned the larger accord, as Eng-fu said."

General Hua contemplated for a moment, then responded, "Mei Lin, I want you to return to the mainland. Fly back to Hong Kong today. Tell General Yong that his answer is unacceptable. That if he wants to see his pilots again, he had better accept our generous offer. We don't want a larger accord!"

Mei Lin broke down and sobbed, "But, Sir. He was very definite about the rejection. He said he had discussed the offer with Premier Deng and that was their answer. Besides, I'm afraid for my life if I return."

General Hua answered imperiously, "Well, you will return anyway! You're the go-between now in these negotiations. You'll be safe. Don't worry."

Mei Lin thought to herself, *Now, that proves it. Neither General Hua nor Eng-fu care about my personal safety, even when I tell them my life is in danger. That makes my defection to Red China easy, especially with Hang-fu waiting there for me.*

Then Mei Lin answered meekly, "Yes, sir. I'll return to the mainland leaving today. I'll give your message to General Yong, General Hua, as you request, Sir."

Eddie handed Mei Lin a big roll of hundred dollar bills and said, "Here, Mei Lin. This should be enough money for your trip. Leave now. You can take a taxi to the airport. Good luck!"

Mei Lin replied, grimly, "Goodbye, Eng-fu. I'll report back as soon as I have any positive information."

After she left the room, Eddie Ching remarked, "Cousin Ding-fua, I don't think Mei Lin's trip will be fruitful. I think we better go to see Uncle Ching-kuo as soon as possible and tell him the news. Call him now!"

General Hua replied, "We need to have Mei Lin keep trying, even if her life is in danger. But, yes, I think you are right. We had better go to see Uncle Ching-kuo as soon as possible. I'll call him right now."

President Chiang's pretty young secretary led the two cousins into their uncle's Presidential Office just after 11 am the same morning. The President invited his two nephews to be seated on the couch in his sitting area. His secretary served the three men tea and cookies.

The President asked, "And how are the negotiations to exchange the enemy pilots for the airplane going?"

General Hua sighed, "Well, Uncle Ching-kuo, not too well so far. But we sent Eng-fu's agent, Mei Lin, back to the mainland to tell General Yong that his response was unacceptable."

The President persisted, "But what was his response? No? Maybe? What?"

Hua answered, "He just said the exchange was interesting, but that such an exchange would have to be part of a larger accord. He also said Premier Deng would be calling you, Sir, with an offer you couldn't refuse."

"I wonder what he meant by that?"

As the three men pondered what possible meanings of the message Mei Lin brought back from General Yong might be, the President's secretary rushed in and said, "Mr. President, there's a telephone call from someone who claims to be Premier Deng from the PRC. I asked him if he were joking, and he said emphatically, *Certainly not!*, and insisted on speaking to you, Sir."

The President said, "I will take the phone call."

He switched the call onto the loudspeaker, and said, "Good morning, Xiaoping, this is Ching-kuo. It's been almost fifty years since I last saw you. I have my two nephews, General Hua and Colonel Chung, listening on the loud speaker phone."

"Good morning, Ching-kuo. It has been a long time, hasn't it? A lot of good men, on both sides, were lost in our great civil war of the 1940's. I have General Yong and Comrade Yung Hang-lee listening on my side."

The President agreed, "Yes, we both lost a lot of good men. And old age has taken a lot more – my father Chiang Kai-shek and Mao Tse-tung. I understand you have an offer to make to me – one I can't refuse!"

The Premier replied, "I see Mei Lin brought back my message. It's a good thing she told the pilot Yung Hang-fu about the October parade plot, or else we wouldn't be having this conversation. The three of us in this room owe our lives to Mei Lin. That was a dumb plot, Ching-kuo. It was destined to failure."

The President answered smoothly, "Of course, I deny that we had such a plot, Xiaoping."

"Of course, Ching-kuo, but we both know what the *real* truth is. Let's put the past behind us, including your *Plans B and C*, and look to the future, for the good of all the Chinese people."

The President responded, "Just what do you have in mind, Xiaoping, for the *good of all the Chinese people*. I don't think I'm going to like it."

The Premier replied, "Just keep an open mind, Ching-kuo. At our age an open mind is difficult, but very important. How would you like to have Hong Kong? I mean part of Taiwan?"

The President was flabbergasted by this question. He responded, "Why, of course, we would love to have Hong Kong. Their vigorous entrepreneurial, capitalistic system would fit well with our system in Taiwan – er, the Republic of China."

"The Premier replied, "Exactly. Of course it's a good fit. Look, Ching-kuo, as you know, we, the PRC, are scheduled to take over the administration of Hong Kong in 1997. Frankly, our Politburo is not very good at administering capitalistic enterprises, yet. We are afraid we'll kill the *golden goose* of Hong Kong. We want to put the creative Chinese capitalists in Hong Kong at ease. We want them to make the transition from a *British Crown Colony* to being a part of China without losing the entrepreneurs or their capital."

The President interrupted, "Xiaoping, you're making sense. The most sense I've heard from you, ever. But, exactly what do you have in mind?"

The Premier answered, "Simple, Ching-kuo. We want Taiwan to become an autonomous part of China and include Hong Kong as part of your super-capitalistic province. We see this arrangement as being advantageous for all parties. In addition, Ching-kuo, to sweeten the pot, so to speak, we would make you Vice Premier of China and make you and two other of your Ministers full members of the Politburo."

The President reflected for a moment and then responded slowly, "Xiaoping, this is an interesting offer. You are getting creative, even entrepreneurial. But, I'm afraid I must say *no* to your offer."

The Premier exploded angrily, "For Buddha's sake, why? I don't understand your thinking at all!"

The President responded, "How do we know that you won't renege on your pledge to leave Taiwan and Hong Kong free to pursue capitalism? You are an old man. So am I. What if your replacement decides your idea was bad? And the agreement should be revoked? What recourse would be have then?"

The Premier answered, "I thought you might have such objections. For that reason, we're willing to let the agreement be administered by a standing committee of the United Nations. The UN committee can ratify the agreement and see that it is adhered to. It may be the best thing the United Nations has done, so far."

The President, warming to this positive stance on the part of the Premier, responded, ""Xiaoping, I'm beginning to believe you have changed. I believe we could live with such an agreement. Let's have a committee established to work out the language of the agreement. We will make the exchange of the seventeen pilots and the UTF as soon as the agreement is signed. Is there anything else?"

The Premier said, "Yes, we would like to produce the Ultra Tactical Fighter here on the mainland. General Yong and General Yung both tell me it's a great airplane."

The President answered, "That sounds fair enough. We would need to get permission from the Israelis to license the use of their MITS/METS/ULS technology. Their license fees are quite high!"

The Premier responded, "We would pay the Israelis well for the license agreement. It would be worth it. Besides it would make them less dependent on the US. I'm sure they would like that. Any thing else?"

The President answered, "Yes, General Hua has a message for General Yong."

Hua said, "General Yong, just tell Mei Lin to ignore my last message to you. Tell her everything is OK."

Yong laughed and said, "Yes, General Hua, I'll tell her. But didn't she tell you she is marrying General Yung Hang-fu next Sunday? That's the real reason she's returning to the mainland."

Epilogue

Is Mainland China Trying to Arrange Taiwan's Future?

During the Fall of 2000 it became quite clear what the People's Republic of China wanted for Taiwan, the Republic of China. The following three events made such intentions clear:

1. Trade agreements reached between PRC, Russia and Argentina have completely left Taiwan, ROC, at the economic discretion of PRC when it comes to doing business with Russia and Argentina.

2. By creating these trade agreements PRC has continued to increase its economic power over ROC. PRC has forced Russia and Argentina to tacitly recognize Taiwan as being part of China. In order for these countries to conduct trade with ROC they must go through PRC. A similar trade agreement was made between PRC and South Africa.

3. During the 1992 Olympic Games held in Barcelona, Spain, the Games Committee was asked by PRC to introduce Taiwan as *Chinese Taiwan* rather than as the Republic of China. Spain complied.

So PRC will continue its plan to implant the idea in the world's mind that Taiwan, ROC, is a part of their country by forcing other countries to recognize this by way of economic contracts.

PRC is not pleased with the United States' criticism of them, (when they say PRC had shown a lack of respect for human rights). Perhaps this is a means for PRC to make a broader accord with ROC in the future. The entrepreneurs in Taiwan would also like to tap into PRC's market.

It seems to your author, based on past history, that PRC will get what it wants, because it is such a huge present and potential economic opportunity for the rest of the entrepreneurial world including the US, Japan, the European Union, Russia and Latin America.

www.ingramcontent.com/pod-product-compliance
Lightning Source LLC
Chambersburg PA
CBHW051145030726
47504CB00004B/1045